PRAISE FOR *IN A FAR-OFF LAND*

Talented writer Stephanie Landsem brings to vivid life the glamour and grit of old Hollywood in this moving story of ambition and secrets, forgiveness and love.

JULIE KLASSEN, author of *A Castaway in Cornwall*

The stage is set perfectly with beautiful prose as Stephanie Landsem takes readers back behind the glamorous curtain of Hollywood, exposing the corruption on the other side. Like an enchanting, enduring motion picture, *In a Far-Off Land* will grip your heart with its timeless truth and captivate the theater of your mind.

MELANIE DOBSON, award-winning author of *Memories of Glass* and *Catching the Wind*

Isn't it powerful how we can get it all wrong, yet God can make it all right? Landsem brings this to life in the retelling of the Prodigal Son. Set in 1930s Hollywood, our heroine goes on the difficult journey of being the prodigal daughter. Decades gone by but relevant still on so many levels. This is a story I'll read again soon, knowing many more life lessons are there waiting to be discovered.

T. I. LOWE, bestselling author of *Lulu's Café* and *Under the Magnolias*

Both gritty and glamorous, Stephanie Landsem's *In a Far-Off Land* digs beneath the sparkle of gilded Hollywood to uncover the true gold of love, mercy, and forgiveness. Don't miss this unforgettable story.

REGINA JENNINGS, author of *Courting Misfortune*

Depression-era Hollywood provides the perfect stage for the desperate and colorful cast of *In a Far-Off Land*. This tale is that of a journey from brokenness to healing, from emptiness to wholeness. Through the eyes of two characters who could not be more different, Stephanie Landsem gives us a timeless story of the prodigal traveling far from home and finding the way back again. Fans of Francine Rivers's *Bridge to Haven* will not want to miss this.

JOCELYN GREEN, Christy Award–winning author of *Shadows of the White City*

From the first page, this remarkable story set in glittering Hollywood during the Great Depression captured my imagination. Aspiring actress Mina Sinclaire's amazing pilgrimage from the dark hollows of her despair into the light of unconditional Love will offer hope to anyone who has ever believed themselves beyond redemption. Bravo!

KATE BRESLIN, bestselling author of *Far Side of the Sea*

One of the best books I've read this year! *In A Far-Off Land* is a beautiful story echoing the power of mercy, forgiveness, and love as it peels back the multifaceted layers of those living in Hollywood during the Great Depression. Stephanie Landsem weaves a heroine with as much spunk and edge as heart and soul. Just a gorgeous, page-turning novel.

HEIDI CHIAVAROLI, Carol Award–winning author of *Freedom's Ring* and *The Orchard House*

With her signature blend of luminous prose and immersive historical detail, Stephanie Landsem draws readers into the dazzle and darkness of 1930s Hollywood. From beginning to end, I was riveted by this masterful retelling of the parable of the Prodigal Son and moved by the poignant exploration of the power of grace in the midst of shame. Superbly written and absolutely stunning!

AMANDA BARRATT, author of *The White Rose Resists: A Novel of the German Students Who Defied Hitler*

Fans of Susan Meissner and Kristina McMorris will be spellbound by Landsem's gorgeously researched historical. Told with heart-wrenching conviction, *In a Far-Off Land* is a lyrical and thematic treatise on redemption, loss, and love and wielded with such surprising grace the reader will have many breath-catching moments. Landsem is a treasure of inspirational historical fiction and *In a Far-Off Land* is no less than a masterpiece.

RACHEL McMILLAN, author of *The London Restoration* and *The Mozart Code*

With everything I crave in historical fiction, Landsem's *In a Far-Off Land* immerses the reader in a world long forgotten yet achingly familiar. Old Hollywood meets *Grapes of Wrath*, and the redemption, romance, and regret are all beautifully written and deliciously authentic. It's still dancing in my head and will be for a while.

AMY HARMON, *New York Times* bestselling author of *Where the Lost Wander*

In a Far-Off Land—an engaging story set in a fresh era—deftly threads themes from the biblical story of the Lost Son through the burlap of the Great Depression and Hollywood's silk. In every age, a distant glitter promising fame, fortune, and self-indulgence tempts us to trade in the gold of family, contentment, and conscience. Thankfully, there is always a way back, as the talented Ms. Landsem shows us, to a happy ending provided through grace.

SANDRA BYRD, author of *Lady of a Thousand Treasures*

IN A FAR-OFF LAND

A NOVEL

IN A FAR-OFF LAND

STEPHANIE LANDSEM

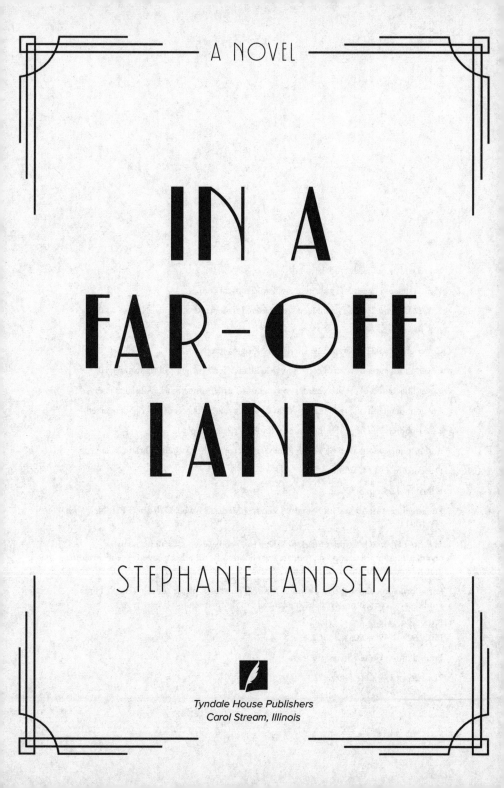

Tyndale House Publishers
Carol Stream, Illinois

Visit Tyndale online at tyndale.com.

Visit Stephanie Landsem's website at stephanielandsem.com.

TYNDALE and Tyndale's quill logo are registered trademarks of Tyndale House Ministries.

In a Far-Off Land

Designed by Eva M. Winters

Edited by Kathryn S. Olson

Published in association with Foundry Literary + Media, 33 West 17th Street PH, New York, NY 10011.

For information about special discounts for bulk purchases, please contact Tyndale House Publishers at csresponse@tyndale.com, or call 1-855-277-9400.

ISBN 978-1-4964-5042-5 (HC)
ISBN 978-1-4964-5043-2 (SC)

Printed in the United States of America

27 26 25 24 23 22 21
7   6   5   4   3   2   1

To Rachel, Andy, Joey & Anna
With love always, no matter what

CHAPTER 1

Los Angeles, California
1931

MINA

Roy Lester's mansion was as ritzy a place as I'd ever seen. I had to pinch myself to make sure I was really there—me, Minerva Sinclaire—at one of the most glamorous parties in Hollywood. This was the moment I'd been waiting for. The part of the story right before the happy ending.

At least that's what I thought at the time.

When the towering mahogany doors swung open, it was like stepping into *The Hollywood Revue*. The high-ceilinged great room sparkled, lit by a chandelier as bright as any studio set. Women in jewel-toned silk took their places with men in midnight-blue evening jackets, all in glorious Technicolor. In the center of the room, a grand piano provided the score, accompanied by the swell of conversation and the clink of ice against glasses. Toward the back of the room, a champagne cork popped, and a woman shrieked a laugh. I half expected to see a cameraman on a moving platform or hear a director with a megaphone call, "Cut!"

Max joined me at the top of three marble steps that led down into the room filled with music and color. "Mark my words, Mina. This is a mistake."

"Don't start."

Max had been grousing since he picked me up at my boarding-house an hour ago. "You're still my agent," I'd told him on the telephone, "and a girl can't show up at the door alone." With how things were between us, I couldn't tell him the truth that I needed him beside me. The thing that had happened between us over a month ago—what I called the New Year's Day Incident—had been a mistake and best forgotten. If only Max were more forgetful. But if Max wanted his 20 percent of the contract I was signing tomorrow, he'd help me out tonight.

Earlier, he'd helped me into his lemon-yellow LaSalle roadster like we were on our way to San Quentin instead of the gladdest party in Los Angeles. He drove into the hills like a madman—as if driving faster could get the party over with. He twitched a cigarette in one hand as we chased the half moon, headlights dancing ahead of us, the roadster spitting gravel behind. When we pulled through the gated entrance to Roy Lester's place, it was too unbelievable. Like one of those English estates had dropped out of the sky and onto the brown foothills of the Santa Monica mountains.

Max threw the stub of his smoke out the window and shifted to low gear on the smooth, winding driveway. He stopped sulking long enough to tell me about the place. "Twenty bedrooms, a theater that seats thirty, and a walk-in fur vault. There's a for-mal English rose garden and greenhouses, and behind there—"

he motioned past an unnaturally perfect lake lit by an illuminated fountain—"is a maze you could get lost in for days."

We sped past sculpted box hedges, giant rabbits, and teapots casting moon shadows on a vast manicured lawn. Sodium lights blazed over two red-clay tennis courts.

"Your friend Roy has a cellar filled with real whisky and gin— the good stuff from Scotland and England. And champagne imported from France. He's got a switch upstairs that locks it up tight if the feds come calling." Max snorted. "As if the law would raid Roy Lester's little haven. They're paid off too well for that."

Max's glum take was starting to rub me the wrong way. "Since when is bankroll and booze a problem for you?" In the four months I'd known Max, he'd never taken offense at other people's cash—or turned down their liquor.

I watched his profile as he maneuvered the roadster around the circular driveway and came to a rolling stop. His scowl really did mar that handsome face. His hair was neatly combed back and his black fedora set at an angle. A dark lock curled over his forehead, giving him a touch of boyish charm, which he used plenty well. He had a jaw worthy of any leading man and a nose with a hint of a crook, as if he'd broken it years ago. His amber eyes, with lashes that would make Greta Garbo jealous, were guarded as he turned to me. "I don't like Roy Lester."

Max played his cards close, and usually I let him keep his secrets, but this time I pushed. "Then how do you know so much about him?" I waved a hand. "And about his place?"

"I just do." The roadster sputtered and went silent. "Be careful with these people, you got me?"

I got him, all right. What was good for the gander and all that applesauce. But my time was running out. I'd learned plenty in the ten months I'd been in Hollywood—to dance, to act, to pretend I fit in. I'd even learned to drink bootlegged whisky—not legally, of course, but nobody cared about that. And I'd learned to take my breaks where I found them—with or without Max's blessing.

Now, faced with a roomful of Hollywood's elite, I wasn't so nervy. My knees wobbled and my palms went damp. A Chinese butler in an embroidered silk robe and satin-tasseled hat greeted us with, "Good evening." I'd heard Oriental butlers were all the rage, but I'd never actually seen one.

I slipped off my fox wrap as if it were a full-length mink. Act like you belong, that's what everybody else is doing. I took a deep breath and passed the fur to Max. Acting had got me this far, and it would have to take me the rest of the way.

"I'm not the coat-check girl," Max muttered, but he took my fur just the same.

"Be careful—it's rented," I whispered.

Max took off his crisp fedora and leaned closer. "At least promise me you'll follow the rules."

That was rich, and I wasn't so nervous that I couldn't fire back at him. "Maybe you should try following them yourself, Max."

At least he had the grace to flush. He turned away, giving his fedora and my fox to the celestial butler, whose expression didn't flicker a jot.

With or without Max's help, this night was going my way. Granted, my plan since I left Odessa hadn't come off without a hitch. I'd stepped off the bus at Central Station as green and innocent as a South Dakota spring. Well, I wasn't green anymore, and I sure as sugar wasn't innocent. But I was at the end of my rope.

I glanced into the ceiling-to-floor mirrors that flanked the entrance. If mirrors told the truth, I would have seen a small-town girl with her knees knocking and stomach churning. But—thank the stars above—mirrors lie, too. The woman looking back at me wasn't a nervous Nelly but a sophisticated Hollywood ingénue. And with any luck at all, Cosmopolitan Productions' next leading lady.

My hair was somewhere between a brunette and redhead—in Hollywood they called it auburn. Bobbed, waved, and as smooth as glass, it was absolutely the thing. Garnet lipstick set off my blue eyes and milk-white skin—no freckles, thank you very much.

Then there was the dress that had cost me my last nickel.

It was an emerald-green sheath, sleeveless and cut on the bias. Pearl beads weighted the cowl neckline and set off my ivory skin— and plenty of it. The slim cut skimmed over my hips and clung to my legs, all the way down to my matching satin heels. An armband of gold wire and pearls—cultured, of course—wrapped above my elbow, and a matching spray gleamed behind my ear. I turned slightly and looked over my shoulder. The back plunged indecently low. Penny would be shocked. In fact, all of Odessa would be shocked.

Max gave me a look that said exactly what he thought of the dress. He knew how much a frock like this cost, and he knew my situation as well as I did. But it wasn't an extravagance. It was an investment. Max was sore because I'd got to this party—the one that would make me a star—without his help. Not only that, but I'd been invited by Louella Parsons herself. The Queen of Gossip, they called her. If she gave a girl the nod in one of her *Examiner* columns or on her radio show, that girl was on her way up. But if Louella took a dislike to a new actress—didn't matter why—she might as well go back to Kansas.

You could have knocked me over with a horsefeather this

morning at the Brown Derby, where I made about enough to keep my cockroaches alive. I brought Louella her breakfast of oatmeal and cream, and she gave me her usual scowl. I won't go into that whole story right now; let's just say Louella and I had got off on the wrong foot.

I poured coffee all around and tried not to look like I was listening to Louella and William Randolph Hearst talking about a party at Roy Lester's that night. I pretended not to notice Louella's husband, Docky Martin, slip a flask from his pocket and dose his coffee. Suddenly, Louella turned on me like she was seeing me for the first time. "Minerva! My dear. Aren't you just the cat's pajamas?" She looked me up and down. "And that hair. Such a pretty shade."

"Thank you, Mrs. Parsons," I managed, clutching the coffeepot.

"Dearest Minerva, how long have you been working here?" she asked, almost like she cared.

I told her four months and waited for her other size-ten T-strap to drop.

"You poor thing," she cooed. "What you need is someone to take you under her wing, like a mother hen." She smoothed a hand over her tan tweed suit. With her matching cloche hat and a spray of crimson feathers, she did resemble a hen I'd known back at the farm—one who'd kept the other hens in line with her sharp beak. "Tell me now, do you know Roy Lester?"

Every red-blooded citizen in America knew Roy Lester. America's Hero, they called him. And everyone in Hollywood knew he was the highest-paid actor in history. "I can't say I've met him, Mrs. Parsons."

"Call me Lolly, darling. And that's going to change tonight. Isn't that right, Docky?" She went on without an answer from her husband. "A soirée at Roy's estate, and you, my dearest, are going to be. My. Guest." She tapped the table with each of the last three words like it was a headline on one of her columns.

I stammered something; I don't even know what. I scooted around the table before Docky could pinch my bottom, while Louella put cream and two sugars in her coffee. Me, Louella Parsons's guest?

She shifted to a stage whisper. "Roy himself told me he's looking for a fresh face for his next leading lady." Her gaze slipped to Docky, who had tipped slightly to eye my backside. He grunted as her foot connected with his ankle. "He'll love you. Leave it to me."

I was speechless. This was what I'd been waiting for. Across the room, Norb, the owner of the joint, was staring at me. He didn't like the help hanging around the guests, especially the big names. I took a cloth out of my apron and wiped an invisible spill.

"Terrific, Lolly," I managed as if I were invited to a millionaire actor's house every day of the week. "I'll be there with bells on." Now Norb was weaving through the tables, his eyes on me, his brow furrowed.

Louella smiled, her bright eyes narrowing to slits. She scribbled the address on a scrap of paper and tucked it into my apron with a plump, jeweled hand. "Trust me, dearest, you won't regret it."

The minute my shift ended, I'd hightailed it back to the boardinghouse I called home. My roommate, Lana, was putting in an early shift at the dance hall so I had the place to myself. Rent was due, and my cupboard held nothing but mouse droppings and a can of sardines, but it didn't matter, not this time.

I changed into my best street dress, a cardinal-red wool number that hugged my figure and fell exactly between my knees and ankles. With a dove-gray roll brim dipped over one eye and suede shoes trimmed in lizard, I looked the part. I pulled my rent money out of the tea tin marked *Do Not Spend!*, tugged on my gloves, and hopped the streetcar for Bullock's on Seventh and Broadway.

Two hours later, I left Bullock's with the emerald dress, boxed and wrapped in tissue. Smaller packages held the matching kitten heels, the pearl armband, and the hair comb. It's an investment, I said to Max as if he were there. I talked a lot to Max in my head. Those days, they were the only civil conversations we had.

I'd made a final stop in Bullock's discreetly placed lingerie department. If Penny could see the rose silk panties with the ruffled petal hem and the new-fashioned brassiere, she'd pitch a fit, but white cotton bloomers and a modest camisole wouldn't do under this gown. And besides, pretty underthings give you confidence—that's what all the magazines said—and I needed all I could get.

I had about enough change for a sandwich and a cup of coffee if I walked home instead of taking the tram, and by the time I got to Broadway and First, my feet were killing me. I didn't give a hoot. I tip-tapped down the street, humming one of those sappy songs I'd heard on the radio.

At the corner, a handful of the down-on-their-luck men stepped to the side, lifting their hats to me. Hand-lettered signs around their necks or propped beside them on the curb told their sad stories.

Will Work for Food.

My Family Is Starving.

My gown and shoes suddenly felt heavier in my arms. Since the crash and what came after, men got off the bus in LA every day to find the same hard truth I'd learned ten months ago: jobs were as hard to come by in the Golden State as they were in the rest of the country. From what the headlines said, it was only getting worse. The lucky men sold apples for two cents each. The unlucky men—and their families—slowly starved to death.

I should have moved on, but I didn't. I couldn't. An old man, his face creased like a well-read newspaper and his pale eyes desperate, stood in the hard sun, a barrel of apples at his feet. He looked like a farmer. Like Papa.

He picked through his bin of apples and chose one, polishing it on his sleeve before offering it to me. "Please, miss."

I looked at the packages in my arms. This man had nothing and would probably have nothing again tomorrow. One more day with an empty stomach wouldn't kill me. Not anymore.

I dumped the entire contents of my purse in his cup. Two bits and a couple of dimes would get him a square meal. I took the apple and turned away as quick as I could, but not fast enough. Eyes bright with tears and a whispered "bless you" gave me a stab of homesickness. Was Papa hungry tonight? Was Penny making ends meet?

When I got home, I wrote to Penny.

Maybe my luck is changing, Penny. Maybe this story will have a happy ending after all. Even if I don't deserve it.

I sealed up the letter and told myself it wouldn't be long now before I could go home to Odessa. First thing, I'd pay off the mortgage and the taxes so Papa would never have to worry again. Then I'd get one of those newfangled tractors that practically planted the corn for you. Maybe I'd buy a closetful of dowdy dresses and the sensible shoes Penny liked. We'd have steak every night of the week and twice on Sundays. That's what I'd do. I'd make everything up to Papa. Even Penny would have to admit I'd come through.

And it would all start tonight—right now—at Roy Lester's party.

Max waited at the top of the marble steps, looking like he was about to get a tooth pulled. The piano swelled to the chorus of "Ain't Misbehavin'," and a trio of men began to sing off-key. I took a deep breath and lifted my chin.

This was it, what I'd been waiting for. So why were my legs wobbling like a soused sailor?

Max looked down at me with what could have been a hint of compassion and tucked my hand in the crook of his arm. "Let's get this over with."

We stepped down, entering the whirl of color and sound. Max's arm under his midnight-blue evening jacket was rigid, his jaw set as if he were going into battle. Was he sore because of what happened between us, or was it something else? You never could tell with Max.

He guided me smoothly through the crowd. The women, all beautiful, moved as gracefully as if they were choreographed dancers. The men made elegance look effortless. Everyone held a glass—dainty bowls of champagne, tumblers of dark whisky, martini glasses of clear gin with the occasional olive. Like everywhere else in the country, the Eighteenth Amendment had not only failed to curb the consumption of liquor, it had made drinking a national pastime.

A maid, a lovely Mexican girl probably no more than eighteen in a black below-the-knee dress and a shapeless white apron, stopped short in front of us, glasses teetering on her tray. She stared at Max. I was used to it—women ogled him wherever we went—but the way her mouth dropped open looked like astonishment. Max took two champagnes and said something to her in a low voice.

She hurried away as if she were being chased.

"What was that about?" I asked.

He gave me one of the glasses and shrugged. "This joint is a waste of time, Mina."

"A waste of—" Changing the subject was one of his specialties, but I fell for it. "Says you." I turned on him, whispering furiously and jerking a nod at the piano. "That's John Gilbert over there." Gilbert, dubbed the Great Lover, earned more in one picture than my father's farm was worth.

Max downed his champagne in one gulp, then put a hand at the small of my back, guiding me toward the center of the room. "Gilbert's a liability. The drinking's one thing, but the women . . . He's probably traded pajama bottoms with every Jane in this room, except maybe your dear friend Louella." Max didn't hide his disdain. "Not to mention his voice. Gilbert's first talkie was his last."

I'd seen Gilbert's debut in talkies and couldn't help but laugh at his high, effeminate voice like the rest of the people in the picture house. I took a sip of my champagne, letting the bubbles dissolve on my tongue. "But look! John Barrymore." My voice fairly squeaked. Me, in the same room as an icon.

Max harrumphed as if the man leaning against the crowded bar wasn't Hollywood royalty. "Barrymore's downed enough gin to sink the *Titanic,* and it's starting to show. The suits in New York—the ones who hold the purse strings—they don't want that kind of trouble, not anymore. If they could break his contract, believe me, they would."

I looked closer at the man they called the Great Profile. Yes, there was a telltale slackening around his jaw. The eyes thousands of women had fallen in love with were bloodshot and puffy. But Max didn't need to be such a sourpuss.

Max guided me around the throng at the bar, to an alcove where we could see most of the room. "See those birds?" He jerked his head toward a trio of women dancing next to a crackling phonograph. Billie Dove, known by every filmgoer as the American Beauty, leaned against Colleen Moore, who had transformed girls' hair across the country with her Dutch boy bob. I'd seen every film either of them had made, sitting in the tiny Odessa Picture House, so caught up in the films I hardly noticed my beaus trying to hold my hand or sneak a kiss. Beside Billie, Norma Talmadge—the most glamorous flapper of all—whispered in the ear of a kid half her age.

"Between the crash, budget cuts, and talkies, they're washed up." Max kept at his lecture. "Rumor has it none of them will work again, unless it's at the Macy's perfume counter."

That brought me up short. Could Max be right? I watched them over the rim of my champagne glass. Their laughs were a bit overloud. And yes, their eyes under the heavy liner and fake lashes held a desperate cheerfulness I knew too well.

"These people aren't who you want to rub elbows with, Mina. The ones who do—" he dipped his head at a set of walleyed young things stumbling through the Charleston—"crash and burn before they get anywhere."

I wanted to ask him how he knew so much, but the hoofers started singing along with the phonograph, and the piano player raised the ante, pounding the keys like he was trying to win a contest. Max leaned closer so I could hear him over the din. "Mina, you need to wise up. Tell me something. Who isn't here?"

He was close enough for me to smell the cologne he always used, clean and lemony. I pushed the memory of the New Year's Incident away and tried to follow. "Mary Pickford," I answered. America's Sweetheart, they called her, and she wasn't here. If she were, she'd be the center of attention.

He nodded. "And?"

I shook my head. What was he getting at? "Douglas Fairbanks?" Pickford's husband. They went everywhere together and unlike some film couples, they were mad about each other.

He acted like I was a schoolgirl finally understanding her lesson. "Buster Keaton, Carole Lombard." He looked at me, his dark brows raised. "The real high-hats, Mina." His eyes ran over the crowd as if assessing them. "Gable and Crawford wouldn't set foot in this place. Not that they don't drink or sleep around—they all do—but not with people like Lester. And your heartthrob, Mr. Chaplin? Wild horses couldn't drag him here."

That was low. I'd only confessed to him my infatuation with Charlie Chaplin in a moment of weakness. It was ungentlemanly to use it against me, but Max always dug deep to make his point.

Max kept at it. "They stay away for good reason, Mina. Nothing but trouble waiting to happen here. And your friend Louella, waiting to jam somebody up on tomorrow's radio show while her husband supplies pills to most of the men in the room and abortions to half the women."

I flushed. Max was worked up, and maybe he was right. But his way hadn't panned out and I was desperate. And desperation put me in a fighting mood. That's when my winning argument perched her famous backside on top of the bar in front of us. "What about Clara?"

Clara Bow, vamped up in thick black eyeliner and a clingy scarlet dress, the three-inch fringe well above her knees. Pencil-thin eyebrows gave her a sad-eyed look, and her hair, a bobbed halo of dark-red curls, caught the glow of the lights. She crossed her shapely legs and raised a highball glass to a gaggle of adoring men.

I'd seen every one of her pictures, from *The Daring Years*, when

I was barely fourteen, to *The Wild Party*, Clara's first talkie. She was the cat's meow. The It Girl. The woman who not only made her own choices but made more coin in one picture than I'd seen in three years of working at the diner in Odessa. Even Max couldn't argue with fame like hers.

Max followed my gaze, saw Clara, and quickly turned his back to the bar, as if he didn't want to look at her. "Do you even read the news rags?" he whispered.

Well, yes. I'd seen the photos of her in court with her current boyfriend, Rex Bell, at her side. "But she's not on trial, her secretary is." Her secretary, Daisy DeVoe, had tried to blackmail her for over a hundred thousand dollars.

"Sure, but it's Clara being raked over the coals." Max kept his head turned away, but his expression was grim and a little sad.

What came out at trial was shocking, even for Hollywood. Drunken parties, cocaine, plenty of men—Gary Cooper, Victor Fleming, the entire USC football team, or so they said—all of it written in letters so explicit, they couldn't be printed even in the seediest tabloid. The newspapers jumped on Clara Bow like hyenas ripping up a carcass. *IT Girl Exposed! Singed Starlet in Ruins!*

Max went on. "Paramount can't handle her mess of a personal life, especially now that it's no longer personal. Not to mention she's the last word in self-destruction. Between the men, booze, and drugs, they won't put up with much more of her, not when she can't even remember her lines." Max snorted. "For the life, I can't understand why these people have to write it all down. They keep letters and diaries like trophies, then they're shocked when some mug finds them and wants a payoff."

Max was a lot of things—stubborn, overbearing, bossy . . . I could go on. But he was rarely wrong about the business. Could the It Girl really be finished? Then I heard her. She'd only been in one talkie, but I'd recognize her voice anywhere. Throaty, with a tinge of a Brooklyn accent.

"Maximilian. Are you going to hide out over there all night, or are you going to come on over and say hello?"

My mouth dropped open. Was she talking to *my* Max?

Max let out a long breath and gave me what seemed to be an apologetic look. He turned toward the bar. "Clara. It's been a long time." He sounded none too pleased.

Max, on a first-name basis with Clara Bow?

Max's grip on my elbow tightened as the circle of men reluctantly parted for us. Clara didn't spare me a glance as she handed Max her empty glass. "Fill that for me, will ya, Maxi?" She turned to the men lounging beside her. "Fellas, this is Max Clark. His father was Dusty Clark, the Kissing Cowboy." She smiled and swayed a bit. "As fine a man as you chumps could ever hope to meet."

Max refilled her glass with a splash from the bottle on the bar. His jaw was rigid, and he didn't even try to look like he was glad to see the most famous woman in Hollywood. "How you holding up, Clara?" He held the glass out of her reach, forcing her to look at him.

She gave him a sultry smile instead of an answer. "So this is who you're spending your time with now?" She kept her eyes on Max. "Isn't she a pretty little thing." It sure didn't sound like a compliment, so I didn't thank her.

Max introduced me with precious little enthusiasm. Close up, I could see what he'd meant. Clara looked worn, like a dollar bill that had passed through too many hands. Her heavy makeup couldn't conceal the bruised circles under her notorious bedroom eyes.

"It's a pleasure, Miss Bow," I got out before she turned away, bellowing for more glasses.

She filled them herself, almost to the rim, and passed one to Max and one to me. "Any friend of Max's" was all she said before raising her glass. "To Dusty Clark." All the men followed suit. "He could drink any of you cake-eaters straight under the table. Didn't matter what there was, gin, whisky, or moonshine." She clinked her glass with Max's and gave him a slow wink. "Down the hatch," she said, throwing back the glass in one go.

I took a gulp from mine. It burned all the way down and made my eyes water.

Max set down his empty glass and took Clara's hand. It was small and pale in his. "Take care of yourself, will you, Clara?"

She looked at him blearily. "I'd rather if you took care of me, Maxi," she whispered with a look that could melt steel.

My cheeks burned as hot as my throat. Was Max one of the long line of Clara's men? I was hardly as pure as the driven snow, but the notion of Clara and Max together made a little fire flare up in the back of my brain.

Without another word, Max moved me through the crowded room.

"You know her?" I whispered, staring up at his tight jaw. Max kept a lot to himself, but when he did talk, he told it straight. I liked that about him, even if sometimes I didn't want to hear it. But at the moment he was looking anywhere but at me.

"My father was part of this crowd." That answer was bushwah, but he had that look on his face that told me not to push it. "Mina, please. Let's go."

Max didn't beg, so I must have misheard that plea in his voice. Besides, I'd just met Clara Bow, and I still hadn't found Louella or

Roy Lester. "Max, I'm not leaving here until I do what I came to do, and that's get this part."

Max turned, grabbing my elbow just below my faux pearls and whispering furiously, "Mina, listen to me for once. These people—" he jerked his head at the whole room—"people like Clara, like Barrymore. They're looking for something—happiness, meaning, I don't know what. They think they can find it in the bottom of a bottle, or with dope, or in somebody else's bed." His honey-gold eyes were bright and close. "They keep looking and looking." His voice hardened. "And then they end up destroying themselves." He put his hands on my bare shoulders. "I'm telling you, Mina, this is a bad idea."

I stared up at him. Honestly, where had this come from? Was this about his father? What happened to Dusty Clark—star roper and rider and in at least a hundred films—had been a tragedy. "Max." I swallowed hard. "I'm not like your father. I can handle this."

Max shook his head, blowing a frustrated breath. "No," he said firmly. "You can't."

Max knew plenty about the business, but he didn't know beans about me. He thought I wanted to make it big, live in a fancy mansion like Lester's, wear furs and designer dresses. But he was wrong.

I had no intention of staying in Hollywood any longer than I had to.

The studios loved new faces and they paid them well. Why, Joan Crawford, the most elegant of all the flappers, had started at seventy-five dollars a week at MGM. My plan was to make my money then get out. A six-month contract as Roy Lester's leading lady would make me enough coin to leave California with ten times what I'd taken from Papa. Enough to make up for everything and keep Papa in peaches and pipe tobacco for the rest of his life. I'd left the farm almost a year ago, and by now the mortgage and taxes were past due. If I didn't make it soon . . . I'd never be able to go home.

But I wasn't about to tell Max that.

My name, sung out in a familiar bleating voice, broke through the tension wrapped around us. Max's hands dropped from my shoulders. Louella Parsons's stout frame pushed through the slim women and swellegant men like a freighter through frothy waves.

"Minerva, my dearest! You came. I knew you would." She was wearing a flowing gown of burgundy silk trimmed in black marabou. Her cheeks were pink, her eyes overbright. She fluttered her lashes at Max. "It's been a long time, Maximilian."

"Louella." The look on his face said not long enough.

So Max knew Louella as well as Clara Bow, and hadn't even told me? He was a dark horse, but this was the clincher. How else had he been holding out on me?

Louella lifted one of my hands, twirling me around. "You. Look. Divine." She linked her arm through mine. "You don't mind if I steal your little friend for a bit, do you, Maximilian?"

Max held out his hand to me, as if giving me one last chance to change my mind. I shook my head. Ever since the New Year's Incident, he'd been in a mood. Sure, he'd got me some auditions, even the promise of a contract with Cosmo, but everything he'd done had fallen through. Sometimes he acted like he didn't even want me to make it in Hollywood.

I let Louella turn me away from him, a lump in my throat. Max was my agent and he wasn't doing his job. That's all there was to it. The crowd closed around me, and the last I saw of Max was his worried eyes watching me walk away.

Louella steered me toward the back of the house like a force of nature, her fingers digging into my arm like talons. "Minerva, dearest," Louella said, "I can put you right up on the screen. You know that, don't you?" I didn't know what to say, but it didn't matter because she went on. "I just need you to do a little thing for me."

"But, what—?" A little thing?

"It's nothing. Just keep Roy Lester busy tonight. And by tomorrow, you'll be signing a contract with Cosmo. I guarantee it."

"But doesn't Mr. Lester make the decisions about his leading ladies? And Mr. Hearst?"

She stopped midstride and turned to me, her voice sticky-sweet. "Don't you worry. I have Mr. Hearst right in my pocket." She patted her breast as if she had a pocket with a miniature William Randolph Hearst trapped inside.

I tried to clear my muddled head. I do this for her, and she gets me a contract with Cosmo? With Louella's help, I could be bringing in hundreds of dollars a week in no time at all. Enough to wire to Papa and keep him in the clear. And what was the harm in keeping Roy Lester company, anyway?

Then, through a tall double door, we entered a party that was far more intimate than the crush in the other room. Half a dozen people lounged on red velvet divans and tufted chairs in front of a massive stone fireplace. The lights were dim, the music muted. A white bearskin lay on the floor, the mouth gaping open to show enormous ivory teeth.

A shiver ran over my bare back.

Louella turned to me, her eyes bright with more than the gin I smelled on her breath. "Here we are, Minerva. I'm telling you, Roy is just going to eat you up."

I ignored the herd of butterflies stampeding in my stomach and plucked up my courage. Roy Lester, get ready to meet your next leading lady.

The murmur of conversation fell silent as we approached, the music and wild laughter of the other room muted and distant. Louella gushed like a little girl, "Minerva, dearest, you remember my friends, William and Marion?"

How could I not? Hearst was propped in one corner of the plush red divan, a full tumbler of whisky in hand. He was forty if he was a day, and Marion had left her twenties behind long ago. Marion was draped over him like a blanket, her famous blonde bob mussed and her lids at half-mast. A champagne bottle dangled from one dainty hand.

I stammered my hello, trying not to gape at how Marion's sapphire dress, with a plunging V-neck and plenty of spangles, had slipped up her thigh, followed closely by Hearst's hand. Marion murmured a greeting, took a swig from her bottle, and hiccupped. Hearst raised his glass to me and winked broadly at Louella's husband, who moved over to make room on the divan. Louella's eyes narrowed and I hoped to heaven she wasn't thinking of the Docky Disaster at this moment.

Louella took my arm in her clawlike grasp and turned me to the man seated on the other end of the divan. Roy Lester wore a white dinner jacket, unbuttoned, and his bow tie was already undone. His classic features blurred behind the smoke of a fat cigar. "Roy, I'd like you to meet Minerva Sinclaire," Louella simpered. "I think you two will just adore each other."

Let me tell you something. Back at the farm, we had a rooster

I'd named Blackie the Pirate, on account of the way he strutted around, his red gobbles wobbling, his swordlike beak ready to strike at any out-of-line hen. Roy Lester made me think of him right off. Roy's dark hair was combed over a thinning crown, and a narrow mustache outlined razor-thin lips. He even had a fold of red-flushed skin inching over his collar. But mostly, it was his eyes. They were sharp and quick, as if looking for a weak spot.

I held out my hand. I didn't have to like him; I just had to keep him company, like Louella said. Roy didn't stand for the introduction, but I guess someone under contract for a million bills a year doesn't have to stand if he doesn't want to. He took my hand and jerked me down into his lap. I yelped in surprise and struggled a bit. He laughed, his hand snaking around my waist as I awkwardly rearranged myself to sit beside him and put my dress back to rights while avoiding the hot ash of his cigar. "Pleased to meet you." I found my voice and gave him a look from under my lashes.

"Miss Sinclaire," he crowed, his eyes swiveling over me. "Louella's told me all about you." His whisky-and-tobacco breath made my eyes water.

I inched away, but Louella settled her bulky form on my other side, trapping me.

"You're dry," Lester bellowed, as if it were a crime. "This won't do at all." He signaled to a waiter—a kid bearing a striking resemblance to the girl Max had spoken to—who proffered a tray of martinis. I tried to remember how many drinks I'd had. Clara's whisky, two glasses of champagne, or was it three? Then I reminded myself I wasn't following Max's rules tonight, accepted a martini, and took a sip. The gin slipped down my throat like a sharp knife, but I figured it would give me courage. Roy settled back, and

Louella started in on who we'd seen in the other room, who they were with, and what they said.

I made small talk and took Roy's hand in mine so it couldn't go any further up my thigh. He wasn't so bad, I told myself, if slurred words and cigar breath were your thing.

Louella leaned into our conversation. "Didn't I tell you? Couldn't you just eat her up?" She laughed as if it weren't the tenth time tonight she'd used the phrase.

Roy buried his face in my neck. I tried to wiggle away as he traced a moist path toward my ear. A flicker of panic started in my chest and I pushed at him. This was too much. Roy leaned back, eyeing me with a hint of disappointment. "Come on, sweet thing, you know the game." He snagged another martini from a passing tray and put it in my hands. His look gave me the heebie-jeebies. Yes, I knew the game. I wished to heaven I didn't. I took a sip, even though I didn't want it.

The party in the other room was getting louder, the singing more off-key, the laughter rowdier. The music on the phonograph competed with the pounding piano. A gal who seemed to be wearing only her underslip scampered past, letting out a small scream and laughing uncontrollably as a man chased her. He caught her up in his arms and carried her out, shouting about the pool.

The room closed in on me, thick with smoke and unnamed expectations. I was definitely in over my head. Oh, how I hated when Max was right. I needed to think, and I couldn't think with Roy so close, with Louella watching me with those bright eyes. "I need to powder my nose." I pasted on a sweet smile and got to my feet. The floor swayed in an alarming way.

Roy grabbed my hand and eyed me suspiciously. "You aren't running out on me, are you, doll?"

"Oh, believe me, Roy, she'll be back." Louella jumped in. She gave me a look that said I better be back.

"In two shakes," I assured Roy, my voice wobbling.

"Lucky man," Docky slurred, and Louella gave him a glare.

I lurched away, my satin heels sinking into the sprawling bearskin. I imagined the bear's glassy eyes watching me as I stumbled out of the room. Panic crept up my throat as I veered around a swarm of dancers. I could hear Max's "I told you so," but I wasn't about to accept defeat. I needed air, then I'd come up with some way to see this through.

Once, when I was a kid, Penny and I dared each other to swim across the lake behind the back forty. Whoever lost had to clean the chicken coop. Penny was older but I was the better swimmer and itching to prove it. I started out strong and was soon yards ahead. By the time I reached the middle of the lake, I was exhausted. Penny turned back, but I pushed on. I made it, but only barely. Penny—the tattletale—told Papa the whole story that night, and I had to clean the chicken coop for a month, even though I'd won the bet. With every shovelful, I reminded myself I'd done what I had set out to do—and I'd do it again.

Sink or swim, isn't that how the saying goes? But how far would I have to swim with Roy Lester? All the way? It wasn't like this was my first time, I reminded myself. It wasn't even my first time with someone I'd just met. I'd thought—and hoped and prayed and promised myself— those days and ways were behind me, but I'd come too far and was in too deep to give up now.

I pushed through the crowd, making a beeline for a set of French doors draped in heavy damask. I could leave now and lose my chance or stay and see this thing through. Papa and Penny were fast running out of time.

Sink or swim? I didn't have a choice anymore.

OSCAR

Oscar plunged his hands into the sink full of hot soapy water. How many more glasses would he have to wash before those *americanos* passed out or ran out of liquor? He hadn't eaten since morning, his hands were as red as a hot pepper, and his head pounded harder than the hammering piano in the big room outside the kitchen door.

"*Ay, ay,* my feet," Francesca complained, shifting her weight from one sturdy leg to the other as she dried a crystal highball glass. "He does not pay me enough for these nights."

Alonso pushed through the swinging door with another tray of dirty glasses, setting them on the counter next to Oscar's elbow. "You should try walking through that crowd with a tray of martinis." He spoke in Spanish, as they all did when they worked in the kitchen. Francesca's kitchen meant Francesca's rules.

Oscar took care with the delicate stems as he transferred the dirty martini glasses to the sink. He'd never make a good waiter. He was too big to weave through a crowded room like Alonso, and he'd probably hit the first drunk who spilled their expensive liquor on him.

"They're winding up in there." Alonso splashed bourbon into three sparkling tumblers. "Clara Bow is dancing on the top of the bar." His mouth curled in what looked a lot like envy. "That blonde, she took off her dress and says she's going swimming. Someday soon, I'll have as much money as John Gilbert. And a swimming pool full of beautiful women."

"Alonso!" Francesca scolded, crossing herself automatically and kissing her thumbnail.

Oscar's headache moved to the back of his eyes. It was always the same with Alonso—to be like the *americanos* with money to burn. Maybe, Oscar thought with a flash of annoyance, if Alonso didn't spend every spare nickel on the picture shows and get-rich-quick schemes, his family would have money enough for rent.

Why did he want to be like the idiots out there? These *americanos* had everything, but they were only happy when they were destroying something—their homes, their bodies, their families. He read enough of their newspapers to see they didn't know the meaning of honor. Give him trees and hedges—no matter how hot and sweaty the work—instead of women dressed like tarts and rich men on the prowl.

Oscar handed Alonso two clean glasses. "*Ándale!* If Señor Lester sees you lazing, you'll be out of a job."

Alonso scowled. "If Señor Lester wants his liquor faster, he should hire more staff." He filled the glasses with champagne. "And someone to help with the gardens."

Oscar didn't disagree. There had been three gardeners when he got this job a year ago, but for months now, Oscar had cared for the grounds alone. Still, a job was a job and he'd take it. As the newspapers said every day, plenty of real Americans were lined up to take his place.

Francesca rolled her eyes. "May God hear you. I've said to the *señora*, I can't keep up with so little help, but she doesn't listen. Ah, my back is aching."

Lupita pushed through the door. Slender and graceful, she moved like a shadow in and out of the kitchen. She was Alonso's little sister, but the similarities ended with their slight builds, curly dark hair, and wide brown eyes. Lupita was as serene as Alonso was discontent. Usually. Tonight, though, her hands trembled as she transferred glasses from her tray to the sideboard.

"Are you feeling all right, Lupita?" Oscar asked. She was only eighteen, too young to be serving drunks, but he knew the Garcias needed the money as much as he did.

"*Sí*, Oscar. I'm fine." She glanced behind her at the door as if a villain lurked outside.

She wasn't fine. And Mamá would expect him to protect a girl her age. Oscar dried his hands on a towel. "Let me go out there this time. You take over here."

Lupita almost dropped a glass, then threw a frightened glance toward Alonso. "No, no, Oscar. I mean, thank you, but I can go."

Oscar eyed her. What was wrong now?

"You need a break, Oscar." Lupita went to the icebox and pulled out a jar of milk. "And you're hungry, I know. Take this." She sliced a wedge from a loaf of bread and pushed him through the door with surprising force.

Oscar could have protested, but he'd been up before dawn, driven his brothers to their jobs at the packing house, then was here by first light trimming the hedges and the ridiculous expanse of green lawn, cutting armloads of flowers for the house arrangements, and making sure the pool sparkled. Another three hours helping in the kitchen for extra pay had done him in. He'd take food and a rest if it would make Lupita happy.

He welcomed the cool night air and the sudden quiet after the noisy kitchen. The English garden stretched out behind the sprawling house—the scent of roses and calla lilies thick and cloying. Paths of crushed oyster shell glowed yellow in the murky light of sodium lamps, and the trimmed hedges took on sinister shapes, like predators stalking through the night.

He slipped behind a copse of rhododendrons, their half-spent blossoms drooping, and settled on the edge of a low wall, away from the spill of lights from the ballroom windows. He took a swig of milk and a bite of the soft bread and rolled his shoulders, loosening the tension in his neck. A muffled giggle came from somewhere in the dark. Guests were no doubt pairing up and finding private hideaways—and not with their wives or husbands. A shriek sounded from the direction of the pool, then a splash and wild laughter.

These people.

He'd be cleaning up broken glass and finding discarded clothing in the shrubbery for days. If there was any justice in the world, these *gringos* would have headaches the size of watermelons tomorrow morning.

He swallowed the last of his bread. Justice. It had no place in this world. At least tomorrow, when Señor Lester paid up, he'd be able to make the rent. Another month knowing Mamá and his brothers had a place to call home.

The patio door opened, letting out the light and noise of the party for a moment, then closed, muffling it again. Oscar leaned back into the shadows. *Por favor,* not a couple looking for privacy. Through the screen of flickering leaves, he saw a woman alone. Her back was to him, long and barely covered in shimmering green wisps. She was slim, her hair dark in the shadows but gleaming like copper when she stepped into the moonlight. She turned, clasping her arms around herself. Her face was the kind of beautiful the *americanos* preferred—deep red lips and flawless milk-white skin. She looked fragile, like the delicate orchids he looked after in the hothouse.

Her shoulders lifted and fell, as if she'd taken a deep breath. Then her fingers brushed at her eyes. She looked up into the stars, her long lashes fluttering as she blinked. What did a woman like her have to cry about?

The door opened again, and this time a man came through, tall, white trousers, dark evening jacket. The light was dim, but his familiar profile—the sharp jaw and slightly crooked nose—made Oscar draw back into the shrubs and hold his breath. The last time he'd seen Max, he'd broken that nose.

The milk soured in his mouth as Lupita's nerves made sense. She'd seen Max and wanted to make sure Oscar didn't. She needn't have worried. The last person on earth he wanted to speak to was Max Perez, or did he call himself Clark now?

Max took a silver case from the inside pocket of his dinner jacket and snapped it open. His mother would be so proud, Oscar thought bitterly. Max even looked like an *americano*. Max drew out a cigarette and put it between his lips. A match flared against the stone wall and he cupped it close to his mouth. He took a deep pull, then handed the cigarette to the silent woman. "Had enough yet?"

She tossed her head, then turned away, putting the cigarette to her red lips. "I'm having the time of my life, no thanks to you."

Oscar watched the scene. It was like a film, the moon turning the colors to sepia, the muted music and the faces of the two actors intense and focused.

"You don't have to go back there." Max jerked his head toward the party.

She let out a small sigh that sounded a bit like a sob. "He's waiting for me. And so is Louella."

"You and Louella good friends now?" His eyebrows went up.

"She's going to see that I get a part in the new film, if that's what you mean."

"That so?" Max didn't sound convinced. "They played you like a piano, Mina." He took the cigarette from her limp hand, dragged in a breath, and turned his head to blow the smoke toward Oscar. "Louella set you up like some kind of pimp."

The girl didn't argue. "Why didn't you tell me about Clara? And Louella? You could have introduced me months ago."

He didn't answer.

Oscar knew Max's silences well. He didn't answer questions unless he felt like it.

She glanced up at him. "I need this part, Max. I need this break."

"I'll get you another part." He offered her the glowing cigarette.

She shook her head. "I'm out of cash and this dress took all my rent." She let out a frustrated breath. "Honestly, it's like you don't even want me to make it in this town. Like you've given up on me."

Max looked away like he had something to hide. "It's a slow time."

"Don't give me that line."

Oscar's hands tightened on the cold bottle. What exactly was he, her lover? Max always could pick the beauties. And break their hearts.

Max blew out a curtain of smoke that veiled them in silver. "Don't tell me you like being pawed by that clown."

"Of course not," she spat out.

"Then wise up. This isn't the place for you."

"Says you." She snatched the cigarette and put it between her lips. The tip glowed bright between them. "Listen. I have a chance with Roy. A big chance." She swallowed hard.

Even in the dim light, Oscar could see Max's jaw clench. "Sure. For a price."

So that was it. *Caramba,* these *americanos.* No marriage, no commitment. Where was this girl's father? Max would stop her if he were any kind of man.

"For a picture," she said firmly. "A big part, like you always say

I need. *Start out at the top, Mina. Bit parts are the beginning of the end.*" She mimicked Max's deep voice pretty neatly.

"Don't fall for that old trick, Mina. You're better than that."

She threw the cigarette on the ground between them. "I know what I'm doing."

He looked at the glowing ember and shook his head slowly. "You don't. I've seen—"

"Oh, you've seen it all. You know it all." Her voice rose and she fluttered a long white hand. "You and your rules. You don't even follow them. Why should I?"

That seemed to stop him in his tracks. Oscar almost leaned right out of his secluded hiding place. He'd never seen Max at a loss for words.

Max rubbed his hand over his face, and in the dim light, his eyes looked like those of a man twice his age. "Mina, if this is about that night—"

"I don't want to talk about that," she snapped.

Max ground the smoldering cigarette out with the toe of his expensive-looking shoe.

The girl turned away from him. Oscar could see her face, but Max couldn't. She looked like she was fighting back tears, blinking her eyes fast.

A prick of conscience surprised him. She didn't want to do this—whatever it was, though he figured he knew. Couldn't Max see she was practically begging him to stop her? If it was something to do with Lester, she was sure to regret it.

She took a deep breath and turned back to him. "I came here to get the part, and that's what I'm going to do." Her voice was sure now.

Oscar hadn't been raised to let women fall prey to wolves—and neither had Max. He wanted to step out of the shadows and tell her about the women who paraded in and out of Lester's bedroom—women with no shame. She didn't want to be one of them, he'd tell her. But why would she listen to him—a Mexican man she didn't even know—when she wouldn't listen to Max? Besides, she wasn't his responsibility. She wasn't even one of his people.

"You give him what he wants, and he'll give you what you want?" Max's voice was like the grind of stone on stone.

She swallowed and eyed the door to the ballroom where a tinny phonograph player screeched. Splashes and laughter came from the pool. "That's how it works."

Max shook his head, his face in the shadows. "Sure. That's how it works." His voice was heavy. He turned away from her. "Don't come crying to me when it goes to the dogs, Mina."

Max walked slowly into the house, opening the door to a burst of noise and slamming it behind him. The record player stopped, and for a moment, it was almost quiet. The moonlight played over the girl's face. She looked sad and young and scared. "Don't worry, I won't," she said in a small voice, as if Max were still there.

Oscar had the feeling he'd just watched something go terribly wrong.

MINA

I cracked open one eye. Sunlight sliced like a sharp blade, and I squeezed it closed again. My body was leaden. My head felt like a fence post taking a pounding. What happened last night?

Think, Mina. The party. Max. Max walking out on me . . .

I moved my hand, as heavy as stone. I was on a bed—I knew that at least. A breeze chilled my clammy skin and I shivered. Why wasn't I wearing my dress?

Roy Lester.

My breath stopped. Oh my stars, don't remember. But it was too late.

Max left me on the patio . . . and I went back to Roy and Louella. Marion snored softly in the corner of the divan, her mouth open to show perfect tiny teeth. The Chinese butler brought a tray of drinks and bent close to Hearst, who whispered in his ear, then handed around the gin and tonics—mostly gin, so I barely took a sip.

Lester pulled me to him. "She's too much," he said, his hands sliding over my bare back and down to my waist.

Louella looked smug. "I knew you'd like her."

I didn't like the way they talked about me like I was a Christmas present and Roy Lester got to do the unwrapping. As if he'd read my thoughts, Roy stood and pulled me to my feet. "Let's take our party upstairs." His words were slurred, but I knew what he meant.

"No, no, no." Mr. Hearst jumped up and grabbed Roy's arm. "The party's just starting, isn't that right, Maryanne?"

Relief almost knocked me over. "It's Minerva," I said, but I didn't care what he called me, as long as he kept Roy downstairs.

"Of course. Here—" He signaled to the pretty maid. "Bring Roy here one of his specials."

"Sure, Billy-boy," Roy said, easy enough to convince. "One for the old road." Roy danced me around the room as the gramophone rasped, the needle stuck on the groove, singing along, his breath hot and moist in my ear, "'All I want is just one kiss, and I have to have one kiss.'"

One kiss? And then . . . what?

I remember we went outside, Roy swaying—lurching—around the courtyard with me in his arms. I felt woozy; the courtyard spun. That's when everything started to run together. Roy dragging me up a stairway, laughing like it was a lark. I guess it was to him. But what happened after?

A familiar shame burned through me.

Had I been what they call "a good sport"? Had we . . ? Don't be a dope, Mina, what do you think we did, play gin rummy? My stomach turned, from a hangover or what I'd done with Roy, I didn't know.

I tried to breathe, to think. How had I come to this? Small steps, small strokes taking me into deeper and deeper water until I couldn't turn back. Now, here I was . . . drowning.

I pried my eyes open. Hard light slashed through dark velvet curtains and glinted off of dozens of lifeless eyes. Antelope, zebra, a huge pig with enormous tusks—all staring at me reproachfully. Roy Lester's trophy room. The silence—the deep, exhausted morning silence—was broken by the low buzz of a fly, bouncing against a window, caught between the heavy velvet drapes and the glass, relentlessly trying to escape.

I'd done what I needed to do. I'd done what Louella had asked, and then some. She owed me, and from here on out, I'd go straight. Follow the rules. I'd sign on with Lester at Cosmo and make all I needed in a few months. Then go home. I'd be home in time for spring thunderstorms, June bugs, the bright green of sprouting corn.

That's what I'd do, I told myself. No one would know.

I sat up, gingerly holding my head.

First I noticed the smell—sharp and metallic—like the chicken house on slaughtering day. Then I saw the body.

On the floor in the middle of the room. And . . . blood, soaking the pale carpet.

I scrambled back, tumbling off the far side of the bed, my knees sinking into thick carpet. I crawled backwards until my back hit the wall. Took a breath. Had I imagined it? I inched around the side of the bed and covered my mouth to stop a scream.

Roy lay on his back, his pale face mottled with blue veins, his mouth sagged open. Those eyes that had charmed women in countless films stared at the ceiling, as glassy as the animals on the wall. I choked. A knife—covered with blood—with a wicked long blade lay beside him.

He was dead. Dead. Roy Lester, America's Hero, was dead.

A rushing sound filled my ears, a drumming in my throat, behind my eyes. The room spun around me. "Think. Think, Minnie." My whisper was queer-sounding in the silent room.

Finally, my brain starting ticking. I couldn't do anything for him now. I needed to get far away, as fast as I could. Out of the house. Home. I'd say I left him alive, late at night. My dress. Shoes. Where were they? I scrambled around the bed. Saw only blood and Roy. There. Green silk in a puddle by the door. I pulled it on. I couldn't be in this room—with him—another second.

Oh, Max, you were right. *Don't come crying to me when it goes to the dogs, Mina.* You were right and I was wrong. I admit it. Please help me. Please help me, Max. Get me out of this horrid fix I got myself into.

CHAPTER 2

MINA

"You'll find your way," Mama always said. How was she to know how lost I'd get?

When I was a kid, before Mama died, I was my papa's shadow. I helped with the milking. In the fields, I talked to Papa as he tinkered with the tractor. Whatever Papa did, that's what I wanted to do, and I loved seeing him smile when I did something just right. "Hard work and determination," he'd tell Mama, "that's my Minnie."

School was something different altogether.

At school, I was good at only one thing. Pretending. Pretending I was following along even when my mind was far from my McGuffey Reader. Pretending I hadn't been looking out the window instead of diagramming sentences. Pretending my pencil needed sharpening again, just because I couldn't sit still for another minute.

Most of all, pretending it didn't bother me when my teachers said, "She sure isn't anything like Penny."

With Mama, I didn't have to pretend. "Don't you give up, Minnie," she'd tell me when she helped me with my schoolwork at night, letting me pace the kitchen as I memorized spelling words and helping me write out my composition papers.

I didn't give up. Not until later, that is.

My favorite part of the week was Saturday afternoon, when Mama would take me to the Odessa Picture House. It was always just me and Mama. Penny didn't like the pictures—not even Charlie Chaplin, which I couldn't understand.

Mama would read the titles in my ear as Douglas Fairbanks saved Mary Pickford from the pirates or Fatty Arbuckle got into one fix or another. Even after I could read well enough to follow on my own, she still whispered in my ear. One afternoon, after laughing ourselves silly over the Little Tramp, as we walked into the sunshine and out of the blue, I told Mama I wished I were more like Penny.

She turned to me and said, "Minnie Zimmerman, if you were like your sister, who would come to the picture show with me?"

I shrugged.

"Don't wish to be like anybody else, sweet thing," she said, cupping my face in her hand. "You have hidden talents of your own. You'll find your way, my girl. Don't you doubt it."

She believed in me, Mama did.

I was sixteen when she died.

She had been sick for most of that summer. Penny was good at taking care of Mama, just like she was good at everything else. She made her eat even as Mama's rosy, rounded cheeks turned sunken and the color of ash. Gave her the medicine the doctor brought, even when it seemed not to help.

I couldn't bear to stay in that room, the smell of sickness, the woman in bed who didn't look a thing like Mama. I knew I should sit with her, read to her, talk to her like Penny did. But I couldn't. I wish now I'd spent every minute with her.

She died quietly on a sunny September day in 1926, the kind of day she called Indian summer—warm and golden with just a hint of crispness in the air. Penny and Papa and I were all there. Mama took my hand in a papery, dry grip. I wanted to tell her I was sorry, that I hadn't been a good daughter to her, that I loved her. But a lump like a goose egg had lodged in my throat and just kept getting bigger. My eyes burned. I buried my face in Papa's shoulder and prayed. *Please, please, please.* I don't know what I was praying for, but when I opened my eyes, she was still. So still.

The next spring, Penny graduated at the top of her class from Odessa Consolidated. She took over the house and took good care of Papa. She cooked and cleaned and made his favorite food. She did everything right, just like the good daughter she was.

I had two years left of school, but without Mama's help, my marks got so bad the teachers told me I'd have to repeat part of my classes. I left at the end of the term and never went back.

I pretended I didn't care.

I felt funny without Mama. Unattached. Like a dandelion seed floating on a breeze, unable to direct my own way and not knowing where I was going. Nothing could really reach me where I was, but I couldn't reach anyone else, either. I tried to not think about it. I pretended I was fine.

Papa didn't want me to quit school and said so. I told him I'd get a job, that we needed the money. I was right and he knew it.

I got a job at the Odessa diner with my friend Ruth. Ruth didn't have the greatest reputation, but she was as different from Penny as night from day, and that was a nice change. I didn't see any harm in bobbing my hair like she did and shortening my skirts. My tips doubled and so did the number of boys hanging around when our shift was over. Ruth and I got to be good pals. She knew a lot about boys, and it wasn't long before I did, too.

The boys were easy enough to handle. Sure, sometimes they stole a kiss or two in the picture house, but I could cope with that without missing a line of dialogue. It was part of the deal, Ruth said. They paid my way, and in return I doled out kisses like change from the cash register. I didn't see the harm in it. Besides, Ruth said everybody did it.

Penny didn't see things the same way. "You're heading for a fall," she said.

I know it was a terrible thing to say, but I figured Penny was just jealous. I'd be lying if I didn't say it was nice to have a new beau take me to the pictures every week while Penny stayed home with her cross-stitching. When I was riding in a boy's auto or laughing at Laurel and Hardy at the cinema, I didn't have to think about Mama or the farm. But if Penny knew how it turned out in the end, she would have said, "I told you so," like she always did.

For eight dollars a week plus penny tips, I took orders at the diner and carried plates loaded with eggs and bacon or steak and potatoes. It wasn't a lot, but I felt like I was helping out. By then, I knew the farm was sinking fast because I'd been doing Papa's books for a while. It wasn't hard, not like grammar and spelling. The money we made on one side, the money we paid out on the other, and at the bottom, how much I could deposit in the bank. Anybody could do it. And it didn't take a genius to see we were just scraping by, just like everybody else.

Way back during the Great War, when wheat was selling at

two dollars a bushel, Papa had borrowed money to buy the sixty acres south of our farm, putting the acres we already owned up as security. Everybody had borrowed then, with demand what it was. But by '27 land prices had dropped so low we owed more than those sixty acres were worth. We couldn't sell it—we couldn't even afford to plant it, what with grain selling so low—but we still had to pay the mortgage every February and October, and taxes on the whole caboodle every March 15. Then came the drought of '29. Everybody said we'd hit bottom and there was nowhere to go but up. But everybody sure was wrong.

In October of 1929, the crash came. Things sounded bad on Black Thursday but got worse on Black Monday. Then came the panic of Black Tuesday.

"Hard times are coming," Papa said. Harder times than we've already had? I remember thinking. But Papa sure was right.

Penny turned even more thrifty, making soap and trading eggs for what we needed at the grocer. Papa repaired the old tractor with baling wire and a prayer. We patched our dresses and darned Papa's socks until they were more darn than sock. We tightened our belts to the last notch, like Papa said, and then we made more notches. I recorded every penny in the columns of Papa's ledger, wishing I could make some more appear, but it didn't work like that.

When the New Year came and everyone was welcoming 1930 with something close to hope, I took a good look at the farm ledger. It wasn't a pretty sight. Sure, we had almost three hundred dollars in the bank, but we'd need more than that to pay the taxes and the mortgage when they came due, not to mention seed for spring and hired hands for planting and harvesting. It didn't add up, and I told Penny and Papa so.

"We'll make do," Papa said. "We have a roof over our heads

and each other." He took my hand and Penny's in each of his own, so we were all linked. "If your mama was here, that's what she'd say."

Penny didn't have Papa's faith. After Papa left for the barn, she grabbed my arm hard. "We have to do something."

Like she expected me to have some great scheme.

"It will kill Papa to lose the farm."

My chest tightened up and I couldn't breathe. I couldn't lose Papa. Not like Mama.

————————

When I missed Mama—and that was a lot, even years after she was gone—I went to the Odessa Picture House. In the cool darkness, I could almost imagine her beside me, whispering in my ear.

Flapper films were all the rage, and I lost myself in the daring stories of women who knew what they wanted and didn't care what other people thought of them. Clara Bow was my favorite. I didn't miss one of her films. *Flaming Youth*, *The Perfect Flapper*, and *It*, the film that made her a legend at seventeen. She made me think anything was possible. Of course, two hours later when I walked out to cold sun and snowbanks, I remembered. Mama was gone and the farm was in trouble and I was far from a plucky heroine. I was almost twenty-one and just a waitress in a diner in the middle of nowhere.

I guess I was looking for something even then. It's hard to know, looking back now, but maybe I thought if I could be like Clara, just a little, things would get better.

The fall I was heading for was named Alex. He had soft hands, slicked-back hair, and a real job selling brushes door to door. He drove an up-to-the-minute Packard Sport Coupe that matched his baby-blue eyes. Alex was smitten, he told me, leaning over the counter at the diner, his hair slicked back and his smile slicker. Even now, the scent of Wildroot Hair Tonic makes me sick to my stomach.

Penny warned me against Alex from the opening credits. "He's trouble, Minnie." She was worried about me, but the way she said it rubbed me the wrong way. I told her to mind her own potatoes and tried not to think about it.

Alex took me to the Stork Club in Pierre on a clear, cold night with the smell of snow in the air. It was a ritzy place with white linen tablecloths and waiters in penguin suits. He ordered us both steak, slipped a flask from his pocket, and dosed me with gin and outlandish compliments. By the time dinner was over, I was dizzy with love. Or maybe it was the gin.

We did the town, such as it was—dancing and drinking cocktails at a real speakeasy. For a few hours, I felt like Clara Bow or Billie Dove, footloose and fancy-free. Well past midnight, Alex drove back to Odessa through the cold countryside, his hand on my leg, the coupe swerving all over the road, both of us laughing.

But he didn't take me home. Not right away.

What happened then was my fault, like he said. I guess I asked for it, like he said.

He pulled the automobile onto a side road, where tall trees blocked out the light of the moon. At first, I didn't mind the kissing—liked it, even. But he kept going, his hands everywhere, his body pressed down on mine. I tried—really, I tried—to push him away.

"Don't be such a tease, Mina." His mouth tasted of liquor and the smell of his hair tonic was all around me. I tried to stay calm.

I didn't want to seem like a flat tire, but my heart was hammering and I couldn't breathe. His body was heavy and his arms were strong, pushing me down on the seat. When he reached under my short skirt, that's when I finally caught on. But by then it was too late.

After he was done, I curled up in a ball as far from him as I could get. He buckled his belt and started the car. I was crying now, my breath sharp and painful like a knife in my chest, my whole body shaking, hurting like I'd never known.

"It's your own fault, Minnie," he said. "What did you think, the way you get all dolled up? A guy can only take so much."

I just wanted to get home. Away from him and the smell of Wildroot.

At home, Papa was waiting for me. Maybe he knew, maybe he was just worried, but I couldn't look at him. How could I, after what I'd done? I ran up the steps to my room, my makeup streaked, my hair a mess.

"*Liebchen?*" He followed me up the stairs. "What's the matter?"

How I wanted to throw myself in his arms, then. Tell him everything. How much I missed Mama, how lonely I was. How Penny had warned me and I hadn't listened. I wanted to tell him about Alex and how I didn't know what to do. But what if Papa told me it was my fault, like Alex said? What if he stopped loving me? What if he told me I was a terrible daughter? It would only be what I deserved, but no, I couldn't bear it.

Shame burned through me. "I'm fine, Papa," I said as I closed my door on him.

It was probably the biggest lie I ever told, and that's saying something.

I tried confiding in Ruth, but she just shrugged. "Don't let it bug you, Minnie. It's not like it means anything." I figured maybe she was right. In the films—with the girls like Clara Bow—it didn't mean a thing.

But it should mean something. I knew it should.

After that, I stopped talking to Ruth and missed my shifts at the diner. I avoided Papa and Penny. I didn't go out with boys but stayed in my room every night. I worried that I was pregnant—and then what would I tell Papa? Penny tried to talk to me, but I wouldn't—couldn't—confide in my sister. She'd never understand, would she? Not perfect Penny. I wasn't pregnant—I thanked God for that on my knees——but by the time I made myself go back to the diner, I'd lost my job.

So you see, when I said I couldn't do anything right, I was telling the honest truth.

I didn't tell Papa about losing my job, but without that extra pay, I knew we'd never make the mortgage. I went to the Odessa Picture House just to make myself feel better, I guess. And that's where I got my bright idea.

The Hollywood Revue of 1929 was playing for the matinee. I'd seen it before—Joan Crawford and John Gilbert, Norma Shearer and Marion Davies—but this time it got me thinking. Joan Crawford, who had her own song and dance at the beginning of the film, had started out at seventy-five dollars a week at MGM and now made ten times that. When somebody asked her how she did it, she answered, "Hard work and determination. And of course, a little bit of talent." And there was Billie Dove. Jean Harlow. Fay Wray. All of them started as nobodies and now made thousands of dollars in a year.

Hard work and determination. A long time ago, Papa had said I had both. Hidden talent—Mama had said I would find mine.

And anyway, wasn't acting just pretending? I could pretend as well as any of them. I had just turned twenty-one and that was no youngster in Hollywood.

I left in the middle of the picture, went home, and packed my bags. I took my savings out of my stocking drawer and knew it wouldn't be enough. I'd seen enough films to know that when things looked their worst, that's when the heroine had to do something drastic, something nobody understood at the time but would thank her for later.

I'm not going to pretend it wasn't stealing. But what was one more sin on my long list?

Papa had counted out the money for the mortgage payment that was due the next week and stowed it with the farm ledger. He never did like bank drafts and would drive it to the bank in Pierre himself. We had some more money put by in the cookie tin above the stove for the upcoming taxes. I told myself I'd pay it all back. That and plenty more.

Papa and Penny would get by, I told myself. I knew from experience that the Pierre bank would give Papa some extra time to make the payment, at least until after the spring wheat harvest. And the taxes? Uncle Sam would just have to wait for my big break to get his due.

Before I left home, I took something else, too. Something that wasn't mine, but I couldn't leave without it. Penny and Papa would have to forgive me for that, too.

I truly thought I was doing the right thing—the only thing I could do—when I got on the westbound Great Northern bus. My goodbyes to Papa and Penny were silent as I watched Odessa get smaller and smaller through the back window.

I'll come back and make up for all of it, Papa. I promise.

I was such a sap back then, me with my plans.

I stepped off the bus and onto the Los Angeles streets lined with cars as colorful as an Easter parade. Palm trees, tropical blooms, the sun so bright it made my eyes water. I bought a pair of sunglasses just like Carole Lombard wore in *Fast and Loose* and told myself all I had to do was wait for a talent scout to find me and drag me to Paramount or MGM for a screen test.

Honestly, what a dumb Dora.

I treated myself to the grand tour for two dollars on a bus with hard seats and a jovial guide who was four feet tall and as wrinkled as an apple doll. The bus swayed and clattered past the Egyptian Theatre's massive statue of Osiris. "Why don't mummies take vacations?" our guide asked the women, children, and honeymooning couples with a twinkling smile. "They're afraid to relax and unwind."

To scattered laughter, we turned onto Santa Monica and headed to Beverly Hills. It was unlike any town I'd ever seen. Majestic palms towered over thoroughfares lined with lush shrubs. Spiky plants with pink blooms looked like birds taking flight. We wound up through the steep pitch of the foothills, catching glimpses of castle-like mansions tucked into valleys.

"On the right, Fred Astaire, ladies and germs."

I craned my neck but could only see a high wall and a glimpse of an ornate peaked roof. He went on: John Barrymore's estate—bought for a cool half million—and William Powell's hilltop castle filled with the most up-to-date gadgets. Then there was the original Beverly Hills mansion, Pickfair: "Built by Douglas Fairbanks for his bride, Mary Pickford," he intoned with reverence.

"Twenty-five rooms of frescoed ceilings, mahogany paneling, and gold leaf trim, plus a complete Old West–style saloon." He looked at us sternly. "Of course America's Sweetheart wouldn't touch a drop of whisky."

We even passed Roy Lester's estate, if I remember right. Ignorance is bliss, isn't that how the saying goes?

When the tour was over, the guide gave each of us his tiny hand as we stepped off the bus. "Watch your step, now, young lady," he said to me, his wise eyes meeting mine.

Add him to the list of people I should have listened to.

I checked into a small hotel on Hollywood and Vine and went right out and bought myself the latest issue of *Photoplay*. I studied it like I'd never studied in school. Clothes, makeup, hair. By the time morning came, I was ready to invest in my plan.

I marched into Bullock's on Broadway. *Photoplay* said it was the most, and it was. The most expensive. But if I was going to get discovered—and fast—I didn't have much choice, so I pretended I knew what I was doing.

"The day of the short skirt is past, my dear," the bottle-blonde salesgirl said, eyeing my above-the-knee frock and figuring me for the country bumpkin I was. "Everyone is wearing their hems longer this year."

She got a titch more friendly when I chose a green bias-cut silk with narrow sleeves, a cinnamon crepe de chine with a wrap-style bodice trimmed in cream, and a blue linen with a low, square neck and ruched waist that made the most of my figure. Of course, no dress would be complete without a hat to match, and Bullock's had plenty. I gulped when I saw the price of a forest-green velvet beret with a divine organdy bow, then an up-to-the-minute turned-brim cloche in chocolate brown that would go well with my dresses. I fingered a tiny wool tilt hat in blue—trimmed with silk flowers that just screamed class—but put it back.

"Two pairs of shoes will do for now," I told the salesgirl as she scurried behind me with an armful. A pair of crocodile T-straps with sensible heels and a matching handbag would be daytime practical, and for evening, high-heeled sandals in cream suede with a tiny matching clutch. I'd stopped adding up the zeros, but anxiety tightened in my chest.

"Stockings for daytime," the salesgirl advised. "But you can still get away with bare legs in eveningwear, depending on *whose* parties you attend," she said with an arched look. I tried to look as if I knew exactly whose parties she meant as she added two pairs of silk stockings and garters to my growing pile. I added three pairs of gloves in white cotton, figuring I'd have to be careful and make them last.

When I fingered the butter-soft silk chemise and knickers the salesgirl brought me, I thought how Penny would have a kitten. I shook my head. I'd have to manage with my cotton underclothes. I stopped at the makeup counter and picked out a cake of mascara. According to *Photoplay*, dark-red lipstick and matching nail varnish were all the rage. I chose one of each and got an approving nod.

My mouth went dry as she totted up the total damage. It was staggering. I eyed the pile of silk, linen, and velvet, wondering what I could put back. My face heated. The salesgirl tapped a shiny red fingernail on the counter. Finally, I pulled all my bills from my handbag and counted them out into her hand. More than half of what I had went into the till. I didn't say much as she boxed up my desperate hopes and piled them in my arms.

I needed to look the part, that's what I told myself. In six months, I'd have enough money to go back to Odessa and make up for everything. I'd have to.

That night, I wrote my first letter to Penny. I didn't beat around the bush.

I guess you know I took Mama's ring, Penny. I'm really sorry. I needed something to hold on to, something of hers. I don't expect you to understand, but it's like a little life preserver out here in an ocean of strangers. I'll bring it back, I promise. I'll bring it all back.

I addressed it to the farm and stuck it in the hatbox from Bullock's. I'd mail it soon—at least that's what I told myself.

The next afternoon, I stepped out of a cab at 6763 Hollywood Boulevard in my green silk, velvet beret, and matching purse and pumps, determined to follow through on my plan.

Under a scrolled canopy, the line at the Montmartre stretched halfway down the street, but that didn't throw me. I took a deep breath and sidled past a group of girls decked out in bolero jackets with ermine trim. Under the canopy at the front door, I gave my brightest smile to a black-suited man with a minuscule mustache. "I'd like a table for lunch."

He eyed me up and down. "Miss, so would everyone else."

"But I have money." I held out my handbag as proof.

His nose went a trifle higher, and his gaze slid past me as if I weren't there.

Just then, a chorus of whispers broke out as a man and woman walked arm-in-arm toward the crowd. She was draped in a white mid-length fox and matching turban. He wore a pinstriped suit with a fedora pulled nearly over his eyes. A girl about my age dressed in a cherry wool suit pushed up beside me. "Who is it?" She had perfect makeup and a beauty mark accenting her full mouth that couldn't possibly be from nature.

I sucked in a breath. Joan Crawford and her latest beau. Straight out of the studio. The snooty waiter parted the velvet cords and ushered the couple into the dark recesses of the café, leaving the rest of us out in the cold. I must have looked as dejected as I felt, because the girl in red gave me a pitying look. "Everybody's after the same thing, sister. Take it from me and don't go thinking you're something special."

I guess I was a slow learner even outside of school, but three weeks later, I was getting the picture. I hadn't been discovered by anyone—unless you count the men on the street corner who wolf-whistled when I walked to the Culver City Pharmacy every day for a small chocolate malt and my big break—and my hotel bill was totting up to something shocking. What had seemed like a lot of lettuce in South Dakota didn't go far in the land of sunshine.

Mama's voice came in my head. *You'll find your way, my girl.*

I packed my bags and took the trolley downtown, where I found a dank-smelling hotel with ten-cent-a-night beds and temperamental plumbing. This sure wasn't what you saw on the picture postcards. Hungry women and children stood in breadlines. Bums slept on benches. Men who looked like they hadn't had a square meal in months begged for dimes. I'd thought California was different, that the hard times didn't dare visit this far-off land of dreams. Boy, was I wrong about that.

───────────

That summer, I tried my best. I really did. Every morning when I got up and waited in the dingy hall for my turn in the lavatory, I wondered about Papa and Penny. Did the corn get planted? Were they getting enough rain? When I stepped outside to the clamor of new construction and honking automobiles, I imagined the morning sounds of the old tractor and the lowing of new calves. I tried not to think of Papa and how he must be worried. I'd be home soon. I'd make it up to him.

I had a system by then. Every morning I scoured the news rags that claimed to have the inside scoop on Hollywood, then I took the streetcar to Central Casting. If I was lucky, I heard about an audition at one of the studios and hotfooted it to the lot. I knocked on doors at RKO, where Fred and Ginger waltzed and tangoed, and hung around Warner Brothers, the first studio to produce a talkie. I lined up with everyone from cowboys to grandmas, all hoping for a bit part. In all of June, I got one walk-on in a western that made me two dollars and a part in a crowd scene at RKO for three seventy-five and a cup of coffee.

I was running out of money and low on luck when I met Lana on a hot July day. Columbia was looking for dancers. I tried out, kicking it up with the rest of the girls, and thought I had a chance. The hot sun had soaked into the paved back lot and I was wilting with only enough change in my pocketbook for fare back to the city, when Lana sauntered out of the audition in seafoam-green gabardine and three-inch coral pumps. She offered me a cigarette, her voice an easy drawl. I wasn't smoking—not yet, at least—but we talked until the assistant director came out and announced casting closed.

I slumped, defeat almost knocking me to my knees. "I needed that eleven dollars."

"Didn't we all, honey?" She crushed her cigarette under her spiked heel. "Don't take it so hard. Come on, I'll buy you a sandwich."

I had nothing to go home to but a five-by-ten room, so I

accepted. Over watery coffee and a stale sandwich, she told me about a place that was hiring. "It's not terrific, but you can make five dollars on a good night. And your days are free to answer the cattle call." She jerked her head toward the studio.

"I'll take it," I told her, and when I thanked her for the sandwich and the tip, she said not to mention it. "Girls like us, we gotta stick together."

It was only later that I realized Lana wasn't much for sticking together.

_____

It's hard to say exactly where you take the first wrong step, but here's the joke: afterwards, you can look back and see it, plain as daylight.

The place Lana brought me was called the Rose, and it was a dance hall just down South Spring Street, five stories high with greasy windows and a garish flashing sign. We walked into a green-tiled entry decorated with a dejected potted palm.

"Bert, this is Minerva, the one I told you about," Lana said.

Bert looked harmless enough, middle-aged and balding with a paunch and ready smile. He jerked his head toward the stairs. "Sure. Fix her up solid, Lana," he said in a friendly way, "and get a wiggle on. Time is money."

"Hold on to your tickets," Lana told me as we walked up four flights of stairs, "and turn them in at the end of the night. We're not supposed to accept tips, but if Tiny and Bert aren't looking . . ." She raised her brows and nodded. "Also, let Tiny know if you have trouble, but only if you can't handle the chump yourself." We reached the top, a little breathless. "Making a fuss over a little bit of groping is bad for business."

Upstairs, windows covered in black curtains lined a long front room. A glum-looking five-piece played in the corner while men in wrinkled suits and faces to match clutched handfuls of pink tickets. A dozen women in evening gowns stood along the far wall, looking bored.

Tiny—I found out quick—kept everything running smoothly. Standing less than five feet on his tiptoes, he had more swagger than a man twice his weight and could wrestle a drunk out the door before a girl had time to say, "Keep your hands to yourself."

We were called hostesses. That night, I danced until my feet ached. The men—short and tall, bald and toupeed, some with bad breath, others smelling like gin—handed over their pink tickets. I figured out quick that the men wanted more than just a dance. They wanted to talk, and their pink ticket bought them three and half minutes of someone to listen. I waltzed and fox-trotted, avoided roving hands, and heard their hard-luck stories, then tucked their tickets under my garter. I hardly ever made the five dollars Lana promised, but it was a respectable job. At least at first.

The next week, I moved in with Lana, splitting the rent at a boardinghouse on Western Avenue. For a while, things were looking up. Some evenings when we were feeling flush, we dressed up and went to the Alexandria Hotel on Spring Street. Lana would flirt with anybody in pants while I helped myself to the free sandwiches and kept an eye out for Charlie Chaplin, who they said liked to come there for supper. I never did see him, but the sandwiches were sometimes my best meal of the week.

I wrote to Penny just about every week. I hadn't sent any of them yet, but I would soon, I told myself.

It won't be long until I find my way, Penny, just like Mama always said. And then I'll be home with enough money to pay everything back. I'll make it up to you and Papa and God and everybody.

In August, I got a couple callbacks from Central Casting that didn't amount to anything and then—finally—I got picked as an extra for a bar scene in a B film. My face ended up on the cutting room floor, but I still got my seven bucks. It wasn't stardom but it was a start. I went out celebrating with Lana and a couple of fellas she knew. My date bought me a steak and got us into a second-rate speakeasy on Wilshire. He got fresh in the back seat after, but that was to be expected and I made sure to put a stop to it before he went too far. I wasn't going to repeat my past mistake—not when I was so close.

Then—it seemed like overnight—rumors turned into a reality. According to the papers, box office numbers dropped by half and unemployment doubled. We'd thought things were bad, but within weeks they got worse. Breadlines swelled and dance partners at the Rose dwindled. Men begging for nickels couldn't spare two for a dance. By the time the Santa Ana winds blew summer into autumn, I was lucky if I made a dollar a night. And a dollar wasn't enough to live on.

I kept trying at the studios—*Don't you give up, Minnie,* I could hear Mama say.

Some days I was too short, others too tall. On Monday my hair was too red, on Tuesday not red enough. It was just too much. Pretty soon I was living off the change in the bottom of my handbag. My face in the pocked mirror at the boardinghouse was drawn, my skin chalky. My hair lost its shine, and gowns I wore at the Rose—they had a rack of dresses in the changing room that all the girls used—sagged where they should have curved. I tried, I really did. I sparked up my smile and perked up my dancing, but I heard from Lana that Bert was looking to send some girls packing, and I was lowest on the totem pole.

Finally, I had no choice. I brought Mama's ring into the pawnshop on Hollywood Boulevard, just down the street from Grauman's Chinese. The proprietor, a fella with a long face and sad-looking eyes, must have thought he was talking to a chump. "Inferior quality," he claimed, holding it close to his face.

I took the ring back, desperation rising in my chest. "It's solid gold." I pointed to the intricately worked gold vines holding a pink-tinged pearl the size of a cat's eye.

"It is unusual, but only eighteen karat." He sighed as if he'd seen this kind of thing before. I suppose plenty of people were down on their luck. "I'll give you thirty, with sixty days to redeem it. Best I can do."

Thirty dollars? I walked out of the store. But the next day I was back, hungrier and not so nervy. That mug took one look at my face and dropped his offer to twenty-seven. I didn't have a choice if I wanted to eat, so I handed it over.

People can be downright horrid, I thought then.

The thing was, I didn't know the half of it.

I'd been in Los Angeles six months when I learned just how naive I really was.

Lana taught me a lot in those days. Like how to make my lip-stick last by mixing it with petroleum jelly and how to make a piece of baloney taste like ham by frying it up on the hot plate. I picked up smoking from her, too. I didn't like it all that much, but it kept you from getting hungry, like she said, and I could make a pack of smokes last almost a week. I'm ashamed to say she also taught me how to ride the streetcar without a ticket and slip a lipstick into my pocket while the salesgirl at Bullock's wasn't looking.

I picked up the lingo from Lana as quick as the cigarettes. When I'd first got off the bus, I didn't know a bird from a bohunk. Thanks to Lana, within a couple weeks, I sounded just like all the other girls out here calling themselves sisters and their fellows macs and palookas.

But what I couldn't figure was how Lana had money to spare for glad rags and bootlegged gin when I worked the same job and couldn't scrape together enough for rent at the end of the month.

On a cool morning in October, I looked—really looked—at myself in the mirror. I wasn't going to get a part in a film unless it was about castaways on a deserted island or victims of drought in an ancient land. I'm not saying I was the only one suffering. Who was I to complain when able-bodied men were selling apples on the corner or praying for a few hours' work in the fields? When women with children clustered at their feet begged for pennies?

That day, I went to one of the breadlines on Broadway. A woman carrying a hollow-eyed infant—with two more children hanging on her ragged dress—stared at my up-to-the-minute frock and fashionable hat. I couldn't bear it. I fished my last quarter from my purse and pressed it into her hand. I wasn't about to take food from children. I'd done this to myself, truth be told, and didn't deserve charity.

Later that day when Lana asked for the rent, I didn't have a nickel. Then she told me how she kept up. Even after six months in the City of Angels, I was shocked.

She fished a cigarette out of her handbag and lit it, taking a long drag. "It's not as bad as it sounds, Minerva. And it will make you ten bucks quick. I can't keep covering the rent for you, you know. There's plenty of girls who could move in here." She offered me a puff.

I said no to the smoke with a shake of my head. I'd known Lana was free with her affection—she called herself a New Woman just like the magazines talked about. But what she was saying . . . No, I couldn't do that. Besides, I wasn't like Lana. She had time working against her. Although the roster at Central Casting listed Lana as twenty-one, I'd seen her in the mornings. She was thirty if she was a day, and thirty was tough to sell in Hollywood. She had less chance of making it big every day that went by.

"I'll find something else. I'll take extra shifts at the dance hall." But we both knew that it didn't matter. Men weren't coming to dance when they couldn't afford a cup of coffee.

Lana shrugged like it was nothing. "Listen, it's not your first do-si-do or anything, right?"

Search me how she knew, but she was right. Alex had taken care of that.

She raised her perfectly penciled brows. "So what does it matter?" My stomach twisted as I realized what she was saying. I was already spoiled, she meant. I guess she was right.

She gave me three days to cough up the rent or get out. I spent every one of them looking for a day job and came up with nothing. I went through my belongings looking for something to take to the pawnshop, but I didn't have anything left. When my time was up, I went back to her. My mouth was dry, and my stomach turned a cartwheel. "Don't you worry about . . . getting pregnant?"

Lana drawled, "Don't worry about it, hon. It's not likely, and if it happens, Bert will take care of you." She eyed me and for a moment seemed to take pity on me. "Honestly, there's no shame in it, Minerva. When you're a film star, this will all be worth it. And anyhoo, no one need ever know." She gave me a sympathetic look. "It's not so bad. Just close your eyes and think of Clark Gable."

Late that night, when my shift ended, Bert was waiting for me. He gave me a couple of shots from his flask—whisky—then introduced me to Cal. The dark-suited man shifting from foot to foot had a sagging, middle-aged face and thick, black-rimmed glasses. He smelled like mothballs and perspiration. My knees shook and the whisky threatened to come back up as Cal led me to his dusty Lincoln touring sedan with a back seat big enough for two.

No one need ever know. No one need ever know. I repeated it like a prayer.

Lana was right. It was quick. It didn't hurt, not like with Alex, but I'd rather have pain than the shame that twisted in me as Bert tucked a damp ten-dollar bill in my hand. When I got home that night, I cried just the same as I did that night in Odessa.

In the morning, I paid Lana and swore I wouldn't do it again.

But I did. God forgive me, I did.

Three weeks later when I hadn't had a good meal in days, Bert took me aside. Cal was coming by again and wanted to see me. It was for the farm, I told myself. For Papa and Penny. I guess I was pretty far gone to believe that hogwash. I drank more whisky, but it didn't make it any easier. When I wrote my weekly letter to Penny, I asked her a question.

Penny, what will God think of what I've done? Does he have something like a big account book, like the one I kept on the farm? With all the good I've done entered on one side, and all

the bad on the other, and in the end he figures if I'm in the
red or the black? I figure I'm in the red, Penny. Have been for
a long time. If I try hard enough, maybe I can balance it out.
I hope so.

I didn't even pretend I'd mail this one but stuck it with all the others in the hatbox.

When the November rent came due and Cal came back a third time, I didn't know how to say no. I didn't think I could, to be honest. That time, I drank everything in Bert's flask, and I don't remember much. But the next morning, I woke with the ten dollars clutched in my hand and asked myself what I'd turned into. I didn't like my answer.

I was between a rock and hard place, as they say, and I didn't know how to get out. I prayed for real then, even though I figured that God—if he was as good as they said he was—wouldn't help somebody like me. But maybe God did hear my prayer, because the next day, I met Max.

―――――――――

When Max found me, I figured he was either the answer to a prayer or the biggest mistake I ever made. Turns out, he was both.

That morning, the room I shared with Lana and the bedbugs smelled like sardines and cheap perfume. Outside the grimy windows, the sky was blanched to the color of dirty linen, as if the November sun itself was tired of shining on Los Angeles. Across the street, a new building was going up like they were all over the city. The pounding of the workers kept time with the hammering in my head.

I dragged myself out of bed and headed for the washroom, hoping it was empty.

The day before, I'd overheard a girl at Central Casting say RKO was looking for a tall redhead for a part in a dance revue. I wasn't particularly tall and not technically a redhead, but I could dance any steps they threw at me. Best of all, it paid twenty dollars. That would give me a little breathing room. I wouldn't have to resort to desperate measures again.

Desperate measures sounded better than what it was actually called.

I washed up and did my hair in the cloudy mirror. Back in our room, I dressed in my blue linen, the brown cloche, and my crocodile shoes. My hair was smooth, my lipstick perfect. My eyes were a little bloodshot from the night before, but there was nothing for it.

When the casting director called me onto the set, I said the lines as smooth as glass and danced like a pro. I got called back with a half dozen other girls. This was going to be my break. I could feel it. A small crowd of spectators gathered as we went through the routine three more times. Finally, the casting director—short and as bald as a lightbulb—gave the nod to the girl on my left. "Thanks, you can go," he said to the rest of us.

I tried to be polite—I really did—but a girl can't keep quiet in the face of that kind of bushwah. "Are you sure about that?"

"Sure I'm sure." He said, drawing himself up to all his five feet.

I could have spit tacks. I'd auditioned for everything from cowgirls to barmaids. I'd pounded the pavement until my best heels were worn to nubs, and now my twenty dollars went to this girl with two left feet? "Listen here, buster. I'm sure she's a sweet girl—" I looked over at her. She snapped her chewing gum and didn't look concerned. "But a potato on a stick can dance better." I pointed to the girl's orange waves. "And she's not even a real redhead."

His cheeks puffed out and his beady eyes narrowed. "Get this—"

he looked down at his clipboard—"Miss Minerva Sinclaire." He said my name like it tasted bad. "The call's final. Now beat it, and don't bother coming back."

Waiting for my trolley five minutes later, I was kicking myself. Word got around fast in this town, and girls who talked back weren't brought back. A woman standing next to me had a cardboard suitcase and shoes bound together with twine. Her dress was at least two sizes too big for her. A panicky flutter started in my chest. Was that what would happen to me? Would I end up like so many of the women here in the City of Angels, desperate, alone, starving?

That's when Max sauntered up, looking like he had nowhere special to go. Every girl on the corner watched him. He was tall with wide shoulders and long legs—a little like the cowboys who hung around Central Casting—but his three-piece was sharp enough to slice a steak, and his two-toned wingtips bright as new pennies. Except for a crook in his nose, his profile was perfect.

One dark curl threatened to make a getaway from his tipped fedora as he tossed a nod toward the studio across the street. "You're not making it easy on yourself, kicking up a fuss."

So, he'd seen my tantrum. Goody for him. I shrugged.

"Max Clark," he said, sticking out his hand.

I took his hand and tried to figure his game. I'd learned a few things about people since I came to Hollywood, the most important being everybody wanted something.

He smiled. "Let me buy you a cup of coffee."

I was pretty sure that smile had nailed more than a few hearts to the wall, but a cup of coffee sounded good, and my feet were killing me. I slipped my hand through the crook of elbow he offered. He steered me along Sunset, past the Egyptian Theatre and across the street, stopping traffic like he owned the road. I tried to be cool as we breezed past the line at the Montmartre, reminding myself to close my mouth as Max Clark handed his hat—a black fedora with silk trim—to the smiling maître d' who had looked down his nose at me all those months ago.

Max guided me into what seemed like another world. The air was cool, as if even the summer heat wasn't allowed in without the proper escort. A small orchestra played in the center of the room, and we angled around the gleaming dance floor where couples tangoed in the middle of the day. Chandeliers sparkled off silver and crystal as a waiter pulled out my chair at a table draped in white linen and stood by while I sat.

"Two cups of coffee, Al." Max eyed me and leaned back in his chair. "And bring the lady a roast beef sandwich and chocolate malt."

He wanted something all right, but in this place I was ready to listen, and I wasn't about to turn down a sandwich.

"So," he said, pulling a silver cigarette case from his jacket pocket, "you want to be a film star?"

He didn't beat around the bush. I liked that. "Yes." The waiter was back like magic, pouring steaming brew into a delicate china cup and adding a splash of cream.

He fixed me with a stare. His eyes were the color of honey, ringed with chocolate-dark lashes, almost as if the makeup artists had a go at him. He took out a cigarette, an expensive foreign brand, and tapped it on the white linen. "Why?"

My reasons swirled together like the cream in my coffee. To hold my head high again in Odessa. To hear Papa say, "I'm proud of you, *Liebchen*." To show Penny I could do something right. To save the farm so losing it wouldn't kill Papa. But I didn't say any of that. The answers that made sense—fame and glory and all that applesauce—I didn't want to say those either. I shrugged. "Because I'd be good at it." It was as good a reason as any.

I sipped my coffee and Max struck a match. The end of the cigarette glowed red.

The waiter came back, carrying a tray covered with a silver dome. He set it in front of me and lifted the cover with a flourish. Thinly sliced roast beef piled high on thick golden toast, horseradish dripping down the sides, a chocolate malt in a frosted glass. I ignored my rumbling stomach. "I've answered your question, Mr. Clark. My turn."

Max Clark leaned back and, crossing his legs, breathed out a curl of pale smoke. "Go 'head, ask me anything. I'll always play it straight, and that's something in this town."

"How do you know my name?"

"I've seen you around at the studios." He took another pull on his cigarette. "How long you been here? Six months?"

My face must have shown him the answer.

"Longer, huh? You have grit. I saw that today. But grit doesn't get you parts. You know what does?"

How was it that he was asking questions again? But I answered quick, "Talent."

He snorted a laugh and tapped his smoke on the crystal ashtray. "That's a good one." He looked me up and down, and a flush crept up my cheeks. "Not talent, sweetheart. Not looks, either, although you've got that in spades." He eyed me from under his long lashes, and my heart did a little number. "Connections. That's what this town is about. And that's what I have."

Just then, my stomach growled so loud I think they heard it on the dance floor.

"Dig in," Max said, looking me over. "You could use a few good meals."

"That's my lookout, buster." I was a little on the skinny side; he didn't have to say it. I used my knife and fork to cut the sandwich into small pieces and told myself to eat slow, but it was the best thing I'd tasted in months. I looked him over as he stirred his coffee. I wasn't some dumb bunny. I'd heard plenty about girls being taken in by handsome con men, and I wasn't about to join their ranks.

Max glanced up as if he knew my thoughts. "Miss Sinclaire, I'm on the level."

I swallowed and wiped horseradish off the corner of my mouth. "Why should I believe you?"

He looked at me sideways and raised his cigarette to the room. "I got you in here, didn't I?"

He had a point. But I still wasn't sold. I had two questions, and he had to answer them straight. I put down my knife and fork. "What's in it for you?"

"There you go, being up front. I like that about you."

He was charming all right, but I'd been burned by charm before. "Cut the baloney."

He blew a silver veil of Turkish smoke. "Twenty percent, off the top."

Twenty percent was a big cut. But one hundred percent of nothing was what I made now.

He watched me think, then added, "If I don't get you a studio contract in six months, we part ways, no charge, no hard feelings."

A studio contract. The words were like gin to a dipsomaniac. I could send money home to Papa for the taxes and the mortgage. After a few months on contract, I could go home with everything I needed. But I had one more question. "Why me?"

He met my eyes, his face earnest. "I've seen you around. You've got determination and you work hard. I think you have what it takes."

Hard work and determination. I covered my flicker of pride by taking a big sip of my malt. It was heaven.

Max waved his cigarette toward the window. "You know that girl today, the one who couldn't dance and got the part instead of you?"

How could I forget?

"She's the casting director's niece. Fresh off the bus from Akron."

I swallowed. "You're saying I never even had a chance."

"Nope. None of you did. He just wanted it to look good, kitten." He stubbed out his smoke and leaned over the table, taking a sip of my malt through the tall straw, keeping his eyes on me.

He was no shrinking violet, this one, and goodness knows I needed help. But could I trust him? "If you have all these connections, why aren't you in films? You know you could be."

"Not interested." That's the first I saw of Max's closed look, the one he had when he didn't want to talk about himself. I got used to it.

"What about your other clients?"

"Until you're set, you're my only client." He tapped another cigarette out of the silver case. "That's how I work."

He handed me the cigarette. I sized him up as I leaned forward for a light. With those eyes and tempting curl, he wasn't the kind of man I'd trust on a good day. But what else did I have going for me? If this fella really was on the up and up, maybe I could get away from the dance hall and everything that went with it.

He eyed me as if he'd read my mind. "How are you set?"

I shrugged. "I make do." I didn't say how.

He raised a brow. Maybe he'd noticed how fast I'd cleaned my plate. "I can get you on at the Brown Derby for now. Doesn't pay much, but the tips will keep you in nail polish."

My heart did a little jig. The Brown Derby would put me in front of all the right people and pay my bills. I didn't have any other prospects knocking on my door. "Six months."

Then he smiled. That was the first time I saw that real, knock-your-socks-off smile of his. It crinkled his eyes and turned his face from handsome to take-your-breath-away. I didn't know then, but that smile would be my downfall. "I knew you were smart. But before we shake on it, I have a few rules."

Was this the catch? "What kind of rules?"

"First rule. Keep your clothes on."

I jerked up and a flutter of panic filled me. What did he know?

He held up a hand. "I get it. You're not that kind of girl. But some girls, they get desperate. Nobody ever made it big by posing for nudies or hopping into bed with a producer. Got me?"

My pulse settled. I nodded.

He held up two slender fingers. "Second, keep a lid on the drinking, and stay away from the rough stuff."

"The rough stuff?"

"Dope, cocaine, pills. They're the beginning of the end. Believe me, I've seen it. Stick to champagne if you can get it. Go easy on whisky and gin. And no more than three drinks for a little thing like you. To make it big, you have to be smart. And anything after three drinks is stupid."

Who did this mug think he was, honestly? I wasn't a kid anymore. "Anything else?" My voice held a hint of sarcasm.

"Just one more," he said, and his smile disappeared. "This is business, you and me. And I don't mix business with pleasure."

"You've got nerve," I sputtered. I didn't know if I was offended or relieved.

He held up his hands, all innocent. "Just being up front. I'm an easy man to fall for." His mouth quirked and that little dimple in his cheek hinted he could be right. "Anyway, as gorgeous as you are, you aren't my type."

"Same back at you," I said. But I had to appreciate his honesty.

He leaned back and tipped his head to the side, considering me. "If you sign on with me, you'll work, Miss Minerva Sinclaire. You do what I say, twenty-five hours a day, eight days a week. Extra and bit parts are for chumps. That's the way down, not up. We're going to the top, the big boys."

I didn't have much else to lose, and everything to gain. I stuck out my hand.

His dark eyes met mine as we shook over the crumbs of my sandwich. "I won't give up on you, Minerva Sinclaire. You can take that to the bank."

He was on the level, just like he said. Max never did give up on me. Turns out, I'm the one who gave up on him.

———————

Max got me a job at the Brown Derby, just like he promised. The owner of the joint, Norb, had me come in and show him my legs before he'd take me on. When he gave me the uniform, I figured why: it was a starched pink dress with white collar and cuffs and a bell-shaped skirt that showed plenty above the knee.

My first shift I brought gallons of coffee to a booth in the corner where studio execs pitched ideas in smoke as thick as Long Beach fog. I tried to get noticed, but all I got was a pinch on the behind and two bits for a tip.

As the morning went on, the red leather booths along the windows filled with more stars than the South Dakota sky. Ramon Novarro and Myrna Loy ordered coffee and eggs just like regular people. Gloria Swanson argued with Cecil B. DeMille over pancakes and pineapple. My head was spinning, and my feet were throbbing by the time I was halfway through my shift.

With less than an hour to go, Louella Parsons herself waltzed through the door with William Randolph Hearst and Marion Davies. A sleepy-looking fellow who had to be Louella's new husband tripped behind them to the corner booth. Florence, an older waitress with bottle-blonde curls and lips painted an improbable tangerine, elbowed me and smirked, "Watch Docky, carrot-top. He's a pill." I wasn't worried. I'd dealt with plenty of handsy men back in Odessa.

I managed to take their orders without a hitch and was hustling a stack of menus to my next table when the front door opened. The menus dropped from my hands as my fingers turned to pudding. The man who walked in might have been the most recognized face in the world if he'd worn his trademark black toothbrush mustache and the comical eyebrows. Without them, he was positively the most handsome: Mr. Charlie Chaplin—genius comedian, director, and notorious ladies' man.

Mr. Chaplin, dressed in a smartly fitted three-piece suit, doffed his fedora. His black mop was streaked with gray, and we were probably the same height in stocking feet, but I went weak as a kitten just the same. The clatter of silver quieted and a momentary hush swept over the room. Even in this restaurant where fame was commonplace, he was something special.

The chatter around me started up again, but I stood there like a bug-eyed Betty. Then Mr. Chaplin bent down, swept up the menus, and set them in my limp hands with a slightly crooked smile and a twinkle in his bright blue eyes. I closed my mouth, my cheeks burning, as he walked to a booth in my section.

I took a deep breath. I could do this. I could speak to Charlie Chaplin, my favorite actor in the world, and serve breakfast to Louella Parsons, the most powerful columnist in Hollywood. I could pour coffee for William Randolph Hearst, millionaire newspaper mogul, politician, and film producer, and his mistress, actress Marion Davies. Just pretend it's nothing.

I took Mr. Chaplin's order without a hitch—a rare steak and eggs. Then Cook barked that my table-three plates were ready. I hustled out of the dining room and around the corner to the service counter. I loaded up both hands with Mr. Hearst's bacon and eggs, a grapefruit and toast for Marion, and a bowl of oatmeal with cream for Louella.

I turned to find the narrow hallway back to the dining room blocked by Louella's husband. He stepped up close. "Aren't you a sweet thing?" His hands went around my waist. I juggled the plates and looked for a polite escape.

"Excuse me, Mr. . . ." I pasted on a polite smile and looked for help, but the hallway was empty. Where was Florence when I needed her?

His hands slid from my waist to my ribs, and he leaned close, his teeth tobacco-yellow and his breath hinting of gin. His hands moved up to places they shouldn't be. I could have called out, but I'd probably lose my job. I could have dropped the plates and defended myself, but I'd certainly lose my job. Panic crept up my throat.

Just then, Docky jerked back, his jacket hiked up to his ears.

Mr. Charlie Chaplin held Docky's collar in his fist.

Without a word, he turned Docky around and marched him into the dining room. I followed Mr. Chaplin and Docky through the now-silent room, every eye on the Tramp and his captive. Docky was six inches taller and at least fifty pounds heavier, but he stumbled ahead of the smaller man like a child caught with his hand in the candy jar.

Charlie reached Louella's table. "Miss Parsons—" he raised his brows—"I believe I've caught your . . . doggy."

Hearst guffawed and Marion giggled. Docky sputtered. Louella's face went red. She said something polite to Charlie while she glared at me. My face burned and I couldn't say a word. I got the feeling this wasn't the first time her doggy had strayed after a pretty girl.

Mr. Chaplin turned to me and gave a polite bow and the smallest of winks before sauntering to his own booth and sitting down. With scattered laughter, the noise of the room rose again, and I went back to my duties with weak knees and stars in my eyes. I forgot all about Louella's icy stare, but what I didn't know was that Louella Parsons didn't forget. And she didn't forgive.

After I signed on with Max, things really started looking up.

Max had a plan and I liked nothing more than a plan.

First, I needed an education. At least twice a week we went to a film. He always paid for the good seats, but I never got to watch in peace. The only thing Max liked more than watching a film was talking about the film. He whispered his way through the opening credits, over the dialogue, and straight through to the happy ending. Honestly, he should have been a professor at one of those high-class universities.

Outside the theater, Max couldn't care less that Joan Crawford was having an affair with Clark Gable or that my hero Charlie Chaplin had been seen at the Polo Lounge with a mysterious new girlfriend. He'd talk about sets and costumes, acting styles and makeup. But what he loved most was the new technology. Sound, lights, cameras. What was coming next.

"Radio killed vaudeville, and films killed radio. Now talkies are killing the silent films. What's next, Mina?" He quizzed me as we walked along Sunset after the film. He had started calling me Mina right away. Minerva wasn't my style, he said.

"Color?" I took a shot in the dark.

He smiled. "I knew you were smart. Color, better sound, they've got stuff coming that we need to be ready for. And not just frame by frame, no sir. It won't be long—maybe by next year—and there'll be color like you can't imagine. Your hair will be terrific, Mina. The camera will love you. Mark my words."

He opened the roadster door for me and helped me in, then came around and slid into the driver's seat but didn't start the engine. "Before the crash, people wanted stories that were real, but not anymore." He nodded to the men standing on the corner in threadbare overcoats, warming themselves beside barrels of burning garbage. "They see enough reality on every street corner. They want to be taken out of this ordinary world, to escape for an hour into a bigger, brighter life." His voice was a little sad. He turned the ignition switch and the roadster roared. "Bringing them that world takes a toll on a person, believe me."

Sometimes I understood what Max was talking about. Sometimes he was tough to follow.

He went on about a friend of his who was buying up all the closed-up cinemas he could get. "People want sound but putting it in is expensive. Lots of places going under. My pal Alfie's buying them for a song, putting in sound, and filling the seats."

"How is that, when nobody's got any money to spend?" Even the cinema in Odessa had been struggling to fill the seats, and that was before things got bad.

"Escape," Max answered. "When your stomach's empty, a nickel will buy you a cup of coffee. Or you can see a cartoon, a newsreel, a B film, and the feature. That's four hours' escape from your worries. A bargain."

I knew about that. Maybe this Alfie was on to something.

The first step in Max's plan was that I was seen by the right people, in the right places. "Just glimpses, I don't want to push you at them," he said. "You follow?"

"Just enough for them to want more?" I said.

"You got it," he said like I'd aced an arithmetic test. "You're going to start out with a leading role. And in an A picture—no Bs or quickies."

I wasn't going to kick about that.

"No more waiting around at Central Casting, either," Max went on. "That's the fastest way down. And you, sister—" he hit me with that smile that made me feel like I was the only woman in his world—"you are on your way up."

I wrote to Penny then.

Dear Penny,

I've met somebody who might change everything. Maybe this story will have a happy ending after all.

I didn't mail it for fear I'd jinx my luck.

Max made sure I was seen all over town. He took me to the

Ambassador for dinner every Friday night, and I gawked when I saw the likes of Buster Keaton and Joan Crawford eating just like everybody else. Monday evenings we were at the Montmartre—the place he'd taken me that first day we met—because that was where everybody who was anybody went on the first day of the week. Once a week we went dancing, even if my feet were aching from a shift at the Derby. Max was light on his feet and kept me smiling with his whispered comments about the clientele.

The first night we danced at the Cocoanut Grove, I bungled a step when we brushed by Jean Harlow locked in a kiss with a much older man. "Don't be shocked," Max said, covering for me with a quick turn. "They're married." He leaned me into a deep dip and whispered in my ear, "Just not to each other." I gulped and tried to look more sophisticated. I don't think I fooled Max.

Fox-trotting at El Jardin in the Beverly Hills Hotel one night, Max whispered, "Look sharp, Mina," and jerked his chin toward a corner table. There sat Louis B. Mayer, his round glasses perched on an eagle's-beak nose, and right beside him none other than Irving Thalberg, the one they called Boy Wonder because every picture he produced was destined for greatness. Before I had a chance to be nervous, Max's hand tightened around mine and he twirled me out, reeling me back in with a wink. Max made sure they saw plenty of fancy footwork before we left.

On the way back to my place, with the scent of lilies in the dark and music still running through my head, Max looked sideways at me with a funny smirk.

"What?"

"You're humming."

"Am not." But he was right. When I was happy, I hummed. Papa had always teased me about it.

The best part was, every night Max took me out, he saw me to the door of Mrs. Perfall's by eleven thirty, wishing me a cordial good night. No funny stuff. It sure was a relief.

I might have been Max's only client, but I sure as shooting wasn't the only woman in his life. Most Saturday nights, I pulled a shift at the Derby, and he was there with one of his ebony-haired gal pals. There were three or four of them from what I could tell—all swanky clothes and red pouts. They weren't hideous, but they hung on him like he was going to make his getaway as soon as their backs were turned. Maybe you should run, Max, I'd think as I dropped menus at his booth with a cheery smile. Max was as gallant as ever, but I never saw him smile at any of them—not his real smile—and I was secretly pleased.

He was always nice about introducing me to his girlfriends. The first one I met was Doris, the next Amelia, and after that they all ran together. For their part, they dismissed me quick in my pink waitress uniform. I got to calling them the Dorises whenever I thought of them, which was hardly ever.

One night, I met one of them in the little girls' room. I was powdering my nose when she walked in and acted like she was surprised to see me.

"Isn't Max just the cat's pajamas?" She smoothed her varnished bob. "You're a lucky duck to be his client." Her tone was as fake as her eyelashes, but her meaning was plain. I was his client and she was his girl.

I was polite, really I was. "Where are you going tonight?"

"Probably to the Cocoanut," she said with a shrug, "but you know Max: he needs to be home before midnight or Julia gets jealous."

Julia? I almost dropped my powder puff. Who was Julia? But I wasn't about to let on I didn't know. I knew Max lived at the

Garden of Allah, but he'd never taken me to his place. Was it because he lived with Julia? I snapped my compact shut and told what's-her-name good night with a smile. I didn't care who he spent his time with because I wasn't stuck on Max. I just wasn't keen on the thought of Max dancing with this sister or answering to a Julia-somebody.

One night in early December, Max took me to the latest Garbo release. I wore a dark-green linen suit tailored to an inch of my life and my best spectator pumps. I'd borrowed Lana's fur collar and pinned up my hair in an elegant knot. I looked pretty good, I thought.

As the story began, Max leaned over and whispered into my ear, "The lighting, see how they fixed it? You can't even tell that she has that square jaw. She owes the director big for making her beautiful."

I ignored his whispered commentary and got caught up in the story. Garbo played a loose Parisian with a long string of lovers. Then she fell in love with Robert Montgomery, a handsome young student, but when he discovered her sordid past, he left her. A shiver washed over me. I knew about sordid pasts.

Max leaned close. "At that angle, her eyelashes look three inches long."

I shrugged him off and sniffed, wiping away the moisture from my eyes with a fingertip so as not to smear my makeup. Montgomery was back, swearing to love her despite her past.

The film ended with Garbo writing a note to her lover as he slept, telling him that she was saving him from ruin, and slipping away into the dark. It was melodramatic and not her best film, but as we walked along Sunset, I couldn't shake the image of Greta Garbo's sad eyes, her heartbroken expression.

Of course, Max was talking again, this time about the new

sound systems that MGM was rumored to have in the works. We passed the pawnshop where I'd hocked Mama's ring, and I stopped to look at it, like I always did. It was still there, displayed front and center. I'd saved my tips from the Derby but didn't have enough to buy it back yet. With a little luck, it would still be there when I could.

I didn't notice at first when Max fell quiet and stepped closer. I guess I looked broken up, because he put a finger under my chin and turned my face toward his. "Hey. That film really got to you."

I shrugged and shook my head at the same time, keeping my eyes on the ring so he couldn't see them fill up again.

Max put his arm around me when I shivered in the cool wind. "People make mistakes. If he was any kind of man, he'd have forgiven her."

I was a little surprised that he'd even followed the story, what with his nonstop monologue, but it wasn't Garbo's lover I'd been thinking of. "Maybe it wasn't his forgiveness that she needed."

He gave me a look I couldn't figure, then tucked my hand into the crook of his elbow and pulled me away from the window. "I wouldn't have pegged you to fall for the sappy stuff, Mina."

I swallowed to clear my tight throat. "I guess I'm just full of surprises."

At dinner, he was even more charming than usual, making me laugh at his sharp comments about the couples parading through the Montmartre. A few times I caught him looking at me oddly, and I tried to shake off my melancholy. It was just a film, for Pete's sake. Not some kind of prophecy.

Then we danced, and all was well when we danced. The sparkling chandelier played across Max's face. One hand held mine and the other rested on my waist, guiding me effortlessly. Our steps were always in sync, Max's and mine. And for a little while, it was only the music and each other, moving in perfect rhythm. No worries, no regrets.

When Max dropped me off that night—walking me to my door like always—I felt something new between us. Oh, I owed him—he was sticking his neck out for me and didn't expect anything more than a handshake. But this was more than gratitude. I hadn't had a real friend in so long, I'd forgotten how it felt. It was the beginning of something good, something I hadn't known I needed.

Even back then, Max wasn't all business. Once in a while, he was just a fella who wanted to have a nice night with a pretty girl. That's what I told myself the night we went to the Tower Theatre. He picked me up at seven, jumping out of the roadster, shiny as a new pin, to open the door for me. It was our usual film night and I'd picked out a soft russet dress. Nothing fancy, but the sweetheart neckline and fitted bolero jacket were the thing for just about any outing. I'd put on some weight and the shadows had disappeared from my eyes. At least at the Brown Derby, I got a square meal every shift.

Max gave a low whistle as he jumped back in the driver's seat. "You get better looking every day." His honey-gold eyes slipped over me, a half smile bending his lips.

I tossed my head and pretended my heart didn't somersault at the compliment. "Then I can't wait for tomorrow."

He laughed and squealed the tires, I grabbed the door handle and let out a little shriek. His driving really was frightful.

He took me to the Tower Theatre crammed on the corner of Broadway and Eighth. He tossed the keys to the valet and helped me out, hustling me under the marquee with its soaring terra-cotta tower topped by a four-sided clock and Indian-head sculptures.

It was a thrill, as usual, being with Max. Women couldn't help but look at him. I could practically see them go weak in the knees. Men recognized him and shook his hand with a glint of envy in their eyes. He had plenty of acquaintances, but I had yet to meet anyone he called a friend.

"Been here before?" he asked as he nodded to the attendant but didn't buy a ticket.

I told him no, getting a good look at the lavish interior as the usher led us up a wide central staircase with carved walnut hand-rails and a stained-glass window that let in the last of the evening sun. I gawked at a chandelier the size of a small automobile before being ushered through a marble-columned doorway. The place looked more like one of those fancy churches in Europe than a picture house.

"It's a monstrosity, isn't it?" Max smiled, tucking my hand in the crook of his arm. "Supposed to be just like the Paris Opera House. Never been there, so I can't tell you for sure." He was jittery and the look he gave me was like a kid with a secret. We entered the auditorium—smallish in size, but boasting a painted dome of a ceiling, carved paneling, and inset medallions of burled wood.

We were directed by ushers to seats in the front section. The picture house was half empty, and most of the audience was men in suits and women in no-nonsense dresses as if they'd just come from work at an office or the studios. A few furs and men in evening wear, so I didn't feel overdressed.

I settled down beside Max and leaned close. "Are you going to tell me what we're seeing?"

"Just relax." He cupped his long fingers over mine on the

armrest, like two upside-down spoons. I liked it, but it didn't mean anything.

I gave him a hard time, partly to cover for the tingles ricocheting up my arm. "You aren't going to tell me about the lighting? Nothing about directors or technique, Professor Clark?"

"Not this time." He smiled as if he'd played me.

I narrowed my eyes. "What is this?"

He smirked. "A sneak preview. Actually, a private sneak preview before the sneak preview."

I raised my brows. "Of?" The suspense was killing me.

"You should know. He's your hero, isn't he?"

I drew in a breath as the screen came to life. *City Lights*, the film Mr. Charles Chaplin had labored over for almost three years—plagued by mishaps, cast changes, and debt, dismissed by critics before it had even been shown. A silent film when talkies were all the thing.

It was too unbelievable. "But . . . it won't be out for weeks yet."

"It's not out. The premiere is in New York next month. This is just for a few people in the business. I pulled some strings—thought you'd like it."

I flushed down to my sweetheart neckline and looked behind us, my pulse jumping. "Is he here?"

Max laughed, low and rumbling. "Settle down. We won't see him." He squeezed my hand. "Just enjoy," he whispered.

The film was marvelous. Funny, of course. Max and I laughed out loud in all the same scenes, but it was also sweet and touching in the most wonderful ways. It was perfection and made me feel like a girl again, with no cares and no regrets. It didn't hurt to have Max's hand cupped over mine for the whole ninety minutes, either.

Max was true to his word. He didn't comment on camera angles or lighting or music. At the last scene, he was completely still, as if holding his breath. I blinked tear-filled eyes at the Tramp's angelic, perfect smile. As the score swelled and the picture faded to black, Max leaned over and plopped a kiss on my surprised mouth.

"That," he said, his face still close to mine, his eyes glinting in the light coming off the screen, "is how a film should make you feel."

I tried to catch my breath. "Like . . . what?" I could barely get a word out, still feeling the press of his lips on mine. The smell of his cigarettes and peppermint.

"Like kissing the person next to you."

I managed to recover the power of speech. "You better make sure you always sit by a girl, then, buster."

He laughed and didn't move away. Around us, people were standing, shuffling to the aisle, but his face was still close to mine, his eyes half closed, as if considering another kiss. "You're something else, Miss Sinclaire. Have I told you that?" His look made me a little breathless.

"Remember, I'm not your type, Mr. Clark." I countered, hoping he couldn't see my fluster, "and you really aren't mine."

He didn't back off, but he looked at me thoughtfully from under those long lashes. "What is your type, Mina?"

"Not the handsome-and-knows-it type, if you follow my meaning." I tried for flippant but my breath was doing funny things and caught in my throat.

He laughed. "I follow." But he said it sweetly and helped me to my feet with a smile, standing back to let me out into the aisle.

By then I had my wits about me. I passed by him, resting my hand against his chest. I leaned up and kissed his cheek, letting my lashes flutter against his skin. "More's the pity." With Max, you had to be able to dish it out as well as he did.

We took our time leaving. Max introduced me to a producer for the new Fox studio and a stunning secretary at United Artists. "She makes the decisions. Don't be fooled by her baby doll face," he whispered in my ear. She flirted with him shamelessly, but it didn't bother me. My lips still felt his kiss.

Silly, I know. It's not like it meant anything, but I caught myself humming the score from *City Lights* as Max drove me home. From his sideways glance, I think he caught me, too.

That was a good night—that night with Max. It helped to remember those good times with Max, later, when everything went wrong.

CHAPTER 3

OSCAR

Señor Lester's party had roared in the small hours of the night and Oscar had slept a precious few hours in the gardener's shed behind the garage. Now, bleary-eyed, he cranked the engine of his automobile for the third time. *"Por favor, Dios mío."* Don't choose today to give up the ghost.

He'd got the Model T—a 1926 with a box—for a good price, and most days he was proud to own his own automobile when most of his neighbors had to rely on the tram or the city bus. But what he wouldn't give for the piece of junk to start on the first try. If he had to get under the hood again, he'd be late to pick up Angel and Roman. The Lord only knew what trouble Roman would get into if he left them with those rabble-rousers at the packing house.

The engine caught and he eased the choke, *gracias a Dios*, then went around to the door and hopped into the car. The sun glinted in the polished rear mirror, a good way above the horizon. He'd be a little late to pick up his brothers. It wasn't good for them to loiter anywhere, especially now. Especially Roman. That boy drew trouble like stink drew flies. Once he got the boys home, he'd come back to do the watering and collect his extra pay for the party last night.

He pulled around the garage. The sun turned the windows over the back garden to gold, the long swimming pool to sapphire. Beauty wasted on *gringos* who'd gone to bed so drunk they wouldn't wake until afternoon. What had happened to the girl Max had argued with last night? Not that he cared, except it proved what he already knew about Max Perez. No Mexican man would let a girl he knew go off with a dog like Lester. But Max was an *americano* now, who only looked out for himself.

Max. He pushed down on the accelerator and the auto jerked. He wished he'd never seen him again. It had been close to four years, but that kind of betrayal didn't fade with time. The gears ground as he shifted into high. If there were justice in the world, people would get what they deserved, Max included. They do good, they get good things, like a place to live and food on the table. If they do bad, they get bad in return. The engine moaned as he reached the main driveway. Instead, *americanos* did bad and got good, and his people worked hard, took care of their women and children, and got back nothing but sorrow.

When Padre Ramirez had given him the inside line on the gardener job, he'd almost turned it down. He'd had all he could take of the film crowd. But Mamá had convinced him otherwise. He needed a steady job, one that didn't ebb and flow with the seasons like everything else available to brown-skinned workers. And it was a good job when Roy Lester remembered to pay him.

He gained speed, passing the tennis courts and the box hedges. The sun glinted off the absurdly perfect lake and he blinked. Then blinked again as a figure lurched from the shadows of the trimmed hedges and onto the road, directly in his path. He jammed on the brakes. *"Qué rayos!"*

It was a woman, as white as death, hair wild and wrapped in rags. A cold hand brushed up his spine as he jerked the auto sideways. Was it *La Llorona*—the ghost woman who roamed the earth, wailing for her lost children? The auto sputtered as he braked. She wrenched open the passenger door and fell inside.

"Please, please," she panted.

No. Not *La Llorona*, but a living woman. Max's woman.

She scooted into the truck and pulled the door shut behind her. She bent over, as if in pain or trying to hide, pulling her dress—the wrinkled and torn wisp of silk—tight around herself. She clutched a pair of ridiculous shoes in her hand.

Oscar stared. He couldn't form words in English.

"Help me, please." Her breath came in short gasps. Her eyes, a startling blue-green, were shot with red.

Miércoles! What to do? He looked back at the house. Would Señor Lester come running out after her? But the house was silent, the windows blank like sleeping eyes. He should tell her to get out, but what could he do—push her out the door, leave her by the side of the road?

"Please—" she turned desperate eyes on him—"please just go."

The auto sputtered and threatened to stall. Then he'd have to crank it all over again. He eyed the girl. She looked like she was running from something. Or someone. She had shrunk down, her lips moving soundlessly, as if she were praying. Last night he thought she looked fragile, but this morning she was like a crushed bloom. He put the automobile into gear and gave it gas, picking up speed. This was a bad idea.

He downshifted as they went around a curve, already cursing himself. He knew seeing Max last night was a sign. Trouble followed Max, and then he dumped his trouble on others. Well, Oscar wasn't going to get fired over Max's floozy. The truck whined as he pulled onto Coldwater Canyon Road. He'd get her away from Lester, but that was all. There was a filling station not far ahead, on Santa Monica. He'd drop her there.

The dress slipped from her shoulder, exposing a pink strap. She swayed, clutching her stomach and closing her eyes. She glanced at him as if she'd just noticed he was still there. "Do you . . . speak English?" she asked in a small voice.

It was a legitimate question, but it rankled. Did every *gringo* think since he had brown skin, he was as ignorant as someone who'd just swum the Rio Grande? Still, he didn't answer. If he said yes, she'd talk to him, and he didn't want that. These *americanas*, they couldn't be trusted.

He tried to concentrate on the curves. This was a treacherous road, even in the light of day. One distracted moment and you could end up tumbling down the steep sides into the gullies or ravines gaping on either side.

"Can you bring me home? Please." She hitched the sorry excuse for a dress up her shoulder. "It's not far, 4242 Western Avenue. You understand? 4242 Western?" Her voice cracked.

He understood all right. And the answer was no. *Absolutamente* no.

Roman and Angel were waiting for him. He wasn't going out of his way for some paramour filled with regret for whatever she'd done the night before. Before he could answer, she took a sharp breath. Her hand covered her mouth. She fumbled with the window crank. "Stop, please." Her voice was muffled.

Now what was the *idiota* doing? He slowed the car. She lurched, coming halfway to her knees on the bench to put her head out the window, and retched. They hit a curve and he jerked the automobile back onto the road.

The dress slipped down her back. He could see a long rip in the fabric, which was why she was clutching it around herself like that. He pulled his eyes away, disgust rising within him. With what he knew about Roy Lester, it shouldn't have surprised him. With one hand on the wheel, he pulled a handkerchief from his pocket. It was clean and smelled like the lye soap Mamá used, ironed smooth. He jabbed it at her bare shoulder. She took it, wiped her mouth, and slumped down into the seat.

"Thank you . . . *gracias*." She pronounced his language in a ridiculous way. She wiped her eyes and clutched the handkerchief. He'd seen hangovers before. Had a few himself. But this bit of a girl had it so bad he almost felt sorry for her. Almost.

On a straight stretch of road, he fished his canteen out from under the bench, the one he'd filled with cold water before he left the estate, and passed it to her. Some *americanos* would hesitate to drink out of his canteen, but she unscrewed the top and took a long drink, gulping the water as if she'd been in a desert. She wiped her hand over her mouth. The truck sputtered and jerked. She put a hand over her belly as if she were going to be sick again.

The filling station was ahead, and he slowed. A greasy-looking kid sat on a stool by the pump, reading a newspaper. He'd drop her there. Oscar looked over at the girl. Her eyes were closed, and she was the color of curdled milk.

She wasn't one of his people. He wasn't obliged to help her.

But neither had he been brought up to abandon a sick woman. If Lupita was in trouble, he wouldn't want someone to dump her by the side of the road. Of course, Lupita was a good girl. She'd never be in this kind of state.

Yet, if he left this girl with a stranger, he'd probably worry all day, not that she deserved it.

He pressed on the gas, picking up speed as he passed the station. He'd get her home, but he'd have to stop for Angel and Roman first. He groaned out loud. What about Mamá? She couldn't know he'd picked up a half-naked woman and let his brothers sit beside her. Angel, he could count on to keep quiet, but Roman . . . he'd need to find a way to make Roman keep his mouth shut.

MINA

Sunlight flashed through my closed lids and my mouth watered. I couldn't be sick again; it was too awful. I swallowed hard. I felt like I'd been hit by a train, then by a bus, then by another train.

You get what you deserve, Minnie Zimmerman, Penny would say right now. She always did like to say that.

I pulled my knees up to my chin and leaned against the rattling door, not sure if the swaying truck or Roy Lester's dead body imprinted on the backs of my eyelids was making my stomach heave.

Should I have stayed? Called the police? Maybe I should have at least said a prayer. But all I could think of was his wife, the press, a scandal. No, I'd been right to get out. It bothered me, though, that I didn't even take a moment to grieve for him. I knew him well enough to go to bed with him, but not to be sad he was dead? I guess that shows how far gone I really was.

I'd left Roy's room, slipping down the staircase—where I'd found my abandoned heels on the top landing— and through the deserted house. Champagne bottles littered the tables and overturned whisky glasses sat in amber puddles. A pair of men's pants were draped over the piano. I told myself I'd get out and no one would ever know I was with him all night. Even with the drubbing my head was taking, I should have known it wouldn't be that easy. Outside, I realized what a mess I was in, miles from anywhere in nothing more than my underthings and a dress that wouldn't stay put.

Dear Lord, help me. As if the God who listened to Penny's prayers would take pity on me at this late stage. That's when I heard the rattle of an engine and saw my chance. And here I was, sitting beside a stranger who didn't speak English. If I could just get home and slip into my room before Lana or my landlady got an eyeful, I could pretend none of this ever happened. I'd get dressed, get some aspirin, and find Max. He'd tell me what to do.

When my stomach stopped doing the shimmy, I opened my eyes, blinking against the bright light. We were on Santa Monica heading toward the city. It wouldn't be long now.

I eyed the man beside me without moving my pounding head. At least now there was only one of him instead of three, like before. He stared straight ahead with a grim turn to his mouth. Like everybody else, he looked like he'd hit hard times. His faded blue shirt was worn, and the tan canvas dungarees frayed at the hems. His cloth newsboy cap looked like it had seen the last century. It was hard to tell, but he couldn't be much older than me—a couple years maybe—and dark enough some women would cross the street to avoid him. No fashionable mustache, just the shade of a day's beard on his jaw. Everything about him was too much: his skin too brown, his hair too curly, his eyes too wide and dark. If he were in pictures, he'd be a south-of-the-border bandit captured by the cowboy hero.

We hit a bump and my stomach lurched. The truck rattled like it would fall apart. It was an old Model T—almost as old as the one we had on the farm. The fabric of the seats was patched in a few places, but clean and smelled like grass. I could almost see myself in the black paneling, shined within an inch of its life.

I couldn't help but notice how he drove, both hands on the wheel, taking the curves like an old man—my queasy stomach thanked him, but I wish we'd go faster. When he glanced sideways, his mouth hardened and his eyes veered back to the road. I looked down to see my dress had slipped again and showed not only my shoulder but most of the scant lacy brassiere made to go under a revealing gown. I pulled it up and closed my eyes, but immediately Roy was there.

Roy's dead eyes. Roy's cold body. Who had killed him? And when? A thought lurked in my mind, one I hadn't even put to words. I couldn't remember anything past dancing with Roy, except that I'd been afraid and desperate and, heaven knows, not in my right mind. I try to be honest with myself—even if I'm not with anyone else—so I made myself think it.

Could I have? Could I have killed Roy Lester? What had my sorry life come to, that I was asking myself if I killed a man?

A punishing bump sent me bouncing against the door. I opened my eyes, expecting to see the familiar streets north of downtown. Instead, we'd turned onto a dirt road. Flat brown fields striped with green rows. Dark-skinned men and women with baskets on their backs. My pulse went into high gear. Where was he taking me? We pulled up at a line of long whitewashed sheds. He jerked the truck to a stop and leaned forward, motioning for me to hunch down.

Where was I and what was he going to do with me?

The Model T had high-set windows and a wide seat. I slumped down like he said—wondering if I'd jumped from the frying pan into the fire, another thing Penny liked to say. He didn't move, just honked the horn . . . two long blasts. I peeked over the lower edge of the open window. Men—all bronze skin and denim work clothes—carried crates to waiting delivery wagons. Two workers with the lanky look of half-grown boys hopped down from a loading platform and loped toward the car. The shorter one was almost at the door, smiling with his hand raised in greeting, when he saw me. His smile fell from his face and his eyes went wide. The other, taller and broader, pushed up behind him and peered through the window. *"Ay, caramba,"* he whispered.

The man beside me barked out a word in Spanish, but the two boys didn't move. He leaned over me and unlatched the door, pushing it open. Then his hand closed around my upper arm and pulled me roughly over the seat next to him. I struggled to adjust my scant covering as the boys slid in beside me, their eyes stuck to me like feathers on a wet hen.

The shorter one—younger, too, now I saw him up close—slid next to me. His eyes were chocolate brown with spiky lashes, his hair a mass of unruly dark curls. The older boy came in next, with lighter hair slicked back with tonic and a shadow of a mustache on his upper lip. They both gawked at me—from my bare toes, my ankles, and my legs, to my naked shoulders and what I could only imagine was the state of my hair and face. The older one let out a whistle through his teeth. The driver said something in an urgent tone that jerked him alert. They all looked toward the men lazing on the platform, but thankfully nobody looked back.

The older boy slammed the door shut, and the man beside me put the auto in low. We jerked back down the rutted road. My stomach lurched as the silence stretched. What was happening? Who were these boys, and how was I going to get home?

The younger boy—the one next to me—stuck out a hand. "Hello," he said with a slight accent. "I'm Angel."

I let out a relieved breath. "You speak English? Thank goodness." I didn't know where to start. "Please, can you tell him I need to get home? On Western Avenue. I—" I realized the hand was still there and he was looking at me expectantly. "Oh." I transferred the grip on my dress to my other hand and shook his. "Minerva." His hand was rough with calluses and gritty with dirt.

The other boy leaned over and took my hand next. "I am Roman." He held it a good moment longer than necessary and gave me a devastating smile. He was too handsome for his own good. Angel's gaze stayed on my face, while Roman's drifted down to my insufficient covering.

"I . . . please." I glanced sideways at the man beside me. "Could you tell . . . him, um, I need to get home? Western Avenue. I don't think he understood me."

Angel frowned at the driver. "He did not understand?"

"I don't speak Spanish. . . and he . . ." I trailed off as the two boys looked at each other, then to the man beside me.

"My *hermano*—that is my brother Oscar," Roman said, and he looked like he was trying to hide a smile.

His brother?

Angel said a few Spanish words to the driver, and he growled back a one-word answer. Angel turned to me. "Oscar says he is glad to meet you." Both the boys snickered. I didn't get the joke. Panic crept up my chest and I blinked to ward off tears. Please, just bring me home.

Angel reacted to my distress. "Are you maybe hurt? Were you in an accident?" he asked, real concern in his voice.

I tried to reassure him. "I'm fine." Except for my heaving

stomach, pounding head, and the dizziness. And I may have killed someone. "I need to get home. Please." My voice broke.

He and his brother—Oscar, was it?—exchanged a long series of words. Oscar's were angry and short; Angel's sounded more like he was trying to make a deal. Roman chimed in with a few sentences that made Angel squirm and Oscar's mouth tighten.

Angel finally turned to me. "Oscar, he brings you home. We go there now." He smiled again, a gentle smile that somehow made me feel better.

Roman nodded, eyeing my bare shoulders. "We get you home, *cariño.*"

"Thank you." I said, letting out a shaky breath. It wouldn't be long, and I could say goodbye to my unexpected—and, at least one, unwilling—heroes.

I'd get home, figure out a story. Nobody would be the wiser.

The man on my left downshifted with his jaw still clenched, disapproval rolling off him like steam from an overheated engine. We turned down Hollywood Boulevard, the marquees dim in the bright light of day, the streets still quiet. We passed Grauman's Egyptian Theatre with the massive columns and barrel spotlights, and the Chinese with its flared copper roof and carved dragons. We veered onto Western and I careened into a hard shoulder. Oscar tensed and shoved me away like I had the plague.

I closed my eyes, thinking of Max. If I'd just listened to him.

On Western, we passed storefronts with gleaming windows showing the latest fashions and green parks bordered with blooming geraniums. The newest models of Packards and Cadillacs parked in front of freshly painted hotels. Angel turned to me and opened his mouth as if to speak, but the man beside me growled a few words in Spanish, and Angel sealed his lips shut with an apologetic dip of his head. The other kid, Roman, grinned and eyed me.

My mind spun with half-formed thoughts as we passed into a neighborhood of modest houses with small green lawns, flower-beds, and older cars. What if Lana was home? Would she ask questions? A few blocks later, weeds replaced the neat flowerbeds. A bum lounged between a boarded-up building and a run-down flophouse. My cheeks heated and I snuck a glance to my left. Oscar was scowling. Why did I care what he thought of my neighbor-hood? Sure, it wasn't the nicest, but it was all I could manage. Actually, it was more than I could manage. Especially as I was wearing this month's rent.

I pointed to an avocado-green house squatting on the corner, framed by a broken picket fence and a junk pile overgrown with weeds. A worn sign tipped drunkenly against a broken window: *Rooms $20 a Month.* "Drop me here, on the corner. Please," I told Angel, and he translated. I prayed my landlady was still asleep. She'd kick me out for sure if she saw who brought me home half-way into a Saturday morning.

Oscar's mouth turned down and I figured he was taking offense. But honestly, if I wanted to tell the story of getting in late last night, I couldn't exactly walk through the front door in broad daylight.

He jerked the auto to a stop and looked around as if he were the one sneaking back home in an evening dress long past dawn. A few words of goodbye from the boys, the rattle of the engine, and I was standing on the curb like yesterday's garbage. I didn't wait around. I slipped through a gap in the leaning fence and darted across the weedy lawn, still damp with last night's moisture. With any luck, I could sneak in, get out of this dress, and nobody would be the wiser. Nobody but the angry man and his brothers. But that couldn't be helped now.

The window was unlatched. I breathed a sigh of relief and listened for a moment. It was still early, and Lana never woke before nine if she didn't have to. Lana was always going on with "girls gotta stick together" when she needed to borrow my clothes, but this was a dead body, and maybe girls didn't stick together over dead bodies. I wasn't about to test her because I had the suspicion she'd fail.

I pushed up the sash and hoisted myself through, less than graceful, I'll admit. My dress caught on a nail, and with a loud rip, I landed in a heap on the hard floor.

"Well, well. Look what the kitty cat dragged in."

I looked up to see Lana, wrapped in her crepe de chine robe, a cigarette dangling from her fingertips. It seemed my only luck was bad luck.

Half an hour later, washed, brushed, and in my gray gabardine, I still felt like somebody was hammering on the top of my head with a pickaxe. I'd spent as long as I could in the washroom down the hall, hoping Lana had somewhere to go, but she was sitting in our one good chair when I came back, looking smug. My shift at the Brown Derby was coming up. If I didn't leave soon, I'd be late, but I needed to call Max first, and I couldn't do that with Lana listening in.

"So who's the lucky fella?" she said as I helped myself to the last of the coffee from our little percolator. "As if I didn't know."

I almost choked. Had I told her where I was going last night? I played it cool. "I don't know what you mean."

"Don't give me that bushwah. You two have been looking at each other with calves' eyes for a month." She exhaled a breath that smelled of old cigarettes and gin. "Don't worry. I won't tell anybody." She stubbed out her cigarette and pulled herself to her feet. She grabbed her bath towel and shower cap from the closet, then opened the door to the hallway. "I don't like the guy myself, but whatever floats your boat."

Max. She thought I'd been with Max.

I took another swig of the bitter coffee as my cheeks burned. She was right, of course. I had been with Max but not like she thought. At least not last night. As soon as I heard the latch click on the lavatory door, I rushed down the hall to the telephone. "West Hollywood 8152," I told the operator.

I let it ring ten times before I gave up.

Back in my room, I sat down and tried to think, taking a gulp of the cold coffee. How long would it take before somebody found Roy's body? Had anyone seen me go upstairs with Lester? Marion, she'd been asleep on the divan. Louella? Why couldn't I remember anything?

My hands started to shake, and I put my cup down with a clatter.

Think, Minnie, think. As far as anyone knew, I could have left anytime during the night. But what about this morning? Oscar. Would he talk to the police? Tell them he picked up a woman and brought her to 4242 Western Avenue? He didn't have any reason not to. If the police asked me questions, I'd need to have answers. Like where I'd slept last night.

Anxiety rose in my chest and I couldn't breathe. I searched through Lana's handbag and found her pack of cigarettes, lit one, and brought it to my lips with shaking hands. I took a puff. What would Max tell me to do? Max, please, tell me what to do.

I let the smoke out in a long stream.

Stay calm, he'd say. Act natural.

I smoked the cigarette down to a stub, ground it out in the ashtray, and buried the butt in the wastepaper basket so Lana wouldn't gripe. I'd go to the Brown Derby, just like any other day. Pretend everything was on the up and up.

I picked up my handbag and keys, let myself out the door, and passed the washroom, where I could hear Lana splashing and humming to herself.

Nobody would know. Nobody would ever have to know.

OSCAR

Oscar put the Model T into high gear. He'd dropped Roman and Angel at the house and told them not to say a word to Mamá about the girl. Angel would keep his word. Roman . . . Oscar wasn't so sure about Roman. Nudging the throttle as far as he dared, he pushed the Ford up Canyon Road until the engine whined and shook. His eyes were gritty from lack of sleep, but if he didn't get back to Roy's estate today to clean up the party, he wouldn't get paid. And he needed the money.

He passed the gatehouse and took the turn on the long drive, then jammed on his brakes and stared. Three black autos, all with white stars on the doors, were parked haphazardly in front of the wide stairs leading to the front door. Next to them, a long black hearse.

Santo cielo. Police. What were they doing here? And the hearse. He crossed himself just like Mamá would have done. It couldn't be Francesca. They wouldn't call a hearse for a housekeeper. He pushed on the throttle and crept past the vehicles to the long garage behind the house. He parked the Ford and turned off the ignition but didn't move. So who was dead?

Whoever it was, he couldn't sit here all day.

Oscar took a deep breath and walked to the back door, feeling like he'd swallowed a cactus. He hadn't done anything wrong. Then why was his heart pounding like he was being chased by a pack of dogs?

He opened the door to the kitchen. It was a big room, with white tile and a large table, cabinets made of dark wood, and every modern appliance from an electric icebox to a gas-powered stove with five burners and two ovens. Two men in suits had their backs to him. Francesca stood near the sink. She saw him and ran stumbling into his arms. "Oscar, *gracias al Dios*."

What was this? Francesca was as white as a ghost. Panic squeezed his heart like a fist. "*Qué pasó*, Francesca?"

The man closest to the door turned to regard him with sharp, flint-gray eyes. He was shorter than Oscar, with a barrel chest and a neatly pressed camel tweed suit. A few tufts of sandy-brown hair sprouted from an almost-bald head, but a luxurious mustache and unruly eyebrows made up for the lack. The second man was tall and thin, with neat blond hair and a bland *gringo* face.

"Oscar Dominguez?" the short man asked, consulting a notebook in his hand.

Oscar's mouth dried to dust. He nodded, snatching off his cap and clutching it at his side. His heart pounded in his ears. Was it a deportation? Francesca wasn't a citizen, and neither he nor Alonso nor Lupita had papers to prove they were born here. But a hearse? It had to be something else.

"Speak English?" the man asked, his gray eyes skimming over Oscar's rumpled work clothes.

"Yes," Oscar answered.

He nodded, then stuck out a broad hand. "Good. I'm Detective Brody."

The hand reaching out to him was as big as a dinner plate, the nails well cared for and clean. Oscar couldn't remember a *gringo* ever offering to shake his hand before, least of all *policía*. He switched his cap to his other hand and shook with Brody. The man had a firm grip.

"This is Officer Adams."

Adams didn't offer to shake.

"Do you know why we're here, son?" Brody asked.

First question and he didn't have an answer. "No, sir."

Francesca put her head on his chest. *"Ay, ay, Oscar. Está muerto . . ."*

Who was dead? His stomach clenched.

"Mr. Dominguez," Brody said, his face a grave mask. "Your employer, Roy Lester, was found dead this morning."

Señor Lester? Oscar's legs went weak and he found himself holding on to Francesca. But he . . . It couldn't be.

Brody pulled out a chair. "Have a seat, please."

Oscar sat, trying to take in a breath. Señor Lester dead. *Qué?*

Brody watched him, smoothing his fingers along his bushy mustache. After Oscar had taken a few breaths, Brody spoke. "If you don't mind helping me out, I have a few questions for you and the rest of the staff. Routine stuff. Nothing to worry about."

Nothing to worry about? They could do anything to him. Arrest him, get him fired, deport him. They didn't even need a reason. He kept his face neutral. "I don't think . . . I don't know anything." He waved a hand weakly. "I just got here."

"Sometimes people know more than they think. And I'd like you to help me talk to Señora—" he checked his notes—"Garcia. If you don't mind." He didn't wait for an answer. "You were both working here last night?"

"For the party, yes."

"Anybody else?"

Oscar hesitated. He didn't want to say, but he couldn't lie. "Alonso and Lupita, they work here. And Señor Feng."

"Feng?" Brody raised his brows. "A Chinaman?"

"*Sí.* At the door." Oscar's mouth twisted. Lester couldn't have a Mexican opening the door for his guests. Feng Li had been hired for the night and had done nothing that Oscar could tell, other than opening the door and looking down his nose at the rest of them.

Brody made a note. "What about the others? Alonso and Lupita?"

Oscar translated and Francesca spoke in a tumble of Spanish. "They don't know anything. I sent them home early this morning on the trolley. They didn't see anything. Tell him." She straightened as if she were facing a firing squad.

Oscar shook his head. "Francesca's children, they went home this morning."

Brody stroked his mustache like a beloved pet. "Just you four taking care of this big place?"

Oscar translated and Francesca answered emphatically. "*Ay, ay.* Tell him. My feet, they are always aching. My back. Señor Lester, he is—"

Oscar cut her off. "Yes. Just us."

A question nagged at him. Something he didn't want to voice, even to himself. "Señor," he said, because he didn't want to answer any more questions without knowing. He ran his tongue over his dry mouth. "How did he—I mean, Señor Lester, how did he . . . ?"

Brody looked at the other *gringo*, Adams, who scowled. Then the detective said gently, "He was murdered, son."

Oscar felt his knees weaken but caught himself before he betrayed any emotion. Murdered.

Brody went back to business. "See anything unusual last night?"

"No," Oscar answered quickly. Too quickly. "I was in the kitchen."

Brody eyed him.

Oscar had seen plenty. Drinking and drugs and lechery. But that wasn't what Brody meant. He meant unusual like a girl running away in a ripped dress. He should tell Brody about the girl. But something had stopped him. Maybe it was something to do with Max, some loyalty that even Max's betrayals hadn't killed. Or maybe it was the girl herself, how she'd looked so broken and terrified. Maybe he was just afraid. Whatever it was, he was stuck now.

Brody watched him. Adams stared bullets. Oscar tried hard not to even think of the girl, as if they could read his mind.

Finally, Brody seemed to accept his answer. "Follow me," he said and started toward the front of the house, glancing over his shoulder. "You too, Señora."

Oscar followed Brody and Adams into the immense front room and up the sweeping staircase, Francesca shuffling behind him, one hand pressed against her hip. Brody slowed his steps to accommodate Francesca's pace, talking all the while as if they were on a stroll in the park. "Now then. Is—was—Señor Lester a good employer?"

Oscar relayed the question to Francesca with a warning glance.

Francesca didn't get the hint. "I ask for more help, but he says no. This house, it does not run itself." She snorted and flipped a hand toward the paintings on the walls, the carpeted hall, the many bedrooms.

Oscar translated a shortened version of her complaints.

At the top of the stairs, a hallway the color of fresh cream with mahogany paneling stretched before them. Half a dozen closed doors lined the hall like somber guards.

Brody threw questions over his shoulder. "And last night. Anybody here didn't seem right? Anything strange?"

Max. A cold knowledge shivered down Oscar's spine. Max didn't belong. He hadn't shown his face at Lester's in the two years Oscar had been here. How much had his cousin changed? Enough to kill?

They walked past an open door. Inside, Señora Lester sat on a satin-covered bed. A well-dressed *gringo*—young and handsome—put his arm around her and pulled her close. She saw Brody and put her hands over her face, letting out a pathetic sob that didn't fool Oscar for a second.

At the end of the hall, a set of double doors was thrown open, a uniformed officer standing guard. Inside, he could see several men, hear murmured conversations. A flashbulb popped, lighting up the doorway.

Francesca stopped, crossing herself and kissing her thumb. Brody took her arm as if to support her. "Sorry you have to see this again, ma'am."

The officer stepped aside, and Oscar followed Brody and Francesca into the room. He thought *americanos* couldn't surprise him, but he'd been wrong. Who had ever known such extravagance?

His feet sunk into thick cream-colored carpet. Mahogany paneling gleamed darkly. A divan of creamy white leather and polished wood and two matching chairs were arranged around a fireplace. The room felt oppressive—airless—even with the chocolate-brown curtains drawn open around the towering windows.

"Through here, please." Brody motioned them on.

The thick carpet continued through double doors, into a room crowded with men and equipment. Animal heads—a lion, a bear, some kind of deer with long straight antlers—looked down from every wall with glassy eyes. A mulberry velvet coverlet and satin pillows lay in disarray on an enormous bed. A gilt-framed picture of Señor and Señora Lester hung crookedly over a writing desk, and the chair lay on its side in the corner.

The crowd of men shifted, and Oscar froze. In the center of the room, Roy Lester's dead body lay sideways, sprawled atop a rust-colored stain, his glassy eyes staring at the ceiling.

"Ay, caramba." Oscar's stomach twisted as he thought of the girl in his auto this morning. Surely she couldn't have done this? The man had been stabbed. A long blood-covered knife lay beside him. Francesca murmured a prayer under her breath. Perhaps he should offer a prayer as well, but Oscar couldn't bring himself to ask God's mercy on Señor Lester's soul. He had no sorrow for the man, and his only thought as he looked at him was that Señor Lester had got what he deserved. He supposed Mamá would be shocked—and Padre Ramirez would be disappointed—but he couldn't help it.

Two uniformed police officers leaned over the body. A suited man stood nearby, his camera clicking in one hand, a flashbulb held high in the other.

Brody barked at the photographer, "You forensics?"

The man took another photo. "Just finishing up."

"Any idea on time of death?"

The man rubbed his chin, his eyes distorted behind thick glasses. "At least eight hours from what I can tell. Maybe more."

Eight hours. A prickle ran down Oscar's spine. The girl. He'd picked her up—what?—just two hours ago? Had she stayed beside a dead body through the night?

"Get the photos to me by end of day today." Brody looked at another man in a tan suit. "What about the weapon?"

The man frowned. "It came from there." He pointed to a wall of swords and daggers. Some looked like they'd been around for hundreds of years, others like they'd come from halfway around the world. Toward the top, there was a gap where the knife had hung.

The officer wasn't done. "And this." He held up a leather wallet. "On the bedside table."

"Any cash?" Brody asked.

The officer raised his brows. "Couple hundred dollars."

Brody stared at the wallet as if it could tell him something he didn't know.

Two officers brought in a stretcher. "Can we get him out of here, boss?"

Brody pursed his lips and shook his head. "Give me a few minutes, boys. Take a break." The room emptied faster than a public square in a rainstorm. The crease between his brows deepened. "Señora Garcia, I'd like you to tell me if you see anything . . . out of the ordinary."

Oscar translated. As if a dead body wasn't out of the ordinary. Francesca looked around the room, her eyes wide. "I cleaned before the party. All was in order."

Oscar told Brody, and they took in the broken vase, the strewn pillows, the overturned chair. Through a doorway Oscar could see another room with gleaming silver fixtures, plush white towels, and a sleek black-enamel toilet—nothing like the outhouse he and his brothers used. Beside a mirror, a wall sconce hung crookedly, the bulb shattered, the silk shade knocked sideways. The window over the sink was open, curtains lifting in the breeze.

Francesca tsked loudly over the mess. "I clean," she said in English and lurched toward the washroom.

Brody stopped her with a hand on her arm, "Not yet, Señora . . ."

Brody waited, his eyes on a picture hanging between the bedroom and the lavatory. Señor Lester and his beautiful young wife. "Adams, bring in Mrs. Lester, please."

Oscar's jaw clenched, and he wished for nothing more than to get away from this opulent room, these men, and now, Señora Victoria Lester. She was all he detested about *gringos*.

She walked into the room sheathed in a silky black dress that looked better suited to a bedroom than a grieving widow. Her short hair was an unnatural shade of platinum and her lips a charlatan red. She clutched the arm of the young man beside her and dabbed a handkerchief at black-lashed eyes that Oscar was sure hadn't shed a genuine tear that day, or maybe ever.

"Mrs. Lester, again I'm sorry for your loss," Brody said. "Just a few more questions and then we'll leave you in peace."

If Oscar had to guess, he'd say the young man was Señora Lester's agent, Grant Manchester. They'd heard his name plenty in the screaming matches that went on between Señor and Señora. She and Grant were in love. She hated this estate and everything in it, including Roy. She wanted a divorce. *Over my dead body,* Señor Lester had roared. Oscar felt a chill roll over him.

Señora Lester put a hand over her lips. "Oh, if only I'd been here. My dearest Roy . . ." She choked out a ladylike sob.

"This must be difficult, Mrs. Lester, but it will only take a moment." Brody sounded like he'd had about enough of her melodrama.

She pulled herself together with a sniff.

"Do you have any idea who might have killed your husband?" Brody didn't beat around the bush.

She shook her head, her eyes as wide as a frightened doe's. Oscar figured she'd used that look a dozen times in her films. "I can't imagine, Officer Brody. Everyone loved Roy."

Oscar had to hold back a snort. Roy Lester wasn't the kind of man everyone loved.

"It's Detective Brody, ma'am. Do you know why someone might have been in his room? Was there something here—valuables, maybe?"

Señora Lester bit her lip and did a good impression of thinking. "Everything of value is in the safe downstairs, in Roy's office. He keeps cash in it, and my jewelry. Only Roy knows the combination . . ." She put her hands over her face. "Oh! I just can't believe he's gone." She started whimpering again.

Grant Manchester stepped forward. "That's enough, Detective. Can't you see she's distraught?"

Brody nodded like he expected as much. "Of course. We can talk again when the shock has worn off. Will you be staying here at the estate?"

She shook her head. "I couldn't. Not now. Not ever."

"Mrs. Lester will be staying at the Beverly Hills Hotel—" Grant Manchester spoke for her—"and the estate will be sold as soon as possible."

Oscar jerked to attention, panic rising. So soon? "Señora," he sputtered, "What about us? You will still need help, at least until—"

"The estate will be closed immediately." Grant Manchester didn't look at Oscar but addressed himself to Brody. "Mrs. Lester no longer requires the services of the help. In fact, if you're looking for suspects, I'd look no further than those in Mr. Lester's employ. I never did understand why he hired those people. And Victoria . . . she never trusted them."

The injustice. Why would any of them kill the man who paid their wages? "But our back pay," Oscar kept at it. "And what we are owed for last night's work—"

Señora Lester buried her face in Grant Manchester's lapel and let out a sob worthy of an actress with twice her talent. "I can't— Grant, please. Oh, it's just too much."

Grant turned to Oscar with a glare, his mouth pinched under a thin line of mustache. "She just lost her husband and you people are badgering her over a few dollars." He put his arms around the weeping woman and led her out of the room. Oscar clenched his jaw hard, wishing he could teach that *gringo* a lesson. A few dollars might mean nothing to him, but to Oscar and the Garcias, it meant a roof over their heads and food on the table. He rubbed a hand over his face and turned back to Brody, who gave him a sympathetic look.

"Not much to go on," Brody said.

"It's as plain as the nose on your face, boss," Adams disagreed. "Robbery gone wrong, as you can see. Somebody thought they'd get some dough. Lester caught them and put up a fight. He lost. Whoever it was went out the window."

Brody stroked his mustache, looking unconvinced. "And left the wallet full of cash?"

Adams shrugged. "Some people aren't too smart." He looked at Oscar like he was *some people*. Oscar's heart jumped in his chest.

Brody stepped toward Lester's body. "Let me see if I follow." Brody held out a hand and counted off his fingers. "Somebody comes up here to rob the place, thinking Lester's downstairs carousing. He gets a surprise when Lester comes in." He pointed to the weapons display. "They fight. Whoever it is grabs that knife from the wall and stabs Lester, then runs. Is that what you're saying?"

"I'd bet my last dollar on it," Adams insisted.

It was Adams who wasn't too smart. Oscar surveyed the disarray of the bedroom. In Spanish, he muttered to Francesca, "Whoever killed him was looking for something, but not the money."

Brody turned his gray eyes on him. "What was that, son?"

Oscar could have kicked himself. He repeated his comment in English.

Brody's eyebrows twitched.

Adams turned on Oscar. "Look who thinks he's Sherlock stinking Holmes."

Oscar sealed his mouth shut. He didn't need to draw attention when he was hiding his own secrets.

Brody didn't comment at all but turned back to Francesca. "Anything else you can tell us, Señora?"

Oscar repeated the question in Spanish. Francesca shifted from one foot to the other, looking uncertain.

"What is it?" Even as he said it, he hoped it wasn't something bad. Something that would get them arrested.

She hesitated, then turned abruptly and left the room. Oscar exchanged a glance with Brody, and they followed her down the stairs, her pace quick this time. She led them to the doors of Lester's office, not far off the main ballroom. "I found it like this," she said to Oscar as she opened the doors and stood back for them to enter.

Oscar had been in the office one time, the day Padre Ramirez had sent him for the gardening job. It looked exactly the same as it had then. Sunlight seeped through slatted blinds, throwing bars of dark and light over floor-to-ceiling bookshelves. A jewel-toned floor lamp cast colored light over a mahogany desk the size of a grand piano.

Oscar turned to Francesca, still standing in the doorway. *"Qué?"*

She threw up her hands. "Do you have eyes? It is a mess." She motioned to the desk. "See this?" A cigar box was tipped over on the desk, spilling a few fat cigars. "And here?" The drawers, a few slightly open, ruffles of papers peeking out. "And see?" She went to the wall of leather-bound books. "All crooked. And the wood—someone has put fingerprints all over. I just polished it yesterday, before the party."

Oscar took a second look. Papers on the desk disheveled, letters and envelopes in disarray. Smudges on the polished ebony shelves. Someone had been in here.

Adams was in the corner, where a tall black safe stood sentry duty. He tugged on the L-shaped handle. "Safe's locked up tight."

Brody examined the top drawer of the desk. He ran his finger over a deep gouge, as if someone had used a sharp instrument to pry it open. He tugged and it slid open, the lock rattling brokenly. Inside was a stack of hundred-dollar bills. "Somebody was looking for something here." Brody rubbed his chin. "And again, it wasn't money."

Oscar glanced at Adams, feeling a tiny thrill of vindication. Adams narrowed his eyes and glared.

Brody straightened up. "Mr. Dominguez, Señora Garcia. You have been a great help. Before you leave, give your particulars to Adams here in case we have more to talk about."

Adams fished a notebook from his jacket pocket and licked the pointy end of a stubbed pencil. "Don't suppose you have a telephone?" he asked after he took down Oscar's address, his tone bordering on insult.

Oscar bit out the number for the *sociedades*. "They'll get a message to me."

Oscar gathered his few belongings from the room behind the kitchen and pushed out the back door. He felt watchful eyes burning the back of his neck as he passed by the greenhouse. What did Adams think, that the Mexican help was going to steal one of Roy Lester's precious orchids? Those delicate flowers would be dead within days with no one to water them, not that he cared.

Let them die and good riddance. Perhaps Adams worried that Oscar would get in Roy Lester's Rolls-Royce and drive it away? Or take the buttercream Packard or the red Mercedes Gazelle? He needn't worry. Oscar didn't want anything from Lester but what was owed to him.

He inserted the crank in his old Ford and gave it a violent twist. Adams was suspicious and that scared him. Oscar hadn't lied to Brody, not exactly. But he hadn't told him everything. He could feel a trickle of sweat on his brow. He pulled out the throttle and cranked again.

Por favor. Start.

Adams was still watching him. Probably itching to pull out his handcuffs.

Oscar's heart was pounding in his ears. Why hadn't he come clean? He didn't owe the woman in the green dress anything. The engine caught. Oscar stood and pulled out his handkerchief, wiping the sweat from his face before he got into the auto. He drove past the gatehouse and turned onto Canyon Road.

When he reached a wide spot, he pulled over and took the Ford out of gear, letting out a long breath. Guilt pricked him. Roy Lester had been murdered while Oscar had slept in the garden shed. Should he mourn the man? He couldn't. Oscar had too many worries of his own to spare more on a *gringo*.

He was out of a job. They couldn't manage on what Roman and Angel made in the packing house and his mother's laundry wages. The rent was due, and it didn't look like Victoria Lester would be coming through with his wages. If he didn't have the money by Monday, they'd be packing up by Monday night.

But the girl. His stomach twisted into a tight knot. Had the girl he picked up really killed Lester? She could have. She'd been shaken and pale. She'd been desperate. And he had helped her get away. What did they call that—aiding and abetting a fugitive?

He could go to prison.

Oscar groaned and laid his forehead on the steering wheel. What had he done? *Estupido.* But all he had thought of as Brody questioned him was that if the girl had killed Lester and the police found out that he'd helped her get away, he'd be arrested. Then, when he saw the bedroom . . . Something wasn't right. And he wasn't so sure she was guilty after all.

The girl he'd picked up on the road was a featherweight, but from the look of Roy Lester's bedroom, there'd been a struggle worthy of Jack Dempsey. And the knife. Oscar was at least three inches taller than the girl he'd had in his automobile, and he would have had to stretch to reach the spot where that knife had hung. How would she have reached it?

Something smelled wrong.

Besides, what did it matter now if she was guilty or innocent anyway? He couldn't turn her in. She'd point right back at him, and the police—Adams, most likely—wouldn't think twice before arresting him. Then what would Mamá do? How would Roman and Angel manage? Oscar rubbed a hand over his forehead. *Miércoles.* Why hadn't the girl listened to Max, who'd warned her not to get mixed up with Lester?

Max.

Oscar straightened up. Max had no love for Roy Lester. He'd made that clear to the girl last night. Could he have killed him? Would he have left the girl there alone? Max Perez wasn't a murderer, but Max Clark was different. Max Clark brought trouble and left pain in his wake. He cared for no one but himself. Suspicion grew in Oscar's mind. Oscar had vowed never to speak to Max again—not in this life or the next. But this was for Mamá and Roman and Angel. This was life or death. He put the auto into gear and threw gravel as he pulled back onto the road. He'd get answers from Max if he had to beat them out of him.

Max had taken enough from Oscar and his family. Oscar wouldn't go to prison for him.

———————

Oscar's heart hammered. A police automobile sat on the corner of Canyon and Sunset, waiting while he passed. It pulled out behind him. He tightened his grip on the steering wheel and tried to stay steady. Two blocks later, the black auto with the white lettering turned onto Glendale. He took a breath like he'd been underwater and pushed his auto as fast as it could go without making smoke.

Sunset Boulevard was already crowded with Cadillacs and Packards, women in furs, men in suits that cost more than a year of his rent. Oscar's stomach clenched tight. He'd heard Max was living in a ritzy place in the middle of Hollywood. The last time he saw his cousin—other than through the hedge at Roy's—Oscar had beaten Max bloody. Max had never shown his face in the *colonia* again.

There. He slowed the rattling automobile when he saw the sign for the Garden of Allah hotel and bungalows. He turned into a driveway guarded by palm trees and a pair of tall cedars. He followed the curved drive lined with sharp-leafed birds-of-paradise and passed a sprawling main house of whitewashed stucco flanked with calla lilies, marigolds, and zinnias. Max Perez had come a long way from the *colonia*. And when he'd had the chance, he'd shed his people—his heritage—like a snake shedding its skin.

Oscar caught the sparkle of a kidney-shaped swimming pool,

and a woman's laughter floated across the manicured grass. Ahead, a line of matching bungalows alternated with overgrown hedges of rhododendrons. A yellow LaSalle roadster—Max's, he knew from *colonia* gossip—was parked crookedly in front of a bungalow like an expensive toy abandoned by a child.

Anger burned like a well-stoked fire in his belly. While Oscar's brothers worked fourteen-hour shifts and Mamá took in laundry, Max lived the high life with fast cars and swimming pools. Was there no justice in this world?

Max had abandoned them all. Mamá, who had treated him like her own son. Oscar, who had fought beside him—defended him—called him his brother when the other boys called him a bastard. Max was an *americano* now, someone Oscar didn't even recognize and someone—Oscar had discovered the hard way, the tragic way—with no honor. Oscar would rather see his children grow up poor with honor than rich and turn out like Max.

Oscar parked beside the roadster and stalked up to the door. He knocked. No answer. He pounded and heard a slurred shout from the place next door. Why should he care if he woke up the neighbors who caroused all night and slept all day?

The door opened and Max stood before him. His sagging pants and an untucked dress shirt looked like they'd been slept in. Lines creased his face. With skin lighter than Oscar's, he could pass for a *gringo*, but his hair gave away his mother's side. Without the oil he used to tame it, it sprung into curls that reminded Oscar of Angel's unruly mop. Max rubbed his hand over his red-rimmed eyes. *"Caramba."* He stepped back.

It wasn't exactly an invitation to come in, but Oscar brushed by him. Max's entryway looked like he'd been robbed. A few picture hooks dangled from walls the color of egg yolk. An arched doorway led to a room trimmed in walnut wainscoting, empty except for a tufted divan the color of a hot pepper and a box filled with books.

Max turned without a word and padded barefoot down a short hallway.

Oscar followed, his heavy work boots thudding on the polished wood floor. He passed a bedroom with a single bed and rumpled blankets. An evening jacket hung from a hook. A bow tie lay like a dead mouse in the middle of the floor. Maybe Max wasn't as rich as he made people believe with his shiny LaSalle and sharp suits. The thought sparked a flicker of satisfaction.

Max led him into a small kitchen, as spotless as Mamá would have expected. A table with a speckled Formica top and two chairs sat on a shining black-and-white checked floor. A sink in the corner, a small gas stove, and an icebox took up the rest of the space. They faced each other, each sizing up their opponent like boxers in a ring.

An open bottle stood alongside a used glass. Oscar picked up the glass and sniffed. Tequila. And cheap. Max delved a hand into an almost-empty cupboard, coming out with another glass. He splashed some tequila in it and handed it to Oscar.

Oscar's nose twitched and not because of the tequila. A mangy-looking calico with one ear lounged in a bright square of sunlight. Oscar drank the shot in one go and set the glass down on the table with a crack. "Still taking in strays, I see."

As a child, Max had a soft spot for lost animals. Dogs, cats, even a baby raccoon at one time. The cats made Oscar sneeze, but Max took them in anyway and Oscar somehow ended up taking care of them. The drink burned its way down to his belly. He switched to Spanish. "Last night, you were at Lester's party."

Max took a wary sip. "It's a free country."

"With a girl, a redhead."

Max frowned. "Yeah, so what?" He drank the rest in one swallow. "You'll be happy to know she left me for the first old man who could get her where she wanted." He wiped a hand across his mouth. "History. Determined to repeat itself."

Oscar didn't have the time or the patience to figure out Max's cryptic remarks. "So you don't know about Roy Lester?"

"I know plenty about him." Max reached for the bottle.

Oscar got in the first hit. "You know he's dead?"

Max recoiled. "Dead?"

Oscar let loose another punch. "Murdered."

Max staggered back. Either he hadn't known or he'd become a good actor.

Now that Oscar had Max in a corner, he asked his question. "Why were you there last night, at Lester's?"

Max ran a hand over his face, then turned his back on Oscar, leaning against the lip of the sink. When he turned around again, his face was shuttered. "Oscar, tell me how he died."

"Answer my question first." Oscar poured them each another shot and got ready for the next round.

Max ignored the drink. "A client of mine, she was invited to Lester's. Now tell me how he died."

"In his bedroom."

Max let out a frustrated breath. "What killed him?"

Oscar sipped the tequila, eyeing Max's clenched fists. "Stabbed."

"Stabbed?" He said it like it couldn't be true.

Oscar moved in for the knockout. "You had something to do with it, Max. You or that girl. I saw her this morning. She was a mess, running from the estate—"

"Saw her? What do you mean?" Max reached over the table and

grabbed the front of Oscar's shirt. "Saw her where? If she came to harm, I swear I'll—"

"Calm down!" Oscar jerked away and tequila splashed. He'd hit a nerve and that meant something. He just didn't know what. "She's fine. At least she was when I left her at her place this morning."

Max's eyes narrowed. "Tell me all of it, Oscar."

"Ask your woman." Darned if he was going to be Max's eyes and ears.

Max's jaw went tight. He strode out of the kitchen.

Oscar followed him to the washroom.

Max stripped off his wrinkled shirt and threw it on the white-tiled floor. He turned on the water, filling a porcelain sink shaped like a clam shell. Steam clouded the tiny room as Max dabbed his shaving brush in a pewter cup and covered his face with lather. "I warned her about Lester, but she wouldn't listen to me. And then I tried—" He closed his mouth abruptly and unfolded a polished straight-edge razor.

Oscar didn't care about Max's regrets. "Just keep me out of your problems."

Max stopped the razor at the side of his jaw. "You think this is my fault?"

"You're around and there's trouble." Oscar's voice was hard. "It's happened before."

Max guided the razor over his cheek and down his neck before he answered. "You're so sure you know it all, Oscar." He rinsed the razor in the sink and met Oscar's eyes in the clouded mirror.

"I know what happened to Maria Carmen was your fault."

Max dropped his gaze and brought the razor up, his voice heavy. "What do I have to do to make it up to you, open a vein?"

As if he could ever make up for what he'd done. "Just tell me, did your girlfriend kill Lester?"

"She's not my girlfriend."

That wasn't an answer.

Max swiped at his face a few more times, then pushed past Oscar. Drawers in the bedroom slid open and shut. The cat wound around his legs, purring loudly. Oscar rubbed at his nose. Why had he even come here? He should have known Max would only think of himself. Max came out of the bedroom, his hair combed, his pressed shirt and silk tie immaculate, every inch an *americano*.

Max rubbed his clean-shaven jaw, as if he was thinking something through. "The police. They don't know about Mina, that she was with Roy, that she left this morning with you?"

Oscar shook his head. "If they find out, and she tells them about me . . . I'm not going to prison. Mamá and the boys—"

"I won't let that happen," Max interrupted. "Listen, Oscar, I need you to keep this quiet."

He didn't like the tone of Max's voice. It reminded him of old times. Him and Max and Maria Carmen. Max, the oldest, always had the ideas. Maria Carmen jumped on any chance for excitement. And then there was Oscar. Somebody had to make sure they didn't get caught. "Listen, I just lost my job thanks to your little floozy—"

"She's not my floozy. And she didn't kill Roy Lester."

Oscar suddenly felt very tired. He let out a long breath. "She was with him last night and this morning he was dead."

"She didn't do it." Max sounded like he was trying to convince himself.

"So who killed him?"

"Could have been anyone. Roy Lester knew how to make

enemies." He turned on his fancy shoe and went into the entry. Oscar followed. Max shrugged into a long wool coat. "I'll find out. Just don't tell anybody anything."

Oscar positioned himself between Max and the door. "What if they come after me?"

Max let out a long breath and put on his hat. "Trust me, Oscar. I'll get this figured out."

"Trust you?" Oscar heard the disbelief in his own voice. Why should he? Besides, the police wouldn't try to deport Dusty Clark's son. What would Mamá do if he were sent to Mexico? Or to prison? And what about Roman and Angel? Max didn't understand any of it, because Max didn't believe in family. "What if I don't?" Oscar ground out. "What if I turn her in?"

"You won't."

Max's confidence set Oscar's teeth on edge. "How do you know?"

Max gave him a look that was part sad and part knowing. "I know because that's how you are, Oscar. You're the hero. You always have been."

MINA

I slipped in the service door of the Derby with my heart in my throat. In the back room, I quick-changed into my uniform and pinned on my cap. I'd spent the twenty-minute ride on the street-car wracking my brains about the party. I practiced my story in case anybody asked. It had more holes than a moth-eaten sweater.

The Derby was packed like usual. The smell of liver and onions—the Saturday special—made my stomach turn an uncomfortable flip, but I switched on a bright smile for Norb as I checked in at the cash register.

"Take the back booths." He eyed me up and down to make sure

I passed muster, just like he had my first day, which had almost been my last.

I stacked the dirty coffee cups on a tray and headed toward the kitchen, remembering how Mr. Chaplin had rescued me from Louella's wandering husband—and his wandering hands—and how Louella had treated me like dirt from that moment on. I stopped suddenly, the cups teetering sideways . . . Until yesterday, when she suddenly became my best friend. She'd invited me to Roy's party and presented me to him like a prize sow at the fair.

Norb barked at me and I double-timed it to the kitchen to do my job. I seated Loretta Young—her name did her justice; she couldn't have been more than eighteen and already a star at MGM—and an older man who must be her agent, and was pouring coffee for a foursome of boisterous publicity types when I looked up to see Max.

He looked terrible. My stomach dropped to my shoes. He knew.

He caught my eye and made a beeline for the back room. I followed him, my mouth as dry as sawdust, remembering what he said last night. *Don't come crying to me.* But was he really going to turn his back on me? He was the only one I could count on.

I pressed my hand over my middle, took a deep breath, and followed him into the room the girls used for changing into our uniforms and fixing our makeup. I locked the door behind me. I didn't need anybody walking in on this scene.

Max leaned against a row of metal lockers, his arms crossed, a look on his face I guess I'd describe as cold. I couldn't say a word.

When I didn't speak up, he bit out, "What happened last night, Mina?"

I swallowed. He waited. So I told him about Louella and Roy, and how she wanted me to keep him company. "After the drinks,

I can't remember. We went upstairs . . ." I stopped, looking at the cracked linoleum floor.

"What happened then, Mina?" His voice was kind of choked.

"I don't—I mean, nothing. I—" I put my hands over my burning cheeks and turned around, walking to the sink so I didn't have to look at him. "I can't remember." I wished I could disappear. "When I woke up, he was dead. I got out of there as fast as I could, but—" There was a knock on the door. Norb's voice calling my name. I didn't move and neither of us spoke until we heard his heavy footsteps fade away. I took a deep breath and turned finally to look at Max.

His face was set like one of those statues in the parks. "You didn't think to call the police, tell somebody?"

He was right. I should have. "No, I—"

"You just left him there and took off?"

I hadn't been able to think. I felt tears brimming behind my eyes, remembering the panic clawing up my throat. "I didn't know—I was scared."

Max turned away and paced across the room. "Good grief, Mina." He turned at the door. "Did anyone see you leave?"

I told him about the man who had picked me up. He and his brothers could go to the police. They knew where I lived.

"Anybody else?" was all Max said.

"No, but Max," I said quick before I lost my nerve, "you were right. About all of it. I never should have—" My throat closed, and my chest felt like a vise. There was so much I never should have done.

He paced back, coming so close I could see the worry in his agate-colored eyes. For a second I thought he'd put his arms around me and tell me it would be all right. Instead, he stuck his hands in his trouser pockets. "Here's the story. You were with me. If anyone asks, we left the party together. Went to my place." His voice was staccato. Unfeeling. That scared me more than anything else. "Did you tell Lana anything?"

I shook my head.

"Good. Don't say anything to anybody." He walked to the door. "Go home after your shift like everything is peachy. Got it?"

I got it.

He walked out the door. No goodbye. No nothing. To be perfectly honest, I didn't deserve anything more.

CHAPTER 4

Odessa, South Dakota

PAPA

Ephraim Zimmerman pulled on his heavy coat and wrapped a woolen scarf around his neck. The winter sun poured through the leaded-glass windows over the door, but he wasn't fooled. It was February in South Dakota—darn cold and they'd see snow by nightfall.

"Papa, where are you going?" Penny stepped into the hall, worry on her face.

He went to her, his boots creaking on the polished wood floor. The scent of baking bread wafted from the kitchen. Penny knew where he was going, and she knew why. "It's Saturday, *Liebchen*."

She crossed her arms over her chest, her mouth pinched tight. "It's cold, Papa."

Ephraim heard what his eldest daughter didn't say. *When are you going to give up on her?* Ephraim brushed his calloused hand over her smooth cheek. His Penny was his no-nonsense girl, from her prim bun to her sensible shoes. But when would she understand that he would never give up? Someday Minnie would come back to them, and when she did, he'd be there to meet her. "I'll keep warm enough."

Penny turned away. "Dinner will be ready in an hour."

He nodded, then tugged on his thick mittens and opened the front door to the smell of snow—a sharp, clean scent. *Ja*, the storm was coming.

He gave the hood of the Ford Model T an affectionate pat, as if it were a favorite horse. Yes, 1920 had been a good year. For Fords, for corn. They'd had a bumper crop and he'd bought his first automobile. Anna had been with him—full of life—Penny and Minnie still just girls. He'd had the world at his feet. Now, the Ford was a little rusty in spots, its joints creaky, its leather cracked. He cranked the old girl up until the engine sputtered. She still had plenty of life in her, ten years later. But 1930 hadn't been a good year.

The bank had come down hard when he didn't have the mortgage payment, and he couldn't blame them, what with the tight corner everybody was in. In the end, Ephraim had put up the rest of his land and all the farm equipment in return for a short-term loan that would tide them over until harvest. If the rain had come last summer, they'd have made do. But the rain never came.

He drove the two miles into town and parked on the main street of Odessa. Through the frosted window of the barber shop, Old Bill raised one hand in greeting, the other guiding a straight-edged razor along the mayor's loose jowls. Ephraim gave them a quick salute but didn't slow.

A battered sign—*Steak Dinner 30 Cents*—blew in the gusting

wind, knocking against the boarded-up restaurant that had once served the best pies in three counties. The picture house next to it had been Minnie's favorite place. Now the *For Sale* sign hung crookedly, and the blank windows made him fancy it was waiting for Minnie to come back, too.

Irma Langer hurried along the sidewalk, clutching her coat close against the wind, but she stopped when they met a few paces before the bus depot door. "Storm is on the way, Ephraim."

"*Ja*, Irma, gonna be a big one."

Irma's gaze went to the depot. Everybody knew everybody's business in Odessa. That morning—ten months ago—when he'd woken to find Minnie's bedroom empty, the news had spread through town. Now, it was common knowledge he came in every Wednesday and Saturday to meet the eastbound Great Northern, hoping this would be the day his daughter came home.

"Don't let me keep you, Ephraim," Irma said, her voice full of sympathy. She was a good-hearted soul.

"You stay warm, now." He nodded back and pushed through the doors into the tiny one-room bus station. An oak bench held a bedraggled man with a cardboard valise at his feet and a worn-looking woman with a toddler clutched close to her side. Timetables and a yellowing map of the US were tacked on the opposite wall. Along the other wall, Gus sat behind a glass-topped counter, reading the newspaper and picking at his teeth.

"Afternoon, Gus," Ephraim said.

"Eighteen inches," Gus answered. "Eighteen inches of snow." Anyone coming in the station to buy tickets, newspapers, or tobacco got Gus's weather report for free, called out like bingo numbers at the church social.

Gus slid Ephraim a copy of the *Pierre Daily*, tapping the

headlines about failing farms and bankrupt banks. "Pencil pushers telling us what we already know."

Ephraim slid a nickel back. "*Ja*, it's a shame."

He and Penny were better off than some, truth be told. They had enough to eat. The potatoes and carrots, even some of the beans, had made it through the drought and the grasshoppers. The chickens were still laying and the cows giving milk. They had a roof over their heads and each other, like Anna used to say. Couldn't ask for more.

Gus glanced at the black-and-white clockface, the main feature on the wall opposite the bench. "Shouldn't be long now." He went back to his paper, his face expressionless.

Ephraim made his way slowly to the bench and settled his creaking bones on the hard seat, smiling at the toddler. He and Penny would get by somehow. Minnie would come home someday, and when she did, he'd be waiting for her.

The following Monday, Ephraim sat in a hard chair at National Bank of Pierre, Penny at his side twisting the strap of her handbag in her white-gloved hands. Behind him, at the marble counter, bank tellers spoke polite words to customers as they doled out bills and coins.

Ephraim couldn't blame his problems on the young fellow in front of him. In all fairness, Robert A. Thomas wasn't that young. Thirty, maybe. Tall and lanky, with a sharp nose and brown eyes that looked like they might have seen some hardship despite his pressed shirt and neat suit.

"I'm sorry, Mr. Zimmerman," Mr. Thomas said, looking down at the papers on his desk, "but there's nothing I can do."

"You mean nothing you *will* do." Penny's voice was a bitter whisper. She glanced behind her as if she worried that someone she knew might overhear. "You don't understand what this will do to us."

Mr. Thomas didn't fidget with his fountain pen or shuffle his papers like some bankers Ephraim had known. He didn't hurry them along, anxious to get on to customers with money, or even seem put out by Penny's outspokenness. That was something, at least.

"I do understand, Miss Zimmerman," Mr. Thomas finally said, meeting Penny's eyes and then Ephraim's with a solemn glance. "And I'm sorrier than I can say."

Ephraim figured it wasn't the first foreclosure he'd handled. Maybe not even the first this morning.

"I've extended the grace period as long as the bank will allow. The loan payment is six months delinquent, as are your taxes. The insurance hasn't been paid in a year."

Ephraim nodded. This day had been coming for a long spell. "I understand, Mr. Thomas."

"I don't!" Penny's voice rose. "You want to get paid, but you're taking away our livelihood."

"I don't make the rules, I'm afraid." Mr. Thomas took off his glasses and pinched the bridge of his nose. "And I don't like them any more than you do, if it's any comfort."

"It's not," Penny muttered, and Ephraim reached over and took her hand in his. These kinds of setbacks were hard on the young. At his age, he'd seen good times and bad. He'd lost plenty. His Anna, and now Minnie. This was just land, he wanted to tell Penny. They'd get on, Penny would see. Right now, she was angry and worried, and he guessed he could understand that, too.

Mr. Thomas continued with the business at hand. "This is your outstanding debt." He tapped a number on the paper in front of Ephraim. A number with too many digits. "The full acreage of your homestead will be sold." He pushed the plat across the desk to show them the markings of the land surrounding the house. "With land prices where they are, that will not, I'm afraid, cover the entirety of what you owe."

Penny's hand clenched his.

"I will oversee the auction in one week's time. It will have to include your livestock and farm equipment to satisfy the remaining debt."

Penny's breath hitched in a sob, but Ephraim had a glimmer of hope. "Not the house?"

Robert Thomas lowered his voice. "The bank manager has agreed that the house remain in your possession."

Ephraim wondered how the young man had made that deal, but he figured best not to ask.

"When spring comes, the bank's land manager will be in contact with you to set up an agreement if you wish to continue farming on a sharecropping basis," Mr. Robert Thomas finished, looking as if he'd rather be saying anything else.

Penny was silent as a stone as they left the bank half an hour later, after Ephraim had signed his name to the papers that would take everything he and Anna had worked so hard to build. He shook the young man's hand and wished him well. They'd see him at the auction.

Ephraim took Penny's arm as they crossed the street and helped her into the Ford. He didn't crank the engine but slid into the driver's seat. Their breath fogged the windshield.

"How will we do it?" Penny turned to him, her eyes bright

with tears. "If they auction off the tractor, the plow, everything—to pay the taxes—how are we supposed to make a living, even as sharecroppers?"

"We'll figure it, my girl." They had food in the cellar, a roof over their heads. Each other.

She clenched her hands into fists. "If Minnie hadn't run off . . ."

"Penny, this isn't your sister's fault." But he didn't figure Penny would see it like that.

"It is!" She turned on him, two bright spots of color on her cheeks. "If she hadn't taken the money . . . If she'd stayed, like I did—"

He leaned over and took his daughter in his arms, wishing he could soothe her anger.

"I hate her, Papa." She pushed her face into his coat. "I hate her," she said again, like she was convincing herself. "I hope she never comes back."

CHAPTER 5

OSCAR

The Ford sputtered and jerked. Oscar prayed the auto wouldn't die before he made it home to the *colonia*. Just yesterday, Roy Lester had been found dead and Oscar's job had gone with him. Today, he had nothing to show for putting his last dollar into the Ford's gas tank. No job, not even a lead, and tomorrow the rent was due.

After attending early Mass with Mamá, he'd gone to the construction site for the Los Angeles Union Passenger Terminal. With his hat in his hand, he'd asked about work, but the foreman had taken one look and told him they were only hiring real Americans. It was all he could do not to punch the man. Even if he had a birth certificate to hand over, proving he was born not half a mile away, it wouldn't change a thing. He clenched his jaw and left without a word. It wasn't fair. This construction site was the very thing that was raising the rent in the *colonia*. With the terminal going in, *gringos* with deep pockets were buying up the surrounding property, tearing down old buildings and putting up new. Landlords saw their chance and raised rent on their brown-skinned tenants until they gave up and left or got evicted. Anger burned in his belly at the injustice.

The fact was, there were plenty of neighborhoods with lower rents, houses with electricity and water and an inside toilet. But those areas were restricted to white families. Their only choice would be the camps on the outskirts of the city, where cholera was as common as hunger, where men found solace in tequila instead of family. Places where even the *gringo* social workers intent on improving the "poor Mexicans" were afraid to go.

He couldn't let Mamá and the boys go there. He wouldn't.

But how could he pay the rent without a job?

After the terminal, he'd gone to the packing houses north of the city and the canneries on the coast, even the fields all the way out in Sacramento County. There were no jobs for men who looked like Oscar.

The Ford sputtered again as he reached Olvera Street, passing the Teatro Hidalgo, its shabby marquee advertising films captioned in Spanish. The Ciudad de México displayed ropes of dried chilis and baskets of Mexican candy. The *farmacia* sold both *americano* medicines and traditional herbal remedies. He turned down his street, lined with the crumbling remains of stucco houses, relics of an earlier age when Los Angeles was a thriving *hacienda*. Now, his people lived in ramshackle assortments of shacks, train cars, and even tents, the stink of the industrial section hanging low in the air.

This was his home. These were his people.

The sight of the deserted plaza stoked his anger like dry grass fed a brushfire. Only a few months ago, La Placita would have been filled with men hoping to be picked for a day job, dozing in the shade, or playing dice. Since the raids, no one gathered outside. Any Mexican man might be arrested at any time. Already they'd lost dozens of men from their *colonia*, and it was the same in all of Los Angeles County.

La Opinión denounced the unjust measures and sent complaints to the Mexican consulate and even Washington, DC. Officials there answered back that the "deportables" were illegals—or even communists and criminals—but everyone knew what their real crime was: taking jobs from *gringos* now that jobs were scarce.

Oscar reached home with the Ford running on fumes, anger and despair warring in his gut. Roman lounged on the front stoop, smoking a cigarette. Oscar slammed the door of the Ford and stomped to the house. "That mine?"

Roman blew out a white plume. "You owe me."

Oscar grabbed Roman's shirt in his fist and pulled him up from the step. "I don't owe you a thing." Hadn't he just spent the day trying to keep a roof over Roman's head?

Roman smirked. "Then I'll just tell Mamá all about the girl you picked up."

Oscar's fist tightened on his brother's collar. He could still beat some sense into him if he had to. "If you think this is funny—"

Roman's hide was saved by a boy tearing between the houses and skidding to a stop, breathless. "Oscar . . ." He took a deep gulp of air. "The telephone, for you."

"For me?" Oscar had only received one telephone call in his life, and that was from Max, telling him that Maria Carmen was dead. He threw Roman back down on the step—"Stay out of my cigarettes!"—then took off toward the *sociedades*.

Oscar caught his breath before pushing through the door. The old storefront building was mostly a social club, a place for men to gather and complain, smoke, and buy the illegal tequila that Raul kept behind the counter. On Saturdays the space was cleared for cockfights or the occasional boxing match. Inside, half a dozen men sat at mismatched tables and chairs. The air reeked of cheap tobacco and chicken droppings, and their low conversations were punctuated by the irregular tap of the old typewriter that sat in the back office. The telephone, paid for by members' dues, was on the back wall, the receiver off its cradle, Raul standing guard beside it.

He'd never liked Raul, who was a few years older than he was. When they'd been boys, Raul had tormented Max with taunts of being half *gringo* until Oscar had grown big enough to ensure that Raul kept his opinions to himself. Now that Raul ran the *sociedades*, he was known to eavesdrop and gossip like an old woman.

Oscar leveled a look at Raul as he picked up the heavy black handset. Raul shrugged and sauntered away. *"Hola?"* Oscar said, turning his back to the room.

"Oscar Dominguez? Detective Brody."

"Sí—yes?" Oscar's heart dropped a few inches. Did Brody find out about the girl already?

Brody didn't waste time. "I need to talk to you." The line crackled and popped. "Meet me at the diner on the corner of Vine and Western. I'll be there in twenty minutes."

He hung up before Oscar could reply. Oscar looked at the silent handset. What could Brody want? Did he know something? He put the receiver back in its cradle. He'd have to go. If he didn't, Brody might just show up on his doorstep.

Santa María. What had he gotten himself into?

On the corner of Vine and Western, the Hard Times diner lived up to its name—a dim luncheonette with grimy windows and a long countertop that looked like it hadn't been washed in a month. A fug of stale cigarette smoke and bacon grease hung in the air. Men in shabby suits hunched over coffee cups. Brody sat in the corner booth, half obscured by a raised newspaper.

Oscar sat down on the other side of the table and Brody lowered the paper. "You want coffee?" Brody signaled to the waitress without waiting for Oscar to reply. She set a cup in front of him and filled it with an oily brew.

"Oscar—you mind if I call you Oscar?" Brody folded the paper.

Oscar shrugged. *Gringos* generally didn't ask what he minded.

"Oscar, you married?"

Oscar's wariness increased. He shook his head.

"I was once." Brody took a sip of his coffee. "Nice girl, but it didn't take." Brody's wiry brows inched together over his gray eyes. He fished a pack of Viking cigarettes out of his jacket pocket and tipped it to Oscar as if they were old pals.

This friendly *gringo* made him nervous. "No, thank you."

Brody tapped out a smoke and stuck it in his mouth, then struck a match. He took a long puff and blew it out. "I'll be straight with you," he finally said. "I need your help."

Oscar's neck heated. "I told you everything I knew." Which wasn't the truth.

Brody raised his brows. "That's not what I'm getting at."

Oscar waited and wished he'd taken a cigarette, at least to have something to do with his hands.

Brody went on. "Today, I had an appointment to take statements from William Randolph Hearst and Louella Parsons." Brody threw the burning match into his coffee cup. He pointed to the front page of the paper, where Señor Lester's picture looked up at him. "Let me tell you how things are, kid. Lester was the highest-paid actor at Cosmo. His wife, Victoria, is a rising star in the same studio." Brody tapped ash over the floating matchstick. "Cosmo is struggling. Box office is down, and they don't need a scandal. They want this case sewn up, and quick."

In the pause that followed, Oscar voiced the first question in his mind. "I thought this was police business, not studio business."

"Kid," Brody breathed out a cloud of bitter smoke, "everything in this town is studio business, especially when William Randolph Hearst is involved."

"Hearst." Oscar made the connection. "He owns Cosmopolitan Pictures."

Brody confirmed it. "And the biggest newspaper in town."

Oscar was still lost. "You think Hearst had something to do with Lester's murder?" Hadn't they been friends? He tried to remember the gossip Alonso was always spouting.

"It's not that simple." Brody shook his head. "Hearst made a statement. His story is sewn up tight with alibis, witnesses, lawyers. It's all too pat. Which means something stinks." Brody narrowed his eyes through the haze of smoke. "Kid, you ever hear of Thomas Ince?"

Oscar remembered some story from years ago. "A big shot. Died of stomach trouble?"

"Stomach trouble caused by a bullet to the brain. On Hearst's yacht. Hearst shut down that investigation before it even started. Louella Parsons was part of that whole bit, too. They say she saw it all but was protecting her buddy Hearst." Brody rested his finger on Roy Lester's picture. "This has the same kind of smell, kid. Like a pig trough in July." Brody considered the cigarette ashes floating on the coffee. "Problem is, we don't know who else is on the Hearst payroll. Don't trust a single one of them, kid."

Oscar's neck tensed. "Why are you telling me this?"

Brody stubbed his cigarette, smoked down to the nib, on his saucer. He leaned back and gave him a long look, as if assessing him. "You need a job." Brody met his eyes. "I need eyes and ears. Somebody people will talk to and I can trust. Everybody from the DA to the cop on the beat is on the take in this town."

Oscar jerked upright. "A job?" He didn't trust Brody any more than any other *gringo*.

"Two dollars a day sound about right?"

Two dollars a day? That was twice what Oscar made gardening. But work for the police? He motioned to Brody for a cigarette, lit up, and took a couple deep pulls while he thought about what Brody had said. If Max's woman hadn't killed Roy Lester, somebody else had. And if they found out who, she would be in the clear. That meant he'd be out of danger, too. But work for Brody? Even if he could, he wouldn't know what to do.

"It's basic stuff," Brody said, as if reading his mind. "Talk to your people first. The Garcias. See what they know."

Oscar tensed. "They don't know anything." And he wasn't a traitor, questioning his own.

Brody held up a hand. "Don't get all worked up. They might know something, more than they told me. Just about the party, who was there. You follow?"

He followed. But he didn't like it. And yet two dollars a day would pay the rent, and asking a few questions wouldn't be so hard. But could he trust this man? "Detective—" he leaned forward—"if the studios pay everybody off, they'd pay you off, too."

Brody raised a brow and might have looked a little impressed. "The bottom line is, you'll have to trust me."

"You just told me not to trust anyone."

Brody flashed a smile. "I knew you were quick."

Brody wasn't like any *gringo* Oscar had known, even if he was police. Oscar needed the money, but he wasn't born yesterday. "If I have to trust you, you do the same for me. I want a week in advance."

Oscar thought he might have seen a flash of respect in Brody's gray eyes before he nodded and fished a worn wallet from his pocket. A ten-dollar bill and a handful of ones came out. Oscar felt a little like Judas with the thirty pieces of silver.

Brody slid the money across the table. "Use your nose, kid. Something smells, ask questions. Look for pieces to the puzzle. You get enough, you start to get the picture. And remember, if it seems like a coincidence, it's not." He threw two dimes down beside the coffee cups. "Call me tomorrow." He pushed a card across the table and picked up his bowler. "And one other thing, kid. Be careful."

Oscar felt another flicker of panic. "What do you mean?"

"Just this." Brody raised his bristly brows. "You and me, we're kicking a hornet's nest. And when you do that, you might find out what's inside, but you're likely to get stung."

———————

Oscar sat in his own kitchen and took a gulp of his too-hot coffee. Ask some questions of Lupita and Alonso. It was easy enough. All his life, he'd lived next door to Francesca, his mother's best friend, to Maria Carmen and Alonso and Lupita. He'd never hesitated to walk across the packed grass and up the two cinder-block steps to their door.

This morning, he couldn't make his feet tread the well-worn path.

There were things he knew: the sun would rise, he would work hard, *americanos* could not be trusted. He knew that Roman would test him, that Angel would try to keep the peace, and that Mamá would always be there for him. Now the steady predictability of his life had vanished. It was like he was creeping close to the edge of his world, and one missed step could send him plunging over the cliff. He'd give much to be at Roy Lester's estate on this Monday morning, groaning and complaining about cleaning the pool. Instead, he was going to question his own people about a murder.

Outside, Mamá and Francesca pulled a cart of dirty linen they'd picked up from the Hotel Estelar. Francesca leaned over, her hand on the small of her back, complaining no doubt. Mamá stoked the fire under the water heater and poured lye and soap into buckets.

Mamá. Oscar rubbed his tired eyes. She wasn't as strong as she pretended.

Papá had died less than a year after Angel was born—an accident at the railyards where he'd worked since he and Mamá had come from Mexico. Oscar had been just nine years old, and Max ten, but they'd quit school and worked in the fields—they'd had no other choice. Then, when Max had turned his back on them, Oscar had been left alone to do his best for the family, and no one could say he hadn't tried. He'd managed to keep Roman and Angel in school until eighth grade, although he wasn't sure if he'd done right by them. Yes, they had learned to read and speak English, but schooling came with a price. *Gringo* teachers fed them *americano* ideas along with the egg and glass of milk they got every morning. They came home ashamed of their heritage, hungry for American ways, and—at least in Roman's case—disrespectful of their elders.

Oscar remembered his own schooling: Don't complain. Don't demand decent wages. Work hard and be grateful. No, the schools full of brown children weren't being taught to be doctors and teachers and businessmen. They were being trained into a docile army of lettuce pickers, potato sorters, and fish packers. Roman had figured out the *americano* shell game quick, and by the time he started working at the packing house, he was already talking about unions and fair wages. That kind of talk could get him on a bus to the border.

Oscar tossed the tepid remains of the coffee into the sink. May God save them from *gringos* who claimed to offer them charity and from their own people who told them to stand up for more. Oscar rinsed his cup and stared through the tiny curtained window above the sink.

The Garcias' house, like many others in the *colonia*, was a cobbled construction of scrap wood and corrugated tin. The cracks were stuffed with rags to keep out the wind, but still they struggled to keep the house warm in the winter months. Francesca's husband, José, had lost his job after a drunken binge and gone north to find work. That was three years ago. No one expected him to return. Maybe that was why Alonso carried on as he did. How could he learn about honor with no father?

Oscar pushed through the screen door and walked purposefully across the grass. It was time to do the job Brody had paid him for. He knocked and waited.

Alonso pulled opened the door. "*Hola*, Oscar," he said with surprise. "Why do you knock? Are you a stranger now?"

Oscar cringed at his mistake. He'd been going in and out of this house without an invitation since he could walk. He followed Alonso into the house. Bedding was rolled along one side of the open room. The other side held a small table and a gas stove as old as Francesca. A pot bubbled on a burner and the unmistakable aroma of beans filled the house.

Lupita looked up from where she sat at the table, breaking off bits of dough and flattening the pieces into tortillas. "Oscar!" She jumped up and smoothed her dress. She poured a cup of coffee from the percolator on the stove and brought it to him.

He took a sip, suddenly tongue-tied. He wasn't a detective like Brody. How was he supposed to question his own friends about a murder?

"Find work yet?" he finally said.

Alonso frowned. "*Nada*. But I have a plan to make some big money."

Oscar didn't put much stock in Alonso's get-rich-quick schemes. He pulled two dollars of Brody's money out of his pocket and gave it to Lupita.

"Thank you, Oscar." Lupita tucked the money in her waistband and gave him a grateful smile.

"Just until I put my plan to work," Alonso said. "What about you? Anything?"

This was the time to tell them about Brody. "Not yet." He took a sip of his coffee. "Tell me, what do you remember about that night at Lester's?" What was wrong with him? He sounded like a *gringo* police officer.

A look passed between brother and sister. Alonso stood quickly and refilled his cup from the percolator. Lupita bit at her lip. The tortilla in front of her was so thin it might drift away in the breeze coming through the back door.

"I know Max was there, if that's what's worrying you."

Alonso turned back to him. "We didn't even talk to Max."

Oscar settled into his chair as if he had all the time in the world. "When did he leave?"

Another look between them. Lupita, nervous. Alonso, more like a warning.

"Early," Lupita said quickly.

"*Sí,*" agreed Alonso, equally quickly. "Why so interested in Max?"

Oscar kept his face impassive. "Just wondering."

Alonso went on, still speaking fast. "We finished with the party. Slept in the gatehouse until the first trolley. Then the police officer came here and asked questions."

"Which one?"

"I don't know. He was blond, not friendly. We told him we didn't see anything and that was the truth. Now you come and act like the police did." Alonso straightened from the wall and walked to the door. "This is *americano* business, nothing to do with us." He opened the door and stood beside it.

Oscar rose. "Thanks for the coffee, Lupita." The door shut firmly behind him. He'd swear on his mother's rosary that they were hiding something.

He sat down on the back stoop of his house, watching the Garcias' door. He wanted a cigarette something terrible, but he didn't light up. The wind turned cold and he was about to give up when Lupita slipped out, looking over her shoulder. She'd come without her shawl, her hair loose and framing her face. She had a worried look he knew. When she got to the stoop, she sat down beside him.

"Whatever it is," he said, "I won't tell Alonso."

She looked down at her feet, clad in soft woven slippers. "He would be very angry if he knew. But I think . . ." She bit at her lip and kept her eyes down.

"What is it?" He tried to be patient, keep his voice calm.

She looked up at him. "That night, Señor Lester wanted his drink, the one he has with the green liquor. But before I brought it to him . . ." She hugged her arms around herself, shivering.

Oscar shrugged out of his jacket and draped it around her.

"*Gracias.*" She looked at her feet. "He . . . put something in it."

"Who?" But he had an idea who she meant, and his gut twisted.

She raised worried eyes to Oscar's. "Max."

Santa María.

"A powder. He said it was better if I didn't ask . . . You know how he is. Alonso saw him upstairs before that, in the hallway."

Max. He should have known. But why hadn't Alonso said anything? "Then what?"

She shook her head and glanced over her shoulder. "He told me to give it to Señor Lester." She blinked as if she were going to cry. "And not to tell anyone." She grabbed his arm. "I did, Oscar. I gave it to him . . . Was it poison? Did I kill Señor Lester? I wanted to tell you, but Alonso—"

"Did you tell the police?"

"No." Her voice shook. "I thought they'd arrest me and then—"

"No, listen to me, Lupita. He didn't die of poison." He took her hand in his. "You didn't do anything wrong." Why had Max got Lupita mixed up in this? Hadn't he done enough harm to her family?

"Really?" She leaned against him, limp and relieved, but his thoughts leapfrogged from one question to another. Oscar had found a puzzle piece, like Brody had asked, but it seemed to be from the wrong puzzle. Lester had been stabbed, not poisoned.

But Max had lied to him. Played him for a fool. Again. And that made him see red.

He left Lupita on the steps, his jacket around her shoulders. He'd get the truth from Max and he'd get it now . . . if he had to beat it out of him.

Oscar cranked the Ford mercilessly, slammed the door, and revved it through the streets of the *colonia*. He worked over what Lupita had told him, a cold lump in his belly. Could Max have tried to drug Lester, then gone upstairs to make sure his plan had worked? Could he have fought with Lester and killed him? But what about the girl? She had to have been in on it, but why did he leave her? And he really had looked surprised yesterday when Oscar had sprung the news. But then again . . . maybe Max had learned to act in the years since he left them.

An old man pushing a cart lurched out of a side street and into his path. Oscar jammed on the brake and the Ford almost sputtered out. *Miércoles.* Max owed him some answers, and he was going to pay up.

The wind gusted in his open window and shivered the tall palms as he turned into the Garden of Allah. Rhododendrons dropped brown blossoms on the sidewalks. Champagne bottles and overturned chairs ringed the ice-blue pool, along with discarded clothing. Oscar's ire surged. These *gringos* with more money than sense, drinking away their nights, sleeping through the days. He jerked to a stop at the third bungalow on the left. The drive was empty, but he got out and pounded on the door just the same.

No answer. A fat man in a woman's dressing gown and cowboy boots stepped onto the stoop two doors down and watched him with droopy eyes. Oscar pounded again. *Nada.*

He got back in the Ford and spit gravel as he turned back

onto Sunset, then north on La Brea. How was he supposed to know where Max would be on a Monday morning? It's not like he lived the high life Max did. He turned back west onto Hollywood Boulevard, passing Grauman's Chinese, the sun glinting off the jade roof and marble columns. Plenty of Cadillacs, Rolls-Royce touring sedans, and Packards, but no yellow LaSalle.

He drove for an hour, his head swiveling from left to right, his anger rising. Women in furs carried shopping bags. Men in suits crossed in front of him as if they owned the street. Then he went to Western Avenue, the girl's place. The roadster wasn't parked out front there, either. He cursed under his breath and turned toward the north. He'd pick up the boys at the packing house and try again. He wasn't giving up until he'd gotten the truth from Max.

By the time he made it back from the packing house and helped Mamá and Francesca deliver the laundry, it was almost the dinner hour and his stomach was making hollow growls. There. The yellow LaSalle, parked crookedly in front of a building with a fancy scrollwork awning. He pulled around the corner and jerked to a stop. Max. Probably eating a big steak. It was enough to set his blood on fire. Letting Oscar do all the work. Have all the worry. Some people never changed.

He was out of the automobile and across the street, the horn of a delivery van blaring as it swerved around him. He wasn't waiting another minute for Max to tell him the truth.

He pushed through a chattering cluster of fancy-dressed women. At the door, a slight man in tails eyed Oscar from his hatless head to his brown dungarees. His pencil mustache twitched. "May I help you?" His tone said he'd help him back to the street.

Oscar squared his shoulders. "I need to talk to Max Clark. I know he's in there."

The narrow mustache quivered. "We don't generally disturb our guests when—"

Oscar leaned a few inches closer and had the satisfaction of seeing the little man swallow hard and his eyes widen. "Disturb him."

The crowd around Oscar had gone silent. Watching him. That wasn't going to stop him. He would see Max or know the reason why.

The fancy doorman scurried away, then came back quick, looking relieved. "Mr. Clark is waiting for you, Mr. . . . ah . . ." He cleared his throat. "Please, follow me."

Oscar followed him up marble stairs and into a room too opulent to be believed. An orchestra played to couples taking turns on a parquet floor. Crystal sparkled and silver gleamed on tables laden with food. This was the life Max had left them for. This was what he did while Oscar and his brothers labored in the hot sun. His neck heated as he wove through a sea of white linen tables, silk dresses, and the *americanos* who turned to watch him. He looked like he'd just jumped off the day-workers truck, but he pulled back his shoulders and raised his chin. He wouldn't let Max see him ashamed.

Max sat in a corner beside a window, his legs crossed, smoking a cigarette, and he wasn't alone. The woman, the one he had thought so fragile—the one who'd maybe killed Roy Lester—was sitting across from him.

When she saw him, her mouth dropped open and her eyes went wide. Good. She should be afraid. Whatever she'd done, it had landed him in plenty of trouble.

The little man pulled out the chair opposite Max. Oscar remained standing. He wasn't here for a tea party.

Max took the cigarette from his lips. "Thanks, Al."

He looked so smug, so cool sitting there, with no decency.

Oscar's anger boiled over. "When were you going to tell me?" he said in Spanish. He didn't give a darn if the whole rotten place heard.

Max straightened a little, surprise in his eyes, and held up a hand. "Listen, Oscar—"

"Did you try to kill him? With the drink?" Oscar interrupted. He laid his hands on the white cloth and leaned over the table. Max's coffee cup jittered on the saucer. The couple at the next table stopped eating. "Tell me the truth or by God I'll—"

"Oscar. Sit down, for heaven's sake," Max snapped in their mother tongue, looking around.

Every eye was on them. The hum of conversation and tinkle of crystal and silver had hushed; even the band faltered their tune. Oscar clenched his jaw and sat down.

Max took a deep breath and switched to English. "Mina, I believe you've met my cousin Oscar Garcia." He tapped his cigarette on the edge of a crystal ashtray. "Oscar, this is Miss Minerva Sinclaire."

The girl stared at him and fumbled, "Y-your cousin?"

Oscar didn't spare her a glance. His business was with Max.

A white-coated waiter appeared at Oscar's elbow. Max raised his brows in question. "You want a steak? It's on me."

Oscar shook his head. He hadn't eaten this morning, and the smell of the food had started his stomach growling, but he'd take charity from Max Clark when hell froze over.

Max held his smoke and leaned back. "Just coffee, Frankie. Cream and sugar." The waiter drifted away. Max fixed Oscar with a look and spoke in Spanish. "I should have figured Lupita would tell you."

Oscar waited. Could he even believe a word this stranger said?

The waiter reappeared with a bone china cup, a tiny pitcher of cream, and a bowl of sugar cubes. He poured the coffee, added a splash of cream and two sugar cubes with a pair of silver tongs. *Caramba*, he even stirred it for him.

Max looked down at his own coffee, still speaking in Spanish. "I was just trying to knock him out, that's all."

Understanding dawned. The girl. The argument in the court-yard. "So you tried to poison Lester so he couldn't—"

"Not poison, Oscar." Max frowned. "It was just Seconal."

"Where did you get it?" he asked Max suddenly. "The Seconal."

"Victoria keeps some in her room." Max looked away.

The girl's gaze went back and forth between them, her face bewildered.

Alonso had seen him upstairs, he said. Oscar didn't want to know how Max knew what was in Señora Lester's bedroom. Besides, he had other questions that needed answers. Before he could ask them, the tuxedoed doorman was back, hovering next to Max with a worried look.

"Mr. Clark, please forgive the intrusion, but—" he cleared his throat and glanced at Oscar—"there is a policeman—two policemen—who would like to speak with you."

Oscar jerked. Police? Here?

Max straightened, giving the girl a sharp look.

"Max," she whispered, panic in her voice and fear in her eyes.

"Al," Max said in a low, controlled voice, "stall them as long as you can." He crushed his cigarette into the ashtray and stood. He spoke in English as the doorman hurried away. "Oscar, I need you to do something for me. We don't have much time."

Oscar's stomach twisted. He'd heard that tone from Max before and it always meant trouble.

Max was talking fast. "I don't know what they want. Maybe nothing. Probably just have some questions. But I need you to get her out of here."

"No." He was not getting caught up in this, whatever it was. Not with the police. Not for an *americana* and definitely not for Max.

"Go out the back door," Max said, as if Oscar hadn't spoken. "Al will show you."

Oscar wasn't listening to any more of this. He moved toward the front door.

Max grabbed him by the arm and swung him around. "If they find you in here with me, they'll arrest you too. You know they will."

"I'm not involved."

"Tell that to the police."

Oscar's heart sped up. He couldn't tell if it was from fear or anger. Max knew as well as he did how likely it was that the police would believe him. He looked around desperately, as if he could find a hiding place in this restaurant full of *gringos*.

At a motion from Max, the girl gathered her pocketbook and stood, her mouth trembling, looking like some kind of frightened animal. Max bent close, whispering something in her ear, then kissed her.

Al was at the table. "Follow me, please," he said, still all politeness.

"I'll stay here, see what they want," Max said, taking the girl and pushing her toward Al. He turned to Oscar. "Go to the church. Wait there and I'll be there soon, I promise." He clenched his jaw and looked toward the entry as if the police could be breaking in any moment.

And then Oscar was following the remarkably calm doorman to a back door, hustling down a staircase, and emerging into an alley with the girl beside him. He heard the man wish them a good day, and the door banged shut behind him.

Oscar let out the breath he'd been holding. The girl looked at him with wide eyes as if she didn't know what had just happened either. He wanted to kick himself. He'd been determined to never fall for Max's game again. Now here he was with this girl on his hands, putting himself—his family—at risk. When was he going to learn?

MINA

I felt like I'd been put in a potato sack and given a good shake.

What had happened in there? The police were looking for me or maybe for Max? Oscar—Max's cousin?—stared at me like I was a stray dog that had been dumped on his doorstep. I never thought I'd see his face again. And why had Max kissed me?

I was thrown for a loop, to be honest. But I didn't have a chance to get my bearings before Oscar pushed me around a corner and shoved me into the familiar old Ford, cranked it, and pulled out onto Hollywood Boulevard.

"Get down," he bit out, and I'd barely ducked my head when three police cars blew past, screeching to a halt in front of the Montmartre. "Stay down," he said, and I did.

It was like what they call déjà vu, I think. I'd been there before. This time, at least, I knew he could understand me. But for the life, I didn't know what was going on. I had the feeling Oscar didn't either from the words he was muttering under his breath. I figured they shouldn't be said in front of a lady, but I didn't blame him a jot.

Max spoke Spanish like he was born to it. That was a surprise.

And Oscar? There was clearly no love lost between them. Even so, before I was hustled out the door, Max had whispered in my ear, "Trust me, Mina. Oscar will take care of you." And then he'd kissed me. I put my hand to my lips. It had felt so natural, so right. That might be the most astonishing part of it all.

Were the police really looking for me? And what had Max and Oscar been talking about? I knew it had something to do with me, and from the look on Oscar's face, it wasn't good.

I straightened up as we left Hollywood and veered through backstreets toward downtown, then a turn into what looked like another country. A narrow street, a patchwork of houses thrown together in heaps, slanted like houses built of cards.

I'd spent the last two days acting like everything was normal, like Friday night hadn't even happened. I'd worked at the Derby on Saturday, gone home like Max had said, and washed my hair. Sunday was about the same. Today I'd had an early shift, then Max had picked me up like he did on Mondays, to see and be seen at the Montmartre. Just like always, he said. Even with things the way they were between us, I'd almost convinced myself Lester's party hadn't happened. What a dolt.

My doubts came back with a vengeance. I couldn't have killed Roy. I knew that at least, didn't I? My stomach twisted and I closed my eyes, fighting back nausea. But if I was innocent, why were they after me?

We pulled up to an old church, older than anything in Odessa. It was simple, plastered in gray stucco with a tile roof and built right up to the street. Three bells hung in a circular window on one side, and over them a steeple.

Oscar didn't turn off the auto, but he did flick the switch that turned off his headlamps.

"What now?" It was the first thing I'd said to him.

"Now we wait."

Oscar rolled down his window. Twilight draped the church in shadows, soft and full of the smells of lilacs and the dry tang of dust. Flowering rhododendrons with thick, waxy leaves bloomed on either side of an arched doorway. Oscar fished a pack of cigarettes from under the seat. He scraped a match against his boot, and the flame illuminated his face for a moment, all angles and dark hollows. He really did look like the bad guy in a cowboy film.

I breathed in the sharp scent—harsh, nothing like the fancy brand Max bought—but I wouldn't have turned down a smoke if he'd offered. He didn't offer.

He kept his gaze in the distance, where the insects had begun their night song in the ravine. He took a puff and blew out the white smoke in a thin stream. "Tell me about Friday night."

I swallowed back the sick feeling in my throat. What did he want me to say? That I'd killed Roy or that I hadn't? I wish I knew. He waited. This man—scary as he was—had got me out of a jam. At least I think that's what he did. I guess he deserved an answer, but I didn't have a good one. "I don't know. Honest."

"I heard you arguing—you and Max out in the courtyard—before . . ."

Before I went upstairs with Roy Lester. So he probably knew what I had gone upstairs to do. I was glad for the darkness, the shadows that hid my face as well as they did his.

He tapped ash out the window. "What happened after?"

After? My face felt like it was glowing in the dark.

He turned to me then, the red tip of his cigarette casting faint color on his face. "Tell me what you remember. All of it."

I swallowed down the lump in my throat. I guess he deserved

the truth, at least what I knew of it. "After Max . . . left, I went back to Roy. We danced . . . and then . . . we went upstairs." My stomach churned with the familiar feeling of shame.

"Señor Lester, did he take a drink—from the maid?"

A drink? He'd had plenty, I was about to say. Then I remembered. "Yes. Something she brought him," I thought hard. "A special nightcap, he called it." The memory was fuzzy. The pretty maid. A green cocktail. Roy, raising his glass to me. *Gin, absinthe, and a touch of bitters. This will put hair on your chest!* He'd winked at me, his face pink and sweaty. Then a bitter taste on my tongue. "Wait. He didn't drink it."

"What?" Oscar straightened up. "Are you sure?"

"Yes, I think . . ." He'd pushed the glass into my hand. *To the next It Girl!* he'd announced, his brows raised in challenge. I hadn't wanted it, but I was stuck. It was time to sink or swim, like they said, and I kept swimming. *Down the hatch,* I'd said and tossed it back. My eyes watered at the remembered burn. What had he said then? *Louella was right, you're a good sport.* My throat clogged. At the time, I hadn't felt like I had a choice, about any of it. The drink, and what happened after. I had, though. I'd always had a choice.

"I drank it."

Oscar straightened up. "Then what?"

I'd almost forgotten. But there, in the dark, details I hadn't recalled—hadn't let myself think on—came to me. Roy pulling me up a staircase. Stumbling, my shoes catching on the hem of my dress, the seam ripping—the dress that had cost me my last dime, ruined. The stairway had spun and . . . had Roy picked me up? Yes, I remembered that, but then nothing. I didn't say any of that, but Oscar must have figured enough on his own.

The tip of Oscar's cigarette glowed bright, then dimmed. "What about when you woke up?"

"What do you mean?"

"When you woke up in the morning. Did you . . . had you . . ." He turned toward the window and the thin glow of the moon caught his face.

My flush turned into a burn as I caught his meaning. I wished I could sink through the floorboards of the car. This was the bitter end. "I don't know." What kind of girl doesn't know if she's been made love to or not? I guess the kind of girl I had turned into.

"He was just dead? When you woke up? That's all you know?"

The blood. The knife. Roy's lifeless eyes. "I—I just had to get away."

He turned sideways and leaned in. I suddenly realized how close he was, and how big. Our shoulders touched and his face was inches from mine. "Is there anything you are not telling me, Minerva Sinclaire?"

My heart was hammering in my ears. Where was Max? He should have been here by now. Had he been arrested? Or maybe he'd really given up on me. I was alone with a stranger and nobody would hear me if I called out. "I swear, that's all I know."

Oscar looked at me like he knew I was lying. He was right. There was plenty I wasn't telling him. About how I'd sunk so low. About Max and me. But none of it had anything to do with Roy Lester. And it wasn't his beeswax, anyhow. But I didn't have the nerve to say that, not with him so big and close.

Finally, he threw the stub of his cigarette out the window and switched the headlamps back on. "We go."

"What about Max?" We had to wait. He'd said he'd be here.

"Max is not coming and I am tired." Oscar looked like a man who wasn't going to talk anymore.

"Where?" The panic that crept into my voice didn't seem to faze him.

"You come with me. Tomorrow, I decide what to do about the police."

Did he mean he'd turn me in? Did he think I killed Roy? I couldn't blame him when I wasn't even all that sure myself. But I couldn't go to jail. It would be the end of everything. I'd never get a film, and I'd never get home. What would happen to Papa and Penny?

I grabbed his arm before he put the auto into gear. "Oscar," I said, "I swear to you. I'm innocent." I had to make him believe me, even if I didn't believe it all the way myself.

"Señorita—" Oscar said the word as if it tasted sour in his mouth—"one thing I know. Girls like you, they aren't innocent."

———————

Señora Sanchia Dominguez decided from the minute she laid eyes on me what I was, and she never changed her mind.

Me sneaking into her son's bedroom in the dark of night probably didn't help.

I had tried to figure out my next move as Oscar drove through the beaten-down neighborhood, but before I could even think, we'd stopped in front of a crumbling stucco house, walleyed windows looking out into the dark street. Oscar turned off the auto and sat as the engine died. He closed his eyes and his lips moved. He might have been praying. Maybe I should have said a prayer too, but I didn't think God was listening to me in those days.

He came around to my side. "Quiet," he whispered, clicking

the door closed behind me. I followed him up the concrete stoop and waited as he eased open the front door. Inside was dark.

He ushered me through and motioned for me to slip off my shoes. I did, and I tried to be quiet, honest I did, but as he pushed me forward, I stumbled, and a squeak left my mouth. In my defense, inside the house was as dark as a midnight prairie.

Oscar grabbed me around the waist, none too gently. He froze, listening.

A woman's voice called out. There was a scuffle in another room. A light flared and glowed. Oscar muttered something that sounded a lot like a curse. And suddenly—as they say—the bush-wah hit the fan.

A woman, her face illuminated by an old-fashioned oil lamp, appeared like a tall, ghostly figure moving down the hall. But this was no ghost, no sir. That woman took one look at me—my shoes in hand, halfway up the stairs with Oscar's arm around me—and opened fire like a Gatling gun.

Oscar stepped away from me and raised his hands, talking in rapid Spanish right over her. A moment later, the brothers from the other morning stumbled into the hall with sleepy, disbelieving eyes.

Roman looked me up and down, then jumped into the clash of words with relish. Angel, the young one, seemed to be trying to calm them all down, but he might as well have saved his breath. The woman's black eyes shot lead. She waved the lamp in my face, making our shadows jump like phantoms on the wall. She pointed to the shoes clutched in my hand and said some words that sounded like a slap in the face. Oscar retaliated, his voice rising. It seemed like everybody was talking at once. Except me. I was just wishing I could disappear.

Finally, Oscar shouted a word I understood. *"Silencio!"*

The old woman sealed her lips and crossed her arms, her foot tapping out a staccato rhythm on the cracked linoleum. She wasn't as tall as I'd first thought, probably about my height, and her cotton nightgown hung loose on her thin frame as if draped over a wire hanger. At one time, she might have been beautiful with that bone structure, but the scowl deepened the lines in her bronze face.

"Please." I just wanted to smooth things over, honest. But boy, I managed to say the wrong thing, didn't I? "Oscar, please. Just bring me to Max."

Three faces turned to me. Three mouths dropped open.

"Max?" Angel and Roman said together, disbelief in their voices.

And the mother . . . well, she sputtered and then choked out a few words. I recognized one: *Maximilian.*

Now I was even more confused. If he was their cousin, why did they look at me as if I'd uttered a curse? Who was Max to these people? And why had he left me with them?

Roman turned to his older brother and raised his brows. *"Ay, ay, ay,* you've done it now."

"You, shut up," Oscar bit out. He let out a breath and rubbed a hand over his face, then jerked his head at the younger brother. "Angel, take her upstairs."

I just wanted out of this house, but I figured it wouldn't help at this point to argue, so I followed Angel up the staircase to a single door at the top. The room was hardly big enough to hold a narrow bed covered in a well-worn quilt and beside it, an overturned crate. A rectangle of thin moonlight fell on a crucifix on the opposite wall. "We will wait here, *señorita.* It is better." Angel motioned me to the bed and pulled the crate over to sit beside me.

I knew what he meant. Better to be out of their mother's sight.

Roman lounged against the doorframe. Downstairs, Oscar's voice was rising again, then his mother's. Angel and Roman shifted and glanced warily at each other.

"What is it?" I asked Roman. "What are they saying?"

"She—our *madre*—says Oscar and you are together." Roman's wolfish look made it clear what he meant.

"But . . ." Of course she would think that, Oscar sneaking me upstairs in the dark.

"Are you?" Roman asked.

"No," I answered quickly. Goodness, no.

"You are Max's woman, then?" Roman said, as if that would explain a lot.

I shook my head and swallowed a sudden lump in my throat.

The mother's shrill voice rose up the stairs but was silenced with a firm word from Oscar that sounded like an order.

Roman grimaced. "Oscar is reminding Mamá he is the head of our family. She will do what he says. And he says you stay here until tomorrow."

Silence ticked by, and then I heard her say something more, her voice like ice. Roman and Angel looked at each other with wide eyes.

"What did she say?" I wasn't sure if I wanted to know.

Roman frowned. "She said you're a—"

"*No sé,*" Angel interrupted, glaring at his brother. "We don't know the English."

But I knew. Like I said, the woman had a sixth sense. In fact, Señora knew a whole lot more about me than I knew about myself, but I'm not going to get into that now. Feet pounded on the stairs and Roman stepped aside for Oscar.

"Don't talk to her," he ordered his brothers belatedly. I could tell Oscar's attitude grated on Roman. Big brother and all that. Then to me he said, "Go to sleep. In the morning, I'll get you out." The way he said it sounded like I was in jail. "You two—" he jerked his head at his brothers—"downstairs."

They both moved to obey, but Angel turned back and took my hand, his voice as gentle as Oscar's was harsh. "All will be well, *señorita*. You will see." He left and Oscar, after giving me a look of barely contained disgust, closed the door with a firm click.

I couldn't possibly sleep. How could I even stay here? Not with that woman who hated me downstairs and Oscar feeling much the same. Not with these questions tormenting me about Max and Roy Lester and the police. Max. I'd kept plenty of secrets from him. I guess I shouldn't be surprised that he was keeping plenty from me.

I went to the tiny window, my only way out of this mess. It looked over a small plot of land—a chicken coop, a garden of twisting dead vines, an ancient oak devoid of its leaves. Beyond, a tangle of brush dipped into a ravine like you saw all through the city—rocky gullies that filled with water during the heavy rains, then dried up for the other eleven months of the year. Beyond the ravine, a glow of light that might be downtown.

The not-so-far-off whistle of a train sounded from the other direction. I was close to the tracks, and that meant in a bad place for a woman to walk alone—and at night, downright foolish. I went to the bed and dumped out the contents of my handbag: my compact of powder and a lipstick, the keys to the boardinghouse, a dime, and a nickel. Not enough for a taxi, even if I could find one. Maybe waiting for daylight was my best option.

I lay back on the pillow and went over every detail I'd told Oscar. The drink, the way I'd barely made it up the stairs. If I could hardly stand up, I sure as spinach couldn't have stabbed a man

Roy's size, could I? Max didn't believe it. And Oscar, who wasn't exactly inclined toward me—he wouldn't bring me to his house if he thought I was a cold-blooded killer.

It was a terrible misunderstanding, that's all. But would anyone believe me? I closed my eyes, but my stomach twisted in a knot of unease. *All will be well,* Angel had said. He was a sweet boy, Angel. But I knew—deep down—he was wrong. All would not be well. All hadn't been well for a very long time.

———————

I opened my eyes to sun pouring through the little window, glinting from the polished crucifix. The air was close and hot. Where was I? Then I remembered. Max. Oscar. The police. The angry woman downstairs. My stomach spiraled. I lurched to the window, pushing it open and gulping the fresh air.

I had to go. And in more ways than one.

I gathered my shoes, ran a hand over my hair, and opened the door. It was time to get out of this house. The sooner the better. At the foot of the stairs, the front room of the house was sparsely furnished. A spotless window draped with a lace curtain, a hard-looking chair. A bright rag rug over the polished wood-planked floor. Three thin mattresses and a few blankets were rolled neatly in the corner.

I had to admit, it surprised me. The newspapers and plenty of the girls I knew had opinions about people from south of the border, making them out as dirty, even diseased. This was a bare-bones kind of place, but any German-born housewife of Odessa would be hard-put to find a speck of dust.

Daylight and the smell of coffee led me to a bright kitchen, where my disposition took a nosedive. Oscar and his mother faced off. His jaw was clenched tight and her arms were crossed over her chest. At my appearance, they both frowned. He bit out a what sounded like a command, and she snapped back something just as bossy. Neither of them looked like they might help me with my immediate concern.

Oscar glanced at me as he picked up his hat from the table, where a pile of newspapers lay beside a dirty plate and a tin cup. "I bring the boys to work, and then I find Max." His English was curt and his accent more pronounced, as if he didn't have the time to work at it. "You stay here. And don't let anyone see you. You understand?"

His look threw me. His mouth was grim and his movements jerky, as if he were afraid.

"Can't I come with you?" My voice had a pleading note to it. I glanced at the woman. She turned away from me.

Oscar jerked his head toward the pile of newspapers. "No." He stepped close, and his voice turned a titch more civil. "You get caught here, we are all in trouble. You understand, Minerva Sinclaire?"

I really didn't follow—what kind of trouble?—but I nodded anyway. He pushed past me toward the front door, muttering for my ears only, "And, *por favor*, don't make her more angry."

The door slammed behind Oscar, and I heard him call for Roman and Angel. I looked out the window to see them jump into the Ford. In a moment, they were gone. I turned to the woman. She looked ready to bite, her chin jutting and her sharp, dark eyes narrowed into folds of bronzed skin.

As intimidating as this woman was, necessity overcame my fear. As I contemplated how to make myself understood and the humiliation that would follow if I could not, the kitchen door opened, and a gust of fresh air breezed in . . . along with a beautiful girl who didn't seem at all surprised to see me.

It was the girl from Lester's party, the one who served the drinks and had gaped at Max, only this time she wore a striped blouse and a long, shapeless skirt that reached almost to her ankles. She rushed to me with brown eyes as friendly as the old woman's were hostile. "You are awake! I am very glad of it." She took my cold, pale hands in her warm, tawny ones.

My heart thumped, thinking of Oscar's fervent instruction. I'd already failed him.

"Don't worry," she said with a smile. "Roman told me of you in secret. I won't tell." She pulled me into the light of the window. "You are so beautiful. He also told me that."

"I'm . . . Minerva Sinclaire," I offered as the girl looked me over from head to bare feet.

"Forgive me." A lovely pink blush colored her dark skin. "I am Guadeloupe Francesca Martina Garcia." She said her long name very quickly, and a charming dimple pierced her cheek. "But you call me Lupita."

"You can call me Mina." Only Max called me that, but somehow it seemed right.

"Mina." Her strong accent made the name musical. "You poor thing. You are hungry, no?"

"Actually. . ." I felt my cheeks redden. "What I need is . . ." I tried to think of a good word, a polite word. I shifted from one foot to the other.

"Oh!" Lupita nodded in understanding. "Of course. You follow me."

That's when I knew this girl was sent from heaven.

Lupita took my hand and pulled me out the back door, saying

something quick to the mother, who responded in a monosyllable. Lupita stopped me in the shade of the small covered stoop. "My house," Lupita whispered, pointing to a boxlike construction of metal, cardboard, and wood. "My brother, Alonso, is at home now. We don't tell Alonso about you."

On the other side of the lot sat a long-handled pump, piles of kindling, and a potbellied stove belching smoke. Lupita left me on the porch and peered around each corner of the house. She came back and led me to a small shed beside a stand of stunted juniper. "You go in there, understand?"

I understood all right. Some of the poorer places in Odessa still had outhouses. When needs must . . . I emerged, still holding my breath, and Lupita was waiting to bring me quickly back to the house, where the old woman sat on her cot, eyeing me like a cockroach invading her kitchen.

Lupita caught my eye and whispered, "You must not let Sanchia's bad temper bother you. She is really a sweet lady."

"Really?" I couldn't help the surprise in my voice.

Lupita's lovely mouth twitched as she glanced back at the woman. "No. Not really. But she does, how you say, get better as you know her?" She covered her mouth to stop her laugh.

Sanchia turned away, her face pinched like she'd eaten something rotten.

"You really are very beautiful." Lupita smiled at me and took a plate from the shelf above the stove. "Roman and Angel are in love with you already." Her dimple flashed. "Of course, they are always in love—it is the way with boys that age, yes?" She said it as if she were much older than the boys who lived with Oscar.

I took a look down at my blue linen day dress. It had been pressed and crisp when Max picked me up yesterday, but now it looked like a flour sack. And my stockings—they were filthy. Not so beautiful, but she was kind to say it.

"Your hair, it is so—how you say?—in fashion?" She opened the cast iron stove that looked like something out of the last century and pulled out a blackened pan. "I so much wish I could cut mine."

Her thick hair would wave perfectly if bobbed, and a short cut would frame her beautiful eyes and perfect features. "It's not hard. I can do it for you." I'd cut my own when I was younger than her.

"No, no." She let out a short laugh. "My *mamá* would never forgive me." She scooped some brown mush onto the plate. "It would be . . ." She shrugged. "I don't know the word. She would call me a bad daughter."

I knew about bad daughters.

She added a few circles of what looked like flattened bread to the plate, put it on the table, and pushed me down in the chair. "Many girls, here even in the *colonia*, they cut their hair. Their fathers beat them, but they don't care."

"Beat them?" Papa had been not so thrilled when I'd shown up for dinner one night with my bob, but he'd never hit me.

"*Sí,*" she said solemnly, seeing my doubt. "Obedience is a good daughter—that's what the papas say."

A good daughter. That's what Penny was, and I wasn't.

Lupita looked down and her lips curved in a soft smile. "Also, I think Oscar, maybe he likes my hair." She flushed. "Oscar . . . he sees me just as a child still, but I am not."

Now I followed. Lupita was a girl in love. But with dour-faced Oscar? That was too unbelievable.

"If I am an obedient daughter, and pretty also, then this year I will be crowned queen of the *festivales*." Her hopeful smile said it all. That then, perhaps, Oscar would notice she was all grown up.

"*Ay!* Listen to me. You eat. And I find something you wear while we get you clean and pressed."

She bounded out of the house. I took a look at the flat bread and what smelled like beans on the plate. My insides weren't quite on the level, but with the old lady watching me with her disapproving black eyes, I wouldn't give her the satisfaction of showing my discomfort. I couldn't see any fork, so I rolled up the bread and nibbled a few bites. They threatened to come right back up. I put a hand on my stomach and swallowed the rest, hoping for the best.

Lupita slipped back in the door with a slew of bright clothes over her arm and a smile that I didn't deserve. I fingered the perfect embroidery around the neck of the green cotton blouse. "It's beautiful. Is it yours?"

Her smile dimmed. "No, this are not mine. But you may keep."

She helped me out of my dress and stockings right there in the kitchen. As I pulled on a bright yellow skirt and the grass-green blouse, Sanchia took my pile of dirty clothes with a scowl and brought them outside. "She will wash, I press," Lupita said as I cinched the sash around my waist. But when I went to the window to get a glimpse of my hair, I let out a squeal. There was Sanchia, shoving my good blue linen and my best stockings into the potbellied stove.

"*Ay, ay!*" Lupita cried out, throwing her hand over her mouth. "*Lo siento,* Mina. She is more angry than I know."

It was too unbelievable. I tried not to think what that dress—now in ashes—had cost me. I looked down at the puffed blouse and full skirt that I'd have to wear until I could get to my clothes at the boardinghouse. I hope it made the old crow feel better, because she sure had got me where it hurt.

"Please, forgive her. She is—I don't know how to say. You keep these, please." Lupita patted my arm. "I must go now. But I come back." She kissed me on the cheek like a sister. "It is not you she no like. It is all this." She waved a hand at the stack of newspapers on the table, as if I should know what she meant. "I do not believe what they say. She will see. Do not worry, Mina. All will be well." Lupita left in a swirl of bright color.

All this? What did that mean?

I glanced down at the newspapers strewn over the table, then dropped into the chair like I'd been sucker-punched.

All this meant my picture. On the front page.

POLICE HUNT FOR MURDERESS—Feb. 24—(AP)
Police have named a prime suspect in the Roy Lester
murder case, sources confirmed late last night. Miss
Minerva Sinclaire of Los Angeles is said to be the last
person with Mr. Lester on the night of his death, reported
Sergeant Bryce Adams of the Los Angeles police. A fur
coat, rented to Miss Sinclaire from Normandie Rental on
Spring Street, was left at the party and led to discovery of
the identity and address of the suspected killer.

I'd forgotten all about my rented fur and the receipt in the inside pocket with my name and address. The *señora*—Sanchia—stood in the doorway now, watching me with her black eyes. She probably believed I was a killer. Was she right? I thought about that night. What I'd told Oscar. How I could barely stand. How Roy carried me up the stairs.

I put my head in my hands. No. It didn't make sense. That's not what happened. But what did it matter when I was the only one who knew? It was all sewn up according to the papers. I'd go to prison, maybe even execution. Did they execute women? Then, almost worse than the idea of prison, I thought of Papa. Would the *Pierre Daily* run the story? Given how famous Roy was, they surely would. My stomach twisted like a June tornado. The whole town would know. Penny. Papa. How could I ever face him again?

I ran to the wastebasket and the little bit of breakfast I'd eaten came right back up.

Sanchia watched me but didn't move a muscle to help. Then she muttered a few words, turned on her heel, and left. I can't say I wasn't glad to see her go. I wiped my mouth and went back to the newspapers. On page two, Louella's column was pure venom. She called me a tramp and described me as some kind of lunatic. Was this the same woman who'd invited me to the party, who'd said, *Couldn't you just eat her up?* and *Roy's going to love you?*

I had to fix this. Please, Max, tell me we can fix this.

What could I do but wait for Oscar to come back?

I paced between the front windows and the back. I watched Sanchia and another woman wash what seemed like hundreds of sheets, crank them through a wringer and hang them to dry on ropes strung between the houses. I bit at my fingernails.

I read the article about me again. Then I read the rest of the newspaper, just to distract myself. On the third page, a headline blared *SEND THEM HOME!* The article reported triumphantly that over two hundred aliens had been rounded up in one week in Los Angeles County. Some were Chinese and Japanese but the real "deportables," as the paper called them, were the Mexicans. Disease-ridden, jobless, criminals. All of them either on assistance or taking jobs that should go to real Americans.

I looked around at the little house, spotless in the sunshine.

A week ago, I'd have believed every word—if I'd bothered to read anything other than the film reviews and gossip page. I suppose that shows how self-centered I really was. Now, I thought of Roman and Angel, of Lupita and her brother, and it finally dawned on me.

This was why Oscar was so worried.

If I were found here—if he were connected to me in any way—it meant a one-way bus ticket to the border for Oscar, maybe for all of them. Or even prison, if they found out he'd helped me get away from the estate.

Oscar should have thrown me out of the auto the minute he saw me. He sure shouldn't have got me out of the Montmartre. Here I'd been just thinking of myself—my studio contract, my big break—while he was risking his family, his very home. No wonder Sanchia looked at me like I was some kind of dirt on the bottom of her shoe. I guess I couldn't blame her. If he ended up in jail . . . it would be my fault. If they all were deported . . . how could I live with that?

By the time the afternoon sun was sinking golden over the ravine, my nails were bitten to the quick and my nerves were shot. Either Oscar hadn't found Max or Max had refused to come for me. That much was clear. I took myself up the stairs and into the little room, peered out the window to what I could see of the neighborhood. Women in kerchiefs, kids playing in the street, a donkey pulling a cart full of wood. I had to leave this place—Max or no Max. Not just for my sake, but for Oscar and Roman and Angel. For Lupita and even Señora. It was only right. I'd wait until dark, then with Oscar's blessing or without it, I'd get as far away from the Dominguez family as I could.

I crossed the room, standing below the crucifix on the wall.

The dark wood was nicked, and the silver figure hanging with outstretched arms must have been passed through generations of pious hands. I touched the naked foot with the tiny nail hole.

Please.

A wordless prayer, since I didn't know what to say. I didn't deserve divine help, so I didn't plead for myself. Just for everybody else. I hoped whoever was listening knew that.

At sundown, Oscar returned to the house in a real temper.

Señora served us more beans and flat bread while Lupita and Angel tried their best to make conversation. My stomach was in such knots I could only eat a few bites. Oscar didn't say a word about Max. I didn't ask. It was honestly a relief when Oscar sent me upstairs like a badly behaved child, telling me cryptically, "Tomorrow, you go. No matter what." Did that mean he was going to turn me in? Or just turn me out?

I wasn't waiting to find out. When everyone was asleep, I'd get out of their lives.

It seemed like an eternity before the house settled and I heard Oscar come inside after his smoke, banging around like he owned the place, which I suppose he did. I counted to one hundred, waiting for him to sleep. Then counted to one hundred again.

My plan wasn't so bad. I'd sneak out and make my way through the ravine until I was out of Oscar's neighborhood. It couldn't be too hard to follow the glow of lights to the city, stay clear of streetlights and streetcar stops. If I headed north and east, I'd hit Hollywood eventually—or at least someplace familiar. Then I'd find a place with a telephone and call Max.

Maybe it would take all night, but when needs must.

What I didn't know was walking a true line through a brushy ravine in the dark wasn't as easy as strawberry pie. I got out of the house nice and quiet and crept past the outhouse and laundry tubs behind the house. A skitter of apprehension got to me as I plunged into the prickly brush of the ravine. I veered around a few dark stands of scrub trees, then detoured around a patch of brambles. After what seemed like an hour of walking, I was turned around. I could make out the glow of streetlights in the distance but didn't know how to get to them. I wasn't scared, though, not yet.

Then I heard the howl—long, eerie, and near.

I froze. I'd heard coyotes prowled the city, had even heard their lonely cry, but I wasn't in the mood to meet one face-to-face. A rustle of brush made my heart hammer like mad. I looked for a tree to climb, a rock to throw—they're more afraid of me than I am of them, right? —but there was nothing. The rustle came closer and a dark shape emerged from the brush behind me.

"Did you lose your way to the outhouse, Minerva Sinclaire?"

Roman. My hand went to my chest and I gulped air. I was never so glad to see anyone, even with his smart grin. "Did you follow me?"

He came closer, a devilish smile on his face. "Are you not glad I did?" He stood closer than he had to, the dim light of the moon making his dark eyes glitter. "That coyote might think you make a good meal."

I wasn't buying his kind of baloney, but maybe he'd help me. "How do I get out of here?"

"Where you want to go?"

"Anywhere with a telephone." It was worth a try. It was hard to tell what went on behind those bedroom eyes, but Roman didn't seem to follow Oscar's orders any better than I did. The coyote howled again, and I jumped. Roman circled me with his arms and pulled me close.

He didn't look at all ashamed as I pushed him firmly away. "Whatever you have in mind, forget it, buster."

His white teeth flashed in the dark. "*Chica,* it's not what you are thinking. But you can't go walking around at night. There's more danger out there than coyotes and snakes."

"Snakes?"

He frowned. "And bums. Police. All sorts of bad."

I put my hands on my hips. "I need out of here. The sooner the better for everybody. I'll call Max and then be gone."

He raised a brow. "Max. He fix everything?" He didn't sound convinced.

Maybe he would. I hoped he would. "Why don't you like him?" I countered. It was like Max was some kind of leper to these people.

Roman took my hand in his and gave me a look from under those long lashes. "You come back with me, *chica,* and I tell you all about Max." He shrugged when I hesitated. "Or stay out here with the scorpions."

I followed him through the brush and right back up to the big oak tree behind his house. Roman sat down, his back to the trunk, and I slid down beside him, checking first for scorpions. He reached into his pocket and pulled out a pack of cigarettes—the same brand his big brother smoked. He scraped a match against the bark and cupped the flame over his mouth. He took a puff, then passed it to me. It felt good to hold one again, a familiar anchor in this upside-down world. I took a ladylike puff—harsh, but I wasn't complaining—and handed it back. I blew out a veil of smoke. Time for him to tell me. "Now, Max Clark."

Roman looked sideways at me. "We play a game, Minerva. It is called *la verdad*."

I was starting to figure why Oscar and Roman didn't get along so well. Roman pushed the limits to the bitter end. *"La verdad?"*

"Sí. 'Truth,' you say. I ask you a question and you must answer it with the truth. Then, you ask me a question."

This sounded fishy. "What kind of question?"

He leaned back, the glow of the cigarette lighting his face. "You tell me about Minerva Sinclaire—" he smiled—"and I tell you about Max Clark."

I took the cigarette back. I could play along for now. "All right. Why don't you like Max?"

"No, no." He shook his head. "I start."

This kid was a real shark.

He looked me up and down. "A beautiful *señorita* like you must have a boyfriend, no?"

That was easier than I expected. "No." I raised my brows. "Now tell me about Max."

Roman took the cigarette back, taking his time. *"Sí.* He is my *primo*—how you say—'cousin.'"

I already knew that. "How? And why doesn't he—"

Roman shook his head. "No, no. Little answer from you, little answer from me."

I let out a frustrated breath.

The wicked look was back. "No boyfriend? So, what is Max to you then? Is he really just your . . . how you say, 'agent'? And you must tell truth, remember."

"You mean is there something going on between us?"

"Sí."

I felt my cheeks heat and was glad for the dark. "He works for me." That was the truth—at least it was now.

Roman lifted his eyebrows. "But you are very beautiful, and Max, he loves beautiful women just like his father did."

"You said the truth. I told the truth." That was all he was getting from me.

Roman nodded. "That is too bad for him. But good for me." His hand slipped down and picked up mine, caressing my wrist.

I snatched my hand back. "My turn. Max. Spill the beans."

Roman smiled good-naturedly and leaned back against the tree. He'd been waiting for this, I could tell. "He grew up here, with us. His mother and my mother were sisters. He and Oscar—" Roman brought his two pointer fingers side-by-side—"like brothers."

Max, the charmer, and Oscar, the guy who couldn't crack a smile to save his life? It was too hard to believe.

"Mamá and my *papá*, with Tía Concha, Max's mother. They come together from Mexico." He waved toward the house. "They move here for Papá to work on the railroad, but Tía Concha . . ." He shrugged.

"What about her?" Max's mother, whom he never spoke of.

He sighed. "She was very beautiful. She was found by the men who made the films and had small parts in the Westerns."

I was starting to get the picture. "And that's where she met Dusty Clark?" He wasn't called the Kissing Cowboy for nothing.

"*Sí*. She became with his child and he did not want her. She came back here, to our house. Max was born and not long after, Oscar. They grew up like brothers."

Max had lived here, not with Dusty Clark? Why hadn't he ever told me?

Roman wasn't playing the game now. "Max, he hasn't been back here since . . ." He shook his head.

I pulled myself together. "Since when?"

Roman looked at the ground, and for a moment he didn't look like the cocky young man, but a child who'd seen more than his share of sorrow. "Since Maria Carmen."

"Who is Maria Carmen?"

Roman pointed to the house where Lupita lived. "The daughter of Francesca." Roman shook his head. "Max and Oscar and Maria Carmen, the three *amigos*." He looked away. "I was very young, but I remember how beautiful she was, like Lupita but also not like her."

Was. I felt a chill over my skin. "What happened to her?"

Roman crushed out the cigarette on the trunk of the tree. "When Max—when Tía Concha died and Dusty Clark took Max to live with him—"

I held up a hand. He'd lost me again. "Wait. Max's mother died?"

"*Sí.* I was just seven year old. I remember a long black auto pulls up, takes Max away right after we buried her."

Oh, Max. I knew what it was like to lose your mother. And I'd thought I was the only one keeping secrets. "So that's when he went to live with Dusty Clark?"

"*Sí.* And Maria Carmen, she left here also. Two years later, when she turn sixteen, she ran away to Max."

"She was in love with Max?" It was like coming in halfway through a film and having to catch up on the story.

Roman shook his head. "*No sé.* Sometimes. And sometimes she was in love with Oscar." He waved a hand toward his own home. "She didn't want to be Mexican, didn't want to obey her father, work in the fields, or do laundry until she was old and bent like the women here. She wanted more."

I had the sinking feeling that Maria Carmen's story didn't have a happy ending.

"She stay with Max and his father. They give her clothes and let her live in the big house. Oscar begged she come back, but she say no. She had chosen Max. Then, three years ago, Max telephoned the *sociedades*. He tell Oscar . . ." Roman swallowed hard.

My heart tightened like a fist. Suddenly, I knew the rest of the story. Three years ago, Dusty Clark had died, rolling his automobile off a cliff on Canyon Road. And not alone. He'd had a woman with him. I'd been sitting in the pharmacy in Odessa when I read it in the newspaper. "She died with Dusty Clark. In the accident."

Roman's eyes were overbright. "And that is not all of it." He looked away, as if wishing he'd never started this game of truth.

"Please, Roman." I grabbed his hand. He had to tell me the rest.

"Max kept it out of the papers but . . . Maria Carmen, she was pregnant."

My mind slowed, stunned by his words. Pregnant. With Max's baby.

"The last time we saw Max was the funeral. Oscar was out of his head. He beat Max bloody, told him it was his fault. Max . . . he didn't fight back. He just let Oscar hit him, over and over."

Oh, Max. I understand now. If I'd been picked up by anyone else on the road but Oscar. And now I was here. And he had to face everything he'd lost.

Roman smiled ruefully. "You win, *chica*."

I slumped down, suddenly exhausted. I hadn't won anything.

Roman looked into the dark. "It is late."

He was right about that. Too late for me to make it up to Max. Losing Maria Carmen had broken his heart and then, when he'd offered it to me, I'd stomped it into the ground. "I have to find him." I didn't know what I'd say, but I had to see Max again, now that I knew.

Roman picked up my hand. "I wake you in the morning when they to go church. I take you to Max then. But maybe you give me little kiss now, to thank me for saving you?"

My look answered that plain. Roman smiled sadly and shrugged. He walked me back into the house, holding the door and tiptoeing past his mother sleeping on her cot in the kitchen. He whispered, *"Buenos noches,"* and I slipped up the stairs to my room. I lay down on the bed, and even as tired as I was, my mind spun like a whirligig.

Max. This was why you seemed so lost.

His father, Maria Carmen, his child, all gone in one fatal moment.

You should have told me, Max. About family you couldn't face. About regrets. If only I'd known.

I stared into the dark. Should haves. If onlys.

I have them, too, Max. And plenty of them are about you.

CHAPTER 6

MINA

If I'd known Max's secrets, maybe I wouldn't have done what I did at Dusty Clark's beach house—the New Year's Day Incident that I remembered with conflicting feelings of wonder and regret . . . but mostly regret. I guess that memory of the beach house is kind of like Mama's ring—it reminds me of what I've lost.

I had wanted so badly to give Max something then—not to repay him, that wasn't it; you couldn't repay somebody for being your friend—but to show him what he meant to me. The sorry thing was, I gave him too much, or maybe just the wrong thing. Then I got scared and I tried to take it back.

I made a horrid mess of it all.

I guess you could say it started last Christmas Eve. That night was something I'd never figured out about Max, no matter how much I thought about it. And I thought about it a lot.

By the time the tinsel stars and silver bells went up on

Hollywood Boulevard and the Bullock's Santa was ho-ho-ho-ing his way through a line of children, Max had become a part of my life. To be honest, the best part of my life. Then, just when everything was going swell, I came down with a whopper of a head cold. I was supposed to work the Christmas Eve shift at the Derby, but I telephoned Norb at noon—sneezing and snuffling—and made my excuses.

Lana had a big date. After she got all dolled up, she moved her radio close to my bed. "At least you can listen to Christmas carols all by your lonely," she said cheerfully. "You mind if I borrow your velvet gloves? It's not like you're going to be using them."

By the time it was dark, my head was hammering, and my nose was running faster than an LA streetcar. I was a sorry sight and felt even worse. I curled up in my bed with a magazine I was too miserable to read and let myself think of home. By now, Penny would have the tree decorated with the precious glass balls that had come all the way from Germany with Papa. She'd probably scraped together enough sugar and butter to make cookies, and the sauerbraten would be simmering. Knitted socks for Papa would be wrapped in newspaper and tied with bright yarn.

And here I was, alone and sick. No presents, not even a tree. It was like Christmas had forgotten this corner of Los Angeles. Or maybe Christmas had just forgotten me.

I was well into my private pity party when I heard a tapping at the window, and Max—his face pressed against the glass—scared the horsefeathers out of me. I yelped, then jumped out of bed and undid the latch. He hoisted himself up to the sill and threaded his long legs through the opening. "What are you doing?" I hissed, as he knocked over a chair and a stack of magazines, making a din loud enough to wake the dead.

Clumping steps sounded down the hall and stopped just outside my door. "What's going on in there, Miss Sinclaire?"

Max grinned and put a finger over his lips.

"Just getting some fresh air, Mrs. Perfall," I called out, shutting the window with a bang. If she found a fella in our room, unchaperoned, she'd put me out in the cold for certain.

I launched into a series of well-timed sneezes. Max covered his mouth with his hand, his eyes crinkling with laughter. Mrs. Perfall's heavy footfalls and mutterings receded back down the hall.

Max looked over my place, the laughter still on his lips. The room was littered with discarded clothes from Lana, magazines, dirty cups and saucers. And then there was me. I put my hand to my hair. I was a fright. Red nose, runny eyes, my hideous pink chenille dressing gown belted over the white cotton nighty I'd had since I was twelve.

"You look terrible," Max said.

"That's bunny, I beel like a million bucks," I managed back, wishing he didn't look so good in his soft wool trousers and navy oxfords. His shirt was pressed, as usual, but the sleeves were rolled up and the top two buttons undone. No tie or jacket tonight. What was he doing here on Christmas Eve, anyway? Didn't he have a family? I climbed back into my bed and pulled the covers all the way over my face. I couldn't deal with Max tonight.

Max wasn't put out. Not a bit.

I heard him rustling through the paper grocery bag he'd dragged in with him and peeked over the edge of the blanket.

"Norb told me you were down with a bug." Before I knew it, he'd found a clean glass, filled it with water, and was handing me two aspirin. "Take these."

He was a bossy one but I didn't have the energy to fight him. He took the glass from my fingers after I downed the aspirin and tucked the blanket back under my chin. "You got a hot plate in this mess?" He kept his voice low—no need to alert the landlady again.

I raised my head weakly and pushed back the covers. "What in heaven's name do you—"

"Ah, ah." He held up his hand. "Stay put."

I obeyed. It was easier that way. I think I dozed, because in what seemed like moments, he was back with a cup and a spoon. He helped me to sit up, plumping the pillow behind my back, then dipped the spoon in the cup and held it out to me.

I eyed the golden liquid doubtfully.

"Don't worry. It's an old family remedy. Guaranteed to make you feel like new." He winked. "Or at least forget how bad you feel. Open up."

I opened my mouth without thinking and swallowed. It was hot and sweet and felt like heaven on my scratchy throat.

He wiped a drop from the side of my mouth with his thumb. "That's my girl." He didn't mean anything by it, but I think my fever went up a few degrees.

"What's in it?"

"Honey and lemon juice. But mostly whisky."

I sank back down on the bed. "Why are you here?" My voice sounded like a frog caught in a drainpipe.

He didn't answer. Not then or later. But he didn't leave either. He stayed, and as my head cleared and the aspirin took my headache to a more reasonable thumping, he told me about the show he'd seen the night before at the Chinese. I was too tired to wonder much whether he'd taken Julia or one of the Dorises, and he didn't say.

"Feeling better?"

I sniffed. "This isn't how you wanted to spend Christmas Eve." Max was a good guy. He probably felt sorry for me and that's why he was here.

"Says you." He smiled his sweet, slow smile. "Besides, I have to take care of my best client."

"You mean your only client."

"That too."

I got the notion that Max just might be as lonely as I was, but maybe that was the fever talking. He spooned me the rest of the medicine and my eyes got heavy. I'm not sure, but I think he leaned forward and brushed his warm lips over my cheek, whispering, "Merry Christmas, Mina." Or maybe I dreamed it. When I opened my eyes again, he was gone. But on the table beside my bed was a tiny tree, decorated in tinsel and gold, with a silver star shining at the top.

I didn't know what to make of it at all.

By New Year's Day, I was back on my feet and working the morning shift at the Derby, where a few desultory patrons slumped over their coffee and eggs, nursing hangovers. The studios had shut down over Christmas and wouldn't open until the big shots came back from their jaunts to Reno and New York. Max sloped in around noon, looking like a walking headache. His usual clean-shaven jaw was shadowed. Instead of his neat suit, he wore slightly wrinkled chinos and a shirt that looked like it had spent the night on the floor.

I asked Cook for a prairie oyster. He cracked a raw egg into an old-fashioned glass, covered it in Tabasco, Worcestershire, salt, and pepper, and pushed it across the counter. "How was your date last night?" I set the glass down gently in front of Max, who drooped over a corner table, and poured him a coffee chaser. I'd spent New Year's Eve at home, washing my hair, taking a blissfully long bath, and thinking about Max. But he didn't have to know that.

He threw back the prairie oyster in one go and set the glass on the table with a grimace. "About as bad as I expected."

"The date or the remedy?"

A smile flickered back at me. Max didn't stay down for long. "Both."

I laughed and secretly exulted. Maybe he'd figure out those girls weren't right for him. "Thanks for the tree." I looked down at the menus in my hand instead of at his handsome face. "You really shouldn't have."

"I do plenty I shouldn't," he said in a voice that sent a rush of heat to my cheeks. When I started to my next table, he caught me by the elbow. "Hey, Mina, let's get out of here." His hand was warm, and the midmorning light turned his eyes to amber. You know that feeling when you take a misstep off the curb? How it knocks you a little breathless and it takes a second to recover? That's what it felt like sometimes with Max.

I managed to play it cool. "To do what?" We'd seen every picture in town except the foreign ones, which Max said weren't worth it.

"Dusty's place in Laguna. I need to check on it."

That's the first I heard of Laguna.

"It's a nice drive." He fiddled with his fork, lining it up with his unused napkin. "I'll buy you dinner."

What about the mysterious Julia? Didn't she like a drive down the Pacific Coast on a bright winter day? "I'm on until six," I hemmed.

He shrugged and stood up, still not meeting my gaze. "Suit yourself."

I watched him saunter to the door, then ran to catch up. "Give me five minutes."

A day with Max was better than serving hangovers at the Brown Derby, Julia be sunk.

I had a heart-to-heart with Norb, promises were made, and it was fixed. I quick-changed out of my uniform and into a peacock-blue day dress with a drop waist and flutter sleeves.

Outside, Max leaned against the roadster. The top was down, and his smile warmed me faster than the thin sunlight battling with the chill breeze. Before I knew it, we were heading toward the coast.

Max didn't launch into a lecture on Louis B. Mayer as we roared past Culver City with its acres of studio lots—or mention again how funny it was that the biggest studio in Hollywood wasn't even in Hollywood—and I was grateful. I didn't want to talk business.

My hair blew wild and caught on my lipstick as we sped through the oil fields of Long Beach, pumps bending up and down like the dinosaurs I'd seen in encyclopedias back in Odessa. Max pointed to a small compartment in front of me. In it, I found a pair of dark sunglasses and a silk scarf. Julia's, maybe, but I didn't care. I turned my new peepers on him. "Looks good on you," he shouted over the wind and roar of the engine.

I watched him, the dark glasses making it easy. He leaned back and stretched one arm along the back of the bench, close to my shoulder. His hat was off, and his hair, teased by the wind, sprung into chestnut curls sun-streaked with copper. He might take after his cowboy father with his long legs and wide shoulders, but the elegant hands draped over the steering wheel were more at home with a cigarette than a six-shooter, and the dark hair and golden eyes had to be from the mother he never spoke of. We all had secrets, I remember thinking back then. Max didn't ask about mine, and that day he kept his confessions for later.

The coast highway was too beautiful to believe—cliffs towering on one side, the ocean and sky stretching to eternity on the other. Seabirds wheeled and shrilled. The sun was warm but the wind off the ocean cut like a blade. I hugged my bare arms.

Max glanced over. "Hold the wheel," he ordered and let go just like that.

I leaned over and grabbed the steering wheel, as if I could do anything else. "What are you—" My heart jumped as we careened sideways. We were on a straight shot, and I got us back in the center of the road by the time Max had shrugged off his coat.

"Put that on." He tossed his jacket toward me and took over.

"I'm not about to thank you for scaring me half into my grave," I groused, but the satin lining of his jacket was warm and scented with his hair tonic and cigarettes.

Max seemed to relax as we ascended the flanks of the San Joaquin Hills. Stands of pine and juniper leaned on one side of the road. On the other, far below, the ocean waves shattered on dark rock. Occasionally, a small home could be seen in the bluffs or nestled close to the beach. Max swerved, and I looked back at the road in time to see a coyote—lonely and lean—staring at us with bright, intelligent eyes. We wound higher into the hills, the trees along the road sparse and twisted.

Max glanced over at me, his lips twitching. "You're humming again."

I stopped humming. "Am not."

He laughed and slowed as we rounded a bend. "Close your

eyes," he said like a show-off kid. I shut my eyes and felt him pull the roadster over and come to a stop. "Now open."

I opened my eyes to a sheer cliff dropping not two feet from my door and making my stomach lurch. Below, a crescent of sparkling emerald curved into the coast. Tiers of white-tipped waves broke on golden sand then retreated, leaving lacy trails of foam.

I let out a long breath. "It's beautiful, Max."

He looked for a few moments more, then zipped down the hill where a tiny store leaned into the base of the cliff. "Back in a jiffy," Max said and hopped out. I listened to the crash of the waves and the call of the seabirds. He came back with an armload of packages and a couple bottles that he stowed in the trunk.

Minutes later, we pulled onto a sand-packed road flanked by sea grasses and pines. After a bumpy ride, the road ended at a bungalow just a hundred yards from a secluded beach.

"This is yours?" I looked at the decrepit gate, the weathered shutters.

"Dusty's," he said. I didn't ask more.

He cranked up the top on the roadster while I waited, then grabbed the packages out of the trunk and led the way. He fished a key out of his pocket, opened the door, and motioned me inside with a flourish worthy of a bellboy at the Ambassador.

It wasn't what I expected from Dusty Clark. He had been one of Cosmopolitan's notorious bad boys, known for parties where champagne and whisky flowed like water, where cocaine and women were passed like party favors. From what I'd heard—not from Max, of course—Dusty had owned a mansion in the hills, a posh bungalow in town, and a ranch over the border in Mexico, replete with women, hangers-on, and plenty of illegal activity.

But this house was more like a home. No grand entrance, but a step down into a big room dominated by a fireplace of river rock. An overstuffed divan and comfy-looking chairs squatted on a slate floor strewn with a couple sheepskin rugs that had seen better days. The opposite wall held a line of shuttered windows. Homey, I'd call it.

Max unlatched the shutters to show the beach and pounding surf beyond. "We came here sometimes, before . . . everything." He let out a breath and his shoulders lowered; his face softened. "Grab that bag, will you?" He led me through a short hallway. I glanced into two bedrooms—pine-framed beds covered in bright quilts—and a lavatory with a claw-foot tub. The kitchen was old-fashioned and dim, with an enameled gas stove and scuffed linoleum floor. I pulled the light switch. Nothing happened.

"Electric's off. Set those here."

I rummaged through the things he'd brought in. A bottle of wine, and one of gin. Tonic and some limes. Bread, butter, a wedge of some kind of cheese. My stomach grumbled. It was late afternoon, and I hadn't eaten since my piece of toast and jam this morning. I lifted the wet towel from a bucket. Tiny gray clams looked like rocks and smelled like the ocean. "Are we going to eat these?"

Max gave me a nod. "Trust me, you'll love them."

A moment later, he'd brought me outside to a patio of uneven flagstone. A pair of weathered wood-slatted chairs cozied up to a stone firepit like old friends. A double chaise lounge—kidney shaped and with a striped canvas cushion—faced the ocean. Across a patch of sea grass, a sand path led down to the crashing waves.

Max faced the wind coming off the water, closed his eyes, and breathed in the salty air. "I love this place."

This wasn't the smooth Hollywood agent that I knew. He was somebody else. I didn't want to break the magic of the moment, so I didn't say anything. Finally, he turned to me. "Let's eat."

I frowned. How was I supposed to cook with no electric? And how did you cook clams anyway? But he patted a chair beside the firepit. "Relax. I'll bring you a drink."

He put a gin and tonic in my hand, and then—you could have knocked me sideways—he made us both dinner. A man, making dinner. He even seemed to enjoy it. I could see it in the set of his shoulders, in the way he padded back and forth, his feet bare, talking easily. And not about studios and Technicolor and how sound works, either.

"This—" he waved at the ocean—"is called Emerald Bay, and further down is Laguna Beach. Kind of an artists' hideaway. Some writers. Real bohemians." He lit a fire in the circle of stones and piled driftwood on top of the flames.

He disappeared, then brought out a tray of bread, cheese, and sliced apples. "There's artists all over on a nice day, with their easels and sketchbooks." He set the food on the small table between the chairs. "But the best part is the beach. There's miles of it."

He put a wedge of cheese and one of apple on a slice of bread and handed it to me. The wind blew his hair into curls over his brow, and the sun, low in the sky now, lit up his eyes.

I took a cautious bite. "This—" and I admit I talked with my mouth full—"is delicious."

Max looked more than a titch smug. Next, he brought out a lidded pan and nestled it into the coals. He refilled my drink as I nabbed another bread and cheese and watched the waves flow back and forth. It was mesmerizing, the ocean. The breeze smelled of salt and brine. The birds rode the azure sky and coral clouds like tiny black kites.

Max fished the clams off the fire. We ate them hot, with our fingers, dipping them in a tin of melted butter. I couldn't get enough.

Max leaned close, wiping butter from my chin and lips with a kitchen towel we were sharing as a napkin. "I told you," he said, and for once I didn't even care.

By the time we washed our buttery fingers, the sun hung above the horizon, setting each wave sparkling like a diamond. Maybe it was the gin, but I was warm and relaxed and not afraid to ask what I'd been wondering since we bumped down the beach road.

"Do you come here a lot?"

He looked down into his drink. "This is the first time since he died." He gave me a sideways glance. "And I've never brought a woman here, if you're wondering."

That was exactly what I'd wondered. I blurted out, "Not even Julia?"

"Julia?" he said with jerk of surprise, and then laughed. He seemed ridiculously pleased. "No. Julia doesn't like the ocean."

I felt a stab of satisfaction. Whatever moxie Julia had, I had plenty more. "Well, I do. Let's go swimming."

He raised a brow. "Do you know how cold that water is this time of year?"

I didn't tell him that I swam in the lakes while there was still ice floating. I just slipped off my shoes and headed toward the beach. "Come on, slowpoke."

My feet sunk into the cool, damp sand as I ran to where the water purled and ebbed. Up close, the breaking waves were bigger than they'd looked from the house. I stepped in up to my knees. An oncoming wave met me, ice cold and with more force than I expected. I yelped as the receding water sucked the sand from under my feet.

Max joined me. We went deeper. I lifted my dress to keep it dry, but it was no use. I turned away from the next breaker, laughing along with the scree of the gulls. Max shouted, and I turned back to see a wave bigger than the rest—much bigger—coming fast. Max grabbed my hand and we started to run, the water dragging us back, the sand moving under our feet. I glanced over my shoulder and let out a screech—or maybe it was a laugh—as the wave crested, the sun glinting through the agate-green curl towering over us.

Icy water crashed over my shoulders, and for a moment, I thought I'd go under. But Max's grip was firm. He pulled me through the seething water to dry sand, and we both collapsed, laughing breathlessly. "That was freezing!" My whole body tingled with salt and cold. My heart raced.

"You were the one who wanted to swim," he said, rolling over on his back.

We lay on the sand, our hands intertwined, and watched the sun touch the water on the horizon. I realized for the first time in a long while that I was happy. Partly because of the sun and the sand. Mostly, though, because Max was happy. I'd never seen him like this before—relaxed and easy. I liked having something to do with that.

The cold waves curled around our feet, receding into lacy foam. The birds circled above us, their cries like shouts of laughter ringing against the cliff. And Max smiled at the sky.

Before long, the wind came up, raising goosebumps on my wet legs and arms and making me shiver. It was January, after all. Even in the Golden State, you couldn't lie around in a wet dress and not get cold. Max heaved himself up from the sand and held out his hand to me. "Let's get you warmed up."

He left a trail of water and sand through the house, padding to the small bedroom. His wet trousers clung to him, and his shirt was flecked with seaweed. I must have looked a mess, but for once I didn't care.

He pulled open a bureau, empty. "We never kept much here," he apologized. After a few more tries, he came up with a heavy brocade dressing gown, a pair of worn dungarees, and a single sock. He gave me a grin. "Toss a coin?"

I raised a brow and took the dressing gown. When needs must. Max left the room, and I stripped off my wet dress and underthings. The silk robe had once been red, now faded to a dull pink with worn velvet trim. It smelled faintly of cigars, but when I cinched the wide belt tight around my waist, the hem fell to a respectable length.

Back on the patio, Max was putting more wood on the fire, blowing on the flame, squinting against the smoke. The soft tan dungarees were a size too big, rolled up to his ankles and hanging low around the waist. Traces of sand clung to his back and shoulders. His wet clothes were slung over the railing. I draped my salt-watered dress alongside, arranging my underthings discreetly out of sight.

Max pulled the wide chaise lounge closer to the warmth of the fire, and I curled up on it as he opened a bottle with the squeak of a cork. "This will warm you up," he said and poured wine into a water glass.

I hadn't tasted much in the way of wine. It wasn't something we had cause to drink in Odessa, and all my LA experience was with bootlegged liquor and champagne. It was strong but went down easy with the tang of earth and fruit.

I watched Max add wood to the fire. I'd seen plenty of shirt-less men working on the farm—Germans mostly, with freckled shoulders and chests like beer barrels—but I couldn't help staring at Max. His smooth shoulders were wide but not bulky, his skin a shade darker than tan. His usually well-disciplined hair rebelled into disorderly curls. He stared into the fire, reminding me suddenly of the coyote we'd seen on the road. *Inscrutable* was a word I heard once. Penny would call that a ten-cent word, but it fit.

He perched beside me on the chaise, and I was thankful he couldn't read my sappy thoughts. He fingered my oversized dressing gown. "That's going to be all the rage next season."

I took a sip of wine, and maybe that gave me courage to pass up our usual banter. This new Max had me hooked and I wanted more. "Why now?" I asked. What I wanted to know was why me, but if I came too close, I figured he'd bolt. "Why haven't you been back before?"

He looked into his glass as if it might have the answer, his forehead knit under his dark curls. "My father . . . he wasn't easy to be around," he finally said, directing his words into the flames. There was pain in his voice, and I wondered then about the mother he never spoke of, but I didn't have the courage to ask him.

He took a deep drink of his wine and looked out over the sea where the stars were starting to glow faintly in the indigo sky. "I had everything you'd think a boy would want. Houses, servants, all the food I could eat." His dark lashes fanned over his cheeks. "He took me to the studios, the parties. I ran for their drinks, drove his car. I learned how to dress like him, talk like him, drink like him." He shrugged.

I shivered. He saw and thought it was the wind. He went into the house, coming back with a soft quilt that he pulled over both of us. He leaned back, pulling me next to his fire-warmed skin. I wanted to ask a hundred questions, but I was afraid to break the spell, afraid he'd stop talking.

"I got older, and I guess the novelty wore off. I was the kid he sometimes remembered. By then, he was usually drunk, or doped, or hungover. That was the worst. That's when you find out how terrible people can be. Even your own father."

An ember dropped and flared, illuminating his face. He looked unfamiliar for a moment, like a stranger. "But sometimes . . . I think it was when he got tired of it all, we'd come here. Just the two of us." He stretched out beside me, his long legs against mine, his arm still keeping me close and warm at his side. "Just beachcombing and eating clams, fishing sometimes. No parties. No women."

I wanted to tell him I understood, but I didn't, so I kept quiet.

He hooked his free hand around the bottle and poured more for me, then emptied it into his own glass. "He was different here. Like the man he wanted to be. Not the drunk that everyone remembers at the end." Max looked down on me. The fire flickered, making his eyes dark one moment and flashing gold the next. "Part of me is glad he's gone." He let out a breath that was a little shaky, so I knew this admission was costing him. "Maybe I'm as bad a son as he was a father."

"Max." I laid my hand against his warm chest, wishing I could bring him back from whatever dark place he'd gone. "You were just a kid." Surely, he knew that. I looked into his eyes, dark and still mysterious, but not as mysterious as they used to be. "He loved you, Max." How could he not?

Max gave me that sideways look that meant he didn't believe a word. "He never said it."

"He said it the only way he knew. He brought you here, where he could be himself, with you." I thought of early mornings in the barn with Papa, before everything broke, before Mama died. When I deserved his love.

"Well, it's the last time I'll see the place," he said. His arm around me was prickled with goosebumps now that the wind had come up.

"What do you mean?" If I had a place like this, I'd never leave it.

"Sold it. Dusty owed a lot of people."

"Oh, Max. I'm sorry." The pop of the fire devouring the driftwood was the only sound other than the rhythmic waves pounding against the shoreline. The moon had risen, illuminating the white sand.

He shrugged but I could see it mattered. "Now you know my sad story, Minerva Sinclaire. Let's hear yours."

Max had told me the truth, given me a look at a real part of himself. That was something in this land of fake sets and thin-lipped smiles. I wasn't sure if anyone else had seen it. Not the Dorises, maybe not even Julia. But I couldn't do the same. It was too much. So I played for time. "Weren't you the one who told me to keep my secrets?"

"I lied." He turned his face to me, mere inches away now. He smelled of ocean and smoke. "Tell me all about Minerva Sinclaire."

My heart flip-flopped and for a moment I was tempted. If I was going to tell anyone about all of it, it would be Max. I'd tell him about Papa and Penny. About how much I missed the open prairie and the smell of the farm. But about Alex? Stealing the money and Mama's ring? Never. And then there was the rest. The dance hall and Bert and Cal. If I started, I might tell him everything.

Max's arm around me was comforting and warm. He'd given me so much. Not just a job and food in the cupboard. Hope. Friendship. A part of himself tonight that I didn't deserve. And I couldn't give him the truth. Maybe my thinking was muddled from wine—more likely from the starlight and the song of the waves—but I figured there was one thing I had to offer.

The sorry thing was, I'd given the same to men who deserved it less.

I leaned in and kissed him. Before this, my kisses had always been something I doled out, like change from the cash register. But this kiss wasn't like that.

He went still, then drew back and looked into my eyes. He lifted a hand and pushed a strand of hair behind my ear. "You're playing with fire, Mina," he whispered with the flicker of a smile. He'd let me off with that if I wanted. We'd go back to being friends.

I kissed him again. If he was looking for permission, I was giving it.

The next kiss was all him, and I'd never been kissed like that. "You know, we shouldn't do this." His eyes were on mine, one hand at my waist, the other at the nape of my neck.

My heart pounded like mad. Under my hand, I felt the beat of his, just as quick. I brushed my cheek over his sandpapery chin. "You do plenty that you shouldn't," I reminded him.

He said my name like he was giving up. He said lots of things then, nonsense, most of it. He murmured against my lips about mistakes, but I didn't answer. His hand pulled at the knot of the silk robe. I squeezed my eyes shut, memories of Alex edging into my thoughts. Max must have noticed, because he stopped.

I didn't move, my heart double-timed, and I held my breath. Was it fear, or something else? I honestly didn't know.

"Mina, look at me," he whispered.

I opened my eyes to his, dark and intense.

His hand cupped my cheek. "We can stop." His thumb smoothed over my lips. "Just say the word."

That was probably the moment I decided. If he'd pushed me, if he'd been at all like Alex, I would have stopped right there. I should have, I suppose. But this was Max. I touched the back of his neck where I knew his hair came to a point and pulled him closer.

His eyes sought mine in the moonlight. "I don't want to hurt you," he said.

I wanted to look away, but I held his gaze. "You won't hurt me." I didn't know it then, but I was the one who would hurt him.

Regret—or something like it—passed across his face. Then he gave in.

I won't say any more about it except it sure as sunshine wasn't what I'd expected. All I can say is neither of us—each for our own reasons—stopped what happened. I knew my reasons. But was I ever wrong about his. Afterward, he whispered sweet things to me, kissing me until we both fell asleep to the sound of the surf against the rocks.

I knew it was wrong, what we'd done, just like it had been wrong with Alex and Cal. But it didn't feel wrong. I suppose I wasn't the first girl to use that old excuse.

Knowing what I know now, would I change what I did that night if I could? I honestly don't know. Isn't that a horrid thing to say? Except for what happened next. If I had it to do all over again, I wouldn't hurt him like I did the next morning. But at the time, I thought it couldn't be helped.

———————

After Max and I . . . after we'd made love—I'll call it that, because that's what it was—I woke in the dark, wrapped in his arms. The waves lapped gently at the shore, the moon's tidal pull spent. The cedars sighed in the breeze and birds chirped. The fire had died, but Max—gallant even in his sleep—cushioned my head with one arm and anchored the quilt over me with the other. His leg weighed heavy over mine, his breath a slow rhythm.

I didn't want to move, to disrupt the warmth that was Max and me, together. This was how it was supposed to be. Well, not really. I was supposed to have a ring on my finger, vows said in a church in front of God and everybody, wasn't I?

As the sky lightened, I could see Max's sleeping face. His long lashes made half-moons of shadow on his cheeks. He looked so peaceful, maybe even happy. That's what I'd wanted, I told myself. To make him happy, at least for a time. Was that so wrong?

Max had made love to me like it meant something. And in the end, it had. More than I expected. More than I could even admit. That was the problem. This could be the start of something new between us, something big that neither of us had asked for. Just the thought of me and Max—together, like that—I couldn't even breathe.

That's when I realized I loved him. And that's when I knew I'd have to give him up.

Maybe Max thought he loved me, but he deserved more. More than a thief and a liar. Sure, he knew that I wasn't a virgin. But he didn't know why. He didn't know about Alex. Or about the Rose and Bert and Cal. He could never know that. Besides, I didn't have a future here in Hollywood with Max. I was going back to Odessa with everything Papa needed. Even back then, I guess I thought I could still become someone Papa could be proud of.

The best thing would be to end this with Max now. Before it went any further. He could go back to Julia and the Dorises. We could go on with the plan, like nothing had ever happened. It was a common story in Hollywood, nothing to get worked up over. That's how I'd play it, I decided, lying in the warmth of his arms. Even if it broke my heart. Problem was, I was going to have to break his too.

Max stirred and blinked awake. His eyes were liquid gold in the rising sun. "Good morning." He pulled me closer and gave me that slow smile, but I wasn't the only woman in his world. I couldn't be.

He bent his head to kiss my forehead, then my cheek, his lips moving to the corner of my mouth. My thinking was already getting muddled as he brushed his lips over mine. I had to stop him but I really, truly didn't want to do what came next.

I tipped my head away from his kiss and pulled out of his arms. It was like stepping into an icy lake after the warmth of the sun. I tried for a light tone. "Looks like we both were a bit sozzled last night."

He went still. An awful, horrid stillness.

I sat up, my back to him, and scooped his father's dressing gown from the ground. "Morning is for coffee and regrets," I said lightly, pulled on the dressing gown, tied the belt. "Isn't that what they say?"

When Max finally spoke, his voice held a world of sorrow. "So that's how it's going to be?"

There was no easy way to do this. The quicker we got it over with, the better. "We made a mistake. Nothing for it now."

For a brief, desperate moment, I wished he'd pull me back and kiss me and tell me I was wrong. But he let out a breath like a surrender, his voice queer and choked. "Sure, Mina. If that's how you want it."

I swallowed what felt like a rock in my throat, and it fell, cold and hard, into my belly. He stood and pulled on his trousers. I kept my eyes on the smooth water, the waves small and lapping at the shore like they, too, were sorry for the way they'd acted last night.

He gathered up my dress and underthings. My eyes were stinging, and I blinked hard, staring at my toes, at the grass poking through the sand between the flagstones. His feet came into view and I was forced to look up.

He stood like a statue, the breeze toying with his hair. He wasn't even trying to play along. The eyes that had looked into mine last night were filled with hurt. He held out my clothes. "They're still damp, I'm afraid."

"It's my fault," I said, taking them. "It was my idea."

"I should have stopped you."

A spark of anger flared in me. "It's not like I didn't know what I was doing." It came out harder and crueler than I'd intended. If I had to hide my heartbreak, why couldn't he?

He dropped his hands to his sides, defeated. "I'm sorry just the same." The naked pain on his face just about broke me.

———————

The drive back to the city was eternal and silent. It started to rain, and by the time we pulled up at my place, fat drops were running down the windows.

Max let the roadster idle and stared at the steering wheel.

I blinked hard, trying to hold myself together. I'd hurt him. I knew it then and I know it now. But honestly, Max, I was trying to save us both a lot of heartache.

"What do we do now?" I asked. I was afraid of the answer, afraid this was goodbye.

He stared at the runnels of water snaking down the windshield.

"See you in the funny pages, Mina." His voice was anything but funny.

Tears stung my eyes, but with the dregs of my control, I answered, "Sure. See you around." I pushed open the door and got out. "I'm sorry," I said again, holding on to the door for dear life. Sorry for not being who he wanted me to be. For all of it.

He didn't look at me. "So am I." He put the auto in gear and was gone. Something hurt inside me then. I'm not sure what, but it was deep and sharp and everything I deserved.

I wrote to Penny that night because I felt so rotten about what I'd done.

You know, Penny, once you start pretending, it's hard to stop. Then one day, you realize you've turned into a stranger. A stranger you don't like very much.

She'd never see the letter, I knew that now, but somehow it made me feel better confessing it all to her.

I wasn't sure what to expect after that. But it turned out, Max didn't hold a grudge.

I'd hurt him pretty terrible, but after it was all said and done, he showed up at my door the next Monday afternoon as if nothing had happened. Maybe he'd thought about it and saw I did the right thing. My relief was like the first breath of air after swimming underwater. "I thought you wouldn't come," I said as he helped me into his roadster.

"I told you from the start I wouldn't give up on you." His voice was easy, but he wasn't quite the same. The set of his shoulders, his hands tight on the steering wheel, said what it cost him to face me. From then on, Max was all business. No more smiles, no more hand-holding. But he was true to his word and didn't give up. By the end of January, I had a screen test at Cosmopolitan for the lead in a film called *She's No Angel*.

I'd never been so nervous in my life. Max coached me through my lines the night before, told me what to wear and even how to do my makeup. By the time I stood in front of Edward Weiss, the casting director, I thought I might faint. Mr. Weiss had a high forehead, wispy blond hair, and a kind smile. In no time, I was as comfortable as if I were in my own parlor.

When I came off the set, everybody said I'd been marvelous. Mr. Weiss said to Max, "Terrific, fantastic. Just like you said, Max. Perfect for this film. I'll let you know as soon as I run it by Hearst."

Max treated me to champagne at the Sunset Tower. I was over the moon at first, but then noticed Max was quiet. "What is it?" I asked, worried now that I'd done something wrong.

"Nothing, kitten. I knew they'd go mad for you." He downed the last of the champagne like it was water. Sometimes, he was just hard to figure.

We waited for word for two weeks. "Don't fret," Max told me, but it turned out I had reason to worry. Max broke the news gently: Ed had called. He'd tried his best, but Hearst had stopped production on *She's No Angel*. "Ed says Hearst hinted at some financial problems. He won't make any new hires, and Ed's gotta use the actors already on contract."

I was devastated.

"This was just the first try," Max assured me. But my cash was running low and so were my hopes. He got me two more auditions.

I did my best, but the films got canned before they were even cast, the economic woes of the country coming to call in Hollywood.

Max didn't seem worried. If I didn't know better, he seemed relieved.

I started pushing. "Just get me a walk-on, a few lines."

"We'll do this my way or not at all," he snapped one night after I'd been harping on him.

I laid off, but Max didn't know what was at stake for me. I had to go back to Odessa with everything Papa and Penny needed—or not go back at all. Maybe that's why when Louella invited me to Lester's, I jumped on board like it was the last lifeboat on the Titanic.

And that's what got me in the mess I'm in now. In a stranger's home, wanted for murder, and all alone. I turned over on the hard bed. The sliver of moon in the tiny window and my own regrets were poor company in the dark night. Max, where are you? Have you finally given up on me? I wouldn't blame him if he had. For the life of me, I wished I could take it all back and start over.

CHAPTER 7

OSCAR

"Bless me, Father, for I have sinned." Oscar knelt in the confessional. Muted light shone through the metal screen, revealing the outline of Padre Ramirez. "It has been a week since my last confession." Roy Lester had been dead for four days, and Oscar felt like he'd lived half a lifetime since.

He'd spent the previous morning driving the city, looking for Max while Minerva Sinclaire sat in his house, endangering his family. Max was nowhere to be found. He finally gave up, cursing his cousin. The afternoon he spent in the *sociedades*, gathering his courage to call Brody. He had nothing to report except what Lupita had told him about the drink, and he wasn't going to throw Lupita to the dogs like that. Finally, he made the call.

"I haven't got much to tell you," he admitted when Brody answered.

"Meet me at the diner tomorrow at noon" was all Brody said before the line went dead.

He hung up the telephone, his gut twisting with worry. He needed something—anything—to tell the detective that didn't put his own people at risk.

Then, when Oscar got home for dinner, he found Mamá was like a volcano ready to blow. Did she think he wanted to bring this *americana* into their home? For all the love in heaven, he had no choice. What was he to do, throw her out in the dark? He spent the evening seething while Angel took care of the girl like a stray kitten and Roman watched her like a hungry coyote. Was it any wonder he hadn't been able to sleep when the rest of the family went to bed?

Now, sun spilled through the stained-glass windows of Our Lady the Queen of the Angels. The statues glowed in buttery yellow, pink, and blue. The altar, draped in white lace, gleamed with gold paint and brass candlesticks. Oscar's head ached as much as his knees. He had an unwanted woman upstairs in his house, an irate mother, and only a few hours before he had to meet Brody at the Hard Times. A few hours to decide what to tell him about Max and the drink, and what not to tell about harboring the prime suspect. But first, he had to confess the sin he'd committed last night, after everyone else was asleep in their beds.

The priest coughed gently. "Go on, Oscar."

Oscar swallowed. What was the point of the screen if the priest knew who you were every time? Before he confessed, he had a question. "Padre, isn't our God a God of justice?"

"Why do you ask, Oscar?"

"I see people who do wrong get rich and good people starve. How can God allow it? It is not justice. It is unfair."

"Is this about Max?"

Every week for three years, Padre Ramirez had asked him to forgive Max. Every week he failed.

"You have much that Max does not," Padre went on gently.

"Like what?" His voice rose in disbelief, but he didn't worry. Francesca and Mamá had confessed before him, and now they prayed the rosary together with the other old women. They would hear nothing from the confessional over their murmuring.

"You have your faith. Your family and our people. He is alone."

That might be, but wasn't it through his own fault that he had lost these things? "Sometimes I hate him," he confessed and not for the first time.

The priest was quiet for a moment. The old women started on the second decade of their rosary. Finally, he sighed. "I will tell you a secret, my son, that I promised I would not. But you need to hear it because perhaps it will help you forgive."

Oscar was sure he wasn't going to like what the priest had to say. He didn't want to forgive Max. Ever.

"You remember when Roman was ill, when he needed the medicine that you could not afford?"

"Yes." What did this have to do with Max?

"And those months when you didn't have enough to pay the rent?"

"How could I forget? The *mutualista* gave us—"

"Not the *mutualista*." Padre let that sit in the silence of the confessional. "And I didn't get you and the Garcias the jobs at Roy Lester's estate."

Oscar went cold. "Why didn't you tell me?" But he knew why. If he'd known any of it came from Max, he wouldn't have accepted it. "He can't buy my forgiveness, Padre. He has to deserve it."

He could see the priest shake his head behind the screen. "Forgiveness isn't deserved, my son. You should know that." He raised his hand for the words of absolution.

Oscar's words came out in a rush. "There's something else."

Last night, his mind had been jumping like he'd had too much of Mamá's strong coffee. After he sent Minerva Sinclaire upstairs and the boys had settled, Mamá started on her prayers, and he slipped out the back door. He lit one of his stash of cigarettes and stood under the shadow of the old oak, trying not to think about the girl putting his family in danger, about Max . . . about Maria Carmen.

That's when Lupita had come outside. She was wearing a white nightdress that glowed in the moonlight, a wool shawl wrapped around her shoulders. She'd taken to coming out at night to exchange a word or two as he smoked. She was a sweet girl, but he didn't encourage her. She stood before him, her delicate feet bare, her hair gleaming blue-black in the moonlight. He felt a rush of something—gratitude, maybe, or relief that there were still innocent girls like Lupita in this world of Minerva Sinclaires.

Lupita was obedient and dutiful. Nothing like her sister. Maria Carmen had been everything Mexican fathers feared: headstrong, outspoken, wild. She lived her life like there was no tomorrow. Until there wasn't a tomorrow for her. Thanks to Max.

Maybe it was the thought of Maria Carmen. Maybe he was just crazy, but before Lupita even spoke, he'd reached out to her, pulling the ends of her shawl toward him. Then he kissed her. She didn't resist. His hands dropped to her waist and he pulled her closer. Her hair smelled of lye soap and lavender and stirred memories of other nights under this same tree. He closed his eyes and felt Maria Carmen's soft lips, her body pressed against his.

"My son?" Padre Ramirez asked.

Oscar looked down at his hands, gripping his rosary hard enough to leave indents of the beads on his fingers. "I kissed Lupita last night."

"Kissing is no sin."

He let out a breath. "I think this one was." He knew it was. Lupita deserved better than a kiss that was meant for her dead sister.

After a long pause, Padre spoke. "Did you ask her forgiveness?"

Oscar couldn't answer past the lump in his throat. He'd left her there, under the tree, without a word. He'd been disgusted with himself, afraid to even look at her, sure she knew what—who— he'd been thinking about.

Padre took the meaning in his silence. "Does this have to do with the woman that you have taken into your home?"

Oscar jerked on the hard kneeler. "How do you know about her?" Was it impossible to keep a secret in this *colonia*?

"You're not the only one confessing this morning."

Miércoles! Had his mother told anyone else? "It has nothing to do with her." It didn't. It was just Max, bringing up old memories. "She is . . . nothing like Lupita. She's an *americana*, Padre. And she'll be gone today." He knew his voice held all the disgust he felt for her and her kind.

Padre Ramirez sighed—a frustrated sound Oscar had heard many times. "For your penance, I give two things. Forgive Max, Oscar. You have held your anger long enough. As for this woman—" He held up his hand, a shadow on the screen as Oscar tried to speak. "Show her mercy. Treat her with the same respect as you would—as you must—give to Lupita."

Oscar had never had a penance more than a few Hail Marys. Once an entire rosary, but that one was also Max's fault. "But how do I do that?"

"You'll know." Padre Ramirez's voice was stern.

Oscar frowned. "But you don't understand—"

"That is your penance." The matter was finished.

Oscar bowed his head. "*Sí*, Padre."

The priest went on with the prayers of absolution, but instead of the easing of his guilt, Oscar only felt more confused. Mercy? What about justice? This girl might not be guilty of murder, but she wasn't innocent, either. He'd kept her from the police. Wasn't that enough?

As he made the sign of the cross, Oscar breathed a prayer that he would find a way to fulfill his penance and then get that red-haired woman and Max out of his life for good. "Amen."

"And Oscar?" Padre poked his head around the confessional screen to look him in the face. "Meet Max at Teatro Hidalgo at noon. And he said to come alone."

Oscar stared at him. "How—What?"

"As I said, you're not the only one who has been to confession this morning."

Oscar left the confessional and sat beside Mamá and Angel in their regular pew. No Roman, of course—the kid was probably keeping company with the good-for-nothing Alonso. Oscar had more to worry about than his brother missing Wednesday confession. He waited for Mass to start, his thoughts spinning. Meet Max at noon? He was supposed to be reporting to Brody then.

Oscar said the responses automatically and hardly listened to the Scripture readings. When Padre Ramirez began to speak on loving your neighbor, Oscar felt the old anger welling up. Love his neighbor?

Yes, some people deserved love. His family. His people in the *colonia*. But what about those who deserved justice? Like the police, who rounded up his people for deportation because "real Americans" wanted their jobs.

A haze of incense clouded the bright colors of the stained glass.

He knelt as Padre switched from Spanish to Latin for the consecration. When would God hear the prayers of parents with hollow-cheeked children and not enough blankets for winter nights? The prayers of the sick who could not work, the elderly with nothing to live on, the children taken out of school too soon?

He found himself kneeling at the Communion rail and realized he'd heard nothing of the Mass, hadn't uttered a word of real prayer. Shame filled him as he filed back into the pew behind Mamá.

And what about Max? Did he deserve this love Padre spoke of?

Max, who'd been like a brother to him all those years, had left his family without looking back. At least that's what he'd always thought. He wished Padre Ramirez hadn't told him anything. What was he supposed to do now that he knew Max had been helping them all along? Thank him on bended knee? Never.

He left the church and hurried toward home, leaving Mamá and Angel lingering in the courtyard. His mother and the other women would sweep floors and polish candlesticks as they did every Wednesday morning. Padre and Angel would talk of theology.

He slowed, his thoughts catching up to him. He had promised during the sacrament of confession to try to forgive Max. To show Minerva mercy. He must at least try, even if neither of them deserved it. He had to meet Max and get the girl off his hands, but it would make him late to meet Brody at the diner. The ache in his head became a pounding.

As he turned onto his own street, the first thing he noticed was the silence. Usually boys played on the street, girls sat in the shade, women called to each other from their shanty houses and washed clothes in tubs. Not this morning.

He looked to his own home and his heart plummeted to his knees.

In front of his house was a black car, *POLICE* emblazoned in white letters on the door. Two uniformed men sat in the auto . . . and leaning beside it, grinning like a cat who ate the canary, was Officer Adams. Above him, the window where Minerva Sinclaire hid in his own house. Oscar made his feet keep walking until he came to a stop in front of Adams. He took a deep breath. Stay calm. Don't say anything. Don't look at the window.

"You know," Adams drawled, "I figured I'd be seeing you again."

Oscar's pulse hammered in his ears, but he kept his face impassive. "What do you want?"

"Just a few more questions. Maybe take a look around." He shrugged.

Oscar felt panic rising. He tried to keep his voice even. "I told your boss everything I know. Go talk to him."

"You're talking to me now."

"And if I don't?" He knew his rights. He could get a lawyer. If he could afford one.

"Smart one, eh?" Adams leaned close and poked a finger into Oscar's chest as he spoke. "Failure. To. Cooperate. Three little words." His smile was like a snake. The other officers—big men with slick hair and pressed uniforms—stepped out of the auto. They watched Adams like guard dogs waiting for their master's signal. "Any questions, wetback?"

In an instant, Oscar could see them all sent to Mexico with only what they could carry. But if they found Minerva Sinclaire, it would be worse. Oscar's legs weakened, but he couldn't show fear to Adams. He clenched his fists. "Call me a wetback again and I'll—"

"*Hola*, officers." Roman's voice was friendly as he opened the front door. "Come in and welcome."

Oscar stared at his brother. Roman had that look Oscar knew, like he had a secret. Usually that look made him angry, but this time he hoped it was more than Roman's usual swagger. It had better be, because Adams went up the steps and into the house, the other two officers on his heels.

Oscar sweated bullets as he followed the officers through the house and into the kitchen. Adams didn't beat around the bush. "This girl we're looking for, Minerva Sinclaire, you know her?"

"No," he said.

"Mind if we have a look around?" Adams said it like he didn't care who minded.

Roman jumped in with a wave around the small house. *"Mi casa, su casa, amigo."*

Oscar prayed to God Roman knew what he was doing.

Adams sauntered into the hall as his men stood, their arms crossed, watching Oscar and Roman as if they were going to run. Oscar heard the tread on the staircase, a creak as Adams pushed open the bedroom door. He dared a look at Roman. His brother winked at him.

Adams came down the stairs and jerked his head to his heavies. They left without another word. As the car disappeared down the street, Oscar let out a long breath and turned to Roman. "Where is she?"

Roman ambled outside, talking over his shoulder. "I was at the *sociedades* when I heard them come in, asking where we lived. So I left through the back. Got her out just when they pulled up."

Oscar clenched his teeth. So Roman was doing God knows what instead of joining them at morning Mass. But when Minerva Sinclaire came stumbling out of her hiding place, her eyes watering, he had to be glad for his brother's fast thinking. Of course a *gringo* wouldn't think to check the outhouse. She was still gasping for breath as he told her to go in the house and stay there or he'd bring her to the police himself.

He sat down on the back stoop and put his head in his hands. What else could go wrong today?

MINA

My stomach felt like it had gone on one of those carnival rides without me.

When Roman had woken me, frantic and breathless, and stuck me in the outhouse—"Quiet, *por favor*, please, quiet"—my heart had just about pounded out of my chest. He was supposed to be bringing me to Max, wasn't he? I couldn't breathe—and not just because of the smell, which was horrid. What was happening? What was wrong? It seemed I was in there for hours before he pulled open the door and let me out and told me the story.

The police. Here. It had been too close.

Now my stomach lurched as Señora slammed a plate of cold flat bread and beans in front of me. I took a couple of bites. Whether it was my rolling insides or the police searching for me—maybe the smell of the outhouse clinging to me—I didn't know, but I must have turned as green as I felt. Señora glared at me.

"Stay put," Oscar said as he jammed his hat on his head. "Roman, Angel, let's go. You'll be late for work."

He couldn't leave me here again. I managed to protest. "But I can't—"

The door slammed behind him.

Max, where are you? I told myself Max hadn't deserted me. He just couldn't face his family after what happened to Maria Carmen. I guess I understood that better than anybody, but still. Please, Max, help me one last time.

Señora took my plate away with a sour face, then left through the back door. I knew the routine by now. She'd go with the neighbor woman to the hotel, bring back a mountain of laundry, and spend the day washing. I wished I could help—just to keep busy—but I couldn't show my face.

I paced through the house, making a circuit of the front window, the tiny sitting room, the kitchen, half expecting the door to burst open any minute and police to swarm the place. But nobody came. Not the police and not Max. If this were a film, it would be the part where the heroine almost gives up. The part where it seems like all is lost. But then she comes up with a brilliant plan and everything works out for the happy ending.

Problem was, I was coming up with zilch.

Just when I thought I'd truly go mad, Señora Dominguez came back and behind her, Lupita, carrying a stack of bright-colored fabrics. Together, they began to sort through the pile, making small tutting noises and fingering pieces of lace.

"What is it?" I asked Lupita.

"It is a dress. I wear it for the *festejos* next week and maybe be crowned queen." She looked at me shyly.

"May I?" I asked.

She passed me the fabric. "It is not fashionable like the clothing you wear," Lupita said like she had to apologize.

I spread the pieces on the table. The skirt, half sewn in crisp apple-red poplin, was layered with ruffles and exquisite white lace. The bodice was in pieces, in the same fabric, and a wide strip of heavy red satin—embroidered with yellow blossoms—would be a sash to show off her tiny waist. From what I could see, the neckline was to be gathered, with puff sleeves trimmed in more lace.

"It is beautiful," I told her. "Or it will be when—"

"I thought I could finish," she cut in, "but I start today at the cannery."

Of course. If Oscar lost his job, so did Lupita. And her brother and mother. It might not be my fault, but it felt like it.

"Sanchia, she says she finish it for me, but—" Lupita's voice dropped even though Señora couldn't understand her—"her eyes, they are not good for the small stitches. And she must do the washing."

"Let me," I burst out. I could do this. At least until Max came to get me. I was no great seamstress, but this wasn't brain surgery. "The sleeves—" I took up a cut piece and laid it along the bodice. "They go like this, right? And the lace over here?" It would be beautiful, perfect with Lupita's bronze skin and curvy figure.

"*Sí*. But I can't ask—"

"Please, Lupita. Let me do this for you. I can't stand—" I looked at Señora and bit my tongue.

Lupita got my meaning but hesitated, stroking the red satin sash. "If . . . you are sure?"

I understood. This fabric and the lace had cost her more than she could afford. There was nothing left for mistakes. But I wanted to do something for her, and really, I could sew a straight seam, even if Penny could do it better. "Don't worry. It will be beautiful."

Lupita sat down beside me and unpacked a small cigar box. Thread, scissors, and a few bright needles. She didn't look at Sanchia. "She has not been so good to you, no?"

I didn't know how to answer. She fed me. That had to count for something.

"Do not let it upset you," Lupita went on as I threaded a needle. "She is afraid."

"Afraid of what?" Sanchia didn't seem like the frightened type.

Lupita looked sad. "Our parents, the ones who come from Mexico, they all afraid. That we will change. We will become like *americanas*—American girls—and leave them." Her eyes clouded. "Many girls have done so—they cut their hair, go out with boys without their mothers to, how you say? Watch over them?"

"Chaperone."

"*Sí*. Or they dress like . . ." She paused as if she didn't want to go on.

Like me.

"And some, they run away with the boy they love."

Like Maria Carmen. I kept my eyes on the needle and began making neat, even stitches. "And then what happens to them?" What would have happened to Maria Carmen, if she'd lived?

"They are disgraced." She smoothed the fabric of the skirt.

I looked up, the needle poised in midair. "Forever?" The answer was suddenly important.

Lupita shook her head. "No. If they are sorry, they are forgiven, taken back into the family after a time." She squinted as if finding the right words. "Mexican fathers and mothers are not so . . . made of stone, you understand?"

I understood better than she could imagine. If a woman could run away and then come back—like Max's mother had, pregnant and unmarried—couldn't Max be forgiven, too?

"Lupita." I laid my hand on her arm. I knew how much a sister was loved, what it would mean to lose one. "Roman told me about Maria Carmen. I'm sorry."

Lupita turned the sash over, picking at the knots and tangles on the hidden side. "Yes. I miss her very much." She tipped her head to where Señora sat ignoring us. "As she does. Max and Maria were like her own children. And she lost them both. This—" she motioned to me—"it is bringing up the old pain. You must try to forgive her for her ways."

I could forgive the old crow when Lupita put it like that.

Too soon, Lupita had to go to the cannery. "Please," she said as she went out the door, "don't let Oscar see it, the dress." Her cheeks colored. "I want to surprise him."

I told her I'd keep it hidden, but secretly I wished her luck with Oscar. She was going to need it.

Señora went outside to wash the mounds of dirty linen. I worked on Lupita's dress and watched the shadows move across the worn linoleum floor. Señora came in just once, to cook her flattened bread and set it in front of me. I guess it didn't matter how unwelcome the guest; her conscience wouldn't let me go hungry. This time I ate everything and wished for more.

The sun shone high in the sky and still no Max. I didn't blame him. Not really. I bit down on a thread to snap it from the knot. Max had done so much for me—saved me, really. Maybe it was time for me to save him. I could give him the chance to make peace with his family, perhaps even to be forgiven, like Lupita had said. All I had to do was get him here. I started to figure a plan. If Sanchia and Oscar had a chance to talk to him, to smooth things over . . .

Maybe—I guess I thought back then—maybe if Max could make things right with his family, someday so could I.

OSCAR

At half past eleven, Oscar was in the back row of the Teatro Hidalgo, waiting for Max while Laurel and Hardy bumbled their way through the nickel matinee. Max didn't show until six minutes after twelve. By then, Hardy was fuming and so was Oscar. "Where have you been?" he hissed at Max. "I've been looking for you for two days."

Max sat down beside him and opened his cigarette case. "I didn't get arrested. Thanks for asking."

Of course not. They wouldn't arrest Max Clark. "You need to take her. Now."

Max lit a cigarette and put it to his lips. "Listen, Oscar. They've been following me since the Montmartre. Put an officer on my tail and staked out my place last night—"

"The police were at the house this morning." Oscar didn't care what Max was facing. "My house, Max. It was only luck they didn't find her."

"Are you listening to me?" Max whispered, "I'm telling you, they're following me. If she's with me, they'll nab her by this afternoon."

"That's your problem."

"And yours. You don't think they'll put it together? You just said they were at your place."

Oscar slumped down in the chair. "Mamá and the boys . . . they'll end up on the busses. I'll go to prison."

"I'm not going to let that happen." Max lit another cigarette off his own and passed it to Oscar. They smoked silently while Laurel got Hardy into another fine mess. "I went to the funeral yesterday," Max said, as if Oscar hadn't just told him that his family was in danger. "Police were there too. Victoria put on a better act than she ever has for Cosmo. You'd have thought she really loved him. Then a detective buttonholed me. Asked me a lot of questions."

That got Oscar's attention. "Guy with a mustache?"

"That's the guy."

So Brody probably knew his connection to Max. If he didn't, he would soon. Would he still want Oscar to work for him or would he want his money back? Part of Oscar wished he could just give him the money and wash his hands of this whole mess. But it was too late for that since the money was spent and Oscar had given his word.

Max leaned forward, his voice lower. "Listen, Oscar. I know how you feel about me, but Mina didn't do this. We gotta keep her hidden while we figure this out—for both your sakes."

Oscar took a breath of the cigarette and weighed his options. Max was smart and he knew people. Oscar didn't trust him— he never would again—but he could use him maybe to get what Brody needed. "You find out anything?"

"After they questioned me at the Montmartre yesterday, I made the rounds. The Ambassador, Beverly Hills Hotel, the Derby."

Oscar couldn't help throwing out a hook. "I hope you had a great time."

Max didn't bite. "Everybody was talking about Lester—but nobody knew much. Except that he was getting paid more than he was worth. A lot more."

Oscar had heard that from Brody, but he still didn't know how it fit.

"Then I ran into a girl I used to take around. She works for Louella now."

Louella, the one Brody had called Hearst's gal pal. "The woman who writes for the papers, good friends with Hearst?"

"That's her. Real chummy with Roy Lester and his bunch."

Oscar sat back and crossed his arms. "And?"

"This girl, Amelia, is a nosy parker and likes to gossip. She said Louella was all burnt up about some kind of note Victoria showed her. I wouldn't have cared, except for the note being so queer and her saying that Louella and Hearst had a terrific row about it over the telephone."

"What did it say?" Oscar asked, and when Max told him, another piece of the puzzle clicked in place. *Dear Mrs. Lester, I have something you want. You pay me $10,000 for it, or I take it to somebody else.* Oscar let out a breath. "That's a lot of money." Enough to kill for. And Louella and Hearst had some kind of stake in whatever it was.

Max took a long puff from his cigarette, letting out a thin stream of smoke. The antics on screen were heating up and a few patrons in front were guffawing. "The note, it was typed up all proper and mailed from downtown. And get this." Max waved his cigarette. "That butler, the big fella?"

"Feng Li?"

"Yeah, except his real name is Felix Young."

Oscar perked up. Something else Brody could use.

"I didn't place him that night, but I knew I'd seen him before, so I checked around the studio yesterday. Turns out he does more than butlering."

"Like what?"

"Little strong-arming, some rough stuff. People are afraid of him, that's all I got, but it's suspicious." Max crushed out his cigarette on the ashtray in the chair arm and met Oscar's gaze. "Oscar, you got to give me another day—that's all I'm asking. Twenty-four hours. Keep her safe for me."

Oscar gritted his teeth. Another day with that woman in his house? He couldn't take the risk. The music swelled. Hardy hit Laurel one more time with his hat and the screen went dark. Max waited. His face in the low light seemed younger, like the Max who had been his brother. Was that Max still there, somewhere under that sharp suit and slick hair? Padre's words came back to him. Max had helped his family when they needed it most. It didn't change what Max had done, or make up for Maria Carmen, but . . . "Twenty-four hours."

Max let out a breath. "*Gracias*, Oscar."

Oscar took a last puff of the cigarette as the house lights came up. Max might deny it, but Oscar figured his cousin had more than a professional interest in Minerva Sinclaire. "You should know, your trick with the Seconal worked, just not how you planned."

"What do you mean?" Max got a worried crease in his brow.

"Your girlfriend drank it instead. Can't remember a thing past going upstairs with him. Says she passed out before . . . anything happened with Lester."

Max let out a long breath. "Well, that's something, anyway."

Oscar dropped the cigarette on the floor and ground it out with his heel. *Americanos*. He'd never understand them.

Oscar hurried along Vine, praying Brody would still be at the Hard Times. How much could he tell the detective? Brody had said it himself: trust nobody. Was Oscar playing into some kind of trap that would land him in hot water? Brody and Adams could be— probably were—working together.

He slipped inside the Hard Times, where smoke hung under the low ceiling lights, giving the place the murky feel of dusk in the middle of the day. Brody sat in the back booth, a plate streaked with egg yolk and scattered with bacon rinds in front of him. Oscar let out a breath of relief.

Brody stood as Oscar approached, brushed toast crumbs off his broad chest, and stuck out his hand. Oscar shook it, then settled across from Brody as a waitress sloped to the table, a menu dangling from her hand.

"He'll have what I had," Brody said before Oscar could refuse. "On my bill."

Oscar supposed he should be grateful; he was hungry. But he didn't like to owe anybody, least of all a *gringo*.

Brody got right down to business. "Got anything for me?"

Oscar started out safe. "The Garcias, Lupita and Alonso, they didn't have much to say." That was the truth at least. He wouldn't say anything about the Seconal. Not for Max's sake, but for Lupita's. It still burned him up that Alonso had tried to hide Max's little trick from him. Did the boy have no loyalty at all? And Lupita . . . he didn't want to think about Lupita right now.

"Did they see this girl, Minerva Sinclaire?" Brody tapped the newspaper.

Oscar tried not to react to her name. He shook his head. "They spend their time in the kitchen."

"Nothing in the morning?"

"They went to the gatehouse about 2 a.m., slept, then caught the early trolley back to town." He blocked out the vision of Minerva Sinclaire appearing like a ghost in front of his car.

"Hmm. About what they told me." Brody rubbed his hand over his eyes. A cigarette propped on the side of his plate had a smoldering tail of ash.

Minerva Sinclaire's face on the front of the newspaper stared at Oscar. The waitress slid a plate full of grease-slicked eggs and burned bacon in front of him, triangles of toast thickly smeared with orange-tinted margarine. His stomach growled but he didn't dig in. He waited for her to fill his cup with coffee and sidle away. "Do you think she did it? The woman in the papers?" He couldn't bring himself to say her name, like it would give away that he'd left her in his house under strict orders to stay put.

Brody grimaced. "Come on, kid. You saw the scene. There was a struggle. From her description, that girl is maybe a hundred and ten pounds soaking wet. Hard to think she took out a man Lester's size."

Oscar felt the tension in his shoulders loosen a little and bit into the toast. A guy like Brody did his homework. It wouldn't take much to connect Max with him. If he didn't know now, he would soon. "Max Clark." He washed the bite down with a gulp of the bitter coffee.

Brody's cigarette spilled a clump of ash on the table. "The girl's talent agent. What about him?"

Oscar wiped his mouth with a napkin then leveled with Brody. "He's my cousin."

"That's a coincidence," said the man who didn't believe in coincidences.

Oscar didn't explain. "He was at the party, left early."

Brody regarded him levelly. Was he suspicious of Max? Or suspicious of Oscar? He was too smart not to be both. "Any reason to think he was involved with her? Romantically? Maybe jealous?"

"No," Oscar lied. There were plenty of reasons to think that, but he wasn't going to talk about Max's personal life. Oscar told Brody what Max said about Feng Li, and how his real name was Felix Young and he worked for Hearst. Then about the anonymous letter sent to Mrs. Lester and Hearst and Louella going at each other on the telephone.

Brody listened, his brows rising like two fat caterpillars. "Hmph. Ties in with the state of the office and the bedroom. Any idea what this thing is that's worth that kind of money?"

Oscar shook his head.

"I'll check around, see if I can find out more about this Felix

Young character." He rubbed a hand over his face. "It's a good start, kid."

Oscar felt a flicker of pride, then remembered it was Max who had done all the legwork. He picked up his fork and started shoveling cold bacon and eggs into his mouth. Max had given him the information, sure, but he was the one bringing it to Brody.

Brody waited until Oscar's plate was clean, then leaned forward. "There's something else, kid, and it ain't good news." He lowered his voice. "The DA, he's got some kind of skin in this game."

Oscar shook his head. His English was good, but he didn't follow.

Brody cleared it up. "I'm off the case. Came from high up. And get this, Adams—the officer that was at the estate—he's on as special investigator."

A buzz of unease crept up his neck. Brody and Adams not working together was good news to Oscar. But Adams . . .

"Maybe I should have told you when you walked in," Brody went on, "but I wanted to hear what you got. And you got plenty to keep me interested."

"But . . . if you're off the case . . . ?" That meant he was off, too, didn't it?

Brody pulled at his mustache. "Yeah, I am. But unfortunately, I've got this thing for the truth. I've seen too much dirt in this job, and a lot of it comes from William Randolph Hearst and his money. One way or another, I'm going to see Hearst go down before I retire to a beach in San Diego." Brody frowned. "But the other thing is, kid, maybe I shouldn't have gotten you into this."

Oscar took another sip of coffee, despite how bad it was. "What do you mean?"

Brody took another long puff from his smoke and kept his eyes on Oscar. "Adams is as crooked as a barrel of fishhooks and he's in tight with Hearst."

Oscar gave Brody a long look. The detective wasn't giving up, but he thought Oscar should. "You telling me to run away?" Would Brody want the money back?

"It's not running," Brody said. "It's stepping back. Nothing to be ashamed of."

"But you aren't . . . stepping back."

Brody shrugged. "I don't have much to lose, kid."

Justice was worth fighting for. Everybody knew that. But was it worth risking his family? That's what Brody was saying. It made sense, but it felt wrong—backing down, deserting Brody. He'd taken the job—and Brody's money—to find the truth, not run away like some kind of scared rabbit. Besides, Minerva Sinclaire was innocent of murder. If people like Adams and Hearst sent her to prison, it would be on his conscience, and what would Padre say to that? He watched Brody watching him. And made a decision he figured he'd regret. "I'm not going anywhere."

"You sure?" Brody raised his bushy brows.

"Yes, I am sure."

They sat for a moment, thinking it through. Brody took out a crumpled pack of cigarettes and tipped them to Oscar.

He took one and bent forward for a light. "So. What do we do now?"

Brody's mustache twitched. He leaned back and cracked his knuckles. "Well now, kid, I guess we go fishing."

MINA

By the time the sun dipped low in the hazy sky of the *colonia* and Lupita's dress was almost finished, I knew what I had to do.

Max needed his family and his family needed him. What nobody needed was me—that was clear as daylight. I was going to get Max back with his family and then get myself out of this place. No more waiting around, thank you very much.

The first part of my plan was Roman. He was easy to convince, just like I figured. The hard part was getting Oscar's auto without him catching on.

Roman had a solution. "Oscar will go to the *sociedades* before dinner, to have a drink and find out the news. He is gone for maybe half an hour." That would just do the trick.

"Tell Max that Oscar sent you. An emergency."

That should get him here. I knew enough about Mexican hospitality by now to know that Señora would have to feed Max if he showed up at suppertime. And then I'd hope for the best. But would Oscar be angry if Roman took his auto? Roman just grinned when I asked him, so I figured maybe it wouldn't be the worst sin. Boy, was I wrong about that.

Lupita came back from the cannery, and we went up to the bedroom, where I'd hidden the dress. We talked in whispers as I fitted it to her and measured the hem. Lupita made a big fuss over it, but it's not like it was that hard to do.

"You'll be the queen of festival. I just know it," I said. If the judges had any sense at all, they'd elect her or whatever it was they did. As Lupita hugged me goodbye, Sanchia muttered a few words and Lupita giggled.

"What did she say?" I asked, not sure I wanted to know.

Lupita shook her head, but her dimple was showing. "Nothing."

"Tell me."

"She said . . . she said you are the devil who has come from hell to torment her for her sins." She caught my eye and winked. "Do not worry. It is just her way."

I laughed for the first time in days. I could almost imagine Lupita and me as sisters, giggling behind our mother's back. Like how Penny and I had been before Mama fell sick.

Lupita left, and by the time dusk fell, my nerves were starting to jump. The sun sank low and golden light filled the kitchen as Sanchia cooked. I couldn't bear to sit upstairs in the stuffy bedroom, so I sat at the kitchen table enduring her glares. But when Oscar came in the door with a frightened-looking Angel, Sanchia was the least of my problems.

"Where. Is. The. Auto?" Oscar bit out each word like a curse, his accent so strong I could hardly understand him. His jaw was clenched so hard I wondered if his teeth hurt.

I figured any answer I gave wouldn't help, so I just stayed quiet.

Angel sat down at the table and gave me a look that he probably thought was reassuring. If this worked . . . maybe they would all thank me later. Please, Roman, come back with Max. And soon.

Oscar dragged a chair across the floor and sat heavily, rubbing a hand over his face in a weary way that made me wonder what else had gone wrong for him today. Señora brought the food to the table and sat. Oscar raised a hand to his forehead, but the prayer died on his lips. He stared as the back door opened.

Max stood in the doorway—neither in nor out—his face in shadow, his hands shoved in his pockets. Roman lurked behind him, a smug look on his face. It had been only a few days since I'd seen Max, but it seemed like years. He wore a pair of dark trousers with a white shirt—no tie, no hat. His glance moved from me to Oscar, Sanchia, and Angel, but he didn't step inside.

Sanchia put her hand over her mouth. Oscar jumped up.

Surprise—*"Qué?"*—followed by concern—"Were you followed?"—he pulled Max inside, then peered to the backyard, pivoted, and half ran into the front room. I heard him shutting windows, locking the front door.

I'd never seen Max at a loss for words, but when Sanchia stepped up to him, he opened his mouth, and nothing came out. She reached out and laid a hand on his cheek. He managed a small smile, like a little boy. My heart squeezed in my chest. Max leaned down and kissed her cheek.

Oscar came back into the room, looking relieved and angry at the same time. "Why are you—you shouldn't be here."

"Couldn't say no." Max looked over his shoulder at Roman. "And Roman's driving gave my tail the slip."

"You—" Oscar gave Roman a look that said he'd deal with him later.

Sanchia said a few words in Spanish, then bustled to the stove to dish up a plate of beans, just like I figured.

Angel stepped up. "Max," he said solemnly, holding out a hand. Max shook it. "You've grown up, Angel."

Angel got a crate from the other room, then we all sat down. They said the prayer, Max joining in easily in Spanish like he said it every day of his life. Sanchia gave him a watery smile and put food on his plate.

Max didn't look at me. I told myself it didn't matter. It felt good, seeing Max here with his family, though his eyes were wary and his words—even in Spanish—sounded careful. I tried to eat, but my stomach was tied up in knots, wondering what would come next.

When the food was gone, Sanchia cleared the plates and went outside for water. Max pulled a pack of cigarettes from his pocket, tapped one out, and offered the pack to Oscar. Oscar took one, frowning and shaking his head when Roman leaned forward hopefully. Max lit his smoke. He didn't hand it to me for a puff like he once would have. I guess I couldn't blame him.

Oscar went to the cupboard, rummaging in the back and coming out with a bottle of clear liquid. He brought five cups, poured a splash in each, and passed them out. Angel took a drink and coughed. Roman took a long swallow. His eyes didn't even water. I took a sip from my cup. The tequila burned down my throat and hit my churning stomach like a firecracker. Now what would happen? Only God knew, and he wasn't talking to me.

"We need to get her out of here," Oscar said bluntly in English, not looking at me. Angel and Roman watched.

Max's elbow was on the table. He held his cigarette between two fingers, hovering close to his mouth. I remembered how his hand had felt on mine, my knuckles fitting into his palm. I told myself I didn't want him to do that again.

"You're right."

Oscar's brows went up. I guess he wasn't used to Max agreeing with him.

"Where?" Oscar leaned forward, pushing a tin can ashtray across the table. "Not your place. And not hers. A hotel somewhere?"

They were talking about me like I wasn't even sitting there, and I didn't like it one bit.

"No." Max tapped his ash into the can. "She needs to get out of California." He looked everywhere—anywhere—but at me, and with his next words I figured why. "I have some cash," he said. "Enough to get to Chicago, or Texas maybe. Start over."

It was like a punch in the face. Leave California . . . and never see Max again? "But I—"

"Run?" Oscar said like I hadn't even spoken. "From a crime she didn't commit?"

"They'll find her if she stays. You don't know what these people are like."

"You think I don't?" Oscar's voice rose. "You tell me she's innocent, then you leave her here for me to deal with."

"You know why I couldn't come." Max's voice was tight. "This is her life we're talking about, Oscar. Prison." He jabbed his half-smoked cigarette into the can. "I can't have that on my conscience."

"And this is about your conscience, is it, Max?" Oscar poked a finger in my direction, but he wasn't talking about me anymore. "Your conscience that is carrying enough already?"

Max's jaw tightened and his hands curled into fists.

Oscar stood and leaned over the table, his accent thicker as his temper rose. "You just trying to save yourself. Get rid of her and go back to your easy life."

Max jumped out of his chair and was around the table in a blink. "That's what you think?"

"Is the truth, isn't it?" Oscar's chair scraped the floor and he was on his feet.

Max's face was inches from Oscar's. "Since when have you cared about the truth?"

They faced off, fists clenched at their sides. Max taller by three inches, Oscar heavier by at least twenty pounds. I stood and stumbled around the table. "Stop it, both of you. This isn't helping."

Angel put himself between them, his voice calm. "Mamá will kill you if you break her kitchen."

Sanchia came in with a bucket, her eyes darting from one man to the other.

Oscar's chest rose and fell. Max scowled, then pushed past me. "This was a bad idea, me coming here." He gave me a look that said it was my fault, then slammed through the back door and into the night.

I couldn't let him leave like this. I'd tried to do something good for him, but I'd made everything worse. I ran out into the dark behind him, not caring if anyone saw me. "Max, please." My voice broke.

Max stopped under the oak tree, his shoulders tense, his back to me. The night was quiet, as if the insects were eavesdropping. "This was a mistake."

"I wanted . . . I thought you could come back," I admitted. I decided to tell the truth, at least this time. "I . . . you seemed so . . . lonely, Max."

He shook his head but didn't turn around. "Do you know, Mina, that in Spanish there's no good word for loneliness? And here—" he threw an arm toward the house, the neighborhood—"yeah, here I was never lonely."

I didn't know what to say to that, but I took a step closer. Softly, carefully, I laid my hand on his shoulder.

He didn't turn. "There was always someone just as hungry, just as beaten. And there was always somebody who stood by you. Even a half-*gringo* bastard like me."

Oscar, his almost-brother. Maria Carmen, the girl he loved. And his mother.

He jerked his head toward the city lights. "Out there is lonely, no matter how many people are around you. No matter how hard you try to fit in."

My heart was breaking for the boy who'd been taken away from his family. "I'm sorry, Max . . . about your mother."

His shoulders rose with a deep breath, and he finally turned to me, his face still in the shadows. "She loved to dance, just like you." The flash of a small smile. "That's how I learned. Dancing with her at the festivals."

I could picture him, young and handsome, much like Roman. "She was lucky to have a son like you."

His smile disappeared. "No. It was because of me that she didn't have anyone else to dance with. She had a child, unmarried, and with a *gringo*. That kind of thing isn't forgotten here."

I had to ask. "Like Maria Carmen?"

He rubbed a hand over his face, looking older than his years. "I guess you know all my secrets."

But I didn't want to talk about Maria Carmen. Not yet. I had to know if Oscar was right. "What he said," I whispered, looking back at the house. "What Oscar said? Be straight, Max. Do you want to get rid of me?" The answer meant more to me than I wanted to admit.

"Mina, I don't want to get rid of you." He tipped my chin up with one finger until I was looking into his dark eyes. "I want to go with you."

My own breath stopped. Go with me?

"We'll get out of here together. Find a place we both belong."

Me and Max. I could see it. Maybe it was the moonlight, but for a moment, I could almost reach out and touch it.

Then he really did stun me. "We could get married. I know—"

My hand went to his mouth, and his lips stilled under my fingers. I couldn't let him say any more. Married. To Max. He'd come here to say this, trying to get up the nerve, and then Oscar had got the wrong end of the stick. Oh, Max.

He pulled my fingers away, folding them in his. "I know you

don't think of me like that. But, Mina . . . I swear I could make you happy."

Of course he was right. He could make me happy. Ridiculously happy. But with the next beat of my heart, I knew I'd make him miserable. He deserved better than that, better than me. And what about Papa? I needed to go home to him, to take care of him and Penny. Running away with Max would mean abandoning them for good. I couldn't do that. I had to make things right.

He looked down into my face. "I don't care about Lester, about what happened." The moonlight lit his amber eyes and paled his skin. "We'll start over, both of us."

Start over. Oh, how I wanted to start over with Max. Leave this all behind . . . Until Max found out about me, about what I'd done—stealing from Papa, the Rose. . . and the rest of it.

He read my hesitation. "Please, Mina. Just think about it."

I'd think about it. Probably every day for the rest of my life. But for now—tonight—I couldn't bear to turn him away, not again. I couldn't hurt him like I did that morning at the beach. So I didn't say anything. I leaned into him, laying my head against his chest. He went still, then his arms came around me. I breathed him in, holding on and wishing . . . wishing I could say yes with all my rotten heart.

It's not my fault, Lana always said when she put me in a fix. *I didn't mean any harm.* I'd said the same to myself plenty of times. But the thing is, even if my intentions were good . . . the whole mess was my fault. And I'd caused plenty of harm.

I was dealt a bad hand. That's another gem from Lana that I could use if I had a mind to. But it's just another lie. The thing is, I could have laid down my cards and stepped away—anytime, really. Instead, I bet the farm and had only myself to blame when I lost it all. That's what Penny would say. If it was just me that I hurt, I'd say that was justice. But it wasn't just me. There were other people I'd hurt—good people—like Oscar and Max and even Sanchia.

Tonight, I'd brought Max here, thinking I was doing something good, that I'd balance the scales. Turned out, I tipped them further against me.

Before Max left, he told me to sit tight. "A couple days," he said. "Think about it, Mina, a new life." Then he smiled, just a flash in the moonlight, but it was the smile I loved. He dipped his head. The corner of his mouth brushed the corner of mine. It was almost a kiss.

I almost broke down.

Think about it, he'd said. I didn't have to. By the time Max had disappeared into the moonless dark, I knew my answer. I wouldn't let Max ruin his life for me. I was feeling pretty low by then, but the horrid part was that the night wasn't over.

When I got back in the house, Oscar and Roman were at each other's throats.

They were speaking Spanish—fast and furious—but from what I could make out Oscar was letting Roman have it for borrowing his auto to track down Max. Angel stood behind the table, his eyes big and worried. Sanchia twisted a towel in her hands, saying words I didn't understand, but the look on her face was enough.

I stepped up, thinking maybe I could help. Boy, I should have known better. "It's my fault, Oscar. I asked him to—"

He rounded on me so fast I faltered backwards. "*Sí.* It is your fault."

Roman switched into English. "I'm not a child. I know how to—"

"Then stop acting like one," Oscar bit out and put his hand in his hair. "You've been pushing me for days, ever since—" He looked at me. We all knew what he meant. Since I messed up their lives. I still was doing it, right now.

Oscar's jaw worked as if he were summoning all his patience. His face was flushed and his words quiet in a way that made the back of my neck prickle. "You will stay at home or you go to work. No more going to Raul's or the plaza or wherever it is you go—"

"You can't tell me what to do."

I thought Oscar's face couldn't get redder, but it did. A vein actually looked like it might burst on his forehead. "You will do as I say."

Roman really should have stopped there. But he didn't. "Or what? Will you beat me up like you did Max?" Oscar grabbed Roman by the collar and wrenched him up against the wall, but Roman didn't stop. "Will you send me away, never speak my name—"

Oscar's fist came out of nowhere. Roman took it hard on the mouth but didn't go down. He came right back at Oscar like a bull with his horns down.

I think I cried out. Señora wailed. Then Angel was there, pushing between them, speaking words that somehow—thankfully—brought Oscar back to himself. He dropped Roman, who wiped a hand across his mouth, smearing blood over his chin. I might have seen tears in his eyes, but I couldn't be certain. Roman pushed past Angel, past his stricken mother, and banged through the door without another word.

Oscar looked like he was going to be sick.

Angel spoke in Spanish to his mother and Oscar and then said to me quickly as he walked to the door, "I follow him, talk to him."

Oscar sank down into a chair, his head in his hands. A wave of dizziness passed over me, my vision darkened, and I clutched for the back of the chair. I felt myself falling, then strong hands steadied me. When the blackness passed, I saw it had been Sanchia who had stopped my fall. She set me none too gently in the hard chair.

"I . . . I'm sorry." My words dropped flat and useless into the silence. I hadn't meant any harm, sure, but I'd brought it on them, nonetheless.

CHAPTER 8

OSCAR

Oscar woke up alone. No Angel. No Roman. Where had they slept last night?

His head pounded and his mouth tasted like the bottom of an ashtray. He rubbed a hand over his stinging eyes. He'd hit his own brother in anger. What was the matter with him? This was Max's fault. If he hadn't pushed that woman on him—put them all in danger—Oscar wouldn't have been so hard on Roman. Max again.

He trudged up the stairs and nudged open the door to the bedroom. Minerva Sinclaire slept curled in a ball, as if she were protecting herself. Padre Ramirez said to show her mercy and kindness, to treat her like a sister. Had he done enough to fulfill his penance? Must he do more? How was he supposed to know?

Coffee. That's what he needed. And then he had work to do for Brody. Maybe, if he could find a lead on who killed Lester, his obligation to Minerva Sinclaire would be fulfilled. And then he would track down Roman and tell him he was sorry.

Downstairs, he found Mamá at the table. Deep grooves etched each side of her mouth and pillows of skin sagged under her eyes. He sat down across from her, touching the tin cup in front of her. It was cold, like she'd been sitting there for hours. "Mamá," he said softly. "I'll find him. I'll fix this." He sounded surer than he felt.

She frowned and blinked, and a tear slipped from her eye.

Oscar covered her hand with his. She'd suffered so much already. Losing Papá, then her sister and Maria Carmen. And Max showing up last night. "He shouldn't have come back."

She looked up at him and her eyes were bright with tears. "Roman will come home. And you will tell him you are sorry."

He nodded.

"But . . . that is not what troubles me." She rubbed a hand over her eyes. "My son, I did wrong by Max and I am ashamed."

"Ashamed?" What was she talking about? It was Max who should be ashamed to show his face in the *colonia*.

"You do not know . . ." More tears slid down the wrinkled pathways of her cheeks. "He begged me not to send him with his father. I made him go."

Max hadn't wanted to go with Dusty? Oscar couldn't hide his surprise. "What? Why?"

"I thought he needed a father, and . . ." Mamá looked away. "I saw how you loved Maria Carmen."

Oh, Madre. His gut wrenched like a fist. She had meant well. But sending Max away hadn't saved Maria Carmen for him. Oscar swallowed hard. How would things have been different if Max had stayed in the *colonia*?

She pulled her handkerchief from her sleeve and wiped her eyes.

"You did what you thought was right, Mamá." Water runs under a bridge and is gone forever. Oscar went to the stove and poured a fresh cup of coffee. He set it beside her thin hand. "Will you tell Francesca? That you saw Max?"

"No." Mamá frowned at her handkerchief. "Francesca, she is . . . I have known her all my life, in Mexico and here, and through it all with Maria Carmen. But I've never seen her like this."

"Do you think she knows about Minerva Sinclaire?" That's all he needed. Francesca didn't keep things to herself. And he didn't trust Alonso farther than he could throw him.

"No," his mother answered with a shake of her head. "But she is keeping a secret from me, as I am keeping one from her. And secrets between friends are not good."

Oscar covered his mother's cold hand with his own. He wasn't about to try to figure out Francesca's problems when he himself had so many. "She's been through much. And now she is without a job. She is worried, that is all." They all were.

She stood before he went out the door, leaning up to kiss his forehead like she did when he was a boy. "Tell Max, if you see him, that he is welcome here."

A twinge he didn't understand went through his chest. Anger, still? Jealousy, maybe? Or guilt? His mother had sent Max away for his sake, misguided as it was. Did he bear some blame for what Max had become? Did they all share some blame in what happened to Maria Carmen? He gave his mother a peck on the cheek and went out the door. His head hurt too much to think any more on it.

Brody had called yesterday with three leads on Feng. "Maybe his people will talk to you," he'd said.

"Mexican and Chinese aren't the same thing," Oscar had retorted.

"You're not a white police officer—that's something," Brody answered.

Oscar would check them out—maybe even find Feng and another piece to the puzzle. Then, he would look for Roman. Maybe it was his pounding head or the threat of the ominous gray clouds, but he had the uneasy feeling he was running out of time.

It took five cranks to start the Ford. As he turned out of the *colonia* onto Broadway, his thoughts returned to Max. Could he be in love with Mina? He'd tried to save her from Lester with the drugged drink. But if he loved her, wouldn't he want to prove her innocence? Maybe that wasn't Max's kind of love.

Chinatown was only a few blocks from the *colonia*, but it might as well have been across the ocean. Narrow streets were crammed with shops and temples with curled rooftops and red globe-like lanterns. He parked the Ford and walked by a shop displaying long curved pipes and tobacco in carved ivory boxes. The next window held a line of scrawny plucked ducks, dried fish, and bins of vegetables. He found the address Brody had given him down an alley not much wider than his shoulders. He pulled a yellow envelope with *Cosmopolitan Productions* written in bold letters from his jacket pocket and knocked on the door.

"Registered mail delivery," he said when an old Chinese woman opened the door. "For Feng Li." The tiny woman eyed the thick envelope and held out her hands eagerly. Oscar pulled it back. "I can only give it to Mr. Feng."

She shook her head and made it clear she hadn't seen her son in a long time. He left with what sounded like Chinese curses following him all the way down the street. The envelope holding nothing but a folded newspaper went back in his pocket.

Oscar got back in the Ford and turned south toward Macy Street. He knocked on the door and replayed the ruse to a dingy blonde in a tattered dressing gown. An unfamiliar odor, sickly sweet and cloying, drifted from her. Feng hadn't been by in months, she said, and the bum owed her money. "You're not the first to come looking for that loser," she said.

"Who else?" he asked.

"Some joker. Looked like a blond John Gilbert, smelled like a cop." She eyed the envelope. "I can help you get rid of that," she said with a brown-stained smile. Revulsion curled in his stomach and he didn't hide it well enough. Her bloodshot eyes narrowed, and he left quick, before she summoned a thug from the dark den behind her.

Back in the auto, he took a deep breath of damp air and headed to the next address—a pawnshop near the Santa Monica Pier. So far, the rain held off but that was all the luck he'd had. He showed a picture of Feng—one Brody had gotten from Central Casting—to a leathery old-timer in a ten-gallon hat and alligator boots. "Yep. The big Chinaman. He came in a couple times," he said. "Always had something to hock." He nodded to a display case. "That cigarette case, jewelry."

"Where'd he get it?"

The cowboy's brown face wrinkled, and he spit a brown stream into a brass jug. "Not my business. Petty thief, I reckon." Nope, he hadn't seen Feng in weeks. Another dead end.

By the time Oscar turned the Ford toward the city late in the afternoon, he was hungry and tired and had wasted a full tank of gas. The clouds had darkened to the color of ash, and he knew he didn't have much time before the rain started.

He pulled up beside Queen of the Angels as the first rumble of thunder rolled in with a damp wind from the west. Padre Ramirez was bending over the rosebushes that ringed the courtyard. He stood, rubbing his back, as Oscar approached. "Oscar, thank the good Lord." He handed him the ball of twine and a sharp knife. "I was just praying to get these taken care of before the rain came, and here you are."

Oscar wasn't sure it was the Lord Padre should be thanking, but he cut a length of twine and set about tying a fragile rose stem to a stake.

"I suppose you're looking for Roman and Angel," Padre said, handing him another length of twine. "They're not here."

Oscar's throat tightened. Did Padre know what he had done? Probably. He was much like the all-seeing God he represented. "Do you . . . did you—"

"All will be well, Oscar," Padre interrupted, propping up a vine heavily laden with blooms while Oscar tied it securely. "You will both cool down and, by tomorrow, forgive each other."

They finished the roses in silence, and Oscar handed the ball of twine and knife back to Padre. "Thank you, Padre. And if you see Roman, tell him . . ." That he was sorry. To come home. Not to get into trouble. "Tell him Mamá is worried."

"Oscar—" The priest put a hand on his arm.

"Yes, Padre?" The wind blew harder, almost taking his hat, and he pulled it tighter on his forehead.

The priest's wispy hair lifted, showing lines of concern on his forehead. "Oscar—" he looked down at the ball of twine—"I hear a great deal of what goes on in the *colonia*. Much of it in the confessional. As you know, I cannot break the seal of confession, but . . ." He glanced up, then plunged ahead. "I can tell you this. You are not the only one hiding something in the *colonia*. I know you are worried about Roman and Angel, but there is another worry here very close to you."

Oscar didn't follow. A worry, here, very close? "Meaning what?"

Padre shook his head. "I can say no more."

Frustration welled in Oscar. Whose confession? His brothers? Mamá? "But you know something."

Padre nodded. "Only that the human heart hides a great deal. Even those closest to us keep secrets."

Oscar cranked the Ford and jumped in. He'd had enough of riddles. He didn't need more puzzles to solve from Padre Ramirez. He'd go home. Maybe Angel had been able to convince Roman to return by now. They would talk and he would tell him how sorry he was. He turned onto Main Street and came within a few blocks of La Placita. Something was happening. He eased up on the accelerator lever. On the street just past the plaza and the statue of Fray Junípero Serra, half a dozen black cars were parked at angles. Groups of bystanders gathered in bunches. Others faced a line of uniformed men holding billy clubs.

Oscar pulled the Ford over and parked, then jumped out and ran toward La Placita. He slowed as he approached a group of old men. "What is it?"

"A raid." The speaker's face was drawn with worry. "Everyone in the plaza is being questioned."

Oscar peered past the black suits. Men and boys from the *colonia* sat in groups on the ground. *Policía* stood, looking at lists and calling names. A police van with an open back held half a dozen of his neighbors. A man with a megaphone called out from the center of the plaza, speaking in English. "Please remain seated. All those detained will be questioned. Do not attempt to cross the line."

Oscar's palms went clammy and his heart hammered. No. They wouldn't be here. He had told Roman and Angel to stay out of the plaza for just this reason.

A hand grabbed at his shirt, and he turned to find Señora Cruz from Queen of the Angels. Her voice held panic, her eyes wild. "My son. Oscar, they took my son."

"Señora Cruz—"

"And Angel, he was here. He tried to talk to the police, but they put him in one of the vans."

Oscar's blood surged. "Angel? What about Roman—did you see him?"

The old woman went on about unions and birth certificates. She was crying now. He helped Señora Cruz to a bench and veered around the crowds. Were they here? Or had they been taken? A police officer stepped up to him, a billy club in his hand. "Get back. Anybody crossing the line will be arrested. That means you, big guy."

Oscar stepped back, his heart a clenched fist in his chest. She could be wrong. Señora Cruz had terrible eyesight. Roman and Angel could be anywhere—at the *sociedades* with Alonso and Raul, or even at home. He'd probably find them eating tortillas and arguing. He ran back to the Ford, his mind bringing forth only one prayer, *Dios te salve, María, llena eres de gracia . . .*

They would be there, at home. They had to be.

———————

Oscar sat in the corner of the *sociedades*, a two-bit pint of tequila in front of him along with a wet newspaper.

LA PLACITA ALIENS AWAIT DEPORTATION—As
part of the biggest drive in the history of California, an
army of police and border patrol officials surrounded
the plaza known as La Placita today in downtown
Los Angeles. Their goal: to round up illegal aliens,
communists, and agitators. Those not able to furnish

proof of their right to be in California were transported to the repatriation facility on Alameda Street. Federal operatives report a bus will take the deportables across the Mexican border within twenty-four hours.

When Roman and Angel weren't at home with Mamá, Oscar had gone straight to the repatriation center. It was crowded with wives, mothers, and fathers—all trying to get answers about the raid on the plaza. The federal officers had taken at least fifty men for questioning. Most were Mexican. A few were Japanese and Chinese. The charges were various: illegal residency, unionizing, criminal behavior. Roman and Angel were on the list as agitators, whatever that meant.

Oscar panicked and telephoned Max at the Garden of Allah. He showed up in his suit and tie half an hour later. His *americano* accent and light skin got them to a border officer, a shrunken man in a threadbare suit. "Dominguez. Yes. Angel and Roman, illegal aliens." He checked his notes. "On the bus tomorrow night."

Max stayed polite, as if this were all a misunderstanding. "They are citizens of this country, born not two miles from where we sit."

The border officer held out his hand. "Birth certificates?"

"They don't have—"

"I can't help you, then." He slapped the file shut and laid it on a mountain of similar files on his desk. "Next!"

Oscar had reached his limit. He leaned over and picked up the little man by his ugly tie. "Let them go or I swear I'll—" Two police officers had him by the shoulders before he could finish.

Max smoothed things over and hustled him out of the office. "Go home before you get put on a bus yourself." He rubbed a hand over his eyes. "I'll stay here and see what I can do."

Oscar poured himself another shot of tequila. This wasn't something he could blame on Max. The fault was all his. He shouldn't have lost his temper with Roman.

The rain had come. It pounded on the tin roof of the *sociedades*. Raul hurried around the room, trying to look sympathetic while totting up the cost of the tequila he was pouring out to fear-stricken fathers and brothers. "We brought them his birth certificate," an old man at the next table said, his hands clenched tight in worry. "No matter. He was sent back for criminal activity."

Another's voice rose over the tumult. "They said my brother was unionizing. He doesn't even have a job!"

"I heard one of the Japanese boys got out. His father gave the border agent five hundred dollars," a younger man said.

"Who has that kind of money?"

Oscar's anger burned along with his people's. It wasn't fair, how they were treated. Like animals. Worse than animals. Suddenly the room fell quiet. Oscar turned his bleary-eyed gaze to the doorway. It was Brody, dripping wet and as out of place as a goose in a flock of crows.

Oscar put down his empty glass. Why was Brody here? And why was the room tipping toward the street? Now Brody was coming across the room to him. Now standing beside his table. Now taking the empty seat and signaling to Raul for another glass. Raul came by, slamming down the glass in a way that said a *gringo*—and a police officer—wasn't welcome in the *sociedades* drinking his illegal tequila.

Oscar didn't care what Raul thought. Maybe Brody could help . . . maybe he knew somebody. Oscar pushed the half-empty bottle to Brody and ignored Raul. "There was a raid on La Placita today," he said, noticing his words came out a little slurred. "My brothers . . ." His throat tightened, and he couldn't say more.

Brody poured a heavy shot in his glass and threw the swig back in one go. His eyes watered but he took it almost as well as a Mexican. "I heard about it. I'm sorry."

"Can you do anything?" It was worth a try.

Brody's bushy brows came together. "Wish I could, kid." He poured them each another shot. "But as you know, they've got no love for me at the Hall of Justice right now."

Oscar knew that. Brody would be lucky to keep his job after this investigation—one that he wasn't supposed to be working. The tequila slipped down his throat easy. He'd better stop soon, or he'd end up on the floor and no use to Roman or Angel. Or to Brody. Why was Brody here, anyway? "I didn't find Feng," he said abruptly.

Brody put down his glass with a grimace. "Somebody else did." He pulled a photo from inside his coat and passed it across the table.

Oscar's stomach dropped to his shoes. It was Feng. Obviously dead. "Hearst's people?"

Brody frowned. "That's my take. He was at a motel out past the city limits, the room ripped apart, like they were searching for something."

Dear Mrs. Lester, I have something you want. "You think they found it? What they were looking for?"

"Maybe. But if they did, why would Hearst do this today?" Brody pulled a special edition from his jacket pocket. He slid it across the table to Oscar, turning it so he could read the headline along the top: *REWARD $1,000.*

"Qué?" He leaned over the newspaper and read as fast as he could. For Minerva Sinclaire? "Why does Hearst want her?" It didn't make sense. Oscar tried to catch up through the haze of

tequila. "Does she have what he's looking for?" Could she have sent the letter? No, she'd been stuck in his house for days.

Brody shook his head. "Whatever it is, he wants her bad. And we need to find her before he does." He tapped the photograph of the dead butler. "Or maybe she's next."

"But . . ." Oscar tried to think, but the thousand-dollar reward nagged at his befuddled brain. A thousand dollars. With a thousand dollars he could bribe the border agent. He could get his brothers home. And the woman was sitting in his home right now.

Brody glanced around the room. It was still quiet, and most of the patrons were watching him. He pulled his notebook from his pocket and scribbled on it, tearing out the paper and handing it to Oscar. "My home number. Find that cousin of yours. He's got to have a lead on where she might be. Ring me when you know something."

Brody left, but Oscar didn't move. He had to do something. But what? He stared at the last inch of tequila in the bottom of the bottle. Then at the phone number clutched in his hand. The newspaper in front of him.

A thousand dollars. For Roman and Angel. He could save them.

MINA

The rain had started with a vengeance.

We sat in the kitchen, Señora, Lupita, and I, each in a private cocoon of worry. Drips of water fell from the ceiling into a tin can, ringing out the moments like an irregular clock, Sanchia's rosary beads clicking in desperate harmony.

Lupita's hands fumbled with her embroidery, taking out more stitches than she put in. I hemmed her dress, the tiny stitches blurring before my eyes, and prayed as if God would hear me. *Please,*

God. Please. I knotted my thread and cut the tail with the little silver scissors. *Let Oscar walk in with Roman and Angel. Please, God. Please.*

I searched the cigar box for more thread but came up with an empty spool.

Sanchia put down her rosary and wrapped her black scarf over her head, covering her hair and most of her face. She said a few words and went out the door. I sent a questioning glance to Lupita.

"She'll get thread from the store on the corner," Lupita told me.

"But the rain . . ." She'd be soaked in minutes.

"It will give her something to do. The waiting, it is so hard. And she will get the newspaper. They have only the English, but I will tell her if it say anything about the raid."

Roman and Angel. Were they afraid, wherever they were being kept? Was Roman still acting the tough? Was God listening to Angel's prayers?

"What can we do? There must be some way to get them released."

Lupita shook her head. "*No sé.* Alonso, my brother, he say we need money to bribe the officers. Five hundred dollars at least, for each." She shook her head and lifted her shoulders. "It is too much."

A thousand dollars? It was impossible. I smoothed Lupita's bright cotton skirt over my lap. "They blame me. Oscar and Sanchia." And they were right to. If I hadn't been here, Roman wouldn't have fought with Oscar, and he and Angel would be home right now. I should have turned myself in from the very first.

Lupita didn't deny it. "Roman was, what do you say—an accident waiting? And Angel will always stay with him. At least they are together." We returned to our silent stitches and the beat of the rain.

Minutes later, the front door opened and Sanchia's hard-soled shoes clacked in the hall. She walked into the kitchen, her face pale as the moon. Not even taking off her dripping head covering, she slapped a newspaper on the table in front of Lupita and spouted a string of questioning words.

"*Qué?*" Lupita put down her embroidery and leaned over the table. Her lips began to move as she read. She glanced at me and there was confusion, maybe even shock in her eyes.

My heart sped up. I put down my stitching. My own face looked back at me from the front page, but that wasn't the surprise. It was the number beside it that took my breath away.

REWARD $1,000. For me. It was too much to believe.

But the two-inch number in the headline didn't seem to be what had Sanchia tied in a knot. She flipped the paper over to the bottom half, where the picture of another woman topped Louella Parsons's gossip column: Lana Love. It was enough to send a sickening jolt through my belly.

Lana. What did you do?

Lupita bent over the paper, her brow furrowed, her mouth moving again. Sanchia started babbling, her voice high and hard. Lupita shook her head and held up a hand while she read. Sanchia went silent but crossed her arms and tapped her toe rapidly on the floor.

"*Qué?*" Lupita whispered again. "It can't be." She looked at me with wide eyes. "It isn't true."

My stomach was doing a slow twist. I sat down heavily and read enough to understand.

SINCLAIRE ROOMMATE TELLS ALL!

No one need ever know. That's what Lana had said. Until she told them. The Rose. Taxi dancing. Liquor and bills changing hands, among other things. The newsprint swam in front of my eyes, details coming into focus. A new man every night, according to Lana. And Bert—the guy who got the biggest cut of the deal—spouting some line about running a decent place, about being in the dark about it all.

Lupita's eyes sought mine, but I couldn't look at her. Sanchia bit out an order, poking at the article with her bony finger. She wanted Lupita to tell her what it said. All of it.

Lupita translated to Sanchia.

Lana. My so-called friend. What happened to *Us girls gotta stick together*? How much did she get to ruin my life? But I should have known. That's how it worked in this town, where friendship was as flimsy as a cheap cigarette and left the same bitter taste in your mouth.

I put my head in my hands, suddenly so weary. Memories I'd tried to shut away . . . Cal's hot hands, the smell of sweat and mothballs. Alex.

My mind whirled like a tornado. Papa. Would the *Pierre Daily* run the story? Then my heart dropped like a brick.

Max.

He would know. He would think . . .

The room tilted. My stomach lurched. I stood up, swaying, and stumbled for the back door, barely getting out before I retched up what little I had eaten. The trees and grass spun around me. The rain wet my face.

I'm sorry, Max. I'm so sorry. I wish I could explain it to you. How desperate and alone I was before I met you. How I felt like I didn't have anywhere to turn. But now, you'll think it didn't mean anything but business to me—at the beach house—and you'll hate me for that. You have every right to hate me, Max. I wiped the rain from my eyes. At least now—after all I've done—at least now, you'll finally give up on me.

When I dragged myself back inside, Lupita was silent, blooms of scarlet on her cheeks. How could I ever have thought we could be like sisters? She was good and kind and pure, and I was . . . not. Sanchia skewered me with a dagger gaze. I was exactly what she'd said from the start. She spit out a torrent of words.

Lupita translated, "She asks if this is true."

I nodded. The gist of it anyway. What did it matter if it was three times or thirty?

Sanchia's lips pursed and her eyes narrowed, looking me over from head to toe. She bit out another question. Lupita gasped and shook her head. Sanchia repeated her words very slowly to Lupita and jerked her head at me.

Lupita turned to me, her cheeks flushing pink again. She swallowed. "She is asking you . . ." She faltered as if she couldn't find the right words. "She is asking who is the father . . . of the child you carry."

My stomach sank even lower. Down to my shoes, if you want to know the truth. I hadn't even admitted it to myself yet, not really. But Sanchia knew straight out.

I looked at her hard black eyes—pitiless, unforgiving. Sanchia would never—could never— know who the father was. Not after everything. And so I said what I had to say. The only thing I could say to protect him. "I don't know."

Lupita didn't translate. Her mouth dropped open.

Sanchia stiffened, then slapped me hard across the face and said one harsh word.

I hung my head, my cheek stinging.

"Oh!" Lupita put her hand to her own cheek. "She said—"

"I know what she said," I choked out. It wasn't anything I hadn't called myself.

Sanchia pointed to the door. "Go," she spat out in English. "You. Go."

It's your own fault, Minnie, Alex had said. And it was.

You get what you deserve, Penny would say. And I had.

Of course, I would go. What else could I do? But I had one request first. Not a request—a demand, a plea. "Please." I raised my head and looked her in the eye, not caring if she hit me again. "Please, Señora. Please don't tell . . ." My hand moved over my middle, my voice cracked. "Lupita, tell her she'll never see me again—I promise—if she swears not to tell anyone about this."

Lupita translated slowly, her voice shaking. She really was obedient.

Sanchia pulled her rosary from her pocket and said a few words, the crucifix clutched in her fist, crossed herself, then pointed to the door.

Lupita took my hand and held me back. "But Mina, you can't—"

I pulled away. The truth was, I didn't care if the police picked me up, if Adams and his goons found me. Lupita had treated me like a friend, a sister. Oscar had risked his family. Even Sanchia had fed me. I didn't deserve any of it. "You won't tell, will you? Please, Lupita?"

Lupita shook her head, tears in her eyes. "But what will you do? You must think of your baby."

Your baby. My baby. I'd been trying for weeks not to think those words.

Sanchia opened the back door and the clamor of the rain drowned her words. Lupita threw her arms around me. "Please stay. I will talk to her, she will—"

Sanchia pushed Lupita backwards and me through the door. Fat raindrops darkened my borrowed blouse. Lupita disappeared for a moment, then was back, throwing her scarf over my head and shoulders, rain and tears on her cheeks. Sanchia jerked Lupita away again and slammed the door between us.

I stepped out into the pouring rain. Where could I go?

Away. Just away. I stumbled toward the road, now a wide river of mud. Away from my dreams and plans. Away from the pain I'd caused good people. I'd told Sanchia I didn't know who the father of the baby was, but that had been another one of my big lies.

I knew. Of course I knew. It was Max who could never know.

———————

I walked out of the *colonia*, putting Oscar and Lupita, Roman and Angel and Sanchia behind me. I hadn't thanked them for all they'd given me. I hadn't done anything but harm. And for the first time since I'd stepped off the bus in this far-off land, I didn't have a plan. I walked aimlessly, cold, wet, oddly disconnected from the danger I guessed I was in. From Hearst and Louella. The police.

I'd stepped into Roy Lester's party five days ago like the leading lady just before the happy ending. But now I knew I wasn't playing the heroine. I was the villain of this story, and this was the part where the villain got what was coming to her. Sure, I had reasons—good reasons—for everything I'd done. But didn't all villains think that?

The rain reached cold fingers under Lupita's scarf and down my back. The hem of my skirt was sodden, sticking to my bare legs. I didn't even try to avoid the puddles forming along the road. I deserved this and much more.

It was full dark now, and I walked from streetlight to streetlight, the sodium glare throwing my shadow long and dark beside me one minute, the next fading it into the surrounding blackness. Cars splashed through the street, people rushed past, everyone intent on getting out of the rain, not looking twice at me.

Max, I pleaded in my mind. Max, please try to understand. But how could a man understand how desperate a woman could be? How could a man understand how I didn't have anywhere to turn?

Max had told me at Roy Lester's house that everyone in Hollywood was looking for something. Maybe we were too, that night on the beach. Maybe the real me and the real Max were looking for each other. We tried. We reached out, but we missed each other. Not by much, but what was it they said? A miss by an inch is a miss by a mile.

Now I stumbled across Temple and turned north along Echo Park, numbly putting one foot in front of another. My head pounded like a timpani drum and the streetlights flickered and swung like a kaleidoscope I saw once in a glassmaker's shop.

Desperation rose inside me, cutting off my breath. A child. Mine and Max's. How could I take care of a child? I couldn't even take care of myself. I was alone, freezing, with nowhere to turn. I didn't even have a dime for the bus.

Plenty of girls got in this kind of trouble, I'd heard.

Mary Astor, Tallulah Bankhead, even Gloria Swanson. Max had told me plenty, on one of his tirades against the studios. "They say it's a 'therapeutic solution,' that they're seeing their actresses through a rough time, as if they're sending these poor girls to butchers like Docky Martin out of the goodness of their hearts.

But they don't want to lose jack on their investments." He looked mad enough to spit. "It's all about the dollar signs."

At the Rose, everyone knew Bert was the man to see. "It's like having a tooth pulled," I'd heard one of the women say. "It hurts for a while, sure, but then you don't even miss it."

Would it only hurt for a while? A child with Max's eyes, Max's smile?

I suspected hurt like that would last a lifetime.

Bert might have dodged the newspapers when Lana told her story, but if I was going to jail, I could put him there, too. He'd get me to somebody like Docky if I put it to him that way. All I'd need was a hundred dollars and a way to live with myself.

A bench emerged from the gloom, the curb labeled in bright white letters: Sunset Boulevard. I sat, the icy cold seeping through my skirt. The rain was ebbing, the glow of the moon struggling through the dark clouds. Weariness washed over me and I swayed, dizzy with hunger and cold and despair.

A man approached, armed with an umbrella and a trench coat. "Miss?" I heard him as if from a long distance. "Miss, are you all right?"

I wasn't all right. And maybe never would be.

"Streetcars stopped running an hour ago," he said. "You lost?"

I'd been lost for a long time.

The man stood, shifting from one foot to another in the rain. Any minute now, even with the scarf covering my hair, he'd recognize me from the papers.

I thought about who I was and who I wanted to be. About Papa and Penny. What I'd done and what had happened to me. About what Max meant to me and what he deserved. And finally, I thought about our child. Our baby.

The man was still waiting.

Don't be a sap, Minnie. There was only one thing to do, and I knew what it was. I stood on shaking legs. "I know where I'm going," I said to the man. "Thanks just the same."

Papa always said my greatest strength was my determination. Once I made a decision, I saw it through no matter how tough. Trouble is, I don't know anymore if determination is my strength or my fatal flaw.

OSCAR

Oscar stared at his empty glass. A thousand dollars.

But . . . Minerva Sinclaire was innocent of the murder. He knew that, at least. He remembered her curled up and asleep like a child this morning. His responsibility and his penance. Could he betray her trust? If he turned her in to Hearst—even to save his brothers—if something terrible happened to her, like Feng . . . could he live with himself?

Show her mercy, Padre had said. Mercy wasn't turning her in to Hearst.

Before he could straighten his muddled thinking, the *sociedades* hushed once again, as when Brody had come through the door. This time, it wasn't a *gringo* detective, but a person even more shocking. Lupita rushed toward him—her hair uncovered, her wet dress clinging to her—oblivious to the outraged murmurs of the men in the room.

Caramba. What now?

"Oscar! *Gracias al Señor.* You must come." She went on, something about the newspaper and Mamá and the rain. Before he could think, she pulled him through the room and out the door.

The rain poured off the brim of his hat. He shrugged out of his coat and threw it over Lupita. She ran through the rivers of mud holding his hand tight. "Come. Hurry."

Alarm shot through his body. Had Minerva been found out? By the time Oscar burst into his house, rain and fear had cleared his head of the tequila. Mamá sat on the straight-backed chair, her arms crossed, looking at the floor. Lupita babbled. Minerva Sinclaire was nowhere to be seen.

"Where is she?"

"That's what I'm saying!" Lupita sat him down. "You must go after her. You've got to find her."

"No. She is gone and good riddance," Mamá said, her voice hard.

Gone? She couldn't be. "Where? How long ago?" His gut twisted. Did they find her? Would someone else get the reward?

"She is all alone," Lupita appealed to Oscar.

He sat down, his head spinning. Maybe he wasn't sobered up yet. "Tell me what happened."

Mamá pointed to the *americano* newspaper on the table. The one Brody had given him, with the headline of the reward. But below the fold . . . He smoothed out the pages and read. The beat of the rain on the roof filled the silence. *Qué?* Minerva Sinclaire, a . . . He knew she wasn't an innocent child, but this? He looked at Mamá, questioning. "Did you . . . Is this true?"

"She said yes." Mamá's words were clipped and short.

His stomach turned over in disgust. She had lived under his roof, eaten his food, and he had believed in her innocence . . . Minerva, a woman who took money for . . . All this time, he'd been protecting her, but she'd played him for a fool. And Max . . . all those things he'd said—about her being innocent, needing help— had he known all along what she was?

Because of this—this woman who sold herself—and her lies, he'd turned on his own brother. And now Roman and Angel were taken from them. How could he have been so stupid?

"I told you what she was, my son," Mamá said.

He didn't need her I-told-you-sos, but he figured he'd earned them. "You were right, Mamá." He crumpled the paper in his shaking hands. He needed something to hit, some way to vent his mounting fury. He'd find her. He'd find her and he'd bring her to Hearst. Then he'd get Roman and Angel back home. His decision was made. "She gets what she deserves now." Even Padre Ramirez couldn't argue with that.

Lupita turned on them both, bright spots of color on her cheeks. "Forgive me, Señora Dominguez, but you are wrong." Mamá's mouth dropped open. Lupita's words came quick and fierce. "And you are wrong also, Oscar. And pigheaded and stubborn and . . . uncharitable." Her eyes flashed fire.

It was like a stab in the back. Sweet Lupita, defending that . . . that *prostituta*.

Lupita went on, her hands jabbing the air as she talked. "Don't you know how lucky we are? We have our people. Our family. But Mina, she has no one. No friends except that woman in the papers. Sometimes people do bad things because they have no other choice."

"How could that—" he poked at the newspaper, his mouth twisting in revulsion—"be the only choice?"

Lupita put her hands on her hips and squared off at him. "You are a stupid man," she said, her voice rising. "A stupid, stupid man! You have no idea what it is like to be a woman. I think about what I would do if I were in her place. It's not so hard to understand."

"You would never—" Oscar sputtered.

"Because I am not alone. But —" she raised up on her toes, her face close to his— "but I do know what it is like to have no choice. Every woman does." Her eyes shone with tears now. "And you yourself have done things not to be proud of, have you not, Oscar?" She stared at him.

He flushed. But a reckless kiss was hardly the same as what Mina had done. What had gotten into Lupita? Was she defending a prostitute? Wasn't Oscar the one who had saved her to start with? Besides, Minerva Sinclaire wasn't alone. "She has Max."

Lupita pointed to the newspaper. "Do you not see? Max is the one who saved her from this—" Lupita stopped suddenly.

"What is it?"

She shook her head, and her hand dropped down. *Nada.* Lupita picked up his sodden hat and coat, shoving them both toward him and pushing him back toward the door. "Go to Max. You will find her there."

At least they agreed on one thing. That's where she must be. He'd find her and turn her in. That's what he'd do. And if she ends up dead like Feng? a small voice—his conscience, he guessed— whispered. Well, then, may God have mercy on them both.

It was almost midnight when Oscar pulled into the Garden of Allah.

When he'd left his house—and the angry woman who used to be sweet Lupita—the Model T was sitting in a puddle the size of a small lake. He opened the ignition, hoping it was dry enough to start. He cranked. Nothing. He tried again and then again, until his arm ached. It was no use. He was under the hood of the Ford for what seemed like forever, cursing and replacing spark plugs before he finally got it cranked into life, then goaded the auto through streets running with water and mud.

Max answered the door in wrinkled trousers and a white singlet. His feet were bare, his hair wild, dark circles like bruises under his eyes.

"Is she here?" Oscar pushed past Max. He yanked open the door to the bedroom, empty. The washroom door was open, no Mina.

"What happened?" Max followed Oscar into the kitchen. The one-eared cat jumped to the windowsill, looking at Oscar with disdain. The feeling was mutual.

Newspapers were strewn over the table, each one showing the picture of Minerva Sinclaire's so-called friend. "Did you know?" He motioned to the newspapers.

Max clenched his jaw.

Oscar felt a twinge—more than a twinge, if he were honest—of pity for his cousin. Minerva Sinclaire had been more than a client to Max. Even he could see that. And now, looking at the state of Max, he figured the answer to his question was no.

Oscar hesitated, guilt twisting his insides, but he wasn't going to change his mind. He'd find the woman and turn her in. "I need to find her, Max."

"Why?"

Oscar didn't answer. He didn't have to because Max already knew.

"The reward." Max stepped closer. "You think you can give her to Hearst? Use the money to get the boys home?"

Oscar didn't meet Max's gaze. The woman wasn't worth saving. Didn't he see that? "I did what I could for her. More than I had to, considering." He glanced at the papers.

Max stiffened. "It doesn't matter what she did before. She didn't kill Lester."

"I take care of my family." Oscar felt his blood heat. "But you wouldn't understand about that." As soon as he said it, he regretted his words.

Max sat down heavily at the table. Despair clogged his voice. "You think you're so noble, Oscar. But you don't know anything." He swallowed hard. "Maybe it's time you heard the truth."

"I don't want to hear your confession."

Max shook his head. "I'm not looking for absolution, Oscar."

Oscar sat down. "Is this about the money you gave us? You looking for thanks?"

Max slammed his hand on the table. "You think that's why I did it? For your thanks? You don't know what it was like, being sent away."

"Must have been rough." Oscar looked out the window into the dark, wet night. The rain sluiced down the windowpane. He didn't have time for this.

"It wasn't like you think." Max blew out a frustrated breath. "All I thought of was you and the boys with nothing to eat. Maria Carmen and her little brother and sister picking oranges while I lived like some kind of prince. It ate me up."

"So you sent us guilt money."

"When I had some. Dusty gave me clothes, food, all the booze I could drink. He wouldn't let me go back to the *colonia*, and believe me, I asked to be sent back. Begged. But he said I was his son now." Max clenched his jaw. "Not that he treated me like one. So yes, I sent you money when I got some. Even though Tía Sanchia gave me away like a stray dog."

Guilt pricked at Oscar, but he pushed it down. Mamá had sent him away, but he'd got his revenge. "You took Maria Carmen."

Max shook his head. "She left on her own. I never—"

"She left me for you." If Max wanted to talk truth, so be it.

Max looked away. "She made her choice, and it wasn't me."

"What are you talking about?" Of course she had chosen Max. That's what killed her.

"I'm talking about the truth. What really happened to Maria." Max stared at his hands. "The baby." His voice dropped. "It wasn't mine."

Oscar jerked, his fists tightening. "She went to you. She left her family for you—"

"Not for me. It was never for me." Max's shoulders sagged, and for a moment he looked older—much older than his years. "It was the life she wanted. The fancy automobiles, the parties, the clothes. I told her to go easy. I'd seen what that life could do, but she didn't listen. It wasn't long before she started up with . . ." The words seemed to stick in his throat.

Oscar's heart pounded. He stood and grabbed Max's arm, pulling him to his feet. "Say it."

Max's face was pale, and the pain in his eyes was sharp and real. "My father."

Oscar's grip tightened. "No. You lie." He had to be lying.

"I didn't know at first, and when I did . . ." Max looked sick. "I loved her, Oscar. You know I did."

Max wasn't lying.

Max went on, his voice harsh. "I wish to God it had been mine. I would have taken care of her. I would have let her have the baby—not push her to have an abortion."

Oscar dropped Max's arm, stepping back like he'd been punched. Maria Carmen would never let one of those butchers kill her baby. "She wouldn't. She didn't."

Max fell into the chair. "She didn't want to. She begged me to help her." Max's voice shook and he ran a tired hand over his face. "He was drunk. I was . . . I was out of my head. We fought but . . . he shoved her into the Bentley."

The Bentley that had gone over the side of Canyon Road. Oscar felt sick, just like he had that day when he'd heard Max's sobbing voice on the telephone.

"I've gone over it a hundred times," Max said softly. "I should have stopped them, somehow."

"You let me put the blame on you." And let Oscar beat him bloody in front of every man in the *colonia*.

"I was the only one left to take it."

"She wouldn't have done it," Oscar said, voice breaking.

Max looked down at his hands. "I'm not sure what she would have done." He shuffled the newspapers. "You think you know someone, Oscar, but it turns out you don't. There are places—parts of ourselves—that nobody knows about. Not really."

Oscar figured he was talking about Minerva Sinclaire now. They'd both been fooled by her. Like they'd both been fooled by Maria Carmen.

What had Padre Ramirez said? Something about the people closest to us hiding secrets. Oscar had thought he'd known Maria Carmen. But the woman Max described was a stranger. He thought he knew Max, but it turned out he didn't know his cousin all that well either. Even Francesca was hiding something, according to Mamá. It seemed only Padre Ramirez knew everyone's secrets, and he was bound by the seal of confession.

Why was this coming to him now, with Roman's and Angel's lives at stake? With Minerva missing? He didn't know, but he couldn't ignore the direction of his thoughts. Padre Ramirez said he wasn't the only one hiding something in the *colonia*. And who went to confession except for him and Lupita and the old women?

"Max." He turned on his cousin. "Alonso . . . he said he saw you. Upstairs at the party."

"Yeah." Max slumped over the newspapers, his head in his hands.

"Where?"

"In the hallway—hey, where are you going?"

Oscar grabbed his sodden hat and rushed to the door, puzzle pieces clicking together.

All this time, he'd been wondering what Max had been doing in the upstairs bedrooms, when he should have been wondering about Alonso and his get-rich schemes.

Francesca, confessing to Padre each week.

The typewriter in the back office of the *sociedades*.

Could it really be Alonso all along? Oscar put Maria Carmen, what Max had told him—all of it—into a corner of his mind. He'd think on it later. Right now, he had somewhere to go. "Max," he said as he opened the door, "find her."

"So you can turn her in?" Max sounded defeated.

Oscar was halfway out the door, pulling his cap down low on his wet hair. "Just find her." He prayed he was wrong. Then he prayed he was right. Then he thought of the dead Chinese butler and prayed that he wasn't too late.

MINA

It was long past midnight. I was lightheaded with hunger and shivering wet. I stood before a meandering drive, identical white bungalows and dripping palm trees lining each side.

Somebody once said—search me who, and I guess it doesn't

matter—that a life lived without regret was a life not lived. Boy, did they have that wrong. Regret isn't something to be proud of. It isn't a one-shot deal like stubbing your toe. No, it's a wound that doesn't heal. You live with it, you keep it covered and try not to think about it, but it's always there, aching.

Maybe Max hated me now and probably always would. Maybe now, he wouldn't mind doing what I needed him to do.

But which place was his?

I'd left Echo Park and walked north through residential areas with modest houses guarded by towering oaks, the occasional mansion screened by black iron gates. I reached the familiar stretch of Sunset. Its garish red and yellow lights reflecting off the wet road threw my shadow first one way, then the other. Hotels, speakeasies, all-night cafeterias. Not many people walked the streets in the rain, but music and laughter—and the occasional drunk—spilled out of the open doors.

I was like a ghost drifting along the sidewalk. At the Sunset Tower Hotel, where Max and I had celebrated with clandestine champagne after my audition at Cosmo, a bored doorman barely looked at me. Farther on at a nightclub called the Kitty Kat—where we'd fox-trotted and tangoed until our feet ached—music and laughter swelled and ebbed.

Was this the person I was going to be now? Lost in this world of in-between. Neither here nor there. Not a bad person—not really—but surely not good. My regrets came visiting then—what I'd done to Papa and Penny, sure. But all the rest. Alex and Cal and Roy. Oscar and his family. And although I couldn't see farther ahead of me than a few steps in the driving rain, I could see one thing pretty clear: I'd never be that girl from Odessa again. I'd never be the person Papa called his daughter. The woman Max thought he loved. She was gone. But who had come to live in her place?

I crossed over Western. A Daimler splashed a curtain of dirty water as it passed by me, the marquee lights reflected on its rain-wet windows. Spotlights cut through the dark sky, throwing bright halos under the lowering clouds. At Vine Street, a right turn would take me to the Brown Derby, the Chinese, the Egyptian . . . the Tower Theatre, where Max had kissed me after the Chaplin film. All that was over now. I wouldn't be breaking into film, wouldn't be making a bundle of cash to bring home to Odessa and Papa. I pulled Lupita's scarf over my hair and pushed my trembling legs on, block by block, leaving my past and my hopes behind.

After what seemed like ages, I spotted the sign: *Garden of Allah Villas*, illuminated in shades of gray as the moon came out from behind the clouds. A sprawling main house in alabaster stucco and black iron, a tiled roof that gleamed like wet charcoal, and the glint of an ink-dark swimming pool.

I stepped under a dripping cedar, hiding in the shadows. The bungalow windows were slate-colored eyes, waiting for something to see. No yellow roadster. No clue to who slept behind the various arched doorways and grated windows.

I couldn't just go knocking on doors now, could I?

That's when I saw the letterboxes. Each had a name stenciled like film credits in white paint. *Swanson* and *Harlow* on the first two bungalows on the left, on the other side of the street a place with a deserted air and the letterbox label of *Marx*. A perfectly groomed lawn with a well-tended rose garden and large letterbox with *Barrymore* in small, precise print.

How long before someone saw me lurking and called the police?

Then I saw it, the faded print on the next letterbox. *Clark.*

Thank heaven. I held my hand over the door for a moment, getting up the nerve. Finally, I knocked, my heart hammering in my throat, my mouth as dry as dust. He'd have every reason to throw me out, but I hoped he wouldn't.

No answer. My pulse slowed a titch and I knocked again, louder. Nothing. No light. No footsteps. I tried the doorknob. It turned, and the door swung opened with a creak. I guess Max didn't worry about burglars in a place like this. My hand found the light button and a dim glow filled a small hallway and spilled into the rooms beyond.

There was a reason Max didn't worry about burglars. He didn't have anything to steal.

The entryway held a brass coat tree with a gray wool overcoat I recognized. The walls were bare but for a few picture hooks and some holes in the plaster. I dripped down the hallway to what must be the sitting room—nothing to sit on but a few boxes filled with books. A white-tiled washroom. A bedroom with an unmade bed.

It felt so . . . personal, seeing this part of Max. Where he lived. The place he slept and ate and lived his life. This was the Max I wanted to know. The Max I would never have. I found the kitchen next. Newspapers covered the table, my shame splashed across every page. A half-empty bottle of gin sat beside a single tumbler. My legs wobbled and tears choked my throat.

Max, I'm so sorry.

I started to shake, the shivers coming from deep inside like an earthquake. I was so cold. I stumbled to the washroom and started hot water running in the claw-foot bathtub. With trembling hands, I stripped off my wet clothes, hung them on the clicking radiator, and stepped into the scalding water. I went all the way under, holding my breath and hoping that when I came back up—somehow—everything would be all right again. It wasn't.

When the water cooled and my limbs felt like melted wax, I dragged myself out of the bath and wrapped up in a towel the size of a bedsheet. My eyes were drooping as I rummaged through a bureau in the small bedroom. I ran my hand over the pressed white shirts. Max's bright silk ties.

I don't expect you to forgive me, Max, I just want . . .

What did I want? I wanted his help, one last time. Then I'd get out of his life for good. But for now, I just wanted sleep. I found a pair of men's pajamas in dove-gray silk—miles too big, but I slipped them on. I lay down on the bed and buried my face in the feather pillow, breathing in the scent of Max's hair tonic. Then I closed my eyes and wished and wished and wished things were different.

If wishes were horses—isn't that what they say?

CHAPTER 9

Odessa, South Dakota

PAPA

It was a cold day for an auction.

Best get on with it, he figured. There was no point in griping. When the banker from Pierre had come to the house with the auction details, Penny had been downright hostile. Ephraim had to give Mr. Robert Thomas his due; he hadn't let Penny's ire get to him and had done his job like a real gentleman.

Ephraim rubbed his hands together and stuck them deep in his wool jacket pockets as he considered the collection of equipment lined up for sale. "Morning." He nodded to Robert Thomas, who shivered in his fancy coat and city shoes. The boy should have known to wear something warmer. Everybody knew that February was raw in South Dakota, and this morning was worse than most. He checked his watch. Wouldn't be long now before the bidders showed up.

The auctioneer, a good man Ephraim had met a time or two over the years, was dressed in heavy dungarees and a bulky wool jacket. He kicked the tires on the tractor and made a note with a stubby pencil. "1917 Fordson. That's a good machine. How about the plow?"

"Bought it used in '26," Ephraim answered. That plow had done some good work. He'd miss it. The auctioneer listed the rest of the items up for sale: a hay trailer, the baler, the old mare he'd had since the girls were little. Ephraim hoped she would go to someone who'd treat her well. Three old Guernseys—Bess, Tiny, and Maddie—all of them still good milkers, though Maddie could be temperamental at times.

They walked past the barn to where the rooster was strutting his way around the coop. "Chickens too?" the auctioneer asked Mr. Thomas.

Robert Thomas looked apologetically at Ephraim and nodded. "Mr. Zimmerman, I'm sorry about this," he said for the umpteenth time that morning.

Ephraim jerked his head toward the house. "How about a cup of coffee?" The young fellow was just doing his job. No need to be inhospitable.

In the kitchen, Penny couldn't manage a civil word to the banker, but Robert Thomas thanked her for the coffee and even offered her a smile. She looked well today, Ephraim thought, despite her rudeness. She was wearing her best dress and a hat that brought out the blue in her eyes. Too bad she was so stingy with her smiles.

The news of Minnie had hit Penny hard and he couldn't blame her.

Ephraim should have known something was wrong three days ago, when Gus didn't call out his usual weather report at the bus station. Nope, Gus had silently peeled a newspaper off the stack and slid it over without meeting his eyes. Ephraim unfolded the newspaper and saw—for the first time in almost a year—the face of his beloved daughter.

Minnie. She was smiling in the picture. That warm, happy smile he loved.

He glanced at the headlines and his old heart faltered.

He read the article, a gossip column it seemed, by some woman in Hollywood. He stumbled to the bench and sat, then read through it again.

His Minnie. How he had loved her. But now that love had changed.

Ephraim pressed her picture to his chest. It was like a knife in his heart, this new love. Stronger and fiercer. A love he hadn't known was possible. He carried that new love with him now, like a treasure. Someday he'd give it to his child, when she came home to him.

If she came home, he admitted to himself. The article said plenty, but he didn't believe half of it. Some such about a murder and a film star, a reward, and what Minnie had done in that far-off land. What was true and what wasn't? He didn't know the whole story, but his heart told him his girl couldn't have killed a man. Not his Minnie.

News got out, and people in town talked. Those who were friends were still friends. Those who weren't—well, he couldn't help what they said and didn't let it get to him. But it was hard on Penny, the gossip about her sister. The speculation. That, and losing the farm. No, Ephraim wouldn't give up hope. Not for Minnie or for their home. Sometimes it was in the darkest times when the Lord opened a door.

The clock on the farmhouse wall clicked to nine. Ephraim, Penny, and Mr. Thomas got up without a word and went outside. Half a dozen autos parked in the farmyard. Old Bill gave Ephraim a friendly wave. Gus and the mayor bent their heads together beside the auctioneer's flatbed truck—Ephraim swore he heard Gus chuckle—while their wives huddled together, whispering and smiling.

Smiling? That was a surprise.

Mr. Langer, the pharmacist, stood with Irma, drinking coffee from a silver thermos. Doc got out of his bottle-green Chrysler sedan and joined a huddle of men Ephraim recognized from town. Doc said something to the men in a low voice, and the other men guffawed. A wagon pulled up with the Webbers and their son, Jonas. Mrs. Webber brought out a covered basket and passed out what looked like hot donuts.

He sure hadn't expected his neighbors to be in such good spirits. Or the townfolk to show up at a farm auction. Why was his farmyard looking more like an Odessa Saturday night social than a foreclosure sale?

Penny stood beside him, bundled in her winter coat, her scarf wound around her neck. "I thought these people were our friends." There was hurt in her voice.

Next to her, Robert Thomas accepted a steaming hot donut and smiled. "I think they are."

The auctioneer read off the notice. With all the legalities observed, he started with the tractor. "Who'll start out the bidding? It's a good piece of machinery."

Nobody made a move.

"Fifty dollars. Anyone?"

Ephraim looked up. The men had made a ring around the auctioneer, but nobody was raising their hand in a bid.

"Forty, then. Forty dollars is a good price."

Again, not a word. Ephraim wondered what was going on. Then Old Bill winked at him. "I'll give you a dollar."

The auctioneer's mouth dropped open. "A dollar? For the tractor? Don't pull my leg."

"A dollar," Old Bill said, sticking his hands in his pockets and looking pleased.

The auctioneer continued, asking for more bids, but none came. He looked to Robert Thomas, who shrugged, and doggone it if he wasn't grinning.

"Going once at a dollar, then. Going twice." The hammer came down. "Sold."

Penny turned to him with a question in her eyes, but he didn't have the answer.

The rest of it went like that. The plow going for seventy-five cents to Gus. The wagon he pulled behind the tractor to bring in the corn went for sixty cents to the schoolteacher with some encouraging clapping. The auctioneer even caught the jovial mood. "Don't you people know I'm working on commission?" he jested, and the men laughed.

The Guernseys went for two bits each, and the mare for a dime.

The auctioneer shook his head as the last item—the cultivator—went to a pleased Irma, who hadn't set foot on a farm since she was a girl.

The auctioneer's gavel fell for the last time. "Pay the man," he said, and those who had bid brought their change to Robert Thomas, who took each coin with a grave nod and wrote out a receipt. The buyers, in turn, passed the receipts to Ephraim, got in their autos with good-natured shouts and laughter, and drove away. The auctioneer took his meager percentage from Robert Thomas and, wishing Ephraim a good day, tipped his hat to Penny and puttered down the driveway in his flatbed.

Robert Thomas was hiding a grin when he turned to Penny. "A penny auction for Penny."

Ephraim had read about penny auctions in the paper—where neighbors stood up to the banks by bidding ridiculously low. He figured they must have blocked the road to the farm early this morning to keep out strangers. Even the auctioneer was in on the scheme, from what he saw. He was grateful to his neighbors, but he had a worry. "What will happen at the bank?" he asked. He didn't want the young man to get into trouble on his account. And he still did owe the bank a debt, even if it wasn't on the books.

Robert Thomas regarded him seriously. "Mr. Zimmerman, you didn't hear it from me, but by this time next week, Farmers and Merchants will be closed for good."

Ephraim opened his mouth to speak, but Robert Thomas held up his hand. "And not because of you, so don't hold yourself responsible." He spoke now to both of them. "I'm just a loan officer, but I have ears and eyes. The bank managers have been keeping their heads above water just long enough to save themselves before we close the doors."

"So why aren't you doing the same?" Penny broke in, her distrust evident in her voice. "Why help us?"

Robert Thomas shook his head. "I'll be out of a job come next week, but maybe I'll have something else."

"What?" Penny asked suspiciously.

Robert Thomas just smiled. Then he tipped his hat to Penny and wished them both a good day before he hopped into his cherry-red Pontiac coupe and drove away.

CHAPTER 10

Los Angeles

OSCAR

Oscar pushed the Ford as hard and fast as it would go back to the *colonia*.

Maria Carmen and Dusty Clark. He didn't want to believe it, but Max was too broken up to be lying. And all these years he'd blamed Max for deserting them, when it had been Mamá who'd made him go. And Maria Carmen . . . Max wasn't the father of her child. His hands tightened on the wheel. She wouldn't have been the first girl from the *colonia* to have a child out of wedlock; Max was proof of that. If only he could have talked to her, asked her to come home.

If only. Were they not the two most sorrowful words in any language?

Somehow, he found himself standing on the cinder-block steps of the Garcias' home, the rain making a racket like machine-gun fire on the tin roof. Was he right to come here? Maybe Padre Ramirez meant something else. Maybe he'd got it wrong.

Francesca opened the door. "Oscar, it's raining pitchers. What are you doing here?" She pulled Oscar into the house and rushed away, coming back with a scrap of towel, mopping the drips as they fell to the floor. "Lupita, she is with your mother. I am praying for your brothers. May God bring them back to you."

Oscar nodded and hung his cap on the hook beside the door. "I came to talk to you. About Señor Lester."

Francesca's face closed like a slammed door and she turned on her heel. She hurried to the kitchen, pulling a bucket from under the cupboard, avoiding his gaze.

Alonso appeared in the kitchen doorway. "What about him?"

Francesca looked fearful, Alonso hostile. Or was it just his imagination?

Oscar took a seat at the kitchen table, where he'd sat thousands of times over the years with Max and Maria Carmen, eating beans and tortillas, drinking coffee.

A tin can caught drips from the ceiling in a staccato beat. He'd have to tell them—Francesca and Lupita and Alonso. They deserved to know how Maria Carmen had really died and who was the father of her unborn child. But not tonight. There was something else he had to know. "I think you have something to tell me, Alonso." He prayed it wouldn't be what he thought.

Alonso's face was blank. Too blank.

Francesca twisted her apron. "He owed us." She said it like it was a reason, glancing nervously at Alonso.

"Mamá!" Alonso said sharply.

"So you took something? Of his?" Oscar stood and in two steps was nose to nose with Alonso. "What was it?"

Alonso stepped back, glancing away.

"Tell me." Oscar's voice was a low threat.

"I-I don't know what you're talking about," Alonso stammered. Francesca crossed herself.

"You remember Feng, the butler?" Oscar reached into his pocket and pulled out the picture Brody had given him. "Whatever it is, they thought he had it." He threw the picture down on the table, beside the glowing lamp. "Do you want to be next?"

Francesca gasped and wobbled. Alonso looked at the picture, and then his mother, his face draining of color. Francesca rushed to the corner of the kitchen and pulled the gas stove away from the wall.

"Mamá!" Alonso said again, but too late.

Francesca fished a blue-bound notebook from behind the stove. She hurried over to Oscar and threw it on the table in front of him as if it had burned her. "Take it. Take it." She crossed herself again and backed away.

"You took this? Stole it?" Oscar couldn't believe it. Alonso and Francesca. His family.

"He hadn't paid us in weeks!" Alonso burst out. "I read the newspapers. These people will pay plenty to keep their dirty secrets. I figured it was our ticket to a better life."

Alonso. Always looking for a quick way to get rich. Always wishing to be like *americanos*. And look what it led to.

Oscar picked up the diary. It opened to a creased page. He struggled to read the English in a messy slanted hand, but after a few sentences, he got the idea. "Did you even read it?"

Alonso hung his head. "I could make out some. I figured it is something bad, from the way they talked."

Oscar couldn't believe it. Just the few words he'd read confirmed it was something bad, all right. He stuck the book in his pocket, feeling like he was carrying a stick of dynamite. "And so you stole this, and what? He found you in his room, so you fought and killed him?"

"No! No, Oscar. That isn't what happened." Alonso stepped back. "He wasn't there. I only found it in his room, I swear. He was downstairs still, at the party. And then the next morning, he was dead . . . I don't know anything about that. I swear that's the truth."

Oscar waited, wanting to believe him. Hoping it was true. "Then what? Lester was dead so you tried to blackmail Señora Lester? You sent the note asking for money?"

Alonso tried to explain. "Oscar, they are bad people—Señor and Señora Lester. I just wanted what was owed me . . . and maybe a little more. What we deserved."

Oscar shook his head. He turned to Francesca. "Where was it?" For all the love in heaven, he was going to get some answers.

She twisted the cloth in her hands. "I clean his bedroom. He keeps it . . . under his pillow."

Under his pillow? This? This book of secrets—what Feng had been killed for—and he'd hidden it under his pillow like a child hiding bad marks on a report card?

Alonso sat down in the straight-backed chair and put his head in his hands. "I didn't kill him, Oscar."

Oscar believed him. Alonso was stupid and greedy and deserved a good beating, but he wasn't a killer. First Maria Carmen, and now Francesca and Alonso. Did he really know anyone? "Did Lupita know about this?"

Alonso shook his head. "I thought . . . she would tell you."

He let out the breath he'd been holding. She probably would have, and they could have turned this over to Brody. Maybe even saved Feng's life and cleared Mina's name. He shook his head. "Don't say anything to anyone. Do you understand?" They both looked at the floor, shamefaced. "I'll do what I can to keep you out of it."

He went back out to the Ford, idling on the street. Alonso and Francesca were good people—he'd known them all his life. But even good people can do bad things if they tell themselves a few lies.

MINA

When I woke it was still dark outside, but a light glowed in the hallway. A quilt was tucked around me, and a cat—patchworked in every color a cat could be and missing part of an ear—curled warm alongside me, purring like a freight train. The cat sat up, blinked at me, then jumped to the floor, looking back as if telling me to follow.

I did. To the kitchen, where Max sat at the table in a puddle of light. The newspapers were folded in a neat pile, and coffee percolated on the stovetop. He was wearing dark trousers and a white dress shirt, but his feet were bare and his hair was damp. Dark circles ringed his eyes, and his jaw was shadowed. He stared at the cigarette dangling from his fingers.

I sat down across from him. "You haven't slept."

Max took a puff, then blew out a white veil of smoke. "You were wearing my pajamas." The smoke cleared and I could see the lines of worry etched on his face. My throat tightened and I swallowed hard. The cat jumped up into my lap, turned in a circle, and settled down, the purr starting up again.

Max still didn't look at me. "I see you've met Julia."

I put my hand on her head and stroked her. I would have laughed because it was funny, how I'd worried about his Julia. As it was, I felt tears prick the backs of my eyes and my breath catch. "Max, about the papers. I—"

"There's no need to talk about it." He stood abruptly and pulled open the icebox. It was empty but for a bottle of milk he emptied into a saucer on the floor.

"You deserve an explanation. After everything you did for me."

"What I did for you?" He sounded like he really didn't know. He leaned against the sink and crossed his arms.

"Taking me on, trying to help me." I waved toward the pile of newsprint, trying to figure how to explain. "I owe you, Max."

Maybe I shouldn't have said that last part because his face went from puzzled to rock hard, his mouth thinned into a line. "Is that what you thought? That you owed me?" The bitterness in his voice cut, and I knew he was talking about the night at the beach.

It wasn't that simple, I wanted to say. There were other reasons. His smile. The waves. The way he knew the real me no matter how hard I tried to hide. But my throat had filled with tears. "You saved me, Max," I choked out.

He shook his head. "I wish I could have saved somebody."

I guess he meant Maria Carmen. Or maybe Roman and Angel. I didn't deserve to be saved, but they did. The percolator gurgled, the dark aroma of coffee drifted through the silent kitchen.

"You want to know what bothers me the most?" Max finally said, looking down at his feet.

I wasn't sure I did.

"That you thought I was like the rest of them."

I must have tightened my grip on Julia, because she stopped purring and jumped from my lap, abandoning me for her breakfast. I couldn't say I blamed her.

"Didn't you get what I was telling you all those times, Mina?" He looked at me finally, and his eyes were filled with something like anger and sadness all at once. "Nobody in this town is walking around whole, without regrets. If they are, they're kidding themselves. Some have done worse. I've done plenty worse. I thought you knew . . ." He swallowed hard. "I thought you knew you didn't have to hide from me."

What he meant was that I should have trusted him. But I'd learned my lessons well in this far-off land. That no one could be trusted. That everybody wanted something. I didn't know he was different until it was too late.

"I wish . . ." He ran an agitated hand through his hair.

He wished he'd never met me. He wished he hadn't tried to help me.

He met my eyes then. "I wish I'd known—" he flicked his hand at the papers and his voice broke—"when we were at the beach house." His shoulders rose and fell. "It would have changed things." He wouldn't have wanted me, then, knowing what I'd done. That's what he meant. And who could blame him? He looked down at the newspaper, where Louella's accusations shouted in inch-high letters. "I'm not . . . I don't want to be this to you."

"You aren't," I choked out in a rush, standing up quick. "Nothing like." A flush burned up my neck, and I wished I could disappear into the floor. How could he not know he—being with him—was as different from the others as a kiss is to a punch in the mouth? But how does a girl talk about a thing like that?

I looked up at him, seeing in his eyes more than I wanted to see. Everything that could have been. Maybe he would have kissed me then. He looked like he might. But I couldn't let him. One thing I wouldn't do—I promised myself—was hurt him again.

The moment—whatever it was—was gone, and he shoved his hands in his pockets. "I tried to save you from Roy. Did you know that?"

I thought I knew what he meant. "You told me not to—"

"Not then. Later." Then he told me what he'd done, putting Seconal in Roy's drink.

"But I drank it." My throat closed so I could hardly get a breath. He *had* saved me. Even when I'd been so cruel, when I hadn't listened to his warning. It might have been the nicest thing anybody had ever done for me. And one more reason why I had to do the right thing now. For him and for his family. I managed one good breath and then said, "Max, I need you to do something more for me. One more thing."

His face took on that guarded look. "What is it?"

I told him my plan.

He stiffened, and that little muscle on the side of his jaw twitched like it did when he didn't like what I had to say. "No," he said. "Absolutely not."

I knew he'd take some convincing. "It's the only way," I said. The only way I could live with myself.

"You don't know what you're saying. What will happen to you."

I swallowed. Maybe Hearst would pin Roy's murder on me. Maybe prison—and not just for me, though I'd never tell Max about the baby. Heaven knows, he'd try something stupidly heroic, like ask me to marry him again.

"We don't even know what game Hearst is playing, why he wants you to take the rap for the murder. Who even did kill Roy. That person is still out there."

He was right. But it was a chance I had to take. "You can help me, or I'll do it myself." I knew I sounded like the Mina he knew. Determined. Stubborn. That Mina was gone forever, but he didn't have to know it yet. "Hearst offered the reward and he'll pay it to you." Maybe if I said it, it would be true.

"Mina, why are you doing this? Why now?" His eyes, full of regret and sadness, were almost my undoing. But I hardened my heart.

"Because it's the right thing to do." And I was ready—more than ready—to do the right thing, no matter what it cost me.

But I didn't have a chance to tell him any of that. Instead, I about jumped out of my skin when the front door burst open. Max moved quick, stepping between me and the hallway as if he was ready to protect me. But it was Oscar, stumbling in soaking wet and panting like he'd run all the way from the *colonia*.

"*Gracias a Dios,*" he said in a whisper, then switched into English. "You found her."

Max relaxed, but he kept me behind him still. "She found me. And you're not taking her."

"Don't worry—I got something." Oscar shut the door behind him and twisted the lock, then brushed by Max and me into the kitchen, shutting the window and pulling the curtain closed. He pulled a blue book from his breast pocket and shoved it at Max like a hot potato. "You look. You tell me."

Max took the book and glanced at the inside cover. He flipped it open and his eyes scanned a page. "What—? Where—?"

Oscar paced back to him. "Is that it? What they are looking for?"

Max flipped through the book, then froze, reading a dog-eared page. He dropped into the kitchen chair, his breath leaving him like he'd been punched in the gut. He read some more, turning the pages quick.

"What is it?" I asked. It was an ordinary diary. The kind that you can buy at any stationery store to remind yourself of your daily appointments. Or record your secrets.

Max didn't answer.

I peered over his shoulder and read just enough to make my blood run like ice water in my veins. *Hearst . . . Thomas Ince . . . Louella Parsons.* "It's not . . . It can't be."

"It is," Max finally said. "Oscar, where did you get this?" Max held the book gingerly, as if it might burst into flames.

Oscar paced between the window and the icebox and told us. About working with Brody. About Feng, the Chinese doorman from Lester's, who was dead, then something about a priest and confession and secrets, and I was lost. I did catch the part about Alonso, Lupita's brother.

Max looked shell-shocked. "You're working with Brody?"

Oscar bypassed the question. "Am I right?" He nodded to the book in Max's hands. "Some kind of blackmail Señor Lester was using on Hearst?"

"This—" Max hefted the book—"any of it, would have got Lester that gold-plated contract." He pointed to the marked page. "But this part would put Hearst—and Louella Parsons—in a real jam."

I was catching up and Max was right. The investigation into the death of Thomas Ince seven years ago had been national news for months. Speculation still put the finger on Hearst, and Louella had been a part of it too. But nobody had ever managed to figure out the real story. If what Roy Lester wrote in his diary was what it looked like, both Hearst and Louella Parsons must be desperate—frantic—to get their hands on it.

Max rubbed a hand over his face, working it out. "So let me get this straight. Feng was working for Hearst? Hired to get the diary?"

"*Sí.* And Alonso also wanted it," Oscar answered. "He'd heard Señor Lester and his wife talk about it—arguing. Thought it was worth something and decided he'd use it against them. He took it from the bedroom during the party. You saw him upstairs, but he swears that's all he did."

"You believe him?"

Oscar nodded. "He's stupid, but not a killer, Max."

Max clenched his teeth and said some words in Spanish about Alonso. "So . . . then who? Feng?"

Oscar rubbed his face and glanced at me. "That's what I think. Hearst sends Feng up to look for it, and he tears the bedroom apart. By then, it's late and Lester goes upstairs with Minerva. He surprised Feng, who panicked . . ." he let his words trail off as we all imagined the scene: Lester carrying me in—passed out by then—putting me on his bed, finding Feng in the room.

"And Feng—what?—killed him in self-defense?" I asked. That was hard to believe, knowing how unsteady Lester had been that night.

"Maybe he was supposed to kill Lester all along," Max said. "That would take care of that pesky contract."

"But Louella . . ." I spoke slowly, as I still didn't understand. "She wanted the diary, too. She'd set me up to keep Roy busy. Why?"

"She must be the one who searched Lester's office," Oscar said.

Max snapped his fingers like it all made sense now. "Because Hearst and Louella, they weren't working together. Hearst didn't tell Louella what he was doing because he wanted the diary all to himself."

I have Mr. Hearst right in my pocket. That's what Louella had said. "And Louella didn't tell Hearst because she wanted to have something on him." I'd been such a fool. "They didn't just want to stop Lester blackmailing them." I looked at the book in Max's hands. "From what's in there, both of them wanted something on the other."

Oscar rubbed his face. "Then Alonso sent the note and they both went *loco*, *sí*? Trying to find out who had the diary. The police, the newspapers, the reward for Minerva—" He looked at me. "They must have thought you had it when they didn't find it on Feng." He paced to the window and looked out anxiously. "Nobody can know we have it or have even seen it. Or that Alonso had anything to do with it." He turned back to them. "We give it to Brody. Get rid of—"

"No," Max interrupted. "We use it. Prove Mina is innocent."

"Wait." I stopped them both, holding up my hand. I had an idea taking shape and needed a minute. "Let me think." I'd been in the wrong place at the wrong time. But now . . . now maybe I was in the right place and the right time to do the right thing. If I could figure a way.

I paced to the hallway and back. I couldn't bring Roy Lester back from the dead or turn back the clock and do everything over. I couldn't mend my heart or Max's—that was done and there was nothing for it. But I could—with some luck and a prayer—do something for Angel and Roman. The details were hazy, but it was coming together. A Plan. And if it worked, I might balance my ledger. At least some.

I stopped in front of Oscar. "This Detective Brody," I said. "Do you trust him?" We'd need his help.

Oscar paused. "I think so."

"What are you thinking?" Max asked, a worried look in his eyes. If Max would cooperate, we had half a chance.

"Max." I tapped the little book. "Everybody in Hollywood is looking for something, right? Including our friends Hearst and Louella."

He gave me the look that said he was listening.

Sink or swim, I figured, and this time it was for real. "You and I are going to give them what they're looking for." I turned to Oscar. "And they're going to give us what we need to get your brothers back home safe and sound."

***

In no time flat, we were sitting at the corner table in the Brown Derby—Oscar and Detective Brody on my left, Max on my right. Two seats empty and waiting. My hand rested on the slick tabletop, icy cold.

It was showtime.

Max cupped his hand over mine, the way he used to, and my heart gave a little jump. "You sure about this?"

I smiled with as much moxie as I could muster. "Sure I'm sure."

I wasn't sure—not by a far cry—and my nerves were stretched as tight as a rubber band. But it was the only chance. For all of us. I couldn't go back and rewrite the story no matter how much I wished I could. But maybe, with a little luck, I could change the ending.

Back at the bungalow, I'd sat down and worked it all out. I told Max what we were going to do. He looked worried, but he didn't object. Maybe because I threw in a happy ending for me, even though I had no intention of being around to see it.

"Oscar," I said, "call Brody. Tell him to meet us at the Brown Derby at noon."

Then I sent Max to Bullock's. He came back in a jiffy with just what I needed. Then, after a cigarette to steady my nerves, I made two more calls and it was done.

I cleaned up and smoothed my hair. Max had brought me a

sophisticated navy gabardine suit with ivory silk lapels and a pair of navy pumps. An ivory cloche with a petal brim hid a good portion of my face. He'd even got my favorite color lipstick and a cake of mascara.

When I was ready, he gave me the once-over and a nod. "Mina." He shut the door of his bedroom, so I figured it was something serious. "I need to ask a question, and I want a straight answer."

My heart fluttered. He couldn't know the last secret, the one I had to keep from him.

"If this all works out . . . is this really what you want?" He waved toward the city. "Films, this life . . . making it in this town?"

I had to think fast, and it was hard with the way he was watching me. I couldn't tell him what came after this—what I'd known since I sat down on that bench in the rain. I didn't want to lie to him again, but what else could I do? "Sure it is."

"You don't want to start over, somewhere else?"

With him, is what he meant. But I couldn't do that. Not now. "Being in films, it's what I've always wanted, Max. You know that." I couldn't tell if he was disappointed or relieved, and I guess it didn't matter since I didn't mean a word of it.

An hour later, Max hustled me in the back door of the Derby with Oscar trailing behind. "You don't need to be here," Max had told Oscar. But Oscar had given him a look that meant business. I had to say, I was glad he was there. He'd set things up with Brody, after all, and another person on our side of the table somehow made me feel better.

Max had a quiet talk with Norb, then tucked me close to his side and tweaked the ivory hat closer over my face. "No need for everyone to see you before the show."

When we took our seats at the back table, a stocky man with

sparse hair and a terrific mustache appeared. Oscar made the intro-ductions. The detective stuck out a huge hand. "It's a pleasure." His grip was firm. Surely, he'd read about me in the paper, yet here he was, acting as if he were glad to meet me. A rush of gratitude for this stranger who was sticking his neck out—and not only for me—had me all but choked up.

Brody took off his hat and sat down. "Miss Sinclaire, fill me in."

It was a nervy plan. Not foolproof by any means, but I didn't have any other ideas and it might save Angel and Roman. I pulled the blue book from my handbag. "This is what they've been looking for."

Detective Brody opened it up, and the pages fluttered, thin and translucent as onion skin, the writing on them bold and dense. I turned to the relevant passage and let him read, then outlined the plan. He rubbed his mustache, considering. "So we don't know for sure who killed Lester?" he confirmed. "Or Feng?"

"No," I said and took a breath. "But we know enough."

He let out a long breath. "Let's hope so, Miss Sinclaire."

I swallowed hard and put the diary back in my handbag.

The little bell over the front door jingled and I about jumped out of my skin. Louella sidled in and, right behind her, William Randolph Hearst. Louella looked like she'd swallowed a rotten egg. Hearst gave us a bored stare, as if he were attending a rather dull business meeting. I had told them to come alone, but another man—tall and blond with a face like the hero's best friend—walked in behind them.

Oscar stiffened in his chair as they approached.

The blond fellow looked at Oscar like he was gum stuck to the underside of his shoe. "What's the wetback doing here?"

In an instant, Oscar was on his feet, nose to nose with the stranger. "Call me a wetback again," he demanded.

The man's hand reached under his jacket. My heart ricocheted to my throat.

"Adams." Brody jumped up quick for a big man. "Hands where I can see them." Brody's voice was easy. "We don't want to mess up Norb's nice place here."

A cold chill went through me. That was a gun under Adams's arm. And if I didn't miss my guess, Brody had one too. My throat went as dry as sawdust and my stomach twisted like a tornado. Oscar sat down but his jaw was clenched tight and his shoulders tense.

"Take a seat," Max said smoothly to Louella and Hearst, pointing to the two empty chairs. "We weren't expecting your goon, so he'll have to stand."

Adams stood, his feet spread wide, staring bullets at Oscar. Louella and Hearst settled down across from us. Florence brought us coffee, giving me a wide-eyed look as she filled my cup.

"Let's get it over with. Where's the diary?" Hearst said in a monotone. He didn't look at me. It was as if he'd never sat on a divan while Roy Lester pawed me, never plied me with drinks or made suggestive comments.

Max's hand tightened over mine. This was my part. "All in good time, Mr. Hearst," I said, my voice as cool as a spring morning. I nodded at Brody. That was his cue.

"Mr. Hearst. I have a few questions," Brody said pleasantly.

"We're not here to answer to you," Louella said with a sniff. I could see a mist of perspiration under the brim of her tweed hat. I'd read the diary and knew why she was hot and bothered.

Brody raised bristling eyebrows at them. "Maybe you'd like to hear a story then. About two murders. It's very interesting, from what I'm told."

Hearst shrugged as if it didn't concern him in the least. Louella looked worried.

Brody tipped his head to Max.

Max pulled out his cigarette case and snapped it open. "It goes like this." He tapped out a cigarette. "Roy Lester, may he rest in peace, had a gold-plated contract that renewed just last month. Guaranteed him over two hundred thousand per film for the next five years."

Brody let out a low whistle. "I've heard the studios can't afford that kind of jingle since the crash."

"You heard right," Max said, putting the cigarette in the corner of his mouth and talking around it as he struck a match and lit his smoke. "With ticket sales in the ditch, and Roy Lester drunk or hungover on the set, you gotta ask yourself who he was black-mailing to get such a plum deal."

"Blackmail." Brody tutted. "Bad for business."

Hearst started drumming his fingers on the tabletop.

Max took a puff of the cigarette, then passed it to me with a wink. A wink! He was enjoying himself and I was about to fall apart. "The thing is," Max said to Louella, "he had something on both of you. Something big."

Louella squirmed like a worm on a hook. "Lies."

"Maybe." Max shrugged. "We'll get to that later. Right now, let's talk about Felix Young."

Hearst leaned back in his chair and crossed his arms. "Never heard of him."

"He's nothing," Max went on. "Just a bit actor at Cosmo. But maybe he does side jobs for you once in a while. Maybe he goes by the name Feng Li and poses as a butler at Lester's place during a big shindig."

"This Feng fellow—" Brody jumped in with questions for Max. "It's his job to get this thing Lester is holding over their heads? The bit he was blackmailing them with?"

"That was Hearst's plan." Max nodded, warming to his role. "But he didn't tell his gal pal, Louella, and as it turned out, she had a plan of her own because she wanted this item just as bad. She wanted it not just to stop Roy from blackmailing her, but to use it against her friend William, if the need arose." He raised his brows. "She wanted to search the office, where she figured he kept it. But she needed Roy kept busy. So Louella set it up to distract Roy Lester with one of his favorite things." He jerked his head toward me. "A redhead."

My face burned. I deserved it, but the humiliation still got to me. How confident I'd been, how sure I'd be the next star at Cosmopolitan. And here I was, just a pawn in a sordid game.

Brody was nodding along. "Meantime, Hearst sees Roy is busy at the party and sends Feng up to search the bedroom for this item. He not only wants to stop the blackmail that's putting his studio under, but it wouldn't hurt to have the goods on Louella if he ever needs 'em."

Max jumped in. "Let's just say—to keep it simple—that the item is a . . ." At this point, Max played it up, looking toward the ceiling as if pulling the word out of thin air. "A diary. A diary where maybe Roy Lester recorded some goings-on that William and Louella want to keep quiet."

Hearst tensed. Louella went pale and swallowed hard.

Max went on. "Unfortunately for Lester, poor chump, he couldn't wait to get upstairs with his prize, not knowing that his bedroom was already occupied."

I tried not to flinch. Louella's worried gaze bounced from Max to Brody like she was watching a tennis match and had money on it.

Max sounded for all the world like he was recounting the plot of a recent film. "So Lester gets to his room and surprises Feng. They struggle, and Feng gets the knife. Kills him. Or maybe killing Lester was the plan all along, seeing as how it solved the problem of Lester's contract pretty neatly."

Hearst jerked upright. "Now see here! I never told Feng to—"

"I thought you didn't know the man?" Brody cut in, his eyebrows hitched high.

"It's Victoria you should be looking at," Hearst blurted. "She's the one who set me up with Feng in the first place. If I'd known she was trying to get rid of—" Hearst shut his mouth with a snap, but he'd already said too much.

Brody looked at Max, then me. The last piece of the puzzle. Victoria had wanted a divorce and Roy Lester wasn't giving it to her. If she'd set Hearst up with Feng, then paid Feng to make sure she was conveniently widowed—that took care of her, nice and neat.

"Be that as it may . . ." Brody laid a finger along his chin and looked quizzically at Max. "I'm wondering, where was Miss Sinclaire when all this was happening?"

I swallowed, ready to speak, but Max beat me to it. "Passed out, after Lester gave her his absinthe nightcap." He put his hand over mine again. "Didn't see a thing until she woke up the next morning."

Hearst made a grunt of derision. Louella looked like she wasn't buying it. Funny how it was the one thing we knew for sure, but nobody could believe it.

Brody pulled at his mustache, but he seemed willing to go along with Max's story. "So then, Mr. Feng didn't get the diary, but did manage to knock off Roy and skedaddle."

"Yep." Max took the cigarette from my fingers and tapped the ash on his saucer. "So Hearst and Louella, here, they still have a problem. They don't have the diary. They figure maybe somebody took it. Either Feng double-crossed Hearst and he has it. . . or maybe Minerva Sinclaire does. She was the last person with Lester at the party, to be fair. Not to mention they need a patsy for the murder—a patsy that doesn't point to Hearst. So Hearst sends his goons to find Feng and sends his friends on the force after Miss Sinclaire."

I chanced a look at Oscar. Nothing about his part in this would make it into the story. That was a sure thing.

"They found Feng," Brody finished the tale, "and maybe it was an accident or maybe he threatened to rat out Hearst. Fact is, Feng's as dead as Roy Lester, and that's pretty convenient for you, Mr. Hearst."

Hearst sat, his face like stone.

"Two murders," Brody said, stroking his mustache, "and both of them pointing to William Randolph Hearst."

Hearst leaned back and crossed his arms. He didn't seem a bit worried. "Good story, Detective. You should make it into a film. But if you had any real evidence, we'd be at the Hall of Justice instead of here." His granite gaze landed on me. "You told me you'd give up the diary, Miss Sinclaire, so hand it over."

My pulse sped up.

Louella leaned forward, her voice breathless. "Minerva, dearest, you assured me I could have that diary. Are you reneging on your promise?"

My heart thrummed in my ears. The two most powerful people in Hollywood, some would say, and I was about to cross them both. Hearst was responsible for at least two murders. Louella had destroyed me with her column and radio show. Adams stared at me, a tough guy with a gun, willing to do whatever Hearst told him. I was glad I was sitting down, because my legs were so weak, they would have buckled.

I lifted a finger at Florence, who was pretending to refill coffee cups that we hadn't touched. "Please bring us a telephone," I asked her. Then to Hearst and Louella, "You'll get what you want when you've both done something for me." I was surprised at how composed I sounded. I guess I would have made a good actress after all.

"And if I refuse?" Hearst growled.

Brody smiled in a friendly way. "We'll make sure your little tell-all gets to the right people."

"It's nothing," Hearst bit out. "Just the scribblings of a drunk old man. One who's dead now, anyway."

"Maybe." Brody gave him a nod like he was conceding a point. "And maybe Marion won't mind the nitty-gritty details about Catalina Island and the showgirls." He turned to Louella. "And Docky won't mind about you and Lester and that trip to Tijuana." He didn't look friendly anymore. "But that part about Thomas Ince . . ." Brody let the name hang in the air, and I saw Louella wince and Hearst's hand close in a fist.

"They can't prove anything." Hearst looked like he could spit tacks, but he'd lost some steam, and anybody could see that he was worried.

Brody put both his huge hands flat on the table and leaned toward Hearst. "Maybe not. And maybe I can't pin Feng's or Lester's murder on you. Or even poor Ince's. But one thing I can do is raise a stink for you and your rising star, Victoria Lester, that will make your eyes water."

Hearst stared at Brody. Louella bit her lip and tried not to look at anyone. Max let out a low whistle through his teeth and looked impressed. Florence came back with a telephone and plugged the cord into the wall next to our table.

Brody picked up the receiver and held it out to Hearst. "We both know Miss Sinclaire, here, didn't kill Roy Lester. So to start, you're going to call your friend the DA right now. Clear Miss Sinclaire's name. Then put the same statement in today's edition, front page . . . above the fold."

Hearst looked for a minute like he was going to call Brody's bluff. My heart went into double time. Then he picked up the receiver and rattled off a number, waited, barked some instructions, then slammed the phone down. "It's done."

I passed Brody the diary, like we'd planned. He paged through as if perusing one of his favorite novels. He tore the dog-eared page—the one about Thomas Ince—from the book, folded it, and slipped it in his pocket.

"See here—" Hearst sputtered.

Brody raised his caterpillar brows. "Settle down. Just until you've come through. Then I'll dispose of the evidence."

"How do I know I can trust you?" Hearst demanded, looking like he could crawl across the table and grab Brody by the throat.

"You don't." Brody smiled. Then he passed the diary to me.

Hearst clenched his teeth and held out his hand for the book.

I took a deep breath. This was the part that needed nerve. "Not yet," I said, squaring my shoulders. "You owe me something more for what you did. The reward you were willing to pay for me should do nicely. One thousand dollars."

Hearst looked at me like I was talking nonsense. "It doesn't work that way, sweetheart."

I straightened my back and looked him in the eye. "Don't call me sweetheart." I let the silence talk for me. Blackmail was a dirty business and I didn't like dipping my toe into it. But this wasn't for me. Not this time.

Louella broke first. "For goodness' sake, William, give her the money so we can put this all behind us."

Hearst pulled out his checkbook from inside his jacket pocket. He scribbled on it, ripped out a check, and slid it across the table to me. I took a good look. *Miss Minerva Sinclaire. One thousand dollars.* Enough to put Papa and the farm in the clear, if that's what I had in mind. I put it in my handbag and saw my hands were shaking.

Hearst tucked his checkbook away and reached for his hat. "Are we done?"

"One more thing," Max drawled. "Louella here is going to do the biggest turnaround this city has ever seen." His voice was thick with disdain. "You were wrong about Minerva Sinclaire and you're going to tell the world. Your column and radio show are behind this girl one hundred and ten percent." Max laid one hand on the diary. "You follow, Lolly?"

"People don't forget," Louella huffed.

Max's voice hardened. "That's bushwah and you know it. Look how fast they forgot your first two husbands. And that little knock-up last year about Docky's work with the studio?"

I had to hand it to Max. He was no slouch in this game.

Louella crossed her arms. "I don't kowtow to the likes of you."

Hearst let out a frustrated breath. "She'll do it. I'll make sure she does. Now give me the book." He reached toward me.

"She said I'd get it." Louella leaned across the table.

Max smiled my way like this was a tea party and it was time for the door prize. "Who gets it, Mina?"

Now for my final scene. If this were a film—like Hearst said—this would have been the good part. As it was, I just wanted it to be over. I opened the blue book to the center and tore it in half, right down the flimsy spine. The front sheaf, I passed to Hearst. "Now William has enough to ruin you, Lolly." The rest of the pages went to Louella. "And you have plenty on him."

Louella's mouth dropped open like a fish. Hearst's face closed up in fury.

"What's a little blackmail between friends?" Brody kicked in. He patted his pocket, where the most important page was safe and sound. "Remember now, kids, keep your promises."

Hearst pocketed his half of the pages, stood without a glance at Louella, and stalked toward the door with Adams on his heels. Louella huffed, struggled out of her chair, and scurried out behind them.

"See you in the funny pages," Max said to their backs. He grabbed my hand and kissed it. "We did it." He smiled at me. "You were terrific."

I let out a long, shaky breath. Sure, we'd done it. But the hardest part of my act was yet to come.

———

Before I knew it, I was sitting in the roadster in front of my boardinghouse, saying goodbye to Max. Our last goodbye.

Problem was, he didn't know it.

I'd always thought that love was hearts and flowers and happy endings. But real love, I guess, is more than that. Real love has to be wanting what's best for the other person. Even if that isn't me. And sometimes it hurts, real love. It hurts a lot.

After the show at the Derby, Max had ushered us out the back door and straight to the bank. It was Hollywood, so the teller hardly blinked as he counted out a thousand dollars to me. I handed Oscar the wad of cash. I wouldn't think of Papa or Penny or the farm. This was for Roman and Angel. I owed them that.

Oscar looked at the bills in his hand like they were going to bite him. "You really doing this?" He looked at me like he'd never seen me before.

I nodded. It felt good, to be honest. Doing something right.

He didn't ask twice. "*Gracias*, Minerva Sinclaire."

"Go to the repatriation center," Max told him, "and wait for me." He gave him a stern look. "Do not talk to the agent without me."

Oscar didn't argue with Max, and I wondered if they had put Maria Carmen behind them. I hoped so. Max would need his family now that he'd made enemies like Hearst and Louella. And when I was gone.

Max helped me into the roadster. "You sure you want to go back to Lana's?"

After what she'd done to me, he meant. No, I didn't. But I wouldn't be there long. "Sure I'm sure. Besides, she owes me." And she'd help me out, if she knew what was good for her.

"I guess she does. But you could always come home with me," he said, cupping his hand over mine. "Julia likes you."

I didn't answer. Couldn't, really, with that lump like a boulder in my throat, and Max must have taken that as a no because he started up the engine and turned down Sunset. I laid my head back and watched him, trying to imprint everything like a film in my mind so I could watch it again later, after I left. Max's voice, talking about who owed him favors. How I'd need to lie low for a few weeks. "You'll see," he said. "This town has a short memory. We'll have you on the big screen before you can say William Randolph Hearst."

I breathed in the smell of his fancy cigarettes and leather seats, felt his hand, warm over mine. I wanted to capture the moment to play again and again in the years to come. In the lifetime I'd spend without Max.

If things had been different, maybe we could have been happy together. If I hadn't done so much wrong. But if I hadn't done what I'd done, I'd never have met Max. Would I trade away those bright moments of joy to undo all the bad?

Like I said before, I just don't know.

I knew one thing, though. The past didn't stay in the past. It crept into every now. Whispered at every turn. Tinted every dream. Papa, Penny, Maria Carmen.

We pulled up next to the boardinghouse and Max killed the engine. I readied myself to say goodbye. But Max, he had to make it harder, downright impossible.

"Mina, I want you to know something." He took my hand in his.

I didn't want to hear it, whatever it was. I knew it would hurt. And I was right.

"It wasn't nothing to me, that night." He turned my hand over and traced the line of my palm with his finger. "I was in love with you." He raised those honey-colored eyes to mine. "I still am. If it matters."

My heart fell to my feet and stayed there. It mattered. It mattered so much I had to say goodbye to him. He was a good man, Max was. He deserved so much more than me, my used body, my sordid past. A child that would tie him to me forever whether he wanted to be or not. Because one thing I knew about Max is that he would do the right thing. The noble thing. He really was the hero of this story. I knew he'd say he wasn't a hero, could hear his voice saying it. But isn't that just what a real hero would say?

It was my turn to do something noble, but when it came right down to it, I couldn't. I took the cowardly way out, God forgive me. "Give me some time," I said, forging a smile and feeling like a heel when I saw the hope flash in his face. Time was something I didn't have any more of.

Always the gentleman, he hopped out and loped around the car, opening my door and helping me out. I stood on my tiptoes—I really meant to kiss his cheek, but my lips touched the corner of his mouth, and he turned to me, enough for a real kiss. You might even call it our first real kiss, if you were sappy that way. Me, I called it a goodbye kiss.

I closed my eyes, my cheek on his, breathing his scent of tobacco and soap. I wanted more than anything to tell him I loved him back and always would. That I was doing this for him. But I couldn't.

Add that to my list of regrets.

I opened the door of my room to find Lana wearing my favorite green dress and suede pumps. She jumped like a jackrabbit when she saw me.

"Don't get your hopes up," I said. "The reward is old news."

She covered her disappointment well. "Oh, Minerva, I'm so glad you're back. You can't imagine what I've been through." She put her arms around me and kissed my cheek, her lips not quiet meeting my skin. "I've been so worried."

"Worried enough to sell a sob story to the papers." I twisted away from her. I wasn't going to let her off easy.

She stepped back and dropped the act. "You have to understand,

Minerva, how it was. The press, they were everywhere. What's a girl supposed to do?" She looked at me with doe eyes. "Really, I didn't mean any harm."

I pulled my cardboard valise from under my bed. I wouldn't need much, but I wasn't going to leave Lana with everything. I thumbed through my closet, where it looked like Lana had been making free. A pair of silk stockings with a small run, white cotton gloves. I'd leave most of the dresses, but I was taking all my shoes.

And something else. "How much did you get?" I interrupted Lana's attempts at explanation.

She closed her mouth fast.

I went to her side of the closet. The tea tin hidden behind her cigarettes held a little more than a hundred dollars. "This is all of it?"

"I had debts, Minerva." She pouted. "You know how it is."

I sure did. I took out as much as I needed. Not enough for what she'd done to me, but it was the least she could do when I was leaving her most of my wardrobe. I was packed in minutes.

I turned to her. "You can do one thing to make it up to me."

"Anything," she said as if she meant it.

I told her and she agreed. It wouldn't be hard for her. She never had liked Max all that much.

I've thought a lot about Lana since then. I could have been like her, if Max hadn't found me, so I can't judge, can I? And I hope, in my better moments, that she will find another way. In my worse moments, I hope her face sags and she gets bunions.

As the bus lumbered out of the twilit City of Angels, I curled up in my seat and closed my eyes. I'd tried so hard. I'd put in everything I had and lost it all. I'd lost my self-respect at the Rose, my hopes and dreams at Roy Lester's—my heart I lost to Max, although he didn't know it. I'd even left my mama's wedding ring behind in a dirty hockshop. I was going back home with nothing. Not even myself. I wasn't the girl Mama and Papa had loved. That girl was gone for good, and I wasn't sure who had taken her place. Maybe I should have been angry—at myself or Lana or Louella—but anger didn't come.

As the road hummed beneath me, I finally realized something. I'd told myself all along I was doing this for Papa and Penny, but that was a lie. Sure, I wanted to help them. But if I were bone-deep honest, I'd have admitted to myself long ago that I'd wanted to show them—Penny, Ruth, Alex, all of them in Odessa—that I was worth more than they thought. I'd wanted to convince myself, too. But I hadn't. I'd done wrong—sinned, I guess you'd call it—against Papa and God and everybody. I'd sinned, and now there was nothing I could do to make up for it. Nothing to balance the ledger.

I must have finally slept, because I opened my eyes to a stiff neck and the rising sun glinting off coral and gold buttes with traces of snow. A road sign welcomed me to Utah.

"Thought you'd never wake up," the man beside me said with a whine in his voice. He had a sharp face and beady eyes like one of the gophers that popped in and out of holes on the prairie.

I moved as close to the window as I could, putting a little space between his stale cigar breath and my face.

"Where's a pretty little thing like you headed?"

"Not far," I answered, pulling out my purse and compact.

"Salt Lake City for me. Got a nice place there," he said, his slippery glance running down to my ankles. He asked questions— Did I have a fella? How about family?— and I answered them as politely as I could, but all the time I was thinking of Papa. What would he say when I showed up at his door? Would he even let me in the house? And Penny. I'd be the talk of Odessa, and not in the way I'd always hoped. *The shame of it,* she'd no doubt say.

The weasel-faced man didn't let up, regaling me with stories of his childhood home—a miner's hut in Montana—and his favorite pet—a snake he kept in a jar—as we passed through flatlands of purple rock and green scrub grass surrounded by shadowed peaks splashed with white. I nodded and murmured at all the right times, I think. It was better than being alone with my thoughts.

The sun set over the Great Salt Lake, streaking the sky with magenta and turning the water to gold. The far side was a dark line of mountains. Rays of light reached up into the sky. My eyes prickled with tears for no reason at all.

When we pulled in at Salt Lake City, he turned his shiny face to me. "I didn't get your name, sweetheart. I'm Frank Malone." He stuck out his hand.

I hesitated, then took his hand. "Minnie." I said, "Minnie Zimmerman." My real name felt foreign on my tongue, but I was done with Minerva Sinclaire. Done with lies. Frank said goodbye and pulled a canvas bag from the overhead rack. I let out a breath of relief and closed my eyes.

At ten that night, I got off in Ogden. The Great Northern, the one I'd be on all the way to Odessa, didn't leave until morning. I saved the cost of a motel room—cash I didn't have—and sat dozing in the diner, nursing a cup of coffee until morning, when the cowpokes came in for their breakfasts and the bus honked. After that, I had plenty of time to think about what was behind me . . . and what lay ahead.

Across the long stretch of Wyoming, nothing broke the view but scattered low ridges and the occasional herd of antelope. Dirty snow clung in patches to colorless land, the sky low and dingy. The towns—what there were of them—had unlikely names in the drab landscape: Green River, Purple Sage, Red Desert.

My thoughts turned with the drone of the engine and rhythmic beat of the tires against the road. What was Lupita doing now? How were Roman and Angel? And Oscar? He was a decent man, a good man. Sanchia . . . well, she had tried, in her way. I wished I'd been able to say goodbye, maybe even thank them for what they did for me.

Shadows lengthened and the horizon disappeared. Darkness curled around me, cold and damp, and I wrapped my arms around my body. The headlights shone on the ribbon of road, sometimes flashing on a charcoal copse of trees or a pale house with lead-gray windows.

Shades of gray, just like in the pictures.

It isn't that easy, I wanted to tell someone. It isn't easy to tell black from white—right from wrong—when so much falls between the two. Somewhere in the dark prairie, I tried to pray. I was pretty sure God was done with me, but maybe he'd hear my prayers for others. For Oscar and Lupita. For Roman, and the hearts he'd break before he settled down. For Angel. Even for Sanchia. And as the darkness deepened, when everyone around me slept and the only light was the tiny, far-off moon, I prayed for Max. A jumbled sort of prayer to a God I hoped was listening.

I sent out a silent plea to Max, too, as if he could hear me. A wordless wish for him to be happy. To understand, somehow, that the last thing I wanted was to hurt him.

I heard his voice as the sun came up over the prairie—so close I could feel the warmth of his breath. *I was in love with you . . . I still am.* It helped, in those dark hours, to believe that Max really did love me. Honestly, if it made me feel less afraid—to picture his face, to remember his voice—I couldn't see the harm in it.

I felt about as ill as I ever had in my life—sick and achy and weak—but I guess that was only what could be expected. I hadn't eaten since somewhere in Wyoming, and my head felt strangely light and disconnected from the jerking and swaying going on around me. At the service station in Cheyenne, I caught sight of a girl with dull hair, bruised eyes, and skin the color of parchment. She could have been pretty once—beautiful, even—and I wondered what had brought her so low. I blinked and realized the girl was me, staring back from the ladies' room mirror.

I climbed back onto the bus, took my seat, and laid my face against the cool glass of the window. This was not how I'd seen myself returning to Odessa. But there was nothing for it now. I'd made my bed and all that applesauce.

The bus slowed as a town appeared on the horizon. "Pierre, South Dakota," the driver called over his shoulder.

Pierre. And after that, Odessa.

I pulled my cloth jacket more tightly around my shoulders as the bitter wind seeped through the bus window. What would I do when we pulled into Odessa, without a coat or a way home? I had made it this far. I'd walk if I had to. I had to get to Papa . . . and I knew what I had to say.

I'm sorry, Papa. For everything. I'm sorry. I don't even deserve to be called your daughter.

After that, I didn't know what would happen.

OSCAR

Oscar sat at his favorite table in the corner. Raul brought him a bottle. The voices around him were a familiar rumble, the sharp scents—tequila, dust, and hard-working men—a comfort. He should be happy. Minerva Sinclair was out of his life—it had been a blissful five days without her presence in his house or on his mind.

Five days ago, they'd celebrated Roman and Angel's return. The boys had turned their capture into a tale that grew with each retelling. What really happened was less dramatic. Max had gone with him to the repatriation office, where the money had changed hands quietly, and the boys were released without a hitch. Mamá and the boys were safe. The rent was paid for another month. And yet he was not at peace.

It was Lupita's fault. Lupita's and Max's.

There had been Max yesterday, pounding on his door and looking like he'd run all the way from the Garden of Allah. "Where is she, Oscar?"

His cousin could only mean one *she*. "Don't look at me. I'm no longer her keeper."

"Have you seen her? Heard from her?"

Oscar let out a frustrated breath as Max invited himself in. "Is she not on Western Avenue?"

"That's the thing." Max fell heavily onto a chair. "Lana, she said Mina wasn't feeling well. Wouldn't let me in to see her. Today, she told me straight: Mina's gone."

"No, no, *amigo*." Oscar shook his head. He wasn't getting involved. Not this time.

Max ignored him and took off his hat, pushing his hand through his hair. "I went to Norb at the Derby, Central Casting. Nobody's seen her. I even checked with that dog at the Rose."

Oscar jerked up. "She didn't go back there?"

"No, thank the Lord." Max clenched his fist. "But I let him know what I thought of him. He won't be breathing through his nose for a while."

Oscar had sent Max away with a wish of good luck and a twist of guilt. What was he supposed to do? The last thing he wanted was to get involved in another of Max's melodramas. And didn't he have enough of his own problems?

That night, after his brothers settled on their pallets and Mamá set to her prayers, he had gone out to his place under the tree. He lit one of his last cigarettes and breathed the smoke into the night air.

That was when Lupita disturbed his peace. They hadn't spoken of the kiss, and he didn't want to, but it was there between them each time he saw her.

Her hair was unbraided and gleamed like a dark waterfall over her shoulders. "I heard Max came to you, looking for Mina."

Mina. Still tormenting him. "She's not our problem anymore."

Lupita fixed her dark eyes on him, her brows raised.

He let out a long breath. "Say it." She would anyway, he knew.

"Max needs to find her, talk to her."

"Why?" Oscar had the sinking feeling he wasn't going to like the answer.

"It's . . ." Lupita looked over her shoulder to the house. "She made your mother swear on her rosary not to tell anyone."

"Madre swore on her rosary? Did you swear also?"

"I . . ." Lupita looked at her bare feet, then back up at him. "I promised her I wouldn't tell." She chewed on her lip. "But not on the rosary."

Then she told him.

"*Ay, caramba!*" Oscar stiffened, stalked a few steps toward the house, then back to Lupita, his temper flaring red hot. "Why can't these people wait until they are married?" If Max were here, he'd give him a good smack on the head. And Mina! Hadn't he just gotten out of a mess caused by Minerva Sinclaire being in bed with the wrong person? "How do you even know it's his child?"

"I just do." Lupita's mouth went into that line he'd seen much of lately.

"Then he can fix his own mistakes."

"Oscar Dominguez!" She stamped her foot. "When will you know that not everyone is as perfect as you?"

Oscar leaned back as if she'd slapped him. "I never said I was perfect."

She tossed her head, her dark hair falling like a curtain across her shoulder. "But you expect everyone else to be. Max. Mina. Even Maria Carmen. And when they are not, you say, 'They deserve what they get'?" She imitated his voice in a way that he didn't like at all. "You have no mercy in you, Oscar."

How could she say that? Hadn't he been the one to find the diary, to clear Mina's name? His fingers burned. He threw down the cigarette stub and ground it out with his foot. What in heaven had gotten into Lupita? "So you are saying I should tell Max?"

"Wouldn't you want to know, if you were in his place?"

"But I'd never—" Too late, he realized his mistake. Lupita threw up her hands and said a word he didn't think she knew. Then she turned on her heel and stomped back to her house.

That had been yesterday, and he still didn't know what to do. Oscar didn't pour himself the tequila. He needed to think straight.

He'd been wrong about Max. About a lot of things. Max hadn't deserted them. And he'd tried to protect Maria Carmen. Oscar's gaze drifted over the men in the *sociedades*, stopping on Raul, who'd tormented Max when they were children. Max had suffered here. Illegitimate. Half *gringo*. He wouldn't want his child to suffer the same fate—of that Oscar was certain. If Lupita was right about the baby, Minerva Sinclaire needed the father of her child. And didn't Max deserve to know? Of course, he'd want to find her, and he'd want Oscar to help him. Just when he'd thought he was done with both of them.

Max didn't deserve his help, but he had a feeling he was going to give it to him anyway. Is that what Padre meant about mercy? Did that mean he'd finally forgiven Max? Would this penance of his never end? *Dios, help me do what is right.*

Max didn't answer the door at the Garden of Allah. Oscar pushed it open and stepped in. The one-eared cat came running and twined around his legs, making noises that sounded a lot like complaints. He found Max asleep on the only furniture left in the bungalow, a narrow bed in a room that smelled like a distillery. An empty gin bottle and an overturned glass sat on the floor beside him.

Max mumbled a curse in Spanish when Oscar shook him.

Oscar cursed him back and heaved him to his feet. "You're heavier than you look, *hermano.*" He half carried him to the wash-room and dumped him into the deep bathtub, clothes and all, then turned on the cold water and left him there.

Max stumbled into the kitchen half an hour later wearing clean clothes and a hangdog scowl. The ugly cat settled on his lap and he rubbed her between her ragged ears. "At least one woman in my life hasn't left me."

Oscar had coffee percolating and was sniffing the milk bottle. He poured it down the drain and gave Max his coffee black. Max groaned.

Oscar found a can of tuna in the cupboard. "How long have you been in love with her?" he asked, working an opener around the can.

Max stared at the coffee. "You really are a pain in the backside, you know that?"

Oscar set the can on the floor. Julia jumped down to investigate, and Max shook his head as if he had expected as much.

"Well?"

Max closed his eyes and dropped his head into his hands. "My heart can't take it again."

"Take what?" Oscar felt something new, something he didn't recognize. Pity, probably. Compassion . . . maybe.

"Someone who doesn't love me back."

Oscar didn't believe that she didn't love him back. He'd seen Minerva Sinclaire look at Max. Of course, lots of women looked at Max like that, but if there was a chance for them . . . Lupita was right. Max needed to know all of it.

Oscar switched into Spanish. News like this should be heard in your mother tongue. "Brother, there's something I have to tell you."

CHAPTER 11

Odessa, South Dakota

PAPA

Ephraim propped the shovel against the Ford and leaned heavily next to it, breathing hard. The snow was wet and heavy for February. He caught sight of Penny watching him through the window and waved, mustering up a smile. She waved back, frowning.

He'd have to hurry if he wanted to make it into town on time.

The Ford took a few cranks, but the engine finally coughed and rumbled. The snow started falling in earnest—fat, wet flakes that made a plop as they hit the windshield. He steered around frozen ruts to the main road and increased his speed.

He was a mile from town when the old Ford gave up the ghost.

He hauled himself out into the cold and cranked. The cylinders didn't even fire. He cranked again. Nothing. Ephraim pulled the sodden wool mitten from his hand and fished the pocket watch out from under his overcoat. Almost four o'clock.

313

He'd have to walk home, get the tractor, and haul the Ford to the barn, where he could work on her. Or he could trudge another mile through the wet snow to the bus station and arrive soaking wet and cold, late for the eastbound bus.

There was nothing for it. He pulled his hat low and started walking.

MINA

Odessa looked different than I remembered.

Smaller, grayer. The streets were empty except for a few old-model Fords parked in front of the feed store, the sky a drab blanket over boarded-up storefronts. Had Odessa changed, or was it me?

My stomach clenched like a fist as the bus lurched to a stop. I took a shaky breath and stood. My knees wobbled as I pulled my valise from the rack over the seat, then walked to the front of the bus.

"Take care, young lady." The driver gave me a cheery wave. I tried to smile but failed, my mouth trembling. We'd been together since Ogden. I didn't even know his name but felt like I was saying goodbye to my only friend in the world. I guess that goes to show how pathetic I really was.

I stepped off the bus and my heels sank into the snow. Wind bit at my jacket and swirled around my stocking-clad legs. The door shut behind me with a thump, the engine roared, and the bus pulled away, leaving me in a cloud of gasoline fumes and doubt.

I'd left home sure of myself and what I was doing. I was coming home sure of nothing . . . with nothing. A terrific wave of despair washed over me. Despair and regret and utter weariness.

Papa had every right to turn me away.

What if he did? I had nowhere else to go. The snow soaked my hair, and cold droplets ran under my collar and down my back.

Don't be a sap, Minnie. You can't stand here in the snow all day. The walk to the farm was long, but there was nothing for it. I started along the street, my feet sinking into the cold snow.

And that's when I saw him. A long way off, so for a minute I thought it was wishful thinking. Then I heard his voice—muffled by the snow but familiar. So familiar it made my breath stop. The way he stood, the slouched hat.

He stood so still, as if he was deciding what to do. Then he broke into a run, shouting my name. I don't know if I ran or waited for him to get to me. All I know is that he was there, so quickly, pulling me into his warmth. His strong arms holding me tight. The scratch of his chin against my temple as he kissed my hair. My chest clenched; my throat closed.

I pulled back to look at him, but all my words—everything I had planned to say—wouldn't come. He was different than the memory I had held all these months. He was older—so much older than when I'd left. His face was thin, almost gaunt, the lines around his eyes etched deep.

Oh, Papa. I did this to you. It hit me so hard my knees buckled.

Papa didn't let me fall. He was still strong, and he held me up. I straightened, determined to say what I had to. What I'd come all this way to say in the cold snow. The truth. No more lies. He deserved that, at least, and then he could do what he must.

"Papa, I'm sorry." I couldn't look at him, so I looked at the buttons on his wool coat, glinting through my tears. "I did so much wrong. I hurt you and . . ." My voice cracked. "And everyone."

I took another breath, pulling air into my aching chest, forming the words I needed to say. I made myself look into his pale blue eyes. "I'm sorry. I took the money and Mama's ring . . . the things I did." Tears filled my throat, but I kept on. "I don't deserve anything from you."

He opened his mouth to speak but I kept going, the words tumbling out before I lost my nerve. "All I want . . . is a chance to make it up to you, Papa. I will, I promise." I blinked back tears. "Someday—" I choked out the last of it—"maybe you can forgive me . . . and maybe . . . you can . . ." *Love me again* is what I tried to say. But I couldn't get it out.

Papa brought my cold hands to his face, laid them against his sandpaper cheeks. "I already have, my girl."

I shook my head. He couldn't. Not really. It wasn't that easy. "But Papa, you don't know what I've done . . ." I looked into his eyes and knew that he knew. At least part of it.

"I forgive you, *Liebchen*." His pale eyes were bright with tears. "It is done."

I wanted to believe it. I really did. But when he knew the rest— the shame of it—I shivered and shook my head. I couldn't hope for that much.

He fumbled with the buttons of his overcoat and shrugged it off. Before I could protest, he'd wrapped it around me. His lingering warmth—the scents of barn and gasoline and the spicy horehound candies he liked—enveloped me.

The snow fell around us, silently landing on my eyelashes as I blinked away tears. He pulled me into his arms again, pressed a kiss to the top of my head, and held me with the fierce strength I remembered from when I was a girl. He whispered close to my ear, "I love you, my girl. Always. No matter what."

Could he? Could he know how terrible I was and still love me?

I looked at him then. Really looked. In his lined face was no anger, not even reproach. Instead, I saw compassion and the love I had always known. There were tears in his eyes, but if I wasn't wrong, I'd say they were tears of . . . joy.

Joy. Because I was back. Even this way? Even broken and ashamed?

I guess it was then I started to understand. It took me a long time to really believe it, but it was this: Papa didn't love me because I was a good daughter. Nothing I did or didn't do changed his love one jot—not even if I had been perfect like Penny. He loved me just because he was my father, and that would never change. Honestly, it was too much to even believe.

I leaned into him. The snow fell but I wasn't cold anymore. Real love. Forgiveness. I didn't deserve either—not one bit. But here he was, offering both to me just the same.

CHAPTER 12

Los Angeles

MAX

Mina shouldn't have given up on me. I'll tell her that when I find her, mark my words.

Maybe Mina thought it would be better for our baby not to have a father like me. But she was wrong. I'll tell her that, too, when I find her.

After Oscar told me about the baby—my baby—after I could breathe, think straight, after my anger at Mina first flared and I broke a few things and Julia hid under the bathtub, it was then that I gave up hope. I'd never find her. My child would be a bastard, just like me.

I ransacked my cupboard for more gin, but Oscar wasn't having that. "Come on, *hermano*. Men in our family don't give up that easy." He said a few more things—about honor and responsibility. He could be a real pain in the backside, Oscar could.

Then Oscar took me to Brody, asked how to find somebody who didn't want to be found. Brody pulled at that outrageous mustache. "You don't know her real name? Not even what state she's in?"

Alone and scared, that's what state she was in.

I paced the small office. I'd told her to keep her secrets, hadn't I? One of the precious few times she'd followed my advice.

Brody leaned over his desk. "I'd put my money on the Midwest, from the way she talked. Minnesota or maybe Illinois. Good thing is, she's not easy to forget. You might get lucky." His attempt at hopeful fell flat but he was a decent mug.

We went to La Grande Station first. I had a picture of Mina, the one she'd had taken by the hack at Central Casting, the one in all the papers. A good likeness, when she was about to laugh, her head tipped a little, that brightness in her eyes. I loved it when she looked at me like that.

The ticket sellers gave us the bum's rush. "A week ago? Do you know how many pretty girls come through here every day, fella?"

Oscar had better luck with a janitor at Central Station. "*Sí*, I saw her. The one in the papers." He described her clothes, right down to her suede shoes, and told us she'd gotten on the 72 bus, a route that went through Salt Lake to Cheyenne.

"She could be anywhere between here and Wyoming," Oscar said, looking at the map covering an entire wall. From Cheyenne, the bus spurs branched east like an octopus stretching its tentacles over these United States. "Or farther. Chicago. New York."

My heart fell clear to the floor.

Mina had given up her dream, just when she had gotten everything she wanted. Because of me. Here I'd told her I'd never give up on her, and wasn't that just what I was doing? I might have been a real heel at the beach house—I know I was—but I wasn't about to run away from my responsibility. I wasn't my father. But how could I track her across the country?

"Let's go back to Lana's," I told Oscar. She had to know something.

We must have scared the living daylights out of her—me and a big Mexican pounding on the door and pushing into her room—but I'm not sorry for it.

"Max," Lana said, backing away from Oscar. "I didn't mean no harm. Like I told you, she came and got her things. I even gave her some money when she asked for it."

That was hard to believe but I let it lie.

Lana was going on. "I figured she was going back home, wherever that is. She asked me to put you off for a few days—to tell you she was sick—until she was gone for good."

Gone for good. Whose good? Not mine. Not our child's.

Oscar grabbed my arm. "You don't think she . . . ?"

From the look on his face, I knew what he meant, and the thought made my legs turn to rubber. It was easy enough to do in this town, but . . . *Dear God, please no.*

I got right up in Lana's face so I could see if she was lying. "Did she tell you about the baby? Did she go to . . . ?" My voice broke and I couldn't go on, but Lana got the idea. Her eyes got wide and her mouth fell open. She wasn't a good enough actress to fake that kind of surprise. She hadn't known.

I sank down on the bed and put my head in my hands.

Please, I prayed. To God, the saints, whoever would listen to a man like me. *Please don't let her think that's the only way.*

"I know I wasn't the greatest friend to her, b-but . . . I did the best I could," Lana stuttered. "I swear, I didn't mean any—"

"Let's go," I said to Oscar. I didn't want to hear any more of her excuses.

"Wait," Lana called before we got out the door. "There was something . . ." She rooted around in the closet and came up with a hatbox. It looked like it had been kicked around a bit. "She left this." Lana put it in my hands like a peace offering. "Maybe it will help."

Oscar and I went outside. He lit a cigarette, and I sat down on the stoop with the box in my lap. The air was cool, and the birds chirped in the trees. I took off the lid. Letters, maybe a dozen or so, sealed and addressed to somebody named Penny Zimmerman in Mina's rounded handwriting.

I don't know where Oscar got to and I didn't care. For the next half hour, it was just me and Mina. I read every letter, then I put them in order—from the day she stepped off the bus in Los Angeles to a short note penned right before Roy Lester's party—and read them again. It was a part of her story she'd never told me. I read the last words of her last letter.

Maybe my luck is changing, Penny. Maybe this story will have a happy ending after all. Even if I don't deserve it.

You do deserve a happy ending, Mina. I'll tell you that when I find you.

"I'm going after her," I told Oscar when he drove me back to the Garden.

"You don't even know if that's where she went," he said. It was a reasonable argument, but I didn't need Oscar to tell me that.

"It's a start."

"You're going to need some cash," Oscar said when he parked in front of the bungalow. "What did your father leave you?"

I told Oscar to mind his own potatoes and set about getting my business in order.

Good old Dusty had left me plenty: Debt. Bad memories. I'd sold off everything I could over the past few years. The houses and cars went to pay his mountain of IOUs. I'd been living off the sale of his furniture for the past few months, and that was precious little. Norb at the Derby and Al at the Montmartre—solid friends of Dusty's even after he turned ugly—never let me pay for a meal. I'd sold the beach house, something I'd waited to do until I didn't have a choice, and paid off the rest of what Dusty owed. I'd cleared a few hundred dollars but that dwindled fast. I was close to broke, except for the roadster . . . and I'd need that to find Mina.

I packed up my few belongings at the bungalow and said goodbye to the neighbors. Then I made the rounds, saying goodbye to Norb and Al, some of the rest of the people who had helped me out over the years. When I'd tied up all my loose ends, I went to the *colonia*.

Tía Sanchia didn't speak of the baby or of Mina. She squeezed me tight and whispered, "May the Lord find you confessed," instead of goodbye. Which was about what I expected from her. Lupita hugged me tight and told me to give Mina her best. Roman and Angel were next, and as I shook their hands, I knew Oscar would take good care of them.

Oscar. We hadn't been brothers for a long time, but it was still hard to say goodbye. He stuck out his hand, but that wouldn't do. I pulled him into an embrace. If I didn't know him better, I'd have said there were tears in his eyes when he turned away. When he wasn't looking, I shoved a few twenties in the money tin on the kitchen shelf. It was the least I could do, after all he'd done for me. Then I took Julia from my back seat and put her in Oscar's arms.

He's such a pushover, I know he'll take good care of her. It still makes me smile to think about his expression.

I said goodbye to the *colonia,* where I'd had a mother who loved me—and a family, too—but had still been an outsider. Goodbye to Hollywood, where I'd tried to be a son to a man who didn't want me, where good people—and a woman I once loved—destroyed themselves in pursuit of fame and money. Goodbye to the bright, hard sun that left you feeling cold and alone.

I made one more stop before I put Los Angeles and the setting sun in my rearview mirror. Just a little something I'd give Mina when—if—I found her.

That was when I still had hope on my side.

OSCAR

Oscar poured a stream of milk into a chipped saucer on the floor. Just like Max to leave him with another mouth to feed. Oscar bent to scratch the ugly animal between her tattered ears, then ran his hand over her arched back as her purring ratcheted up a notch.

"I thought you said we weren't feeding it."

Oscar straightened quick to see Roman lounging against the kitchen wall with a smirk. Oscar put the milk back in the icebox, but he didn't snap back at his brother like usual. Since Roman's release from the repatriation facility, they'd danced around each other, not fighting but not talking either. Roman's face had healed, but every time Oscar thought about that night, his chest tightened with regret.

Of course, he'd gone to confession, and this time Padre Ramirez gave him just an Ave María for his penance. "You're not telling me to go to Roman, to beg forgiveness?" he'd asked before absolution, just to make sure.

"I think you know what God wants from you," Padre had said, and Oscar did. But it was harder than he thought, and almost a week had passed.

Now Roman sat at the table, eating a leftover tortilla filled with beans, that cat in his lap licking up the crumbs he offered.

"Roman," Oscar said. His mouth was a little dry, so he took a sip of his coffee. "About that night." He studied the gouges in the old table.

Roman talked around the food in his mouth. "I deserved it."

"But I want to say—"

"I know. You don't have to."

"Roman!" He raised his voice, his temper flaring. "Shut up and let me say I'm sorry."

The cat gave Oscar a disappointed look.

"You said it, then." Roman's voice was soft.

Oscar studied the scuffs on the linoleum floor. He did not deserve to be forgiven. "I don't expect you—" he swallowed hard—"to forgive me for it. But maybe in time, you can find it in your heart—"

"I forgive you, Oscar. Don't worry about it."

Oscar looked up quick. Roman took another bite of his tortilla and chewed. His usual smirk was gone. His eyes on Oscar were without grudge. "Just like that?" Forgiveness wasn't that easy. He should know.

"*Sí.*" Roman brushed the cat gently from his lap and stood. "Let's face it, Brother. You and me? We're going to be at each other's throats until I get out from under your roof. We'll be lucky if we don't kill each other. But we're brothers. We forgive each other, right?"

Oscar gave a nod, his throat oddly tight. He stood and pulled Roman into a hard embrace. "I can put up with you a while longer."

His voice came out gruff, and he grabbed his hat and left out the back quick, before Roman said something smart.

Forgiveness. It had been easy for Roman, the work of a moment.

He strode down the street toward the *sociedades*. He thought about Max, heading to God knows where in search of that woman, and no anger came over him. No resentment. It was gone. He wished only good for Max—happiness in whatever way he found it. Somewhere along the way—maybe because of Minerva Sinclair, or Mamá and Lupita—he had forgiven Max.

Gracias, Señor. What a relief it was.

He reached the *sociedades* feeling ten pounds lighter and with almost a smile on his face. Perhaps today's *festivales* wouldn't be as terrible as he had thought. The mood in the *colonia* was not what it had been in past years, what with so many men taken in the raid on La Placita and more raids likely to come. Yet it was the one day in the year that work and the struggle against poverty were put aside to celebrate their own people with parades, music, and the food of their homeland—that warm and beautiful place that most of them had never seen except in the memories of their parents. He took his place along the street lined with his neighbors to watch the parade.

First came the *caballeros*, ten men in *charro* suits and *sombreros* riding splendid horses. Then, a strolling *mariachi* band playing guitars, trumpets, and violins. Next came the floats. The floats had been crafted by the women of the neighborhood, and each one was a spectacle of spring blossoms and rippling banners in red, white, and green sponsored by the neighborhood businesses—the *farmacia*, the *sociedades*, and even the Hotel Estelar.

The final float was preceded by a roar of applause and murmurs of expectation. It was the honorific society, from whom would be chosen the queen of the *festivales*. Oscar had little interest in the women who vied for the coveted prize, but when the float stopped in front of the master of ceremonies, he blinked, shook his head, and blinked again.

Ay, caramba. Was that Lupita?

The master of ceremonies was speaking into a megaphone, but his flowery speech did not penetrate Oscar's thoughts. Lupita did not look like Lupita, and yet she did. She stood upon the float—no—she reigned upon the float. She wore a bright red skirt with some kind of ruffling, with a belt and a full lacy top, and her hair gleamed like a black waterfall on her shoulders. She looked— she didn't look like the girl he knew.

". . . the young woman who most exemplifies the qualities of the Mexican maiden: honor, beauty, and obedience." The announcer's words began to make sense in his addled mind. "Miss Guadeloupe Francesca Martina Garcia!"

The crowded erupted in applause. The *mariachi* band struck up a new tune, and Lupita smiled sweetly—the smile he knew so well. Of course she deserved to be crowned queen. Of course she was honorable, beautiful, and obedient—he could have told them that. So why was he suddenly filled with a desire to whisk her off the float and wrap her in a blanket? It was ridiculous. He forced himself to join in the clapping and told himself he was happy for Lupita. Of course he was.

The float continued on and he stood straight, craning to catch her eye but to no avail, and as the crowd surged onto the street to follow behind, his heart did a curious dip and his mood dimmed as if the sun had unexpectedly stopped shining.

He didn't see Lupita again until evening, at the street dance.

"I thought you weren't coming tonight," Angel said. He held

a tall glass of watermelon drink in one hand and a churro in the other.

"Somebody has to keep an eye on Roman," Oscar grumbled. The boy ran with the rowdy crowd and probably snuck some tequila into their punch. Angel didn't look like he believed him. Oscar stood at a good vantage point, where he could see Raul make a fool of himself dancing with a woman old enough to be his mother. And there was Lupita, surrounded by men old enough to know better and boys not old enough to shave.

"Ask her to dance," Angel said gently.

Oscar scowled. He'd been watching long enough to know she had danced every dance and hardly had time to catch her breath between songs. She certainly didn't have time for him. Angel patted his arm—*santo cielo,* he didn't need comforting—then went off to pay his respects to Mamá and the church women, who sat in straight-backed chairs overseeing the dancing.

Oscar went home, even before his mother, and lay down in his bed. The house was silent except for the muted strains of the trumpets and guitar coming from the street. He wouldn't worry about Roman, or about Lupita being plied with compliments. Why should he care? And yet sleep was a long time coming.

Oscar stood beneath the oak tree two nights later, congratulating himself for successfully avoiding Lupita since the festival. He'd spent his time looking for work, as he should. Brody had given him some leads on jobs—one in Santa Monica looked hopeful, driving one of the bigwigs from the cannery around. He'd go there tomorrow and hope they didn't mind that he was a Mexican.

He was glad Lupita didn't come outside to see him in the

evenings anymore. It seemed like every man in the *colonia* between twelve and fifty had knocked on Lupita's door in the past two days. She'd received so many bouquets of lilies and roses that she'd taken to giving them to Mamá, and now his house smelled like a cheap perfume factory.

But when he saw the crack of light spill between their houses and a slight form coming across the grass toward him, he straightened up and his heart jumped in a strange and unwelcome way. Then it plummeted straight to his knees. "What in the name of heaven did you do?"

Her hair—her beautiful long hair—was cut short, just below the line of her chin. It shone like a dark cap in smooth waves. How could she?

"You don't like it?" She didn't seem surprised or at all worried about his reaction.

"I . . ." The cut framed her face and made her eyes even more luminous, the curve of her face more pronounced. He most certainly did not like it. And the dress. It was something Minerva Sinclaire might have worn. Robin's-egg blue with short, fluttery sleeves that showed Lupita's smooth arms. A cut that was reasonably modest, he had to admit, but still revealed her curves more than he thought was appropriate. "Why would you do such a thing?"

She didn't answer the question. "I saw you at the parade."

So she had seen him. Somehow that didn't make him feel better. His brain didn't seem able to form a response. "The parade, *sí*. Congratulations, you were very . . ." He didn't know what he had in mind, but the curve of her lips made him forget whatever it had been.

She laughed, probably at how tongue-tied he suddenly was with her. "Very what?" she asked.

"Pretty." It wasn't what he wanted to say. Womanly? That sounded wrong. "And at the dance. You had . . . many admirers." Why had he said that? It sounded like he'd been watching her. Which he had. He stepped back and stuck his hands in his pockets.

Lupita smiled even wider. "I do not care about those boys. They are children."

He heart felt like lead in his chest. It was exactly what he feared. With the prize money from the *festivales*, the new clothes and bobbed hair. "You will leave us."

Lupita frowned. "Leave you?"

He tried to work up anger but all he felt was fear. Fear, and an ache somewhere close to his beating heart. "Why else all this?" He motioned to take in the dress and hair. "You want to be an *americana* like Minerva Sinclaire, like . . ." Like her sister, Maria Carmen. "You will run away, and we will never see you again." He could hear panic in his own voice and was past caring.

"Oh, Oscar." Lupita stepped closer to him, shaking her head. "You really are a stupid man."

Then she stretched up on her toes and kissed him.

Lupita kissed him. And it wasn't like the other kiss, the one that had been meant for Maria Carmen. This was sweet and short and wise. Just like Lupita. He didn't have time to react. Didn't know what he would have done had he been able to think. His hands stayed in his pockets, his eyes open. He didn't even kiss her back.

His mind spun like a tornado. Was this goodbye? He couldn't bear it if it was. Why hadn't he seen before that Lupita was leaving them? Why had he not known what it would do to his heart? Could he stop her, or was it too late?

She pulled back and looked into his face. Waiting.

Oscar didn't move, but he also didn't draw back. He had no inkling what to say.

But Lupita did. Almost as if she'd planned this whole scene. "Now do you understand?"

He shook his head, his mind still fuzzy from the kiss. "I don't think so."

She smiled like he was a child trying to understand a lesson in school. "I don't want to be *americana* or any other thing that I am not. Yes, I cut my hair and I have a new dress. I am a woman and we do those things. But, Oscar—" here she looked up at him until his eyes met hers—"I am not my sister."

No. She was surely not. She was something else. "If you don't want to be *americana*, then what do you want?"

"I want to live here, with you. To make a good life here but not to forget where we come from and who we are."

"With me?" He understood that part. That she wanted to stay with him. Here, in the *colonia*. "Even if I am a stupid man, as you say?" He meant it. He was far from perfect. She knew that—she'd known it before he did.

She let out a small laugh. "Yes, with you. You have a good heart, Oscar." She placed her hand on his chest where that heart was beating like a drum. "And that is why I love you. That, and you aren't as stupid as you sometimes act."

She loved him? Lupita really loved him? Even if he hadn't understood until now what she meant to him? He unhooked his hands from his pockets and raised one to her hair, smoothing the short waves. It was all he could think of to do. He felt a smile breaking out and couldn't stop it.

She smiled back and looped her hands around his neck. "Now.

You will tell me that you love me—if that is true, and I think it is. And then you will kiss me and ask me to marry you."

She was right, of course. And so he did.

MAX

All through California, I talked to Mina as if she were right beside me, her hair blowing, giving me the sidelong look like she did, that mysterious half smile. I told her she was stubborn, misguided, mistaken.

For once, she didn't talk back.

The road beneath my tires took up the rhythm. *Gone for good. Gone for good.*

"You should have trusted me," I whispered to the photo on the seat next to me. She looked back at me, and this time I saw reproach in her gaze. She had trusted me, that night at the beach. And what had I done?

My hands tightened on the steering wheel until my knuckles were white.

I'd taken advantage of her.

I hadn't meant to make love to her. I'd tried not to think of her that way since the day I met her. Sure, I'd been lonely, but I could have called any of the girls I knew—those pretty birds had seemed like what I wanted until I met Mina. I should have kept my distance.

Should have. Words that came with a mental kick in the backside.

With Mina, keeping my distance was impossible. It wasn't the aquamarine eyes, that laughing mouth, or her smarts. Don't get me wrong. Those were all terrific. But it was something else. Underneath that beauty, that moxie and quick wit, there was another woman. I saw her in flashes, like when we waltzed and her face went all soft, like she was in another world. Or when she pretended she wasn't crying at sappy films, when she laughed until she snorted at Chaplin.

And the humming. She didn't even know she did it.

I had seen just enough of that woman to know I wanted more. Who was she, really? And what was she hiding? She was hiding a past. Just like the rest of us.

The thing was, I wrote the book on hiding your past, on trying to change who you are and how people see you. I had kept the boy from the *colonia* under wraps since the day Dusty Clark took me. Until that day at the beach, when I'd shown Mina a part of myself I hadn't shown anyone. The boy who never fit in. The bastard kid who'd lost his mother and loved a father who couldn't love him back.

I'd wanted Mina to love me, that night at the beach house. I won't deny it. But I'd gone about it all wrong and before I knew it, we were in too far. And then . . . finding out she felt she owed me, that she was paying a debt. That hurt. It still hurt. I'll tell her that, too.

The sun went down over the desert in a kaleidoscope of pink and orange, and the wind cooled my fevered thoughts. I'd let her down, and not only at the beach house. The more I fell in love with her, the less I wanted to share her. She'd been right when she'd accused me that night at Lester's. By then, I didn't want her to make it in Hollywood. It was too tough, too dangerous. Every audition brought her closer to what she wanted and took her further away from me. I couldn't lose her to that town like I'd lost Maria Carmen.

I couldn't pretend it didn't bother me, what she'd done at the

Rose. But I knew a thing or two about how women were treated and what they had to do to survive. And I knew plenty about regret. But I hoped I knew something else about Mina. Mina wouldn't harm our baby. She might have done a lot of things, but she wouldn't do that. I knew that, at least, didn't I?

Darkness fell, but I kept driving. *Please, God, let me be right about that.*

My eyes were heavy as the moon rose and I told her how I really felt. "I'll take care of you, Mina," I said to the black sky as I crossed into Nevada. "I'll take care of both of you." I'd find work. I'd make her happy. And maybe, if I was luckier than I deserved to be, I could make her love me. "Just give me a chance."

The rhythm of the road still beat in my head. *Gone for good. Gone for good.*

Please, Mina. Please, not gone for good.

The roadster broke down just outside Salt Lake City.

With the help of a couple of mugs, I pushed the auto to a repair shop and waited while a mechanic as old as Methuselah checked out the engine.

"You burned up the belts, and your gearbox is shot," he said, wiping his gnarled hands on a rag covered in oil.

"What'll it take to fix it?" I had a couple of twenties and some change in my pocket. I'd been hoping it was enough to get me to South Dakota.

He rubbed his whiskery chin. "Pretty fancy auto, this is. Have to order the parts from the catalogue." He spit into a bucket in the corner. "Two weeks to come in, give or take. Not sure, but you're looking at fifty dollars up front, then the rest when you pick it up."

Fifty dollars. Two weeks.

I sat at a diner in Ogden, a thousand miles away from Mina and no way forward that I could see. I took out Mina's picture, creased and curling at the edges, and laid it beside the cold cup of coffee I wished was tequila, but I'd given that up. It hadn't done any good and had done plenty of harm.

An old-timer on the stool next to me leaned over. "That your girl?"

I wished I could say yes. "Maybe. If I can find her." Then I told him about Mina and South Dakota. Not about the baby, no sir. Just about the auto sitting in the repair shop across the road. I'd given the mechanic most of the money I had and promised I'd be back with the rest. That left me with enough change in my pocket to pay for my coffee and leave a tip for the waitress.

The old cowboy eyed my pinstripe suit and two-toned wing-tips. "You know how to work?"

I had a spark of hope and sat up straighter. "Yes, sir."

"Humph." He didn't look like he believed me. "Can you ride?"

I nodded, figuring he meant a horse. I was Dusty Clark's son, after all.

He pursed his lips. "It's hard work. Pay's a dollar a day, three squares, and a bunk."

I stuck out my hand. It was a better offer than I'd get anywhere else. "I won't let you down."

They called him Ostringer. I never got his first name and maybe he didn't have one. He was a foreman on a big spread about ten miles out of Ogden. And when he said hard work, he wasn't kidding around. He gave me an old pair of dungarees, some worn boots, and a place in the bunkhouse with twenty other cowhands.

The other hands called me Clark. Nobody knew my father was

a film star and my mother wasn't his wife. I don't think they would have cared anyway. They knew I was just passing through, on my way to find a pretty girl. They gave me a hard time about that, but on the whole, they worked hard and took a man for what he was worth and nothing more.

Every day, I got up with the sun and did whatever Ostringer told me. Repaired fences and chopped firewood, mostly. Spent a few days patching a leak in the bunkhouse and a week hunting a pack of wolves that had been attacking the herd. I was glad for the riding I'd done with Dusty, and that he'd taught me how to handle a rifle. Every night I fell into bed and my last thought—before I fell into a dead sleep—was of Mina.

March turned into April, the grass greened, and by the time I saved up enough lettuce to get the roadster back and fill it with gas, it was almost May. I thanked Ostringer for taking me on; he said, "Don't mention it."

I got back on the road and my doubts hit hard. What if Mina hadn't gone to this place in South Dakota? And that wasn't even the thought that made my gut churn the most as I pulled back on the road stretching east. What if I found her, and she didn't want me?

MINA

That day I came back to Odessa—it seems like a long time ago now—well, it wasn't such a sweet reunion with Penny.

Papa, cold and wet with me wearing his coat, had telephoned Penny from the barber shop. She showed up on the tractor, covered with snow and hopping mad.

When we got home, Papa had brought me into the house and stoked the fire.

And then—all at once before I lost my nerve—I told them

about the baby. Papa didn't say much, just took my hand and held it tight. *I love you, my girl. Always. No matter what.* I guess he really meant it.

As for Penny, well, I don't blame my sister for what she said. She'd seen the newspapers, just like everybody else. She called me a thief, a tramp, and plenty worse than that. She told me I should get what I deserved. She was right about it all. I'm not proud of what I did, and I sure as sugar don't expect her to forgive me. She's barely spoken to me since. And why should I expect more?

I don't deserve it, do I?

If I could, I'd tell Penny how sorry I was, how I heard her voice in my head with every mistake I made—wrote her all those letters but didn't send them because I knew what she'd say back. She was my conscience, I guess you'd call it. But she didn't want to hear it.

"I can live out in the barn," I told Papa. "Where the hired hands were. I'll fix it up. That way, Penny won't have to . . ." *See me*, I was going to say, but Papa shook his head.

"You are my daughter, just as she is, *Liebchen*. You'll sleep in your old room."

"But when the baby comes—"

That's when Penny turned a queer shade of purple and ran up the stairs to her room.

"Don't worry. She'll come around," Papa said, but I wasn't so sure. There's nothing like a hopping-mad German woman for giving the cold shoulder, and I felt the freeze coming off Penny even as the snow melted and the spring sun warmed the fields. Her silent anger reminded me each day that I hadn't paid my debt to my father, that I didn't deserve his mercy.

I was thankful the wedding had her in such a tizzy. Her dress. The house. The luncheon and cake. I tried to help, but everything

I did was wrong. That much hadn't changed. Robert Thomas was clearly gaga over my sister, even when she carped about all she had to do with no help at all, giving me the side-eye. I caught him giving me a sympathetic glance after one of Penny's stinging remarks had me brushing away tears.

To give Penny her due, I think the part that had her in such a lather was leaving Papa. She and Robert Thomas had one whirlwind romance, from what I'd heard. And that wasn't like the Penny I knew. And then, when Robert got the job in Minneapolis, I thought for a few days that she was going to call the whole thing off.

"How will you take care of Papa and the house?" she fussed at me, giving my middle—now starting to show—a glare. "In your condition?"

In my condition. I'd heard that phrase enough times to sink a sailboat.

Overnight, it seemed my dresses didn't fit anymore. They stretched tight over my belly, the bump as plain as a cat under a blanket. I didn't ask for new clothes. I couldn't, with how little we had in the way of money. I took to remaking the dresses I had in my closet, but letting out seams would hardly make do much longer.

Then, a few days before the wedding, Papa came home with a package wrapped in brown paper. "I hope it fits, *Liebchen.*"

I unwrapped it to find a soft green dress, midcalf, a wraparound style to accommodate my growing belly. Bright embroidery on the square neckline and belt matched the trim on the deep hem. "It's beautiful, Papa." I felt tears prick my eyes—not unusual these days. I'd given up fighting the waterworks.

He shoved his hands in his pockets with a smile like Christmas morning. "Go on, there's more."

Under the dress was a carefully wrapped hat—last year's style, but I didn't mind—and a matching swing jacket in lightweight wool.

I leaned over and kissed Papa's cheek, scratchy with graying stubble. "Thank you." I didn't deserve this, any of it.

Penny picked up the packaging, her lips thinning in that way of hers. "Where did you get this? Not from town?"

"*Ja*, at the dress shop. Frau Fischer picked it out. Helpful as anything." Papa gathered up the strewn brown paper and tissue.

Penny's face had gone white. "Mrs. Fischer? So the whole town—they know about her . . . condition?" She looked at me as if I were a toad she'd found sitting in the butter. A pregnant toad. "Papa! At least you could have waited until after the wedding."

"*Liebchen.*" Papa took Penny's hand. "That's why she needs it. For the wedding."

Penny made a choking sound and stomped out of the room.

My throat had a lump as big as a goose egg, but I didn't blame her a bit. Of course, Penny wanted to be the star of her big day—instead of her pregnant, unmarried sister. The shame of the family. I gathered up my new things and put them away, wishing I could make it up to Penny, but knowing I never could.

I still thought of it like that—like I had a lot to make up for. Like I didn't deserve Papa's love or to live in the house with him. But I was learning to believe him when he said he loved me, and that's all that mattered. I got up each morning trying to remember that. Some days I did better than others.

The morning of the wedding, I wore my new dress for the first time. I admit, it was a dream to have a pretty frock, and the wrap-around skirt was far more comfortable than my remade dresses. But Penny was like an angry bee buzzing through the house ready to sting anyone in her path. Robert's mother had come early to help her dress and do her hair and makeup, and Penny shooed me away like I was an embarrassment. Of course, I was. Maybe I'd feel the same way if I were in her sensible ivory lace-ups, but it still hurt that she didn't want my help. I escaped outside and gathered all the lilacs I could find, Mama's favorite. Maybe they'd make her feel like Mama was watching over her today.

An hour before the ceremony, I'd arranged them in vases and the house smelled like heaven. I was moving the dining chairs into the parlor when Penny simply went loony.

"Minnie, stop this instant!"

I looked at the setup. It seemed right to me. We'd have about twenty people, and with the hall bench and the kitchen chairs, we should be able to seat them all. But she stood, red-faced, in her bridal dress, her hands clenched at her sides.

"What's wrong with it?" I'd do whatever she asked, even if it meant arranging the chairs upside down. It was her big day, after all.

"Everything is wrong," she said through clenched teeth.

Papa appeared in the doorway. *"Liebchen—"*

"No, Papa." Penny turned on him. "I mean it. All this time I've been here, not once did I ask anything of you. Just this day that I want perfect. But she—" she lifted a trembling hand at me—"she takes your money, uses it for God knows what, and then comes back like . . . *that*." She huffed. "She took Mama's ring. The one I should have today. She . . . ruined . . . everything."

Papa didn't say anything, but he put his hand on my shoulder and squeezed.

"I'm sorry" was all I could say. I slipped through the kitchen and up the stairs. I'd just stay up there until it was all over. It was the least I could do for her. Penny was hurt, I told myself. And she had a right to be. She'd done everything she was supposed to do, been a good daughter—no, a perfect daughter. She deserved a wedding day without me.

Her going-away clothes were laid out on her bed. I found a run in one of her stockings and mended it for her, then checked her valise one more time to make sure she had everything she needed for the short honeymoon trip to St. Paul—a honeymoon that included looking for a place to rent when Robert's new job started. The two of them were nothing if not practical.

I could hear Maura Fischer, who'd offered to play the wedding march on our old piano, begin to warm up with a few discordant notes. The minister's voice floated up the stairs. Robert answered with a nervous laugh.

I sat on the corner of Penny's bed and thought about what she had said. I'd done everything wrong, made so many mistakes. Hurt so many people I loved. Papa, Penny, Max.

Did I wish I could take it all back?

Yes, part of me wished I'd never left Odessa. But the thing is, if I hadn't run to that far-off land, if I hadn't ended up lost and broken, if I hadn't done everything wrong and come back with nothing . . . would I know about real love? About mercy and forgiveness? The thing I learned—after everything that happened—was you don't deserve mercy. And you can't earn forgiveness. If you deserved it—if you earned it—well, I guess then they'd call it something else.

It doesn't make a lot of sense, but all that bad I did? The side of the ledger that weighs against me? I can't change it one jot. But it can change me. And even those horrid things I did can work good in my life if I let them. If I accept Papa's forgiveness and let that forgiveness and love change me into the daughter I want to be—the daughter Papa had known was there all along.

It's a tall order, but I'm trying. I'm really trying.

The strains of the wedding march sounded downstairs. It was starting, and the wedding spotlight would be on Penny. I hoped it would be as beautiful as she ever imagined. I smoothed Penny's chenille bedspread, following the pile and running my fingers in the ridges as if following a map across the country. The piano stopped, midchord. I heard the snap of heels on the stairs and the door behind me clicked open.

"What are you doing?" I asked as Penny came in and closed the door behind her. Did she have more to say to me? She sat down on the bed, right on top of her carefully pressed traveling suit, and burst into tears. She leaned into me, sobbing into my shoulder. She was ruining her makeup. She blubbered something about lilacs and Mama and how she couldn't walk down the aisle feeling like she did. I wasn't sure what to do, but I put my arms around her.

A long minute later, she gave a shuddering breath. "I tried," she said, her voice muffled in my shoulder. "I really tried, Minnie. I said to myself, *I forgive her.*" She pulled away but didn't look at me. "I've said to God, *I forgive her.* Then I see Papa. And I think of those days, after you left, and how he—" She shook her head like she couldn't get the words out.

My own throat closed. I knew what I'd done to Papa.

"And now, he's so . . ." Penny pressed her lips together.

Happy. Every day he smiled at the breakfast table. Every day he kissed the top of my head on his way to the barn and said, "I'm glad you're home, *Liebchen.*" I hadn't thought how that must hurt her. To see how much my coming back meant to him when she'd been here all the time.

She leaned back, picking up a corner of the bedspread and wiping her eyes. "I *want* to forgive you." She hiccupped. "Is that enough?"

I felt my own tears welling up and spilling over. "It is for me."

She held on to me tight, both of us snuffling like old hound dogs. A knock on the door broke us apart, and Robert's low voice was urgent and worried. "Penny, you in there?"

Penny glanced at the door, rubbed her red nose, and smiled. "Let him wait."

That was the sister I knew. I called out to him that she'd be down in a minute, then grabbed the powder and comb from her bureau. "Let's get you fixed up."

The wedding was beautiful. The minister said all the right words; Maura hit only a few wrong notes. I stood beside Penny, and if tongues wagged, then they could keep on wagging all the way back to town.

Now, I stood in the kitchen, making sure the cake was perfect, the chicken ready. Not exactly hiding, just staying out of the way. I didn't want to push things with Penny. We had a ways to go, and I wasn't so daft I didn't know it. It would take time—work—to get us back to what we had been.

Forgiveness is a tricky business. Maybe for some it's simple, like with Papa. And like Papa says it is with God. Papa says God never stopped listening to me and never stopped loving me, even when I was at my worst. All that time, he was just waiting for me to come back to him and tell him how sorry I was. Waiting to forgive me. But maybe for others, it's not so easy. Some people have to work on forgiveness for a long time, like Penny. As for me, I have to accept it and try to forgive myself at the same time. And maybe that will be the hardest part of all.

MAX

The roadster was running on fumes when I pulled into a lonely filling station south of nowhere. Dust covered the shiny paint job, and the tires were worn as smooth as Stan Laurel's forehead. I pushed open the door and stretched as I got out, bone-weary from two long days driving across Wyoming and Nebraska, with a six-hour stop to sleep on the side of the road when I crossed the border into South Dakota. The kid who ambled out of the tiny shack next to the pumps gave my wrinkled suit and coffee-stained shirt a long look.

"Fill her up." I handed him a dollar that was close to my last. "Where am I?" I spread a map on the hot hood. It was torn and falling apart from too many struggles against its folds.

He raised his brows and set his dirty finger down close to a place called Pierre.

"Town around here called Odessa?"

He twitched the finger. "Sure. 'Bout here. Not much to speak of."

I didn't need much. Just one redhead and a second chance. Then I was back on the road, the one-pump station disappearing behind me, the road stretching out before me, bright and empty. I was used to being lonely—had been since that day I left the *colonia* with Dusty Clark. But that was nothing like the loneliness since Mina left.

I'd had a lot of time to think. Days and weeks with nothing but my regrets to keep me company. I'd done plenty I wasn't proud of, those years with Dusty. Parties and drinking and pills. And women. I'd learned fast none of it led to any good. By the time I turned twenty, I'd seen too much ruin. Men ruined by drink, women ruined by men. Booze and cocaine turning good people into bad. After Maria Carmen, I'd vowed not to be like my father. I put it all behind me—the women, the pills, the hard drinking. Well, mostly. But I tried to do right. Then that night at the beach with Mina, I was the worst kind of heel.

If she didn't want me, I could understand it. Heck, I wouldn't blame her one bit. But I'd ask her—beg her, even—to give me a chance. The least she could do was listen to what I had to offer. Which—as I really thought about it and my palms turned clammy on the steering wheel—wasn't a whole lot of anything.

The town was so small that if I'd blinked, I would have missed it. I tried to work up some hope that this was where she'd gone. But it looked to me like Odessa wasn't the kind of town people came back to. It was the kind of town people left. A shabby diner with no cars parked outside. Beside it, the Odessa Picture House was boarded up, a *For Sale* sign flapping crookedly in the arched doorway. I parked in front of the bus station—just a tiny storefront with a single bench outside—and left the motor running.

There was nobody sitting behind the glass window. A hand-written note said *Closed.*

I went back out to the empty street, unsure where to go next. The diner? Or maybe the dress shop with a frock at least five years out of date in the window? A dirty-faced kid came around the corner on a creaking bicycle. He stopped and pulled a stack of newspapers out of his basket, throwing them outside the door of the bus station. "You looking to buy a ticket, you'll have to wait. Gus'll be back by two o'clock."

"Maybe you can help me." It was worth a shot.

The kid eyed me, and I didn't blame him. I hadn't had a haircut since before the ranch, and I could have used a shave. Not to mention a bath. I probably looked like a bum just coming off a bender.

I pulled Mina's photo from my pocket. "I'm looking for someone who lives around here. Goes by Minnie, I think."

He leaned down to examine it, then glanced up at me in surprise. "Well, sure she does, mister. That's Minnie Zimmerman."

345

He handed the photo back and swung a leg over his bicycle as if he was going to start pedaling.

I stepped in front of him, my heart jumping. "Where is she?" I said, loud enough to make his eyebrows go up to his widow's peak. "I mean, do you know where I can find her?"

"Sure I do, mister," the boy answered, as if I were daft.

I took a breath. "Where?"

"Oh. You head out of town here, then take a left 'bout two miles up. You'll see the mailbox." He raised his voice as I headed toward the roadster. "Better hurry," he yelled out. "Wedding's about to start."

My heart stopped, then thudded into high gear.

Did he say *wedding*?

I clicked at the starter and the engine caught. No, no, no. Could Mina be marrying some farmer? Someone to take care of her and the baby? Maybe some kid who'd waited for her to come back? My thoughts jumbled, my tires squealed, and gravel flew.

Everything I'd said to her on this never-ending road, all my arguments and explanations, my lectures and pleas, dissolved like the dust behind me. My mind was a blank, except for a prayer: *Please, let me not be too late.*

Was it wrong to pray that way? Selfish, maybe? Especially since God and I weren't on the closest terms. And maybe Mina wanted to get married. Maybe the guy was a good egg—a better prospect. Maybe I'd be a sorry excuse for a husband, a worthless father who'd never had a father. A half-Mexican bastard with nothing to his name. I might be the last person on earth Mina wanted to see.

I pushed the accelerator lever as far as it would go. If that was the story, so be it. But I'd come too far to give up easy. A couple miles out of town, I found the mailbox at the juncture to a long dirt road. Faded white letters spelling *Zimmerman*. My stomach did a nosedive.

Fields stretched on each side. They were brown and untilled, and the scent of wet earth mingled with the smell of spring grass. Behind a line of spindly trees, I could make out a house, a rust-colored barn, and tall silos like the ones I'd seen dotting the countryside since I'd rolled into the Dakotas.

In front of the house, a line of parked autos blocked my way. Old Fords with boxes, a Plymouth, two newer sedans, and a wagon—an honest-to-goodness wagon with horses nibbling at the new grass.

I wasn't in Hollywood anymore.

I parked behind the Plymouth and was out the door before the engine was done sputtering. I felt like I hadn't taken a breath since the kid said *wedding*, and I wouldn't be able to until I saw Mina.

I followed the hum of voices and a beaten path to a pretty backyard filled with lilac bushes and people. Then I saw her, not five feet from me, turned to the side. I glimpsed her profile beneath a wide straw hat with a puff of veil, and my knees went weak. Actually weak. Her dress—pink and lace and down to her ankles—wasn't what I'd pictured when I'd let myself picture Mina in a wedding dress. Neither was the groom . . . because he wasn't me. He stood beside her wearing a suit so crisp it could stand on its own. His hand slipped around her waist, the gleam of gold on his finger.

I was too late.

I must have made a sound—maybe I said her name. She turned around.

She wasn't Mina.

I felt like I'd stepped onto the wrong film set. This woman looked like my Mina, but the fringe of hair under her hat was gold instead of auburn, her eyes cornflower blue instead of aquamarine. Relief washed through me, then the crush of despair. The kid had steered me wrong.

Not-Mina eyed me from the tips of my dusty spats to my wrinkled suit and overlong hair blowing in the breeze. "Hello," she said, holding out her hand as if I were a guest come late. I took it in mine, feeling like the biggest fool, but she smiled, and again the resemblance to the woman I had sought for the past nine weeks hit me like a punch in the gut. "You're looking for Minnie."

Yes. I was looking for Minnie. But I didn't say that. I just nodded like a dimwit.

She tipped her head toward the back door. "She's in the kitchen."

I looked around, suddenly aware of the other guests, silent now and watching me. A schoolteacher type with glasses. A stocky kid with a shock of blond hair standing beside a balding, older version of himself. An older man with Mina's eyes, green-blue and considering me with curiosity and something else . . . maybe sizing me up.

I'd figure that out later.

I walked to the propped-open back door, my heart beating fast and furious as my eyes adjusted to a dim kitchen smelling of cinnamon and vinegar. A pot boiled on an old black stove and a woman stood over it, her back to me. She wore a green dress, a narrow-brimmed hat hiding her hair. If this was another dead end, my heart couldn't take it. If it wasn't . . . I didn't know if my heart could take that, either.

Then I heard it. The humming—the wedding song, the one they played when the bride walked down the aisle—and I knew I'd found her.

I couldn't say a word.

Mina turned, still humming, a flour-sack towel in her hand. Her eyes flew wide and she let out a squeak of surprise. The towel fell from her hand. My eyes fell from her shocked face to her waistline. The curve of her rounded belly took my breath away.

Gracias a Dios. Thank the good Lord I've found you both.

MINA

It was Max. My Max. Here. In the kitchen.

I blinked. He was still there.

He looked terrible. His clothes were rumpled, his head bare, his hair longer and curlier than I'd ever seen it. He took one look at me, let out a breath, and put his hand on the doorframe, leaning against it as if he might fall over.

I turned away, my back to him. I couldn't bear it. I braced myself against the cold lip of the sink. I breathed in and out. In and out. No, Max. Why did you come? How did you find me? I pressed one hand protectively over my tummy, as if to hide the baby from him, but it was too late.

His step scuffed across the linoleum floor. "Mina." The word was soft, barely a whisper.

I shook my head, biting hard at the inside of my mouth. Oh, Max. It had taken all I had to give him up. I couldn't do it again.

Sounds drifted through the open window—birdsong, Penny's voice, Robert's laughter—as if the world hadn't turned upside down when Max appeared. His hands touched my shoulders and his sigh brushed my neck. I breathed in the scent of his cigarettes, hair tonic, gasoline. My throat was clogged with tears, but I didn't know what to say anyway. I guess he didn't either, and that was a wonder.

He tugged at me, but I wouldn't turn to face him. I couldn't bear to look into his face to see the question on it. He'd be right to think maybe this was some other man's child. How I wished he'd been the only one. He deserved so much better.

Why didn't you just let me go?

He pulled me back against his chest. One hand slipped down my shoulder and around my waist. I closed my eyes. I could picture his hand, the way he had intertwined it with mine that perfect day on the beach. In the Tower Theatre while we laughed. Now it curved over mine, like he was holding our baby with me. I thought I'd known what a broken heart felt like, that day I said goodbye, but this was the real thing.

"Mina, please," he whispered. "Please give me a chance."

I closed my eyes, a sob caught in my throat. "That's what I was trying to do," I whispered. A chance for a real life, without someone like me.

He pulled me gently around and I couldn't fight him. "Look at me," he whispered, his breath brushing my cheek.

But I didn't. I couldn't. If I did, I'd be lost.

"Mina, look at me."

I opened my eyes. A stubbled chin, straight-edge lips, crooked nose. Honey eyes, bloodshot and earnest.

"I told you I wouldn't give up on you, Mina."

"You should have," I said. I laid my cheek against his chest. "You really should have." I knew I'd lost and that's when I cried. Heaven help me, I cried out my regret or relief, sadness or joy. Maybe all of those things. Max held me tight and whispered— promises or prayers, I don't know. It was all the same to me.

That's how Papa found us.

Max straightened and stepped back. I took a breath and wiped my face, then introduced them, my voice shaky. Papa eyed Max from the top of his head to his fancy shoes. Max pulled down his cuffs and ran a hand over his hair, then stuck out his hand, stammering a hello.

Papa shook his hand solemnly. He knew who Max was to me, and why he'd come. I could see it in his face, in the way he held Max's gaze. But the voices outside reminded me this was still Penny's wedding day.

Max followed, seeing us both glance toward the guests. "Sir, if you don't mind, I'll go get cleaned up, and then I was hoping—" he swallowed hard, glancing at me and back at Papa—"I was hoping to ask you . . . both . . . a question."

Papa said he was welcome to come back in the evening. Max gave me one last look and went out the way he had come. My stomach twinged and my doubt returned with a fury. A question. I knew the question he wanted to ask. Of course I did.

Problem was, I knew what I had to answer.

MAX

They must have thought I was crazy, those people in Odessa. They'd be right.

Crazy about Mina.

I wasn't sure what I'd feel when I saw her. But then . . . the way she looked at me. The way she put her hand over her rounded middle. She loved our baby. Maybe she could learn to love me too. She could say what she wanted—and I figured she would after she caught her breath—but I wasn't going anywhere.

It was time for a battle plan.

After a couple hours in Odessa, I had the lay of the land. A haircut and shave from Bill at the barbershop filled me in on

Mina—Minnie, that is—and her family. The little mercantile had a scant selection of shirts, but the saleslady got me set up and tutted about all the fuss with the wedding.

At the diner, I had a sandwich, coffee, and a short talk with a waitress named Ruby. She took my order and came back with my coffee and one less button done up on her too-tight blouse. I didn't encourage her, but she was happy to tell me a thing or two. "Poor Mr. Zimmerman. Minnie was always a trial. And now she's—" her voice dropped to a whisper—"in the family way." She raised her penciled-in brows. "She should be ashamed." I paid for my dinner, refusing both her offer of pie and something else after her shift. Ruby didn't deserve the quarter I left for a tip, but I hope she used it on a better-fitting blouse.

Odessa wasn't as different from Hollywood as I'd figured.

Feeling more like myself, I stood in front of a boarded-up building for a long time. The Odessa Picture House. Then I went back to Bill's and asked if I could make a few calls on his telephone. One call was to the *sociedades*, where I had some luck and Oscar was there. I told him I'd found Mina and what I was going to do. He wished me luck, then recounted a few goings-on in the *colonia*. I don't know why, but I felt better after that, like I had somebody in my corner.

The sun was sinking along the western horizon by the time I'd finished my business. I took a deep breath and started the roadster. I'd paid a kid two bits to wash it while I was gone, and it shone like a new penny. I turned east and, with the sun blazing a trail of gold and crimson in my rearview mirror, headed back to the farm.

This time, heaven help me, I was going to do the right thing. And the right thing just happened to be what I wanted more than anything in the world.

MINA

I thought I'd got good at waiting, but I was wrong. I paced the length of the parlor as nervous as a girl watching for her first date.

The guests were gone. Penny and Robert, too, in a shower of rice and good wishes. Penny had hugged me hard when she left, and I know she wondered about Max. "Don't worry. I'll take good care of Papa," I said.

She looked at me long and hard and pressed her hand on my cheek just like Mama used to. "I know you will." That warmed my heart, to be honest.

Now it was me and Papa, who'd gone out to check the animals as if this were just another day on the farm. I heard the roadster and ran to the mirror to check my hair, then told myself it didn't matter. *Give me a chance, Mina,* he'd said. There weren't any more chances. I was home and I was going to do the right thing—for the right reasons—like I should have a long time ago. I would be strong and send Max on his way.

The knock on the door made me jump. Max looked good with his hair combed back and his jaw smooth. His suit was pressed and clean, shoes shined. He'd never fit in here in Odessa with the farmers and field hands. I'd always known that. Go home, Max. Please go home. I still talked to him in my head. I figured I always would.

"Hello." He smiled when I stood in the doorway staring at him like a dumb Dora.

"Come in." I moved aside, full of my unsaid words. "How are . . . how are Roman and Angel?" was all I could think of to say. And I really wanted to know.

He laid his fedora, which showed some wear, on the hall table. "Roman? Getting into trouble, no doubt." He stepped close, close enough to lean down and kiss me. Don't kiss me. Please don't kiss me. "Father Ramirez is working on getting Angel into the seminary."

"I'm glad," I got out as I stepped away quick. "About Angel, that is." The world needed people like Angel. Roman needed people like Angel. "And Lupita?"

Max wasn't letting me off that easy. He closed the gap between us. "She was crowned queen of the *festivales*, and the next day, she cut her hair." He raised his hand and brushed a strand of hair from my face, pushing it behind my ear. My heart cartwheeled. "Oscar says it looks a lot like yours."

I almost groaned. Oscar blamed me, no doubt. Sanchia, too. Even half the country away I was making trouble for them.

"I think there's something going on with her and Oscar," Max speculated.

"You think?" I laughed, the tension in my neck easing a bit. Men could be such slowpokes.

Papa came in, scuffing his boots on the rug in the kitchen and thudding into the hall. Max stepped back with a jerk, running his hands down his trousers. It hit me then. It wasn't just me that was a mess. Max, who'd dined with the Barrymores and played pool with Fred Astaire, was nervous about talking to my father. It was too unbelievable.

After they shook hands and said polite words, Papa gave Max a long, thoughtful look. "Let's go for a walk, son."

Max glanced back at me like he thought I might run off but followed Papa through the kitchen and out the back door that led to the hay barn, the chicken pen, the little plot of land we still owned. And I was alone. Waiting again.

I couldn't bear it. What was Max thinking? What was Papa saying? I went to the front porch. A porch swing hung from the rafters on a set of heavy chains. I sat, setting it to creaking and groaning under my weight.

Max wanted to marry me. I knew that, and I knew why. He always pretended he wasn't the hero, but he was. He really was. Still, nothing had changed since I got on that eastbound bus in Los Angeles. Max deserved more. Better.

He came to find you, a small voice reminded me. That meant something, didn't it? And he hadn't been surprised about the baby. I figured that was Lupita's doing. It was no good telling him the baby wasn't his, even if I could pull off a lie that big. If Max wanted to do right by me—and I knew he would—he'd leave me here. I'd give the baby his name, if that's what he wanted, but I wasn't going back to Los Angeles with him.

I was here for Papa. I was here for good.

The night was deepening when Max found me curled up on the swing. The peepers had started their evening song, filling the air with their hypnotic chirp. I was glad for the dark. It would be easier that way.

He sat down next to me. Warm and familiar and far too close.

"I like your father," he said.

I could hear the smile in voice. His hand found mine. There was a lump like an egg in my throat.

"I told him about me. My mother and Dusty. I wanted him to know." He raised my hand to his face and laid his cheek against my knuckles. "He asked me if I loved you."

My eyes burned with tears. You'd think I wouldn't have any left after the day I'd had.

"I do, Mina. You know that, don't you?"

"Don't, Max." I snatched my hand away and stood, making the swing creak. "Don't say that."

"Mina, let me ask you—"

"No, Max. Please." I walked to the far side of the porch. Clasped my hands together to keep them from shaking. I had to get it out or maybe I never would. "No."

"He said you'd say no." Max didn't sound worried.

"I can't leave him."

"He said you'd say that, too." Max let out a breath. "He knows you pretty well. And he loves you, Mina. It's really something, how much he loves you."

He did. And I wouldn't leave Papa, not again. But I heard the wistfulness in Max's voice and thought of Dusty Clark and how much that young Max had wanted to be loved. My throat constricted. "You don't know everything, Max. If you did—"

"I wouldn't want you? Is that what you think?"

"That's what I know."

Max stood up and strode across the porch. He pulled me around to face him. "Is it about the Rose? Bert and those men? I don't care about that, Mina. I've told you—"

"There's more than that."

That stopped him. But not for long. "Then tell me." His voice held a hint of anger. "Tell me and see if I walk away like you want me to."

I didn't answer. I couldn't. I swallowed hard.

Max was too close. I stepped back. "It's about what . . . why I left."

Max turned soft then. "Tell me, Mina. Tell me all of it." He took my hand and led me to the swing. He sat and pulled me down close. "But know this, Mina," he whispered. "Nothing you can tell me—nothing—will change how I feel about you."

I wasn't sure if I wanted him to be right or wrong about that.

But I told him. I spoke into the dark, his arm warm around me. About Mama. About Papa and Penny and how I'd left school and done everything wrong. When I got to the part about Alex, I felt him tense.

I choked out the story I'd never told anyone, my throat thick.

Max jumped up, paced across the porch, then back, biting out words I can't repeat. I was crying by then, and he sat down and pulled me into his arms, holding me tight, burying his face in my hair. "Mina," he whispered. "It wasn't your fault."

I wasn't sure if he was right. It felt like my fault. But as Max held me tight, rocking us both in the dark, he said it again. "It wasn't your fault, Mina." I let his words sink into me and maybe that's when I started to believe—a little bit—that they might be true.

But I wasn't done. I had to be honest with him. "The rest of it—running away, stealing from Papa . . . and the dance hall." I made myself say it. "I won't pretend *that* wasn't my fault, Max. It was." I had to say the rest before I lost my nerve. "And at the beach house . . . with you. I was so . . ."

That's all I could get out. I buried my face in his shirt. I'd hurt him. I'd told myself I was doing it to save him, but really, I was just trying to save myself. "I'm sorry, Max. I'm so sorry."

He drew back, gently. This was it. This was when he'd get up and leave. He moved back just far enough to look at me, his eyes serious and dark in the moonlight. "Mina, I know about regret. I've done plenty I wish I could undo. That night at the beach, I wish I'd done things different, but now—" his hand rested on the bump of my belly—"maybe it's the grace of God or just good luck, but we have something I don't regret. Not for one second." He slid off the bench and knelt in front of me, his hands folded around mine like we were praying together. "Let's start over, Mina. Let's do it right, both of us."

No. I couldn't do this. Maybe he could forgive me for all that, but there was still Papa. I put my hand over his lips before he could say the words. "I can't leave him. I can't leave Papa. He lost the farm because of me, and now—"

"I'm not asking you to leave." He took my hand in his and kissed my fingers, flashing a glance at me. He looked like he had a secret.

"You'd never be happy here. On the farm." I couldn't see it— Max feeding calves, planting corn. It would never work.

"You forget I worked plenty hard before Dusty claimed me. I can do it again. And something else . . ." He smiled. "We're going to open up that old picture house, you and me."

"What?" He'd lost me.

"The picture house in Odessa. I made a call to my pal Alfie. He's all for it. He'll put up the money and we'll run the place." His hand tightened around mine. "We'll take care of your father, have our baby . . . maybe even a few more. Your father would like that, wouldn't he?"

He'd bowled me over. It was really too much. The farm and the picture house. Papa and Max and our baby, all here in Odessa. "You've got it all planned out, sounds like," I managed to get out. It was a good plan, to be honest.

"Except you haven't said yes yet." He fished in his pocket and then slid a familiar weight on my finger.

I didn't think he could surprise me one bit more, but he'd gone and done it. Mama's ring, the pearl luminescent in the moonlight. That ring. A sign of my past. Of what Mama had wanted for me. Of how I'd failed her. Now it was something different. A promise. A new beginning. *You'll find your way, my girl.* Had I found my way at last?

"Take it, Mina. And marry me." His voice trembled a little.

I realized suddenly with a flip in my heart what this meant to him. Everything. Just like it meant everything to me. I turned the ring on my finger. Could we really start over, both of us? Could we find our way—after all we'd done wrong—together?

"We'll do it up right—tomorrow if you want, or next week." He put his hand on the bump of my stomach and something changed in his eyes. "Or when our baby comes." Then the poor sap smiled at me. It wasn't fair play, that smile that made me feel like I was the only person in his world. But this time, that smile wasn't just for me. It was for the two of us.

So I said yes. Of course I said yes.

He kissed me then, but I won't tell you about it. That's between Max and me.

Looking back, you could say it wasn't fair, just like Penny told Papa that day I came home. I did everything wrong and I should have got what I deserved.

Sometimes, though, you don't get what you deserve.

Sometimes you get so much more.

THE HAPPY ENDING

DISCUSSION QUESTIONS

1. Mina had some bad things happen to her—the loss of her mother, the actions of Alex. Other things, she chose to do, like stealing her father's money and her decisions at the beach house with Max. When and how are we culpable for our actions, even when they stem from something that isn't our fault?

2. Mina asks herself about the nature of mercy and forgiveness: "The thing I learned—after everything that happened—was you don't deserve mercy. And you can't earn forgiveness. If you deserved it—if you earned it—well, I guess then they'd call it something else." Do you ever feel like forgiveness is a ledger that has to balance on both sides? How is Ephraim's forgiveness more of a gift than a reward?

3. Oscar finds himself frustrated and angry at injustice: "If there were justice in the world, people would get what they deserved, Max included. They do good, they get good things, like a place to live and food on the table. If they do bad, they get bad in return." Do you ever feel like Oscar? Does that frustration make it harder to forgive?

4. Lupita further challenges Oscar about his expectations of perfection in those around him, accusing him of having no mercy for others. In what ways do we see this in the story? How have you experienced this attitude, either from others or in your own thoughts and feelings? Why is it sometimes easy to fall into this pattern?

5. Even after Mina returns home and tries to make things right with her family, her sister has a hard time forgiving her: "Her silent anger reminded me each day that I hadn't paid my debt to my father, that I didn't deserve his mercy." Have you ever been unable to forgive someone for something they did to someone you love—a child or a parent? Is it harder than forgiving someone for a wrong you've suffered yourself?

6. In the end, Penny wants to forgive her sister, but she still feels anger. How do we forgive when we don't *feel* forgiveness in our heart?

7. Many parents are much like Ephraim, waiting for their children to come home—children who have turned away from their families or their faith: "Papa didn't love me because I was a good daughter. Nothing I did or didn't do changed his love one jot—not even if I had been perfect like Penny. He loved me just because he was my father, and that would never change. Honestly, it was too much to even believe." For those who are waiting for the return of a child or other loved one, what can we do as we wait and hope?

8. Both Max and Mina struggle with unspoken assumptions and past shame. In what ways does this affect their relationship? How do they finally move beyond it? Looking

ahead, how might they continue to feel the effects of their past choices and continue to heal from them?

9. Hollywood's excesses during the 1930s were the stuff of legend—fashions and furs and expensive cars, lavish houses and jewels—while a large portion of the population was suffering from the Great Depression. Why is it that so many people turned to films and the glamor of Hollywood to escape the realities of their daily lives? Do we still do that today?

10. Because of rampant unemployment during the Great Depression, the United States forcibly "repatriated" somewhere between five hundred thousand and two million Mexican people in the 1930s. At least half of these were American-born citizens who were intimidated into leaving the country. What do you think should have been done instead? What kind of similar practices are we using at our borders today?

A NOTE FROM
THE AUTHOR

Dear reader,

My hope for this story is that, when the last page is turned, you might say, "Wasn't that like the story in the Bible, the one about the Prodigal Son?" For that beautiful parable of compassion has been my inspiration.

Jesus was a teacher with radical ideas and unconventional ways. The Parable of the Lost Son, which he told to his disciples and the Pharisees, started out as a story they all knew well: a story of justice—of a bad son who did bad things and got his come-uppance, and a good son who followed the law and in return received his father's favor. But to the Pharisees' shock—and, no doubt, dismay—Jesus turned the story on its head. In his upside-down version, the terrible son who squandered his father's money on a life of dissipation was forgiven! And not only forgiven but welcomed home with rejoicing. What kind of father, they surely asked themselves, would reward a sinful son with the father's own cloak, the ring from his finger, and a feast? The wayward son didn't deserve forgiveness, they surely argued. He wasn't entitled to mercy.

And yet he received them just the same. Because the Father Jesus showed us in the parable defies our understanding. His mercy is infinite. His forgiveness is without measure. His love is beyond all reason.

My hope is that through this reimagining of the Parable of the Lost Son, we can see ourselves in one—or all—of the characters: Max, seeking redemption and forgiveness; Oscar, obsessed with justice; Penny, unable to forgive; Ephraim, a parent faithfully waiting for the return of a wayward child. And most of all, Mina, who longs to return to her father and be forgiven.

For aren't we all wayward children hoping to return to the arms of our Father? And don't we long for him to say, "I forgive you, my child. I love you. Always. No matter what"?

With love,
Stephanie Landsem

HISTORICAL NOTE

When I start a book, I spend months in research, a process I love as much as the writing. This book being set in the 1930s (as opposed to my previous biblical fiction) allowed me to study a plethora of resources: not only books and maps, but newspaper articles, magazines, photographs, films, interviews, and biographies. While I can't list all the sources that contributed to the plot and setting of *In a Far-Off Land,* there are several that may be of interest to readers who wish to delve further into the general history of the times and the specific themes of this story.

As I was inspired to write this story in the course of a trip to Monterey, California, it's only appropriate that I read the novels of John Steinbeck to acquaint myself with the period and place in which he lived and worked, and especially with his commitment to the issues of labor exploitation and immigration. As I did, the characters of Oscar and his family—and the prejudices they experienced—came to life, as did the desperation of the Great Depression. I'd recommend any of Steinbeck's books to get more insight into these issues and for the beauty of his prose.

Somewhere between five hundred thousand and two million

Mexican people were forcibly repatriated to Mexico between 1929 and 1936—and an estimated 60 percent of those were American citizens. These forced deportations were most often carried out by city and county governments, but with the tacit approval of federal lawmakers. To learn more about Mexican migration, culture, and repatriation, please see *Rebirth: Mexican Los Angeles from the Great Migration to the Great Depression,* by Douglas Monroy.

Almost anything you wish to know about Los Angeles in the Great Depression can be found by perusing *Los Angeles in the 1930s: The WPA Guide to the City of Angels.* This book was written as part of the Federal Writers' Project of the Works Progress Administration. The WPA was a government-funded project that provided jobs and income to writers during the Great Depression when such jobs were hard to come by. It resulted in a series of detailed guides of many cities and states of our nation, all of which are invaluable now to historians and writers of historical fiction. To look at the Great Depression from a new perspective, I suggest *The Forgotten Man* by Amity Shlaes.

The period of the Great Depression is often overlooked in our history, coming as it did between two great wars. It deserves our attention perhaps now more than ever, for it was a time of great uncertainty and fear, much like recent years. Difficult times such as these can be—and often are—met with charity and love, a coming together of communities and neighbors. Unfortunately, hard times can also cause desperate people to lash out in fear and prejudice. May we strive for the former and avoid the latter as our country continues to meet unprecedented challenges.

I endeavor always to be historically accurate. Any small liberties I've taken for the sake of the story or mistakes made through my own ignorance will, I hope, be forgiven.

ACKNOWLEDGMENTS

Readers might picture me in a room with nothing but a laptop, a window, and a cat, tapping away with wild abandon, but no author truly writes alone. There are many others to thank, for without them this book would never have come to be.

Thanks must go first to my husband of many decades, who is the most generous and encouraging person I know. Without you, Bruce, I would not be who I am today. Thanks also to our children, Rachel, Andy, Joey, and Anna, to whom this story is dedicated. You are our greatest joy.

To my family, especially my mom, whose strength and faith are a constant source of inspiration, and to my sister, Rachel, who keeps me sane with frequent phone calls and texts. We may live far apart, but I've never felt far away.

I am grateful to my many friends in Stillwater, Minnesota, especially the priests and parishioners of St. Michael's Catholic Church, which has been my spiritual home for almost thirty years. Thank you for your deep faithfulness and for sharing your many talents, encouragements, and smiles. A special thanks to the women of my book club, with whom I have read, learned, cried, and prayed over many years and thousands of pages.

To my unflagging critique partner, Regina Jennings. You are always ready to lift me up with your humor and gently guide me to clearer writing, better characters, and a deeper faith. This book was a particular challenge; thank you for your patience with its many iterations.

With deep gratitude to my agent, Chris Park of Foundry Literary, who is continuously supportive of both my writing career and each book. Someday, Chris, we will meet again in person! To all those at Tyndale House Publishers who have been so supportive and encouraging: Jan Stob, thank you for championing this book, and Kathy Olson, thank you for smoothing the flaws and polishing the prose that brings Mina to life.

And not least, a heartfelt thanks to my faithful readers. You are the reason I get to do this amazing job of writing the stories in my head. Your personal and virtual encouragement keep me inspired. Each time I hear how one of my stories has touched your life, I am renewed. Thank you from the bottom of my heart.

ABOUT THE AUTHOR

STEPHANIE LANDSEM writes historical fiction because she loves adventure in far-off times and places. In real life, she's explored ruins, castles, and cathedrals on four continents and has met fascinating characters who sometimes find their way into her fiction. Stephanie is just as happy at home in Minnesota with her husband, four adult children, two cats, and a dog. When she's not reading, researching, or writing, she's avoiding housework and dreaming about her next adventure—whether it be in person or on the page.